LOVE,
HONOR,
BETRAY

MARY MONROE

LOVE, HONOR, BETRAY

DAFINA

www.kensingtonbooks.com

DAFINA BOOKS are published by

Kensington Publishing Corp.
119 West 40th Street
New York, NY 10018

All Kensington titles, imprints, and distributed lines are available at special quantity discounts for bulk purchases for sales promotion, premiums, fund-raising, educational, or institutional use. Special book excerpts or customized printings can also be created to fit specific needs. For details, write or phone the office of the Kensington Special Sales Manager: Attn. Special Sales Department. Kensington Publishing Corp., 119 West 40th Street, New York, NY 10018. Phone: 1-800-221-2647.

The DAFINA logo is a trademark of Kensington Publishing Corp.

ISBN: 978-1-4967-3265-1
First Kensington Hardcover Edition: April 2023
First Kensington Trade Edition: March 2024

ISBN: 978-1-4967-3266-8 (e-book)

10 9 8 7 6 5 4 3 2 1

Printed in the United States of America

This book is dedicated to Jacqueline Battle, Randy Carlo Willis, Liz Lando, Sheila Sims, Maria Sanchez, Vella Mae Woods, and Ellen "Pinky" Tate.

Acknowledgments

I am so grateful to be a member of the Kensington Books family. Esi Sogah is an awesome editor. Thanks to Steven Zacharius, Adam Zacharius, Michelle Addo, Lauren Jernigan, Robin E. Cook, Norma Perez-Hernandez, Samantha Larrabee, Alexandra Nicolajsen, the wonderful crew in the sales department, and everyone else at Kensington for working so hard for me.

Thanks to Lauretta Pierce for maintaining my website and doing such a great job.

Thanks to the fabulous book clubs, bookstores, readers, and magazines for supporting me for so many years.

I have one of the best literary agents in the business, Andrew Stuart. Thank you, Andrew. You are still the best!

Things changed dramatically when the pandemic hit. I miss meeting in person with all you wonderful book club readers, bookstores, and libraries around the country. In the meantime, I love doing Zoom meetings!

Please continue to e-mail me at Authorauthor5409@aol.com and visit my website at www.Marymonroe.org and my Facebook page.

All the best,

Mary Monroe

PROLOGUE
Hubert

January 19, 1941

I shot and killed Blondeen Walker last month, but it seems like it happened yesterday. I still couldn't believe I had actually took somebody's life, especially since death had caused me so much grief. I'd lost my first wife, Maggie, and our twenty-one-year-old-son, Claude, on the same day a little over a year ago. I was still having a hard time dealing with such a big loss, because my parents was the only other kinfolks I had in Lexington, Alabama.

Maggie and Claude had died of natural causes, but if somebody had killed them, I wouldn't have been able to go on. I shuddered whenever I thought about how Blondeen's death had devastated her family.

But she was as much to blame as I was.

Blondeen was one of several women I'd spent time with after Maggie died. She'd refused to accept the fact that I'd ended my relationship with her to marry Jessie Tucker, a widow who had been Maggie's best friend, and a good friend to me for more than twenty years. Jessie was a fine specimen of a woman with a well-proportioned petite body and a cute face. Her copper-toned complexion was flawless. Blondeen, who was still in her twenties at the time and probably the best-looking colored woman in town, couldn't believe that I'd chose a woman in her forties over her.

While everybody else was preparing to celebrate Christmas last month, Blondeen was preparing to kill me and Jessie. She had been bad-mouthing us all over town and harassing us whenever we bumped into her in public ever since me and Jessie got together. But her plan had backfired. When she broke into my house in the middle of the night and barged into our bedroom with a gun in her hand, she was the one who ended up dead. Even though I had accidentally shot her during a scuffle, we agreed that the best thing for us to do was to cover it up.

We'd put Blondeen's body in the woods, where a maniac had dumped five other colored women he'd killed in the last year. Since everybody assumed he had also killed Blondeen, me and Jessie didn't think anybody would have a reason to suspect us. We tried to go on with our lives like nothing had happened. It wasn't as easy as we thought it would be, though.

CHAPTER 1
Hubert

"Hubert, do you really think we're going to get away with murder?" Jessie asked in a meek tone. We had just started eating breakfast. I knew something was bothering her as soon as I got in the kitchen and seen the distant look in her eyes.

I looked up from my plate and gazed at her with a mess of grits, bacon, and scrambled eggs still in my mouth. She had only ate a smidgen of her grits and half a slice of bacon. I swallowed hard and replied, "We done already got away with it. It's been over a month. And it wasn't really murder. It was a accident while I was trying to defend myself." I stared at the dark circles around Jessie's eyes. "You don't look too good. It's going to be a long day, so you should finish your food and take a pill. You'll feel better."

"I done lost my appetite and a pill ain't what I want," she insisted in a much stronger tone.

"Then what do you want?"

"I want to talk about what happened."

"I declare, talking about it ain't going to help. It'll just make the situation seem worse and that much harder for you to get over it. It's been a couple of weeks since we talked about this, so I thought we had laid this subject to rest. Why are you bringing it up again now?"

Jessie's shoulders drooped and she let out a loud sigh. "Because I dreamed about Blondeen again last night. She had a gun and was chasing me around in the graveyard," she mumbled with her voice trembling and a terrified look on her face. I hated seeing Jessie in distress because it distressed me. "Before last night, I hadn't dreamed about her since the night of her funeral."

My stomach knotted up. I rubbed the back of my head and groaned. "Looka here, I still dream about her too. When I wake up, I find other things to occupy my mind with, so I won't have to think about her too much."

"It's hard to keep her off my mind, even when I have a lot of other things to think about. I have to walk past the house she used to live in to go catch my bus to work every day. Then I have to pass it again on my way home. I done seen the curtains at the front window move a few times—and that house is still empty. Everybody knew how she would sit in her living-room window, crack open the curtains, and gawk at folks walking by."

I rolled my eyes. "Jessie, what are you getting at?"

"I think . . . I think Blondeen's spirit is in that house."

"Pffftt! If it was, she'd have shown herself to me or you by now. It ain't nothing but the wind making them curtains move," I insisted.

"There wasn't no breeze nary one of the times I seen them curtains move."

I rolled my eyes again and tried not to sound unsympathetic. "If that house spooks you so much, start walking a different route to and from the bus stop."

"I tried that a few times. Going three blocks out of my way takes me ten minutes longer to get to work, and to get home.

And it seems like almost every time I go out in public, I bump into some of Blondeen's kinfolks. Last week, I ran into her mama at the market. Lord, was she a sight! Her hair was a frizzy mess, and she didn't have on no makeup. The last three times I ran into her, she had on the same dress. Jesus would weep if He was to see her these days. I ran into her again yesterday at the fabric store. When she hugged my neck and started to talk about how well you handled Blondeen's final arrangements, I ended up crying along with her." Jessie sniffled and went on. "It's a shame Blondeen had to die so young. I'm glad she didn't have no kids. I would be feeling even worse."

"Jessie, if I hadn't killed her, she would have killed us. Don't you ever forget that."

"I just wish we could have talked some sense into her."

I looked at Jessie like she was crazy. "Nobody can talk sense into a maniac. You was married to one, so you should know that." I snorted, rubbed my nose, and silently prayed that this conversation would end soon. "I'm sure we'll be fine when enough time done passed, sugar."

Jessie sucked on her teeth and gave me a weary look. "I don't know about that. Year before last, I read a newspaper story about a pig farm worker in Georgia who chopped his wife up and fed her to the hogs. He was able to convince their kids and everybody else that she had run off with another man. It took eight long years for his guilt to get so bad, he couldn't deal with it no more and he turned hisself in. They put him in the electric chair."

"I remember that case. What we done ain't half as bad as what that fool done. So there ain't no reason for you to believe we'll end up feeling guilty enough to turn ourselves in. Not even in eight years or longer. All we have to do is keep our mouths shut. And so long as we continue to read our Bible and pray regularly, we'll be just fine. Now get a grip and let's finish breakfast so we can get to church on time for a change. Daddy wants me to sing a solo before his sermon."

While Jessie was getting dressed, I stayed at the table and reflected on what I had become since Maggie and Claude died: a rapist, a bigger liar, and now a killer. I wouldn't allow myself to spend too much time wondering what folks would think about me if they knew my secrets.

Me and Maggie had been best friends since childhood. She was the only one I trusted enough to tell that I was attracted to men. I was the only person she trusted enough to tell that she had been sexually abused by one of her daddy's friends when she was a little girl. That experience had been so traumatic, Maggie was terrified of sex and decided in her teens that she didn't want nothing else to do with it. She also decided that she would only marry a man who wouldn't expect any. And I wanted a wife I wouldn't have to have sex with. No normal man or woman would marry us on our terms. Therefore, we was perfect for each other. I married Maggie when I was twenty and she was seventeen.

I had never seen Maggie as happy as she was when she became a member of the Wiggins family. Her parents had led unsavory lives before they died, and she'd been looked down on by most of the folks we knew. Marrying me had put her as high up on the food chain as she could go. Daddy was the most respected and adored colored preacher in the small country town of Lexington, Alabama. Mama was a hairdresser with a lot of customers and friends, so everybody looked up to the Wiggins family—especially me.

I had a good job supervising the colored workers at the turpentine mill. And when my uncle died shortly after me and Maggie got married, he left his house to me, which he had paid off in full. I had assisted him in his undertaking business, and I'd inherited that too. His two loyal employees, cousins Tyrone and Floyd McElroy, had come with the business. They'd assisted my uncle for years and years and knew a lot about undertaking, so I wasn't about to reorganize and replace them. I was glad they had decided to stay on and work for me, because at the end of the day, I didn't know what I'd do without them. There was only one other colored funeral home in town. It was run by the Fuller Brothers, Ned and Percy. They was a little older than me and more experienced, but I treated people better, so I got most of the business.

Before Maggie died, she had been a great prop to help me keep my relationships with men a secret. She gave me her blessing to have as many boyfriends as I wanted, so long as I didn't get caught and scandalize her.

Despite me and Maggie's sexless marriage, we desperately wanted a child. But we could never create one together. That wasn't no problem, though. We searched around until we found a stranger with features similar to mine and set him up to get Maggie pregnant. Our son, Claude, was born the year after our wedding.

Once Maggie and Claude was gone, I didn't like living by myself. And I didn't want to move in with Mama and Daddy. That was when I decided to focus on developing a relationship with Jessie that would benefit us both. I never expected to find another wife as accommodating as Maggie had been, but Jessie was close enough. She was a upstanding, well-respected Christian woman who lived a biblical life. Just like me. We followed *almost* every rule in the Bible as much as we could. I had some flaws, but the only one I could see in Jessie was that she liked to gossip. So there was no way in the world I could tell her my deep, dark secrets.

To reel her in, I had gave her a good reason as to why I couldn't have sex with her. What I told her was so believable, I had a hard time believing it was a lie myself. I claimed that the deaths of Maggie and Claude had traumatized me so much, I had lost my urge to have sex and couldn't even get aroused.

Jessie had bought it hook, line, and sinker. But that was only because she believed my manhood would be restored one day. I couldn't tell her that day would never come . . .

Things was going just fine until my birthday rolled around last year. Me and Jessie had drunk more alcohol than we should have during the celebration at my house that February night, and I'd blacked out. I woke up the next morning in bed with her in my arms. We was both naked. She told me that I had raped her while she was too drunk to fend me off. But since I'd been under the influence of alcohol and the Devil, she didn't get upset or want to end our relationship.

I had never had sex with a woman and never thought I'd have the desire to do so. I didn't remember nothing about the incident, so I had no idea if I'd enjoyed having sex with Jessie or not.

About a month later, she told me she was pregnant and that I was the daddy! I immediately offered to marry her, if she could live with a man who had lost his manhood. She still believed that my condition was temporary and insisted that she was a very patient and understanding woman. So she was more than happy to become my wife. My daddy married us a few days later. Unfortunately, Jessie had a miscarriage in May.

I knew that me and Jessie would be very happy for many years to come, so long as I kept my secrets hid, not to mention the one me and her shared about how Blondeen died. The only other thing I was concerned about was holding her off in the bedroom, *permanently*.

Chapter 2
Jessie

When I got back to the kitchen, Hubert was still at the table with his coffee cup in his hand. He was sitting so still, it looked like he was in some kind of trance. Even with half of his hair gray, a few noticeable wrinkles on his honey-colored face, and a slightly overweight body, Hubert was still a handsome man. I loved looking at him, even when he was in a trance. He didn't realize I was standing beside him until I cleared my throat and nudged his shoulder. "Oh! I didn't hear you come back in here."

"Why are you still sitting here? You better hurry up and get ready for church," I told him in a stern tone. "What was you so deep in thought about?"

"Huh? Oh! Nothing serious." Hubert set his coffee cup down and stood up.

"You sure looked mighty serious to me. You didn't even know I'd come back into the room until I let you know."

"I was just thinking about work at the mill, that's all." He chuckled and rolled his eyes. "Some of the men I supervise done got so lazy, I'm surprised they even come to work at all."

"Well, you'd better remind them that even though they say the Depression done ended, it's still hard for a lot of folks to find work." I looked Hubert up and down and stomped my foot. "Shake a leg, lickety-split, so we can get going. I done already laid out your blue suit and a shirt and tie."

"Good! It won't take long for me to get ready. I done already shaved and took my bath."

"Hubert, I'm sorry about bringing up what happened to Blondeen again this morning."

He heaved out a heavy sigh, took my hands in his, and gave me one of his warmest smiles. "And I'm sorry I scolded you for doing it."

By the time we left our house fifteen minutes later, I was in a better mood, and the short ride to church helped. I knew and liked everybody in our neighborhood, from the doctor who lived in the biggest, nicest house on the same street we lived on, to the field hand who lived in a shack two streets behind us on a dirt road. Except for work, almost everything else was within walking distance. We could go north from our house and walk to church, the few restaurants that served colored folks, my in-laws' house, and the market. Carson Lake, where folks fished and had picnics, was at the south end of town, which was also within walking distance.

The sun was bright for it to be January. It was still a little chilly outside, though. I wore a thick tapestry shawl over my short-sleeved blue silk dress. Hubert's dark blue suit was thick enough, he didn't need nothing else to keep him warm. He was so dapper, I liked to gaze at him when he wasn't looking. There was times when I had to pinch myself to make sure I wasn't living in a dream.

Even though our church was within walking distance, we usually drove there every Sunday in case one of the elders needed a ride home or we wanted to go someplace else after the service ended. As we moseyed down the street in Hubert's well-kept Ford, I looked out the window at the tall magnolia trees standing in front of some of the houses. The trees would be even more beautiful in the spring when they bloomed and perfumed the air with a wonderful fragrance. The only thing I didn't like about our house was that we didn't have no magnolias in our yard. But the pecan tree, which we had, made up for that. Every year we collected so many pecans, I made enough pies to feed a lot of our friends.

"How come you being so quiet now?" Hubert asked.

I whirled around to look at him. "Huh? Did you say something?"

He glanced at me for a few seconds with a mild frown on his face. "You was on me about sitting at the kitchen table deep in thought. Now here you are doing the same thing. I complimented you on that new fragrance you got on. I tell everybody you got a knack when it comes to picking out the best smell-goods."

"Yeah. Um, I was just thinking about a few new ones I wanted to check out." I coughed and cleared my throat. "It's a shame we live in such a beautiful, serene little town, but . . ."

"But it would be even more beautiful and serene if it wasn't for them five colored women getting killed?"

"Six," I corrected.

Hubert slapped the steering wheel. "All right, then. *Six* dead colored women. How many more times will I have to tell you to forget about Blondeen?"

"I'll drop the subject, but I'll never forget about Blondeen. And I know you won't neither." I had scrubbed the spot where she'd bled out and covered it with a rug, but every time I moved the rug to sweep, I cringed and got sick to my stomach. There was no way I could forget completely about what happened to Blondeen.

"It ain't helping none if you keep bringing her up."

"Hubert, when they catch the man who killed them other

women and they blame him for Blondeen, what we did won't bother me no more."

Hubert sighed and sucked on his teeth. "I guess that's when it won't bother me no more neither," he admitted.

We didn't say nothing more the rest of the way.

We got to church ten minutes before the morning service started. Being Reverend Wiggins's immediate family, me and Hubert was expected to sit on the first pew.

Before Maggie died, I used to sit on the first pew because I was her best friend. But I hadn't enjoyed church since she passed, so I only went once or twice a month. I was glad Hubert felt the same way.

While the choir was getting situated, folks was roaming around, hugging and greeting other members of the congregation. I was glad nobody had come up to me yet. It was probably because of the tight look on my face. I couldn't help myself. Blondeen was back on my mind.

I didn't like to speak or think ill of the dead, but I was glad she was out of my life for good. I was sorry she had to die for that to happen, though.

Ten minutes after Hubert had sung his solo, "Swing Low, Sweet Chariot," he slumped back into his seat and dozed off. Nobody would have noticed he had fell asleep if he hadn't been snoring so loud. I got embarrassed every time I looked around and seen folks gawking at him, snickering and shaking their heads. I was glad Hubert wasn't the only man snoozing. I noticed at least half-a-dozen others. While the choir was singing the last of eight songs, I jabbed him in the side with my elbow and woke him up. "I don't want to stay for the afternoon service," I whispered. "I need to get home and do my ironing."

He snorted and muttered, "I ain't staying neither."

When Pa Wiggins finally ended the last prayer, me and Hubert bolted, but a elderly birdlike woman named Sister Quigley intercepted us as soon as we made it outside. She stood in front of us adjusting her wide-brimmed hat, looking from Hubert to me and back. With a side-eyed glance, she said, "Jessie, I noticed how worried you looked all through the service. A woman in your shoes shouldn't have nothing to worry about, especially during a church service." Then she looked at Hubert and added in a sarcastic tone, "Ain't that right, Hubert?"

"You're right as usual, Sister Quigley. Um . . . you'll have to excuse us. Jessie ain't feeling too good, so I need to get her home."

"You sick? What's wrong with you, gal? You ain't got nothing catchy, I hope." Sister Quigley moved a few steps back and looked at me with her eyes popped out as far as they could pop without rolling out the sockets.

"No, it ain't nothing like that. It's my job at the nursing home," I answered. "We lost three patients on Friday. They was all real nice to me, so their passing really got to me."

Sister Quigley shook her head and gave me a pitying look. "As long as you been working at that place, you ought to be used to that by now. We all know that a nursing home is the last stop on a person's journey before they reach the graveyard. By the way, I didn't get a chance to talk with you at Blondeen's funeral last month, but I wanted to mention how surprised I was to see you there. Everybody knew she didn't like you . . ."

It was going to be harder for me and Hubert to put Blondeen out of our minds if other people was going to be bringing her up too. "Me and Blondeen had our differences, but I was just as upset as everybody else when she got killed," I replied in a stiff tone.

"Jessie attends most of the funerals I handle. With Blondeen dying in such a wretched way, even folks she didn't like felt duty-bound to be at her home-going," Hubert tossed in. A few moments of silence passed. I didn't know what else to say and I didn't want to hear nothing else Sister Quigley had to say. I was glad Hubert continued. "You'll have to excuse us. You have a blessed rest of the day."

We didn't give Sister Quigley a chance to say nothing else. We got into our car and took off.

There was times when I still couldn't believe I was married to a handsome, prosperous man like Hubert. I didn't waste too much time after Maggie's death before I started scheming to get him. My first husband, Orville, had been so mean and violent, I was relieved when he died the year before last because of a lifelong heart condition.

Anyway, I had schemed like mad to become the new Mrs. Wiggins. Since I had been close friends with Maggie and Hubert for years, naturally I'd helped him get through his grief when she died. He was so distressed; he was having a hard time functioning. I offered to cook and clean for him on a regular basis. He not only went for it, he also paid me every week. But I knew that so long as he was still single, there was a chance that one of the other women who had wanted to be more than friends with him might woo him away from me. The only way I could have him all to myself was to become his wife. That wasn't as easy as I thought it would be. He took me out and we spent a lot of time alone, but that was all.

I was dumbfounded when he told me that losing Maggie had traumatized him so much, he had lost interest in sex and wasn't sure he'd ever want to do it again. Well, I had my own ideas about that. I told him that I believed his manhood would eventually be restored. It didn't take long for me to realize he was going to need some assistance from me. On the night of his birthday celebration at his house last year, I drugged him with a double dose of some tranquilizers that I took from the nursing home. When he became conscious the next morning, I didn't have no trouble at all convincing him that he'd raped me while he was drunk. He was so remorseful. We agreed to forget about what had happened and remain friends.

A month later, I told him I was pregnant as a result of the

"rape." He didn't waste no time asking me to be his wife. We got married right away.

To this day, he ain't never attempted to make love to me. That was the reason I had got involved with the handyman at the nursing home last year. I didn't find out until later that the same man was also Blondeen's live-in boyfriend.

Since I was never pregnant by Hubert, I had to fake a miscarriage. He was heartbroken about losing a child he'd wanted so desperately. *I* desperately wanted to have his baby and prayed that he'd be able to make love to me before I got too old to conceive. With a baby in the mix, I could have a hold on him for life.

My boy, Earl, was the only child me and my first husband had been blessed with. He was twenty-one now, but he had the mind of a child around seven or eight years of age. Maggie used to babysit him for me while I was at work, and never charged me a dime. I didn't make much money working at the nursing home, so I would not have been able to pay a babysitter. Once Maggie was no longer around to watch Earl for free, my oldest sister, Minnie, took him to live with her in Toxey, a nearby town that was even smaller and more country than Lexington. She had several grandchildren and Earl enjoyed their company so much he rarely wanted to visit me and Hubert. When he was happy, I was happy.

Matter of fact, even if me and Hubert never consummated our marriage, I'd still be happy. The thought made me smile.

"Jessie, I'm talking to you," Hubert said in a loud voice.

I whirled around to face him so fast, I almost lost my breath. "Huh? Did you say something?"

Hubert pulled into our driveway and turned off the motor. "While you sitting here, smiling like a new bride, I was saying that if you want to go back to church for the evening service, you'll be going by yourself. I'll drive you back over there, though."

Just the thought of sitting through some more of Reverend

Wiggins's rambling speeches in the same day made my head throb. "I'd rather spend the rest of the day at home."

I followed Hubert into the house, and we went straight to the living room and flopped down on the couch, him at one end and me at the other. After the "rape," he never got too close to me again. It was bad enough that he never made love to me, but he rarely showed me any other affection at all. He didn't give me passionate kisses, like every other man I had known. He usually just hugged my neck or kissed me on my jaw. "I enjoy us being alone. We have fun together, don't we, Hubert?"

"Sure enough. I'll go get the checkers and we can play for a while before you have to get busy cooking supper. After we eat, we can play checkers some more, or dominoes, until it's time to go to bed. That suit you?"

"That suits me." As soon as he looked away, I rolled my eyes. I couldn't think of nothing I hated more than checkers and dominoes. But I would do anything I had to do to keep Hubert happy.

CHAPTER 3
Hubert

Maggie's and Claude's birthdays had been a few days apart earlier in January. I'd had a hard time getting through them days. By February, I was feeling much better. I made up my mind to focus more on the future and less on the past. With me and Jessie's history, only God knew how things was going to play out.

I didn't realize today was Valentine's Day until Jessie brought it up at the breakfast table this morning. It was a holiday that never meant too much to me. But Maggie and most of my used-to-be boyfriends would get all giddy when it rolled around every year. They would buy frivolous gifts for me that I would have never bought for myself. One year, Maggie had the nerve to buy me some see-through socks that she had bought from a mail-order outfit in New Orleans. That was not a practical gift for a man with bunions on each foot almost as big as walnuts. To keep her and my boyfriends happy, I'd go with the flow and buy them something just as silly.

"Let's do something special together today. We can go shopping after we get off work, and you can help me pick out some new curtains for the living room. If you feel like it, we can eat out this evening too," Jessie suggested as she dipped a spoon into a jar of the blackberry jelly she made last year. She dumped a second helping onto my plate and a third onto hers. I had almost finished the grits, bacon, and eggs.

"I don't want to go shopping, and you know how busy the restaurants will be with folks celebrating Valentine's Day this evening. And why can't you make some new curtains on that Singer sewing machine you made me buy for you?"

"We don't have to eat out then, and I made curtains for our bedroom. I want to buy some new ones for the living room. Besides, I get tired of sitting at that sewing machine making quilts, pillowcases, and whatnot. I just thought that since today is a special day, to some folks, you might want to do something special."

"Um . . . I don't really want to do nothing today. We'll be doing enough celebrating for my birthday next week." I was going to turn forty-four on Monday.

"God willing." Jessie screwed the lid back onto the jelly jar and flopped down in the seat across from me. "Your mama wants to cook the cake this year. And she wants to cook supper for us." She let out a loud breath and gave me a serious look. I squirmed whenever she did that, because I knew she was about to say something I didn't want to hear. "Hubert, do you ever think about what happened last year on your birthday?"

"What do you mean?" I already knew exactly what she was talking about, another painful subject we had to deal with.

"You getting drunk and—"

I held up my hand. With all the scrumptious food still on my plate, I suddenly lost my appetite. "Hush up, Jessie. Please let's not travel down that dark road again." I rubbed the side of my face and let out a weary sigh. "We got too many other things to be concerned about."

"All right, then. I keep forgetting," she mumbled with the

kind of pout on her face I only seen on toddlers. I didn't like it when she did that. It made me feel like a bully, so I didn't waste no time changing the subject.

"Oh! I couldn't go with you this evening nohow. I forgot to tell you that I'm leaving the mill early today to go to Hartville. I have a meeting tomorrow with the man I buy a lot of products from. We need a new embalming table and a pallbearer casket carriage. And there is a restaurant over there that I like to eat at. I want to get there before they run out of them turnip greens with okra, fried green tomatoes, hush puppies, and smothered chicken, like they did the last time I went there."

"I can cook the same things for supper this evening. I got everything I'd need in the icebox. That way, you can go later or wait and go in the morning."

"Jessie, you know I don't like to be on that highway too late in the day. Besides, it's a hour-long drive from here to Hartville. And it being the weekend, the motel I usually stay at might run out of rooms for colored people tonight before I get there if I leave later. The same is true of the other motels. I need to get a good night's rest before I meet with that vendor. He claims he can give me a better deal on embalming tables than the folks I met with over there last week. With times still being hard, we need to be careful with our money. We need to have enough saved up to be comfortable in our old age." I gave her a glum look and added, "And enough to pay for our funerals."

Jessie shuddered and screwed up her face like a snake had bit her. "Did you have to say something so ominous?"

"What's 'ominous' about reality? We ain't going to live forever."

"I just don't want to hear about it if I don't have to. We spend enough time talking about things related to death."

"Jessie, what do you expect? I'm a *undertaker*, not a schoolteacher."

"I'm sorry. But I wish you didn't have to be so grouchy."

I gasped. I had always made it a point to be as pleasant as possible to Jessie and everybody else. This was the first time I'd ever been called "grouchy" to my face, and it bothered me. Especially coming from my wife. "Jessie, I'm sorry too. I declare, I didn't realize I was acting that way. I'll be more mindful in the future."

"I know you have your moments just like everybody else, and I should have chose a better word. It's just that . . . well, I didn't want to spend Valentine's Day alone."

"Jessie, please don't pout. We'll do something for Valentine's Day and my birthday at the same time next week." I gobbled up the last piece of bacon on my plate and stood up. "I need to get my tail over to the mill and you need to get to that nursing home. I go out of my way not to be late. I ain't going to do nothing to put my job in jeopardy."

"I ain't neither. It don't take much for them white folks that run the home to chastise one of the colored workers." I braced myself because I was afraid the next thing she was going to bring up was the fact that the nursing home had fired Blondeen the year before last. A patient had accused her of stealing and Jessie had refused to lie in her favor. Every time I heard that woman's name now, my ears burned. Jessie surprised me this time by going in a different direction. "I declare, I don't know how you can keep up with your undertaking commitments and your responsibilities at the turpentine mill and be so good at both. That's so wonderful."

"Uh-uh. That's so Jesus," I insisted with a firm nod. I was relieved she hadn't brought up the incident at the nursing home with Blondeen.

"All right, sugar. You have a blessed day and drive careful this evening."

It warmed my heart to finally see a smile on Jessie's face. It got even bigger when I leaned over and kissed her jaw.

I was glad she had stopped asking questions about my frequent overnight trips to Hartville, and a few other towns I told her I had to go to for business. More than half of them trips was ruses I used just so I could visit my boyfriend, Leroy Everette. He owned a barbershop in Hartville and rented the two-bedroom apartment upstairs in the same building. I was also glad she hadn't asked to go with me since that weekend I took her to Hartville last year. I'd made sure she had a miserable time so she wouldn't ask to go with me again. She was mortified when she seen the seedy motel I took her to. And none of the so-called friends I claimed I spent time with over there was available for her to meet because they didn't exist. I couldn't get her back to Lexington fast enough. She made it clear that she never wanted to get in my business again. Having such a understanding woman was very important for a man in my position. It was the only way I could continue to keep her in the dark and maintain my relationship with Leroy.

Leroy had closed up his barbershop early so he could have time to get to his apartment and have supper ready when I got there Friday evening. When he opened his front door, I was pleased to see him in the green flannel bathrobe I gave him for his birthday last June. Just looking at him made my heart skip a beat. He was the most handsome, well-built, middle-aged man I knew. Every time I gazed into his shiny dark eyes, raked my fingers through his thick black hair, and admired his butterscotch-colored skin, I was ready to go at it with him. Looks was important to me. I had decided when I was much younger that if I was going to risk my life to have relationships with men, I wasn't going to get involved with no baboons. "Hello, sugar." I hugged his firm neck and kissed him on his forehead. Leroy was so serious when it came to romance, he usually didn't bother with itty-bitty things like pecks on the forehead. That was for little old ladies and their grandkids. But I done it just to get a rise out of him.

"Get yourself on in here." He was so giddy; I was surprised he didn't scoop me up in his arms and cover my face with kisses. Instead, he wrapped his arms around me and kissed me real hard on the lips.

I didn't want to rush nothing, so I gently moved away. "Slow down now, sugar. We'll have plenty of time to get cozy." I chuckled.

"I can't help it. It ain't easy for me to keep my hands to myself."

"I feel the same way. But let's just sit for a little while first."

"Anything you say . . . *anything*," Leroy cooed. He let out a giggle as we plopped down onto the living-room couch. "How was your day?"

I waved my hands in the air and shook my head. "Oh, Lord in heaven! Today was a mess on wheels! My stomach knotted up right after I got to the mill this morning when I seen all the chaos that had already started." I softened my tone and started massaging his thigh. "Thank you for asking. I feel much better now." I was still massaging his thigh as I went on. "We had some mighty big orders to get out today. I think every merchant in town ran out of turpentine at the same time. Two of my men called in sick this morning, so we had to work real hard to make up for them. One of our delivery trucks had to turn back around and come back because the driver hit a mule that had got loose and wandered onto the road. It took us two and a half hours to get the truck running right again. I didn't even have time to take a lunch break. Then about half-a-dozen rats got loose on the main floor. We had to hunt them down and dispose of them."

"My goodness. With all that going on, I'm surprised your boss still let you off early today."

"Mr. DeBow is one of a kind, for a white man. He's honest, fair, and almost agreeable to anything I want. I couldn't ask for a better boss."

"Good. Get comfortable and I'll go get you a glass of cider. Supper is almost ready. Mustard greens with okra, fried green tomatoes, hush puppies, and smothered chicken."

"No dessert?"

Leroy winked. "I'm the dessert."

I licked my lips and rubbed my palms together. "Mercy me! I declare, you do spoil me."

"And you deserve it." Leroy kissed me again, and would have done more if I had let him. But I was hungry, so I wanted to put something in my stomach before we took to his bed.

After supper, we cuddled on the couch. But it didn't take long for things to get serious enough for us to move to the bedroom. It was just beginning to get dark, but I knew we would be in bed for the rest of the night. We cut off the living-room and kitchen lights and walked hand in hand to the bedroom.

Every room in the apartment was always neat and organized. But Leroy was so anxious to go at it with me, he dropped his bathrobe and underwear on the floor by the side of the bed. I did the same thing with my clothes and shoes.

We fell onto the bed at the same time, giggling and kissing like teenagers. "Let's make this a night to remember," Leroy panted.

"That's the way I feel about every night I'm with you."

I had no idea that before the night was over, I was going to experience my worst nightmare.

CHAPTER 4
Hubert

M e and Leroy had just finished making love and was basking in the afterglow. "I'm thirsty. Is there any more of that cider left in your icebox?"

"I think so. I wouldn't mind wetting my whistle a little. I'll go get it. You want something to nibble on too? I can heat up some of them hush puppies we had left over from supper."

Just as I was about to answer, somebody started pounding on the front door. Leroy sat bolt upright. I froze. I managed to sit up a split second later. "Who in the world could that be?" I had been seeing Leroy for over a year and nobody had ever knocked on his door while I was at his apartment.

"Oh, it's somebody that came to the wrong address," he suggested. "*Nobody* knocks on my door this time of night."

Before we could say anything else, a woman with a husky voice boomed, "Leroy, let me in!" She pounded on the door some more.

"Oh, Lord! It's Sadie!" he whispered. I had never seen Leroy look so frightened.

"Your used-to-be wife?" I whispered back.

"Yeah! What the hell is she doing here? I'd better see what she wants before she wakes up the whole damn neighborhood." He rolled off the bed and grabbed his underwear and bathrobe off the floor. He was struggling so hard to get dressed, he put his bathrobe on inside out.

I had told Leroy up front that I never wanted him to meet none of the folks I knew. It would have only complicated things for us. He felt the same way about me meeting any of his friends or family, especially his used-to-be wife. If she found out about us, his life wouldn't be worth a dime no more. And mine might not be neither. At least not in Hartville. Other than Leroy, the only other folks in this town that I interacted with was the merchants I bought products from. I considered the fact that if Sadie found out, and if her tongue was long enough that the scandal reached the businesses I dealt with, they probably wouldn't want to deal with me no more. That would be a blow to my undertaking work. I would have to do business with folks in another town because nobody in Lexington sold the products I needed.

Now it looked like I'd have to face his used-to-be wife anyway! Just the thought of that sent shivers up my spine. "Pretend like you ain't home," I suggested. "She'll get tired of knocking and leave. There ain't no telling what she'll think if she finds me in your bedroom."

Leroy started to wring his hands. "This is the first time Sadie came back here since the divorce. There's got to be a good reason. If I don't answer the door, she'll come back."

"She don't have a key, right?"

"No, but you know I never lock my door. Besides, my car is outside, so she knows I'm home. I have to go talk to her. This might have something to do with one of my sons." Leroy paused and gave me the most hopeless look I ever seen on his face. "Do you mind hiding until I get rid of her?"

"I don't mind at all. I'll stay in the bedroom—"

Leroy held up his hand. "No, she might come in here! Get in the closet! You ain't got time to get dressed, so take everything with you. First chance I get, I'll bring you a bucket to use for a toilet." He was looking around the room to see if there was something else that belonged to me other than my clothes and shoes on the floor. I had left my jacket on the arm of the living-room couch. But I didn't think it was anything to worry about, even though it was two sizes too big for Leroy. I scrambled out of the bed and scooped up my clothes and shoes and headed toward the closet.

Leroy waved his arms and shook his head. "Wait! She might look in there!"

"There ain't no place else in here to hide," I protested. "We're on the second floor, so I can't go out the window. But I can crawl through it and slither onto the roof of the barbershop."

"Oh, hell no! You hiding on the roof is crazy. The neighbors or somebody walking by would see you. Besides, I don't know how long she'll be here. It's cold outside and you could catch your death of cold." Leroy looked at me with a desperate expression on his face and then he glanced at the bed. "I declare, I hate to ask you to do this, but do you mind hiding under the bed until she leaves?"

My jaw dropped. I couldn't believe my ears! "Say what? *You want me to hide under the bed?*"

Leroy was so frantic his jaw was twitching and sweat covered his face like a veil. "Dagnabbit, Hubert! This ain't the time to put up a fuss. I can't let that woman find you in my bedroom. Look, we been careful for so long—"

I cut him off. "All right! I'll get under the bed. But you better get rid of her quick!"

Of all the boneheaded shit I'd ever done in my life, sliding on my back to hide under a bed was the worst. Naked at that!

It was a good thing I hid when I did. Before Leroy could make it to the living-room door, Sadie let herself in. "Leroy, I hope you ain't got company! Me and the boys need your help!" she yelled. Then she started howling like a stuck hog. "Aaarrrggghhh!"

The walls in the apartment was thin, so I heard everything that was being said in the living room. "What y'all doing here?" Leroy asked. I couldn't believe how composed he sounded. If I'd been in his shoes, I probably would have been cussing up a storm.

Sadie stopped crying, but she didn't say nothing.

"We got kicked out," his eldest son, Raymond, piped in. I'd never met him and his younger brother, Woody, but once when I'd called Leroy's apartment, Raymond had answered the telephone, so I recognized his voice. I'd pretended like I'd dialed the wrong number.

"We didn't have no place else to go," Woody added. He was thirteen, two years younger than his brother, so his voice hadn't changed yet. He sounded more like a girl.

"Sadie, how come you didn't call me to let me know y'all was coming?" Leroy asked. He didn't sound composed now. I had never heard so much fear in his voice.

"I didn't think I needed to do nothing like that. These young'uns belong to you, and you are still responsible for them!" she growled. "Besides, that beast I married rushed us out the house so fast, I didn't have time to call you."

"Why did your husband kick y'all out? What did you do to him?" Leroy asked in a calm tone.

"I ain't done nothing I ain't been doing since I married him. He's just a . . . he's just a BEAST!" she roared. "He suddenly decided I was spending too much of his money and told me to either stop, or haul ass. So here we are." Sadie let out a cackle that grated on my nerves like fingernails scratching down a blackboard. "And you better know I didn't leave without a fight. While he was trying to usher us out the door, I picked up a flowerpot and bounced it off his head."

"Ooh-wee, Daddy. You should have seen it. Pieces of that

flowerpot, and the flowers that was in it, went everywhere!"
Raymond yelled.

"Well, I'm sure that when your husband calms down, he'll
come to his senses and y'all can go back home soon."

"Pffftt! What's wrong with you, Leroy? You sound like the
same idiot you was when I left you! I don't care if that sucker
comes to his senses or not, I ain't in no hurry to go back!"
Sadie cackled again. "How come it took you so long to come to
the living room? You got a woman up in your bedroom?"

"Uh, no. I'm alone. I was asleep."

"I ain't never knew you to go to bed by nine o'clock. You
look wide awake to me!" Sadie barked.

"Well, I had a long, busy day and I was tired. I decided to
turn in early." For Leroy to be such a normal-sized man, I
couldn't believe how small he sounded.

"My throat is bone dry. That long-ass bus ride from Branson
and the walk to get here from the bus station was torture! My
booty is numb, my back is aching, my head is about to split in
two, and my feet feel like bricks done fell on them. Let me go
in the kitchen and get some water. I can't wait to get to bed."
Sadie stopped talking for a few moments and then she yelled
from the kitchen, "Why is there *two* dirty plates and silverware
in your sink?"

"Huh? Oh! I had company this evening," Leroy explained.

"Was it a lady?" Woody asked.

"Um, yes, it was," Leroy answered.

"Humph! Well, I hope she ain't one of them straight razor–
toting heifers from the valley that might come up in here and
cut my throat. I ain't never fought over no man, and I ain't
about to start now. Especially over a sorry hound dog like
you." Sadie and the boys laughed. I could already tell that this
woman was a ball-breaking battle-ax. What I couldn't figure
out was why a quiet, easygoing man like Leroy had married
her. He hadn't told me much about her, so I had no idea what

she was like in person. He had never even told me what she looked like, and I'd never seen a picture of her or the boys. But Leroy had told me that his sons both looked like him.

"You know me better than that. I would never be involved with one of them kind of women," Leroy insisted. "And you ain't got to worry about my lady friend. She left for Detroit right after we ate the going-away supper I cooked for her."

"Humph. Ain't that a blip. I could count the number of times on one hand that you cooked for me. When is she coming back?"

"She ain't. She's going to live with her sister and get a job so she can start a new life. She's a nurse."

"A *nurse*! Zowie! How could a lame duck like you get a woman in such a honorable position? She must be butt ugly, stone crazy, or both."

Sadie and the boys howled with laughter.

"She's a good-looking woman and she ain't crazy," Leroy said in a firm tone.

"She moved to Detroit, huh? I guess you couldn't hold on to her neither. She had to be a fool to be with you in the first place, but she'll be glad she didn't stay with you as many years as I did. Well, I'm happy to hear she ain't coming back." Sadie sounded relieved. "Boys, y'all put your suitcases in the spare bedroom. I'll put mine in Leroy's room."

"You want me to put your suitcase away?" Leroy asked with his voice cracking.

"Naw. I ain't cripple. I can do that myself. All you need to worry about is making me and these young'uns comfortable. If you got some whiskey, go fix me a hot toddy."

"I ain't got no whiskey."

"You better buy some as soon as possible because I'm going to need a buzz every day to put up with you."

CHAPTER 5
Jessie

Hubert was one of the hardest working souls I knew. I didn't know how he was able to work all day—five days a week at the turpentine mill—and still have enough energy in the evening to drive all the way to Hartville four or five times a month, and sometimes more. It was a shame we didn't have no merchants in Lexington that sold the products he needed to do his undertaking work. His meetings with the vendors usually took so long, he checked into a motel and spent the night. I was glad he did that, because I didn't like the idea of him driving back home too late in the day. There was more than one bogeyman along the highway just waiting to accost a prosperous-looking colored man traveling alone. Especially one that drove a Ford that was only a few years old.

Every now and then, the gossipmongers would hint to me that maybe Hubert wasn't going to Hartville just for business. They had the nerve to imply that maybe he was going to fool around with a woman! I ignored every single one of them busybodies. But the truth was, because of his condition, the only thing his tallywhacker was good for was emptying his bladder. So him going at it with a woman these days was about as likely as me going at it with President Roosevelt.

I was probably the only woman in town who trusted her man completely. Hubert never lied to me about nothing. I lied to him, but only when I had to. I wasn't proud of that at all. And being a liar wasn't easy. I had so many secrets, sometimes I felt like I was two different women.

I had finished eating supper and gone into the living room. I planned to relax on the couch, turn on the radio, and listen to a weekly gospel program that came on every Friday evening. Before I could stretch out on the couch, my neighbor and best friend, Yolinda Crandall, opened our front door and rushed in. Most of the folks in our neighborhood was also friends to one another, so we rarely knocked before entering somebody's house. I didn't even know anybody who bothered to lock their doors, day or night. I'd only heard of one case of a thief breaking into a house and stealing something. And that fool had been too drunk at the time to realize what he was doing.

Yolinda scurried across the floor like a squirrel with a wild-eyed look on her face. "Girl, with what's going on, how can you be sitting up in here looking as blasé as Cleopatra on one of her best days!" she hollered. She stopped and stood in front of me. The brown corduroy housecoat she had on was buttoned up to her chin. Underneath it was a long flimsy white nightgown that almost touched the floor. Yolinda was the only colored woman I knew who had freckles. And with her being high yellow, they really stood out. But she had nice enough features and kept her black-and-gray hair looking good, so she was still attractive for a woman who was well into her fifties. Mr. Crandall had died years ago, but Yolinda still got a lot of attention from other men. She'd been with the same boyfriend as far back as I could remember.

I wasn't in the mood for company, but uninvited guests was one of the prices we paid for leaving our doors unlocked. I wobbled up off the couch and folded my arms. "What's the matter? Did somebody die?"

"Sure enough," Yolinda answered with a sniff. "They found one of the Puckett boys dead."

"My Lord! Where did they find him and how did he die?"

"He was *lynched*. He just turned twenty-one and hadn't even been married or had no kids." Yolinda fished a large white handkerchief out of her brassiere and dabbed her teary eyes.

I gasped so hard, I almost choked on some air. I started to rub my bosom. My heart suddenly beat so hard, I was scared it was going to explode. *"Lynched!"*

"That's what I said," Yolinda replied, sniffling. "His brothers found him a little while ago hanging from a fig tree near the highway. A half-burned cross was left a few feet from the tree. The South is getting too dangerous for me. And these murderous white folks down here got the nerve to call themselves *Christians*! Jesus must weep every time He hears them claim that! I been thinking about packing up and moving up North. The only reason I ain't already hauled ass is because I'm a fool in love with a old goat that don't never want to leave this place."

Yolinda lived in a two-story house directly across the street from us that she shared with several of her kinfolks. She only worked doing laundry and housekeeping when she felt like it. She had recently let it slip while she was drunk that her late husband had left her quite a bit of money. Yolinda blabbed everybody else's business, but she never told any of us how much money she had hidden in socks and pillowcases somewhere. But she was a good friend, so I enjoyed spending time with her.

Before I could gather my wits and respond, my telephone rang. I ran to the kitchen to answer it. It was the eldest sister of the lynched man. Between sobs, she told me that the family wanted the body picked up right away. I always felt terrible for the loved ones of a deceased person, but I hated telephone calls like this one. Now that I'd been married to a undertaker for a while and had took a heap of calls of this nature already, I should have been used to them. But I wasn't.

Right after I hung up with the Puckett woman, my sister Minnie called. "Jessie, we just heard about the Puckett boy getting lynched," she sobbed.

"I just heard about it myself. Hubert had to go to Hartville this evening. I can't talk long because I have to get in touch with Tyrone and Floyd. They need to go to the funeral home and pick up the hearse and go collect the body." I didn't realize I was crying myself, until I felt warm tears sliding down my face. "I don't know what I'll say to that boy's mama and daddy." I could hear Minnie's grandkids making noise in the background. Her divorced daughter with three kids lived with her and her meek husband. They helped look after my son, Earl, who was in no hurry to move back to Lexington.

Minnie sighed. "The Puckett family done had more than their share of misery. There's them other two sons in prison, a uncle battling cancer, and one of the daughters fixing to marry a Bluebeard with four dead wives everybody suspects he killed. Now the youngest boy getting lynched. What a mess."

"I feel so sorry for that family. But they don't let nothing break them down and keep them down for too long." I didn't want to change the subject, but I was getting depressed. I wanted to lighten up the conversation, so I asked, "Is my boy behaving hisself?"

"Earl is fine. You know that boy ain't got a unruly bone in his body. You ain't never got to worry about him causing no trouble over here."

"Well, if he ever causes a ruckus, you just let me and Hubert know and we'll bring his tail back home."

"Hold on. He just came in the room. I'll put him on the

phone and you can say something to him," Minnie said. "He's been giving us the silent treatment all week until today." My son would often go for days and weeks at a time without saying a word. He'd been that way since he first started talking. When I asked him one day why he didn't like to talk sometimes, he told me he didn't talk when he didn't have nothing to say. I was glad to hear that he had something to say today. "Right after he ate breakfast this morning, he started yakking away like a mynah bird. He told me my pancakes was too soggy." Minnie laughed. "You better say something to him now if you want to conversate with him before he zips his lips again." The next voice I heard was my son's.

"Hey, Mama. What you doing?"

"Hello, Earl. I'm just sitting here talking with Yolinda. What you been up to lately?"

"Everything!" he yelled.

Earl was very slow, but he was still smart in some ways. He couldn't read or write, but I had taught him quite a bit. He enjoyed looking at the pictures in our Bible and listening to me read the stories that went along with the pictures. He also loved for me to read fantasy stories to him, especially about creatures from other planets, and fairy tales. But the ones about animals was his favorites. He'd had several pets when he was growing up, until taking care of them got to be too much work for him.

"Everything like what, son?"

"Like *everything*, Mama!" Even though Earl had the mind of a very young child, he sounded like a grown man. He looked like one too. He had his daddy's peach-colored complexion, handsome features, and muscular build. One of my fears was that some shameless hussy would take a shine to him and lure him into something he couldn't understand or handle. But as soon as Earl started talking, it only took a few minutes for anybody to realize he was limited. My boy was so innocent, whenever he talked to me, he usually said something that made me smile.

I made sure not to sound impatient. "I hope you had fun doing everything."

"I did. We drove to Branson yesterday to visit a lady that used to live next door. On the way back, we came to a horse farm and the farmer let me ride one of the lady horses. Oh, Mama. That horse was so pretty! She was brown and had great big eyes. She looked just like you."

If anybody else had told me I looked like a horse, I would have been upset. But Earl was paying me a compliment. Even with the bad news Yolinda had just delivered, his comment made me laugh. I didn't laugh long, though, because I didn't want Yolinda or Minnie to think I wasn't as distraught about the lynching as they was. "Thank you, baby. Put your auntie back on the phone."

Earl didn't say nothing else. He just handed the phone to Minnie and went back to doing whatever he had been doing. "Excuse that boy. You know he didn't mean no harm," Minnie snickered.

"Oh, I know that. At least he took my mind off that Puckett boy for a few minutes."

"Listen, I got to go finish washing out my bloomers. Call me as soon as you know when the boy's funeral is. I declare, y'all must still be reeling from Blondeen's murder a couple of months ago, and now y'all got another one. Lexington is becoming a dangerous place to live. Well, one good thing about this lynching is, Hubert will have some more business. Since he didn't charge Blondeen's family for her funeral, I'm sure y'all could use the money."

"Yeah," I agreed in a tired tone. "We sure can."

CHAPTER 6
Jessie

Before I could make it back to the living room, two more folks called me up to vent. I'd been getting a heap of calls like these ever since I became Reverend Wiggins's daughter-in-law. Folks would go on and on about one thing after another. No matter how many times I interrupted and promised I'd pray for them, that didn't stop them.

I didn't mind too much. Being a sounding board made me feel important, especially when it involved something as serious as a death. One of the callers today was a man who lived down the street that me and most of my neighbors bought live chickens from. He was so mad. "Them damn peckerwoods! They ain't nothing but devils! And every last one I know spend half their time in church! Praying to the same damn God we pray to!" I agreed with the chicken man, hoping he wouldn't stay on the phone too long, but he was on a roll and went on for five minutes.

One of my coworkers called right after I got off the phone with the chicken man. She cussed up a storm too. The first time she paused, I jumped in and said, "Let's pray together.

That'll make you feel better." We prayed for two minutes, but she was crying like a baby before I ended the call.

I knew I'd be getting more calls like these because everybody would be talking about the lynching for a while. I was prepared to offer prayer assistance and spiritual guidance for as long as I had to. One thing that almost made me laugh was the fact that I needed just as much prayer assistance and spiritual guidance as everybody else.

Two minutes after I sat back down on the couch, my front door flew open. It was Ma and Pa Wiggins. I cringed. As much as I adored my in-laws, being in their presence was not the most pleasant thing for me to endure, especially when there was a major crisis like a lynching.

"Good evening, Reverend Wiggins, Sister Wiggins," Yolinda greeted. Yolinda was a hypocrite, but she was always gracious when she was around preachers and other folks deeply rooted in the Church. "It's so good to see y'all again. I enjoyed your sermon last Sunday, Reverend. I felt Jesus go through me all the way to the bone."

"Good! And that's the way you're supposed to feel," Pa Wiggins said. Him and Ma Wiggins nodded at Yolinda before they turned their attention to me. "Jessie, where is Hubert at?" my hefty father-in-law shouted as he waddled across the floor in my direction. Him and my mother-in-law was in their seventies and suffered with arthritis, obesity, and a heap of other afflictions, so they couldn't move too fast. Pa Wiggins was a older version of Hubert. Ma Wiggins had nice features on her heart-shaped face, but she was just as overweight and sluggish as her husband. By the time they made it up to me, they was huffing and puffing like racehorses.

"He went to Hartville this evening to see a man about some new products for his undertaking business," I answered as I glanced from one face to the other. I got along real good with Hubert's parents, despite them being pushy and gruff sometimes. That didn't bother me because they was still two of the sweetest, most loving folks I knew. They was happy as pie when they found out me and him was going to get married. They treated me as good as they had treated Maggie. Pa Wiggins pastored his own church and was still employed as a part-time butler for our used-to-be mayor's brother. My mother-in-law dressed dozens of women's hair in her kitchen every month. Every single one of them women loved her to death, so she had a lot of friends. Despite them being physically limited, my in-laws was still very active in everything. Especially my marriage. But I didn't mind that either, because Hubert was their only child and they doted on him. So long as he was happy—and I made sure of that—Ma and Pa Wiggins was happy.

"We been trying to get in touch with Hubert and ain't had no luck," Ma Wiggins whined. She was wringing her hands so hard, I was surprised she didn't rub the skin off.

"Is this about that Puckett boy getting lynched? Yolinda just told me."

Ma Wiggins started talking loud enough for the folks in the next county to hear. "Yeah, it is about him! The family laid his body on a pallet in their pantry. But everybody in that house is so grief struck, they want to get things rolling as soon as possible and put this behind them."

"We called here a little while ago, Jessie. More than one time. Where was you at?" Pa Wiggins wanted to know.

"I was in the bedroom ironing a few pieces. It's hard for me to hear the phone when I'm back there," I explained.

"Well, you need to get ahold of Hubert so he can pick up the body and get it out that house before everybody in that boy's family go crazy," Ma Wiggins advised.

"I went over there and did a laying on of hands to his mama and daddy, but it didn't do much good," Pa Wiggins said as he shook his head and wiped sweat off his face with the back of his hand. "Them poor folks is on the verge of a nervous break-down."

"There ain't no way for me to reach Hubert. The motels in Hartville that rent to colored folks don't have telephones in the rooms, and they only take messages at the front desk for white folks. When he goes to Hartville on a Friday, sometimes he don't come home until Sunday morning."

"Then you need to get in touch with Tyrone and Floyd lickety-split," Yolinda tossed in. "Hubert don't never let a body sit for too long before they start working on it."

Her words made me wince. "I know he don't. He is going to be so distraught when he gets home and finds out what done happened. He needs the business, but he is downright squeamish when it comes to handling *murdered* folks."

"Tell me about it. Especially after all the misery Blondeen's murder caused last year." My mother-in-law choked on a sob and shuddered.

Just hearing about Blondeen's death *again* made my head throb. It seemed like this subject was never going to go away. I didn't waste no more time talking. I sprinted into the kitchen to dial Tyrone's number. I was so keyed up, I reached wrong numbers twice before I got his. I was glad he answered right away.

"I'm so glad I caught you at home!" I hollered. "You and Floyd need to go get the hearse and pick up a body."

"Oh, I just heard about what happened to Brother Puckett. Poor soul. The boy led a rough life, fighting and drinking and whatnot. It's a good thing he got saved in time so he can be with Jesus. I seen Reverend Wiggins baptize him myself."

"How soon can y'all go get the body? Pa Wiggins just came from the Puckett house and everybody over there is prostrate with grief."

"Jessie, you ain't got to fret none. I'm fixing to go pick up Floyd as soon as I get off this phone. We'll go straight from his house to pick up the hearse. I sure do hate for Hubert to come home to this mess! Them white devils ain't going to stop until they done killed us all!" Tyrone boomed.

"Hubert probably won't get back from Hartville until Sunday, so y'all need to start preparing the body as soon as possible."

"You ain't got to worry about nothing! Get some rest and let me and Floyd do what Hubert pays us to do."

"Tyrone, I can't tell you how pleased I am that Hubert's got folks working for him that he can count on. I'll make sure he gives you and Floyd a nice bonus when he settles the payment with the Pucketts."

"Thank you, Jessie. Me and my cousin love our jobs. As Christians, we feel duty-bound to do them well."

CHAPTER 7
Hubert

I held my breath when I heard Sadie come into the room. From her heavy footsteps, which sounded like they belonged to a Clydesdale, even without seeing her, I could tell that she was a mighty big woman. Just how big, I didn't know. When I'd asked Leroy what she looked like, all he'd told me was that she had a pretty face for a "big-boned" woman. To me, that was a nice way of saying she was the size of a full-grown cow. And from her loud menacing tone of voice, I had a feeling she was right vulgar too.

The closet door creaked when Sadie opened it and set her suitcase down with a thud. "Leroy, I'm glad to see you cleaned out this closet after I left, but it still needs a little more work," she growled. "And the same thing goes for the rest of this place."

"How long do you think y'all will need to stay?" Leroy asked in a tone so low and meek I could barely hear him. It was heartbreaking to see a man as strapping as he was cower to a woman.

"What difference do it make? We'll stay as long as we need to."

"What I need to know is, what do you plan to do if you don't go back to *your husband*?" He sounded much stronger this time, and I liked how he emphasized "your husband."

"I ain't had time to make no plans yet. And I'm too tired to think about that right now." Sadie paused and moaned. "I'm so sore, I feel like I been run over by a mule. That bus ride was pure-D torture! I'll have to sleep in the bed with you."

Leroy gasped and I almost swallowed my tongue. The thought of him sleeping in the same bed with Sadie was *pure-D* torture for me! "That won't be necessary. I'll sleep on the couch. You can have the bed."

"What's wrong? You scared I might bite you? Or do you think you might want some affection?"

"No, that ain't it. I . . . I just don't think us sleeping together would be appropriate."

"Appropriate, my foot. I know how much nookie it took to content you, you nasty devil." She snickered. "All I got to say is, when you ready for some, just let me know." I had to press my lips together real tight to keep from letting out a yelp.

I heard a slap and then Leroy hollered, "You stop that, Sadie! Keep your hands to yourself."

"What's wrong with you? You never slapped my hand away all of them other times when I squeezed your pecker," Sadie whined. "You used to like it."

"Well, I don't like it no more!" I was glad to hear Leroy sounding more aggressive.

The thought of Sadie fondling my man made me want to scream!

They returned to the living room. Fifteen minutes later, Sadie came back to the bedroom alone and closed the door. She plopped down on the bed with a groan. The bedsprings sunk so low, they almost touched my face.

It was the longest night of my life and the most traumatic. I didn't sleep a wink. Several hours later, Leroy entered the room again. "Good morning, Sadie. You awake?"

"Yeah, I'm awake. But I'm still so dog-tired, I need to just lay here for another couple of hours."

"I'm sorry to hear that. The boys got a itching to go over to that little café on Morgan Street for breakfast."

"Y'all can go without me. I'll fix myself something here."

"No, I want you to come with us. The boys do too. Get up and get dressed so we can get there before it gets too crowded. Besides, I ain't been to the market yet, so my icebox is almost empty. I ain't even got no bread or eggs."

Me and Leroy had planned to go to the market yesterday evening. I was glad we'd decided to put it off.

"All right, then. Let me get some clothes out of my suitcase. I'm pretty rank and I know the boys is too, so we all need to wash up before we get dressed."

"Okay. But don't take too long."

Right after they both left the room, Leroy came back in a couple of minutes later and shut the door. He trotted over to the bed, squatted down, and lifted the covers so he could see my face. "Hubert, you all right?" he whispered. He looked hopeless, and that made me feel even worse.

"I done had better days," I replied in a sarcastic tone. "My bladder is about to bust open, and I could use a glass of water."

"I am so sorry about this! I'm taking everybody out to breakfast. I'll keep them away as long as I can and you can crawl out, put your clothes on, and leave. I will call you at home when I can. If you don't hear from me, call me at the shop."

"All right," I mumbled. My throat was as dry as a week-old bone. I could barely speak. "What time is it?"

"Half past eight."

Sadie had arrived around nine o'clock last night. "Do you mean to tell me I been up under this bed for more than *eleven* hours?"

"Uh-huh. Baby, I am so sorry about this."

My jaw was twitching when I spoke. "I'm sorry about it too."

"I swear to God, I'll make it up to you as soon as I can. I know your birthday ain't until Monday and I probably won't get to talk to you on that day. So, happy birthday in advance." Leroy tried to lighten the mood by adding, "You don't look like a man about to turn forty-four."

"I might not look it, but after what I went through last night up under this bed, I feel twice that age."

Leroy laughed. I didn't.

It was another thirty minutes before I heard the front door slam. I wanted to make sure the coast was clear, so I stayed under the bed another ten minutes. Then I slid out, jumped into my clothes and shoes, and ran to the bathroom to empty my bladder. I made it by the skin of my teeth.

I was so disoriented and sleepy when I got in my car, I was scared to drive. But I couldn't sit in front of Leroy's building and fall asleep. Me and him had come too far for me to end up letting Sadie catch us anyway.

After I had made it completely out of his neighborhood, I pulled to the side of the street and took a lot of deep breaths before I headed toward the highway. I drove slower than I normally did, so it took me almost twice as long to make it back to Lexington. My back and legs felt like a mule had stomped on them. My head was throbbing so hard, my ears was ringing. All I could think about was how Sadie's sudden appearance was going to affect my relationship with Leroy.

When I pulled into my driveway, Jessie opened the front door. "Hubert, I'm so glad you came home today instead of to-morrow," she started.

I held up my hand. "I'm so tired, I just want to get in the house."

"Well, I'm glad you are here because—"

"Because my birthday is Monday and you want to get to the market today and get the things you planning on cooking," I said in a weary tone. I dragged my feet across the living-room floor and flopped down on the couch. "I don't know if I feel like doing any grocery shopping today. I had a real bad experience."

"Oh? Did something happen? I thought you was supposed to go check out them caskets and pallbearer carriages today? Did the place burn down or something?" Jessie sat down at the other end of the couch.

"No, but the man had a family emergency and had to close up for today. Um . . . I got chased by some Klansmen on my way home . . ."

Jessie's eyes got big. "Oh, my Lord! Them devils is really on a rampage!"

"They was on horses, so I was able to get away before they caught up to me. What do you mean about them being 'on a rampage'?"

"Hubert, they done lynched one of the Puckett boys."

After the night I'd had, this news almost pushed me over the edge. My mouth dropped open, and I had a hard time catching my breath. "W-when?"

"I don't know exactly when. The boy's daddy said he left the house to go do some night fishing Thursday evening and never came home. His brothers found his body hanging from a fig tree near the highway yesterday."

I jumped up off the couch and started waving my hands. "I can't believe it!"

Jessie got up and put her arms around my waist. "Calm down. You know these things happen from time to time. There ain't nothing we can do about it." She let out a loud sigh and shook her head. "Just be grateful it didn't happen to you."

"Me?"

Jessie gave me a surprised look. "Hubert, what do you think them Klansmen chased you for? They are probably the same ones that lynched that boy."

"Yeah, you're right. Praise God I made it home safe and sound. The whole Puckett family belongs to Daddy's church. I'm sure they'll want me to handle the arrangements."

Jessie nodded. "That's for sure. One of the Puckett sisters done already called here. I got in touch with Tyrone, and him and Floyd went to pick up the body last night. Now you sit back down and try to pull yourself together. I'll fix you some breakfast."

While Jessie was in the kitchen, I went in the bathroom and shut the door so I could think in private. Lynching was the most heinous crime colored folks had to be concerned about. I felt as bad as I could feel about what had happened to the Puckett boy. I was going to go visit his family right after I took a bath and put on some fresh clothes. That and the thought that my relationship with Leroy might be over was too much for me. I leaned over the sink and cried like a baby.

I was grieving for the dead boy, as well as myself. With Leroy's used-to-be wife in the picture now, I felt like my life was over in a way too.

CHAPTER 8
Jessie

It was a shame that the lynch mobs always got away with murder. Not a single one of them devils had ever been arrested for lynching a colored man. We knew that the police wasn't going to do nothing about it because some of them was involved in the killings! And it wasn't just grown men them devils lynched. Two years ago, they killed a thirteen-year-old boy who was retarded. The family had kept tabs on him all his life, as much as they could, but it hadn't been enough. One day he snuck out of the house to go swimming in a creek deep in the woods near where the Klan held some of their cross-burning meetings. The boy had told a couple of his friends where he was going. When he'd been gone longer than he should have been, his friends went looking for him and found him. The murdered boy's family didn't belong to our church, so they'd had the Fuller Brothers handle the final arrangements. Every time I thought about that poor boy, I couldn't hold back my tears.

Hubert had been in the bathroom so long, I got worried. I dried my eyes and before I knocked on the door, I stood outside for a few moments. When I heard him crying, I knocked.

"You all right in there?" One thing I liked about him was that he wasn't afraid to show his feelings, like some men I knew. The day Maggie and Claude died, and when I had my miscarriage, he cried more than anybody else.

"I'm okay," he muttered, choking on a sob.

"Hubert, I know how you feel. Almost getting caught by the Klan, and then hearing the news about the Puckett boy is enough to drive somebody stone crazy. But you got to be strong. Come on out so we can eat. That should make you feel better."

When the door eased open, I couldn't believe what I was seeing. His eyes was red and so swollen, it looked like somebody had beat him up. "Good God!" I yelled before I took his arm and led him to the living-room couch. "I'm going to go put some ice in a sock for you to put on your eyes."

"Jessie, thank you for being so concerned. You always work on me like a pill when I'm feeling low." He sniffled and took a deep breath. "I . . . I feel a little better already."

I wrapped my arms around his neck and patted his shoulder. "We'll all feel a lot better in a few weeks."

I was glad he had composed hisself before Tyrone and Floyd showed up a few minutes before noon. Hubert was so pleased to see them; he even got a little giddy. "Hello, y'all come on in here," he greeted, and waved them to the couch. He plopped down in the wing chair facing the couch and I stood next to him with my arms folded. "Y'all done talked to the Puckett family about the final arrangements?"

"Yeah, boss," Tyrone answered. "They was in pretty bad shape when we left that house. I'm sure they'll be glad to see you." Him and Floyd had gone to school with me and Hubert. But their long, mulish faces, leathery skin, and droopy shoulders made them look much older than us. They wore overalls most of the time, so they looked more like field hands than undertaker assistants. But they was real important to the business, especially since Hubert had to go out of town as often as he did. They was also the closest things to male friends Hubert had in Lexington.

"Y'all remember Brother Puckett's brother that moved to Chicago some years ago and started making money blowing his trumpet in them white nightclubs?" Floyd asked.

"Yeah, I remember him. There's a framed picture on their living-room wall with him standing next to that famous criminal named Al Capone that we used to read about in the newspaper years ago. What about him?" I said.

"Well, he's already on his way down here. Sister Puckett told us he said for the family not to worry about nothing because he's going to cover all the expenses."

"In that case, it's bound to be a lavish funeral," I predicted. "I never knew no colored man who liked to spend money like that trumpet player."

"I never knew no colored man who made the kind of money he makes," Hubert added.

"I'm just glad the boy was a member of your daddy's church, Hubert. Otherwise, them Fuller Brothers would be handling everything," Floyd said.

"And getting that trumpet man's money," Tyrone added.

The smug expressions on their faces concerned me. I had to say something. "Y'all don't seem too broke up about this tragedy." My tone was firm and loud.

Hubert whirled around to look at me with his mouth hanging open. "Jessie, what done got into you? When you been working at a funeral home as long as these two boys, you don't react to tragedies like everybody else. You need to cut Tyrone and Floyd a little slack."

I didn't like being chastised by Hubert, but I decided not to say nothing about it. I thought it would make matters worse.

Hubert turned back to Tyrone and Floyd. "This ain't about how much money we'll make, y'all. It's about us doing our Christian duty. The main concern should be us doing a dignified job. If Brother Puckett's brother hadn't already said he'd be paying all the expenses, I probably would have let the payment slide."

From the corner of my eye, I seen Floyd poke Tyrone's side with his elbow. Then Floyd screwed up his face and shook his head. "Boss, you didn't charge Blondeen's family nothing for her final arrangements. You keep doing free funerals, sooner or later every family in town will be expecting a free ride."

"Well, I don't want nobody to think I'm greedy. Besides, I got *both* of the boy's grandparents' bodies last year in the same month. That set the family back a pretty penny, even though the trumpet player helped pay for them two funerals too."

I had to put in another two cents. "Floyd, at least you and Tyrone still got jobs. Be thankful for that. The Fuller Brothers just laid off one of their assistants last week."

Hubert gave me a stern look, so I decided not to say nothing else. He snorted and looked from me to Floyd and Tyrone. "All right now, y'all. Let's move on. Floyd, you and Tyrone meet me at the funeral home in two hours and we'll get the ball rolling."

The room suddenly got so quiet you could have heard a pin drop. I couldn't stand the silence and the deadpan expressions, but I had to bring up something else that was distressing. "Hubert, I know you want to forget about what happened to you this morning, but tell them about that scary run-in you had with the Klan."

Tyrone and Floyd gasped. *"What scary run-in?"* they said at the same time.

"Oh, it wasn't no big deal," Hubert replied, waving his hand. "I put a little heel and toe to the gas pedal and left them boogers in a cloud of dust."

I didn't think his smug attitude was fitting and I had to say something about it. "Hubert, don't make light of nothing like that. Anything that involves colored folks and them bedsheet-wearing monsters is a big deal. They just lynched another colored man!" I turned to Tyrone and Floyd and told them everything Hubert had told me about his encounter with the Klan.

Floyd yelped and scooted to the edge of the couch. He would have slid to the floor if Tyrone hadn't grabbed his arm. They both looked so scared, you would have thought the Klan had chased them too.

"I wish I could sneak up on one of them Klan boogers while he was fishing or hunting by hisself. I could do him in and get away with it!" Tyrone blasted. "And *buh-lieve* me, I wouldn't feel the least bit guilty!"

"And I'd get the next one!" Floyd roared.

"Y'all stop talking crazy," I scolded. "I been knowing you two since we was kids, and I ain't never seen neither one of y'all even hurt a fly."

CHAPTER 9
Hubert

After spending so many hours naked under Leroy's bed last night and part of this morning, I was pretty wore out. I still felt like hell when I joined Floyd and Tyrone at the funeral home.

"Just look at what they done to this poor boy," I said as I gazed at the body laying on the embalming table. I had to turn away after a few seconds because he was not only close to my dead son's age, but he also even looked a little like Claude.

"His uncle will get here from Chicago tonight. He's supposed to come over here and pick out the casket first thing tomorrow morning," Floyd told me with a sniffle.

"If you ain't here, we'll make sure he sees only them fancy new models you bought," Tyrone added. "Like the bronze deal that Webb Street moonshiner's family picked out for his funeral last month. If Brother Puckett's brother is going to cover all of his nephew's final expenses, we might as well milk that cow as much as we can."

I gave Tyrone the harshest look I could come up with. "Hold on now. I keep telling y'all, the service we do ain't all about making money. If we start looking at it from a money angle, we'll lose our perspective." I rubbed my face and shook my head. My knees felt weak, and I was still aching throughout my body. "The news about what happened to that Puckett boy done wore me down to a frazzle. Since y'all got everything under control, I better go home and take a pill and get some rest before I fall out."

"I declare, you do look terrible, boss. Go on home and take care of yourself. Sister Puckett told us to come back to her house tonight to pick up her son's burial suit," Floyd told me. "We'll call if we need for you to come back."

When I got home, I took a pill, but it didn't make me feel no better. I nibbled on one of the chicken legs Jessie had cooked, but only to keep her from fussing at me. She did it anyway. "Hubert, you need to eat more." She pointed at my plate with her fork. "Just look at all the food still on your plate you ain't even touched. I don't want you to get sick and have to miss work. And I don't want to have to stay home to doctor you."

"Don't worry about me getting sick. Once I get a good night's sleep, I'll be as robust as a prize-winning hog. Even if I do get sick, Mr. DeBow won't have no problem with me taking off from the mill. And Tyrone and Floyd can keep things running at the funeral home. I'll eat something else later."

It had just got dark when Jessie decided to go across the street to help Yolinda clean some chicken feet. I watched out the window until I seen her go inside. Then I sprinted to the phone and dialed Leroy's number. I was surprised nobody answered.

When Jessie came home two hours later, I was already in bed, but I wasn't asleep. When she got in, it didn't take long for her to doze off. I tossed and turned for quite a while before I was able to.

I woke up Sunday morning before daybreak. Jessie was sleeping like a log, but to make sure she wasn't playing possum, I shook her shoulder. "Jessie, you still asleep?" She didn't move or say nothing. I waited a couple more minutes before I gently eased out of bed and tiptoed into the kitchen.

I immediately dialed Leroy's number again. Since I knew he was sleeping on his couch, he was only a few steps from the kitchen, where his telephone was. When Sadie picked up on the fourth ring, my heart felt like it was about to turn upside down. Her tone was just as gruff as it had been the first time I heard it. "Hello!"

"Is Granny there?" Even though Sadie didn't know me, I used a high-pitched, fake voice.

"No, there ain't no granny here!" she barked.

"I'm sorry, ma'am. I guess I dialed the wrong number."

That miserable sow didn't say nothing else before she hung up.

A hour later, when Jessie went across the street to borrow some grits from Yolinda, I dialed Leroy's number again. I was so relieved when he answered. "Can you talk?" I asked.

"Not right now. Don't call again until you hear from me," he whispered. He hung up so fast, I didn't have time to say nothing else.

Almost three weeks had gone by, and I still hadn't been able to see or talk to Leroy. I didn't know what to think. Even though he had told me not to call him until I heard from him, I decided to call him up anyway Saturday morning. Jessie was in the bathroom sprucing herself up so we could go shopping and eat lunch at one of our favorite restaurants. I tapped on the bathroom door to make sure she'd be occupied for a few more minutes. "Sugar, how much longer do you think you'll be?"

"Hold your horses, Hubert!" she snapped. "Give me about ten more minutes. We got a lot of shopping to do and there ain't no telling who we'll bump into. You know how the women in this town like to gossip and low-rate other women. I need to make sure I look my best."

"All right, baby. Take all the time you need."

I scurried to the kitchen, grabbed the telephone, and dialed Leroy's number at the barbershop. His business days was normally Monday through Friday, but when business was real busy, he opened up on Saturdays. I didn't think Sadie would be in the shop with him. The telephone was picked up on the second ring. I was fit to be tied when she answered. "Hello there! This is Leroy's Barbershop." She sounded so dainty, if I hadn't known what a miserable, low-down mule's butt Sadie was, I would have thought she was as prim and proper as Jessie.

Just hearing her voice made my blood boil. I clenched my fist and forced myself not to cuss and hang up on her. "Yes, is Mr. Everette available?" I could hear Leroy talking with somebody in the background.

"He's busy right now. Can I give him a message?"

"I don't have no appointment, but I need to come in and get my hair cut as soon as possible."

"When did you want to come in, dearie?" She sounded even more prim and proper now. If I hadn't known no better, I would have thought she was flirting with me—with Leroy in the same room. This woman had no shame.

"Um, let me figure out when and I'll call back."

I was stunned when Leroy came on the line. "Hello, this is Leroy Everette. How can I help you?"

"It's me. Please don't get mad. You told me not to call, but I . . . I just wanted to hear your voice."

"Hello, Brother *Franklin*! I'm glad you called," he said with his voice cracking. "I'm booked up for today and all next week, but I hope to see you soon. Could you give me a call again one day next week just before I close, Brother *Franklin*? That's usually when I get cancellations."

Hearing him say that made me feel a little better. "I'll do that, sugar. Bye." I didn't know how much longer I could go on without him before I went off the deep end.

CHAPTER 10
Jessie

I told Hubert yesterday that somebody had called our house and hung up on me several times in the last couple of weeks. He'd brushed it off and told me not to worry about it because it had to be somebody who was calling our number by mistake, or some kids playing on a phone. When it happened again this morning at seven o'clock, five weeks after the Puckett boy's funeral, I decided to mention it to him again. "Them hang-up calls is coming too often, for it to be wrong numbers," I said at the breakfast table this morning. I gazed at him from the corner of my eyes and asked, "Is there something going on that you don't want me to know about?"

He stopped chewing and gave me a guarded look. "I ain't got nothing going on that I don't want you to know about. Why in the world would you think that? You know I tell you everything."

"When folks keep calling and hanging up, something sneaky is usually going on," I insisted.

"True. But it ain't nothing going on with me. The only thing I can think of is that one of them women I used to spend time with before we got married is playing pranks."

I gasped. "Blondeen was the only one that gave us a hard time."

"True again. But sometimes folks let things fester before they take any action."

"I agree with you about folks letting things fester, but why would one of them other women wait over a year to start pulling pranks on me? And I've seen each one in public a heap of times since we got married, and nary one seemed upset with me. Anyway, all but one of your used-to-be lady friends married somebody else."

"Well, it could be the one that ain't found a husband yet." Hubert shrugged and sipped from his coffee cup. "I don't know what to tell you, sugar. But I wouldn't worry about them hang-up calls."

I took a deep breath before I asked my next question. "Do you think that maybe a woman you never told me about is the one hanging up on me?"

Hubert's jaw dropped so low it was a wonder it didn't touch his plate. "Jessie Wiggins, I can't believe you actually said that. I didn't cheat on Maggie with another woman, and I ain't cheating on you with another woman. I'm scandalized that you would even think I was." He looked so hurt, I thought he was about to cry.

I held up both hands. "Get a grip now. You don't have to get so upset. I believe you. I had to ask, because that's what the women who was fooling around with my dead husband used to do."

He wagged his finger in my face and said, "I ain't nothing like Orville was. Don't you never bring up this silly subject again. I got too many more serious things on my plate to be concerned about. I don't need to add my wife suspecting something so unholy of me. If I wasn't such a restrained man, I'd get righteously indignant. Do you hear me?"

"I hear you," I mumbled. There was times when I was so confused, I didn't know if I was coming or going. Even though

Hubert was telling me the truth, did he think I was so gullible I wouldn't get a little bit suspicious? I wasn't in the mood to get him, or myself, more rattled right now, so I decided to forget about the hang-up calls and change the subject for the time being. If and when them suspicious calls started up again, I'd deal with them then. "It's a little chilly outside today. Make sure you wear your wool jacket."

When we ate supper this evening, I got rattled all over again. But this time, it was because Hubert seemed like he was worried about something. He was real quiet, and no matter what I asked him, he gave me one- and two-word answers. I seen him staring off into space several times. Every time there was a noise outside, he jerked his head around to look at the kitchen door. When the telephone rang, he leaped out of his chair like a frog to answer it. It was Floyd calling to tell him he'd found some insurance papers that had been misplaced. Hubert seemed relieved, but when he sat back down, that worried look was back on his face. I didn't want to rile him up again today, so I didn't ask him about it. But I did want to conversate with him so it wouldn't look like I was too concerned about the way he was behaving. "What are we going to do for my birthday next week?"

My question caught him off guard, because he reared back in his chair and looked at me like I had just fell from the sky. You would have thought he was hearing this information for the first time. "Your birthday is next week?"

Now I knew something was going on with him. Since my birthday was also April Fools' Day, him and everybody I knew teased me about it every year. "It's every year on April first. To be honest with you, when a woman reaches my age, she don't want to be reminded that she's another year older." I let out a heavy sigh. "I don't care if we don't do nothing. We didn't do much for your birthday this year."

"Do you want to bake a cake and have Mama and Daddy come over and celebrate with us? You can invite your mama too."

"I don't really care. It's just another day to me. I'd be happy if just you and me spent the evening together alone. You ain't even got to buy me no presents. We can skip having cake and a bunch of other fattening snacks. I done gained so much weight lately, my butt looks like it belongs on a horse." I chuckled. Hubert didn't. But I was pleased to see he didn't look so worried now.

"What's wrong with you gaining weight, Jessie? You ought to be thankful the Lord done blessed us with so much abundance. Don't you know there are folks in Lexington, and everywhere else, scrounging around for food?"

"I know a lot of folks are still struggling to get by. Every time your mama and the church sisters ask me to cook some pies or casseroles to donate to the poor, I do. But I been eating enough for myself and a few other folks. I ain't got but three pairs of bloomers I can still squeeze into."

"Go buy some in a bigger size," he suggested.

That was not the response I expected or wanted to hear. As much as I didn't want to ask the next few questions, I knew I had to do it now. "Hubert, what's bothering you? You having problems at the mill? Or is Tyrone and Floyd neglecting their work at the funeral home?" I couldn't think of any other things that would put him in the doldrums. I was sure that if he was having another health issue, he would have told me by now.

"Naw, I ain't having no problems at the mill. And you know I ain't never had no problems with Tyrone and Floyd. They are so dedicated and competent; they could take care of business with their eyes closed. It's just that I got a few other things on my mind."

"Well, I'm your wife. Anything that involves you, involves me. So, why don't we talk about it?"

He gave me a wide-eyed look. "Jessie, I don't want to worry you."

"You are already doing a pretty good job of that! You been sitting around this house looking as grim as a pallbearer lately."

I didn't want to make him feel worse by hollering at him. I gave him a hopeful look and softened my tone. "Is it another medical issue, or ... did the current problem get worse?" I couldn't believe the last part of my sentence. Hubert's pecker had been as dead as a doornail ever since Maggie died. How much worse could it get? I immediately tried to backpedal. "What I mean is—"

He cut me off. "The problem I told you about, before we got married, ain't no worse or better. The rest of my body is in perfect health." He pushed his plate to the side, with most of the fried chicken and pinto beans still on it. "I think I'll leave now so I can go get some gas. After I do that, I might buy a mess of flowers and put them on Maggie's and Claude's graves."

"All right, then. I would go to the graveyard with you, but I'd just get depressed and then I'd be walking around looking like a pallbearer. Get enough flowers so you can put some on Blondeen's grave too."

Hubert looked so mortified; you would have thought a snake was crawling up his leg. "Why? That woman wasn't no kin to us!"

"No, but she wouldn't be where she's at if it wasn't for us," I said gently.

"Oh, Lord. I thought she was a subject we'd put behind us. I don't know why you won't let it go. I have."

I hunched my shoulders. "I know I should have, and I will eventually. But it still pops up in my mind from time to time."

"All right. If I go to the graveyard, I'll put flowers on Blondeen's grave too. Happy?"

I nodded. "I ... I just feel so bad about us being responsible for her death."

"Jessie, quit whining. Did you forget who the bad guy was that night? Would she be putting flowers on our graves if she'd killed us?"

"No, because she would be in jail."

"Humph! Do you think for one minute that the police would have tried to find out who killed us? That woman would be walking around as free as a bird."

"Just like us," I reminded.

CHAPTER 11
Jessie

Hubert had been offering to drive me to work ever since we got married, but we was rarely ready to leave the house at the same time. Then he offered to use part of our savings to buy me a car. I told him I didn't mind taking the bus, no matter how bad the service was sometimes. I was more concerned about us saving money for more important things. The bus that I took home from work Friday evening was running a hour late. I got home just as Hubert was getting in the car. "Where you going?" I asked.

"One of my men at the mill is out sick and I need to take him his paycheck."

"You want me to go with you?"

"No, you go on in the house before the mosquitoes come out and eat you alive. Him and his family live way out in the sticks near the county line, so I could be gone for quite a while."

"All right, then. I'll cook supper and put a plate for you in the oven."

"You don't need to cook unless you want to. I'm sure my

worker and his wife will want me to stay for supper. They don't have company that often, and when they do, they practically hold them hostage."

"Maybe if I go with you, they won't expect you to stay long."

"Uh-uh. His wife is more into making quilts than you. She'll put you to work on one right away. I'll see you when I see you." Hubert left and I went inside.

After I got out of my uniform and ate a baloney sandwich, I got restless, but I didn't feel like visiting nobody. And I sure didn't feel like working on no quilts or anything else. I decided to take a walk and get some fresh air. It was almost 7 p.m. I wasn't planning to go no place in particular. But I ended up in a neighborhood eight blocks from my house, close to the edge of town. This was where a lot of rowdy folks lived, and the homes was not as nice and well-tended as the ones on my street. One of the residents was a moonshiner named Glenn Hawthorne that I'd known all my life. He used to be a share-cropper until he realized he could make a lot more money selling homemade liquor and hosting nightly "parties" at his house. Glenn was Hubert's age, and his wife Carrie was a year younger than me. But we'd all attended Lexington's only elementary school for colored kids at the same time. Glenn and Carrie had dropped out before they got to high school. They belonged to my father-in-law's church, but they only went to attend weddings and funerals.

I rarely went to a moonshiner's house. My first husband, Orville, used to visit various ones on a regular basis, mostly to meet up with one of his numerous girlfriends and pick fights with men he thought had slighted him in some way. When he got too unruly, somebody would come get me to drag him home.

There was several houses like Glenn's in the colored section of town. Prohibition had been over for a while, but it didn't make no difference to colored folks. Things was still the same for us when it came to drinking. The white store owners that sold liquor was not only mean to us, but when they had stuff on sale, they made us pay full price. The colored moonshiners sold homemade liquor and they sold it cheaper than the stores. Besides, we got treated like human beings when we did business with our own kind.

When Glenn opened the front door to his small house, with some of the red shingles missing in the front and on both sides, he looked at me like I was a ghost. "Jessie Tucker? W-why, I thought you was dead!"

I gasped. "I don't know why you would think that!"

"Well, since I ain't seen you in a coon's age, what else could I think? Colored women are still getting killed left and right in Lexington. I thought that killer might have got his hands on you." Glenn laughed and gave me a bear hug. "Aw, don't pay me no mind. You know I'm just kidding. It's good to see you again! You are one of the most righteous women I ever knew. Come on in and give this place some class."

Glenn had a charming personality, but he wasn't no Prince Charming. He had a short, lumpy body, bug eyes, and a cone-shaped bald head. But he'd never had trouble attracting women. His third wife, Carrie, was a thin mulatto woman with plain features and limp brown hair that she always wore in a ponytail.

"My last name ain't Tucker no more," I told him as he steered me into the living room. There was already a small crowd drinking and having a good time. A cross-eyed man in a plaid suit was sitting on a wooden crate blowing on a harmonica. Two women was dancing together with the same man, staggering like they'd been drinking all day. And they probably had. One thing everybody knew about Glenn was that he encouraged his guests to drink as much as they could afford.

Less than a minute after I'd walked in, Carrie came out of

nowhere. "Glenn, your memory is getting worse and worse. Jessie married Reverend Wiggins's son, remember?"

Me and Carrie used to hang out a lot together until she married her first husband. She had three children with him, and six with Glenn. I had always been so jealous of her because she'd been blessed with a slew of children, and I'd only had one, so I'd started avoiding her years ago. I was still a little jealous, but I was able to hide it tonight. I gave Carrie the biggest smile I could come up with, and I hugged her neck so tight, I almost strangled her. "It's good to see you again," I gushed.

"It's good to see you too, girl. I guess being married to a preacher's son slowed you down!"

"I wouldn't say that. It's just that me and Hubert spend a lot of time socializing with folks from church and work." My statement couldn't have been further from the truth. Me and Hubert had never socialized with any of the people we worked with, and we only "socialized" with church members after funerals, weddings, and other church events. I didn't count the time we spent with Tyrone and Floyd because they only came to the house for something related to the funeral home. Sometimes they'd sit and drink a glass of cider, nibble on a pig foot, and maybe play a few games of checkers or dominoes, but that was it.

"What brings you to our neck of the woods this evening, Jessie?" Glenn asked.

"Hubert had to go visit one of the men who works under him at the mill to take him his paycheck. He's been out sick for a few days. I was at loose ends and feeling kind of lonely. With nothing better to do, I decided to take a walk, and ended up over here," I answered. "Me and Hubert gave up alcohol a while ago. But I still take a sip now and then. I thought a drink or two would perk me up this evening."

Glenn and Carrie looked at each other and then at me. "I guess it's hard for a preacher's son—who is also a undertaker—to keep his wife perked up. Dealing with all of them church activities and processing dead bodies must really limit Hubert's spare time," Glenn said with a grimace.

"We don't spend as much time at the church like we used to. And handling dead bodies don't bother him one bit. It's just that he's at the age when—"

Carrie interrupted me. "Hubert's at the age when he ain't fun no more, right?"

Glenn shot Carrie a hot look. "Me and him close in age, and I'm still fun, ain't I, Carrie?" he whined.

"When you stop being fun, I'll let you know," she snapped as she punched the side of his arm. "Jessie, if it's fun you looking for, you came to the right place," Carrie told me with a wink. "Do you remember my half brother, Amos Meacham? Him and his mama moved to Montgomery thirty years ago and he just decided to move back here last month. He's got a itching to get reacquainted with everybody. I'll go let him know you came to visit. I'm sure he'll be tickled to death to see you again."

"I remember Amos. He used to chase me with lizards when we was kids. I'd love to see him again, but I need to empty my bladder first." I went through the kitchen and out the back door to a outhouse a few feet from the porch. I had to shoo away a hound dog stretched out on the ground asleep in front of the outhouse door. At least half of the folks who lived in Glenn's neighborhood didn't have indoor plumbing. They got water from a backyard well not too far from their outhouse. The only other times I used a outhouse and got water from a well was when I visited my mama. She lived one street over from Glenn. I hadn't even considered visiting her tonight. Mama liked to stick her nose into me and Hubert's business, and she borrowed money from me on a regular basis. I wasn't in the mood to deal with that tonight.

I was glad Glenn and Carrie kept their outhouse clean, but

the stench was unholy. I had to hold my breath the whole time I was doing my business.

When I got back to the living room, I didn't see Carrie. I took a long pull from a tall glass of moonshine that was so strong, my head started spinning right away. I couldn't remember the last time I felt so giddy and young. The next thing I knew, I was dancing with the same man who had been dancing with them other two women. When the music stopped, Carrie came from around a corner and grabbed me by the hand. "Come on. Amos is in the kitchen."

When we got to the kitchen, there was a tall, well-built man looking out the back window. "Amos, say hello to Jessie. You used to chase her with lizards."

Carrie's brother spun around and looked from her to me. I couldn't believe a plain Jane like Carrie had such a good-looking brother. He had been fairly cute when we was kids, but now he looked like a film star. Most of the men I had known when I was a young girl had lost a lot of their hair by now. And what they had left was thin and streaked with gray. Amos still had a head full of curly black hair and there wasn't no gray in sight. But he had a few wrinkles on his walnut-colored face. His shiny dark brown eyes was his best feature. He was so handsome, I couldn't take my eyes off him. It was nice to see a man close to my age that still looked this good.

"Y'all two are the only ones up in this place tonight that came by yourself. Amos, I thought you'd like to talk to a woman you wouldn't have to worry about getting punched in the nose about. We got some mean, jealous rascals here tonight and it don't take much to set them off when they think somebody is trying to move in on their property. The same goes for the women. They wouldn't waste no time going after a woman with a straight razor for even looking at their men. So, Jessie, I advise you to confine your attention to Amos." Carrie laughed.

"Hi, Amos," I said in a low tone. "It's good to see you again."

"It's good to see you again too, Jessie." He had a deep voice that was very sexy to me. He paused and looked me up and down. "You looking mighty nice tonight."

"Amos, don't you get no ideas. Jessie is a happy married woman, and you are a happy married man." Carrie grinned and went on. "Amos and his wife, Nita, just had their sixth child. But since he needs to get reacquainted with Lexington, I thought it would help if he started off with some of the folks he used to know."

Amos winked at me. "Especially one that turned out to be so pretty."

Being close to a luscious man who thought I was pretty made me nervous. If I hadn't already gone to the outhouse, I probably would have peed on myself.

"I hope you plan on staying in Lexington, Amos." I couldn't believe how shy I sounded. I was anything but that.

"That all depends. So far, settling in Lexington for good is looking real good to me . . ."

I couldn't remember the last time my stomach felt like a swarm of butterflies was fluttering around in it.

CHAPTER 12
Hubert

When I left the mill this evening, I went straight to my worker's house to drop off his paycheck, but I only stayed a few minutes. I'd told Jessie that fib about him making me stay for supper because it would cover what I really wanted to do. I had decided last night to drive over to Hartville after work today and see if I could get a glimpse of Leroy. Even if I couldn't speak to him, I knew it would do me a world of good just to look at him.

Friday was usually the busiest day at the barbershop, so Leroy always stayed open longer when it was necessary.

When I got to Hartville, I checked into the same motel where me and Leroy had first got together. The hour-long drive always made my legs stiff, so I rested for about fifteen minutes. After I splashed some cold water onto my weary face, I got back in my car and drove to his street. When I got a block from the barbershop, my heart felt like it was trying to bust through my skin. As soon as I got in front of the shop, I slowed down. I wanted to see Leroy, and I wanted him to see me.

He was cutting a customer's hair when I gazed through the

window. He didn't glance in my direction, but my eyes flooded with tears as I stared at him. I was glad there wasn't no cars behind me, so I was able to sit in the same spot for a few moments.

While I was admiring Leroy, something told me to look up toward his bedroom. A chill ran up my spine when I seen Sadie's scowling, pie-shaped face in the window looking out. That bitch! Oh, how I detested that loathsome woman. I slapped the steering wheel, let out a few cusswords I rarely used, and sped off like the police was chasing me.

I cussed all the way to the grocery store three blocks away, where me and Leroy shopped. I bought a pig foot and some crackers to snack on, and then I went back to the motel. Since I'd already paid for the room for the whole night, it didn't make sense for me not to spend more time in it. Besides, I was so distressed, I didn't think I'd be able to hide it from Jessie if I went home tonight.

I didn't eat the snacks I had picked up because I had lost my appetite. It didn't take long to make up my mind to go back to Leroy's barbershop. I was due for a haircut and that was the excuse I planned to use when I got there. I splashed some more cold water onto my face and got back in my car. I prayed that Leroy hadn't already closed up for the day.

He was working on a different man's hair when I walked in. He looked up at me like he had never seen me before! My confidence sunk as low as it could go. "Good evening, sir. Do you have a appointment?" he politely asked.

"Um, no, I don't. But I'm going to a wedding tomorrow and I wanted to look nice. I been so busy with work all week, I couldn't come here before now."

"Well, I can accommodate you if you don't mind waiting. I got one more customer to take care of first."

"I'll wait." I plonked down into one of the metal waiting chairs with such a thud, my butt felt like a mule had kicked it.

Time seemed to stand still. And my butt was getting numb sitting in that hard chair. I didn't care if I turned to mush and slid to the floor, I wasn't about to leave.

A couple of seconds after Leroy finished cutting my hair, I slipped him a note that I had wrote on a piece of paper before I left the motel. The note let him know where I was staying at and invited him to join me if he could. I knew he couldn't spend much time with me if he came, but I was willing to settle for even a few minutes. If he came and thought he could come back after Sadie went to sleep, but didn't know what time, I would spend the whole night. The only thing I was concerned about was Jessie. If I didn't go home tonight, she'd be all up in my face when I got home in the morning. I'd add on to the original lie and explain that my sick coworker's wife and kids suddenly had to go somewhere tonight. They didn't want to leave him alone and had practically begged me to stay with him until they got back.

Another customer came in and sat down in the same chair I'd been sitting in. I thanked Leroy for cutting my hair and handed him a dime tip, which was twice as much as I usually gave for a haircut. He looked into my eyes and winked.

I had a hard time sitting still when I got back to the motel. I paced around the room so long, I was surprised I didn't walk a hole in the floor. A hour dragged by, and I got even more restless.

Finally, a few minutes past 10 p.m., somebody knocked on the door. I didn't even ask who it was before I opened it. It was Leroy.

We didn't say nothing at first. He just rushed in, pulled me into his arms, and kissed me. And then we started taking off our clothes. "I can't stay long," he told me in a hoarse tone as he stepped out of his underwear.

"I figured that. I'm just glad you came. Every minute I can spend with you is a blessing."

Ten minutes after we'd pleasured each other, he leaped off the bed and grabbed his clothes off the floor. I gasped. "W-what's this? You leaving already?"

"I told you I couldn't stay long. Sadie thinks I'm picking up some barbecue." Leroy shook his head and let out a disgusted breath. "That woman ain't never liked to cook. That was one of the reasons me and her didn't get along. And I got a feeling that's one of the reasons her new marriage fell apart."

I laid on my side and watched Leroy get dressed. "So, if her marriage is over, does it mean she'll be staying in Hartville for good?" I thought it was in my best interest to ask, "And she'll be staying with you permanently?"

Leroy suddenly looked so frightened; I became frightened too. "I . . . I don't know what her plan is. But the bottom line is, I can't put her and my boys out on the street."

"Now don't get mad, but I need to ask you something and I hope you'll tell me the truth."

"Hubert, I ain't never told you nothing but the truth. You can ask me whatever you want and I ain't going to get mad."

"Is Sadie still sleeping in your bed?"

Leroy blinked real hard and bit his bottom lip before he answered. "Um . . . yes, she is."

"You still sleeping on the couch?" Leroy looked down and didn't say nothing. He didn't have to. Leroy couldn't have looked more guilty if he tried. The thought of him making love to that woman turned my stomach inside out.

"Hubert, Sadie is the kind of woman that don't take no for a answer."

I started to grit my teeth. I was mad and I wanted him to know it. "You making love to her!" I snarled. It wasn't a question, it was a statement. When he didn't deny it, I knew it was true. I sighed. "You told me once before that having sex with her was a 'unique experience,' even though you never wanted to do it. Is it a *unique experience* with me?"

Leroy flopped down on the bed and massaged my thigh. "Please don't make things no harder than they already are." He stood back up and faced me with his hands on his hips. He looked so pitiful, I felt worse for him than I felt for myself. "I can see you as often as I can, but it'll never be for more than a hour or two each time. Does that suit you?"

"I guess it'll have to. So long as you see me."

"Then we need to come up with a plan."

We decided to get together every Tuesday and Thursday evening for as many hours as possible. I'd leave the mill early and get the motel room. If I had to check into a different motel than the one we was in now, I'd drop by his barbershop and slip him a note. He'd tell Sadie he had to drive to Mobile to pick up some products for his shop that he couldn't find in Hartville.

Tuesday and Thursday was the best days in the week for Leroy because every Tuesday Sadie went to play bingo with some of the members who belonged to the church she'd attended before she left Leroy. On Thursday nights, one of the local moonshiners had a "buy one drink, get one free" deal that she and some of her female friends liked to take advantage of. We would also get together on weekends when we could. We would figure that out each Thursday when we got together so he wouldn't have to call my house too often and have to hang up if Jessie answered.

Even though I agreed to this arrangement, I didn't like it. But my feelings for Leroy was so strong, I was willing to settle for crumbs at this point. I had heard about men who would settle for so little. But they was either real old or ugly, so I couldn't understand what was happening to me, unless I had slipped into one of them categories and didn't realize it.

CHAPTER 13
Jessie

I had a good time at Glenn's place last night. I drunk two glasses of moonshine, danced with Amos several times, and when I got ready to leave, he borrowed Glenn's truck to drive me home.

Just recalling the conversation I'd had with him on the way to my house made me smile. It had been a short ride and he'd done most of the talking. After a loud snort, he asked me with a tight look on his face, "So, what is it like being married to a undertaker?"

I reared my head back and gave him a puzzled look. "That's a odd question. Why do you ask?"

"I'm just curious. Everybody I know, me included, get real nervous when it comes to dead bodies. It's downright ghoulish. I've only been around corpses at funerals. But your man has a personal relationship with dead folks on a regular basis. With all that embalming fluid and whatnot that he has to put his hands on, some of it is bound to splash on him from time to time and make him smell to high heaven. My daddy worked on a farm tending to hogs for years. He'd come home and scrub off in the hottest water and strongest lye soap we had, and he would still smell like hog manure." Amos laughed.

I didn't think his comment was the least bit funny. "Well, Hubert never comes home smelling like embalming fluid or nothing else. His regular, full-time job is at the turpentine mill. Some days when he comes home, he smells a little like turpentine, but it don't bother me. I love my husband." I sniffed and gave Amos a serious look. "Since we are already on the subject, what kind of work do you do?"

"Me? Well, if you recall, I had to drop out of school in the sixth grade and go work on the farms to help out at home. I had to give that up when I fell off a tractor and injured my back one day, about fifteen years ago. Since then, I been doing jobs that don't involve nothing too physical. My last job was taking care of a dying man. I had to bathe and feed him like he was a baby. And let me tell you, that wasn't no picnic."

"Jobs for colored folks is limited. It must be doubly hard for you to find work if you can't do nothing too physical."

"That's true. But I ain't starving and I got a roof over my head. My wife's mama and daddy still work and they help us out a lot. And I get what I can from Carrie. As long as she don't let Glenn know. When do you plan on coming back to their house?"

"Why?"

"I like the way you dance, and I enjoy conversating with you."

"I don't know when I'll visit Glenn's place again. I ain't been to one of them kind of houses in quite a while."

"Was tonight a special occasion?"

"Not really. I was just bored and wanted to get out of the house."

"Hmmm. Don't you and your husband get out much? Like to a restaurant or the movies or something?"

"He takes me out to eat from time to time, and we go see a movie when it's something we want to see. But we're really homebodies. My birthday is this coming Tuesday. We'll eat some birthday cake at home, listen to gospel music on the radio, and probably play checkers or dominoes before we go to bed. That's what we did for his birthday this year."

Amos snickered. "If that's all you plan on doing for your birthday, why don't you and Hubert swing by Glenn's place later that night? I only vaguely remember him from when we was growing up. I'd like to get reacquainted with him too."

I gave Amos a surprised look. "What for?"

"So I can congratulate him for landing such a beautiful wife."

I laughed. "You need to quit all that. You done flattered me enough for one night. The bottom line is, Hubert is a very pious and straitlaced man. His daddy is a preacher, so he wouldn't be caught dead drinking at a moonshiner's house. He used to take a sip of champagne on special occasions we celebrated at home, but now he don't drink nothing stronger than cider and coffee."

"Well, *excuuuse* me. I didn't know he was one of them folks that think moonshining is the mark of the beast."

"He ain't that extreme," I defended. "He just ain't interested in things like that."

"Looka here, I'm going to be at Glenn's house on Tuesday night anyway. I'll be thinking about you while I'm there."

I decided to change the subject. "If you don't mind, can you stop at the Seafood House so I can get me a catfish sandwich to take home? It's coming up in the next block. It's the only restaurant colored folks can go to this time of night."

"No problem. I wouldn't mind nibbling on some catfish or oysters myself. The only thing is, I ain't got but a nickel to my name."

I waved my hand. "Pffftt! Don't worry about it. I'll treat you for bringing me home." I didn't mind paying for Amos's order. If he hadn't told me he was low on money, I would have offered to pay for him anyway.

There was only four other customers in the dingy little restaurant on a dead-end street. They all occupied booths near the back. I cringed when I realized that two of them was women who had hung around with Blondeen. Both of them wenches had kept me tensed up by relaying nasty things that Blondeen had said about me. I was glad they was busy, hunched over their table, conversating—probably talking trash about somebody—so they didn't notice us standing at the counter. We got our orders and was back in the truck within fifteen minutes. "Turn right at the next corner and my house is on that street in the second block."

"Okay." Amos glanced at me. "I can't get over Carrie having such a good-looking friend-girl. The ones that I've met so far ought to be sleeping in doghouses." He slapped the steering wheel and laughed.

I thought making fun of folks' looks was very disrespectful, but I had to force myself not to laugh. "You shouldn't talk about women like that. Some people can't help the way they look."

"You're right. Anyway, I'm glad I bumped into you tonight. I hope we can be friends."

I hesitated before I said, "I don't see why we can't be."

"I promise not to chase you with lizards no more." This time, I laughed with him.

"You'd be wasting your time if you did, because they don't scare me no more. My son used to play with them when he was a little boy, and I helped him catch a few." We laughed again. It had been a long time since I'd laughed so much in the same night. It felt good.

I didn't have that many men friends to speak of, and I wasn't sure I wanted Amos to become one. He was too good-looking, and I was too weak. I was so glad when we reached my house. He parked in front and shut off the motor. "Thank you for driving me home. But I could have walked." I had my hand on the doorknob and was about to pile out when he started talking again.

"Uh-uh. I heard about that maniac going around killing colored women. There was no way I was going to let you go off in the dark on foot and get snatched."

I was liking Amos more and more. "I appreciate your concern."

"I don't do much walking myself no more, so I can only visit Glenn and Carrie when I get a ride with somebody."

"I don't mind walking. I do it a lot. It's good for you." My hand was still on the doorknob, and now it was sweating. It seemed like the more I looked at Amos, the better-looking he got.

I was about to start squirming when he said, "I agree with you that walking is good for you, but when you get to be my age, everything that's good ain't so *good* no more. Too much walking makes my feet and legs hurt."

I narrowed my eyes and gawked at him. "Just look at you. You ain't that old!" I pointed out. I was a little more relaxed, but I was anxious to get away from this gorgeous man now, because my crotch had started to itch. If he got me any more worked up, I wouldn't be responsible for my actions.

"I doubt if you'll think that when you reach your forties."

My jaw dropped. "How old do you think I am?"

Amos snorted and stared at me for about ten seconds before he answered. "Well, I would guess thirty, maybe thirty-one. That's how old you look."

I smoothed back my hair, hoping he wouldn't notice the few strands of gray. His last compliment made my head swell up like a balloon. Now I wanted to stay with him longer to hear more. "I'll be forty-three on Tuesday."

"I declare, I never would have guessed that."

I gave Amos a side-eyed look. "Come on. Don't be messing with me. When you was chasing me with them lizards, how old did you think I was? Besides, me and you went to school at the same time."

"School was so long ago, I had forgot about that."

"Well, me and you are about the same age. But I appreciate hearing that you think I look much younger," I said shyly.

"Don't thank me. Thank your mama and daddy and the good Lord. I know I ain't the only one you get compliments from. Carrie tells me that your husband is crazy mad in love with you. He ought to be praising you every night before y'all go to bed."

I sniffed and puffed out my chest. "My husband treats me like a queen. I wouldn't trade him for five of these other men in Lexington."

Amos looked disappointed for the first time tonight. "That's a lot for a regular man to live up to."

I liked him more than I wanted to admit to myself. I wished he wasn't married. But marriage usually didn't stop folks from fooling around. It hadn't stopped me last year. I still thought about that handyman at the nursing home that I'd been such a fool for. Not to mention the lie I'd told Hubert about a man taking advantage of me at one of Yolinda's parties last year when I thought I was pregnant by the handyman. Thank God it had been a false alarm and Hubert forgave me.

I was glad when Amos left. I couldn't remember the last time a man had made me feel as good as he had done tonight.

CHAPTER 14
Hubert

I hated having to tell Jessie so many lies. Especially since she was so open and honest with me. But I had to lie to her if I wanted to be happy. The older I got, the more I hated the fact that I'd been born the way I was. I would have gave anything in the world to be a normal man. That way, I could have been the husband Jessie deserved. I wondered why God allowed such things to happen to some of us, and why He chose the ones He did? When I was a teenager and seen other boys my age going fishing, playing sports, and chasing girls, I would feel left out and sad because I never wanted to do none of them "mannish" things. If Maggie hadn't spent so much time with me doing girly things, like making pot holders, raising flowers, and baking tea cakes, I probably would have lost my mind. What could the Lord have been thinking when He made me? I even asked my daddy one time why God made some of us different when He knew we'd suffer because of it. Daddy's answer didn't help me none. And he said it with his thick finger wagging in my face the whole time. "Boy, He had His reasons for making some of His children colored."

"I'm talking about different in other ways. If God made man in His own image and He's perfect, how come every human ain't flawless too?" I was too scared to go into more detail. Daddy had been condemning folks like me in his sermons for as long as I could remember.

"It don't matter what kind of different you talking about. The bottom line is, don't you never imply again that the Almighty got something wrong. God don't make no mistakes! That's how He got to be God." Daddy's words rung in my ears for years.

I didn't like to reminisce about my past, but I couldn't control my thoughts. I did have some pleasant ones, though. One was, I had just had the best weekend I'd had since Sadie roared into Hartville. Leroy had been more passionate than he'd ever been before.

After he left the motel Friday night, I decided to stay in Hartville another night, just so I could savor the experience. I could still smell his scent on me when I woke up Saturday morning, so I took my time washing up.

I didn't have much of a appetite, so I didn't want to go out and eat no breakfast. But a couple of hours later, I did want to nibble on something. I went to the closest store and picked up a loaf of bread and some baloney. Just for the hell of it, I drove past the barbershop again, hoping I'd get another glimpse of Leroy before I headed back to Lexington. The shop was closed, so I went back to the motel, ate two baloney sandwiches, and laid around in the bed until I went to sleep.

I was in such a good mood when I headed home Sunday morning, I actually hummed one of my favorite spirituals for about twenty minutes as I drove down the highway back to Lexington. About ten miles from home, I got behind a man driving a mule wagon. He was moseying along like he had all the time in the world to get where he was going. Cars was com-

ing toward me so fast in the opposite lane, it was a while before
I could pass the mule wagon.

I walked in my front door a few minutes before nine o'clock
on Sunday morning. When Jessie heard my footsteps walking
across the kitchen floor, she whirled around from the sink and
did a double take. "Great day in the morning! Where you
been?"

I rolled my eyes. "I told you I was going to take one of my
sick workers his paycheck."

"That was Friday. *Two* days ago."

"And I told you that him and his wife would probably want
me to stay for supper. Well, as it turned out, I ended up staying
for supper Friday evening and then we played checkers. I was
enjoying myself so much, I lost track of time. The next thing I
knew, it was so late, they talked me into spending the night.
They ain't got no telephone, so I couldn't call you. It was too
late for me to drive five miles down that pitch-black dark road
to use their neighbor's phone like they do."

"Okay. So, you stayed with them Friday night. Did you have
to stay all day and night Saturday too?"

I sighed and flopped down in a chair at the table. Jessie
stood by the side with her arms folded. "Oh, Jessie. You know
how countrified folks behave when they have company. I spent
most of Saturday morning fixing their busted butter churn.
After that, they needed some things from the store in town, so
I did the Christian thing and obliged them. It was so late when
I got back, I decided to stay another night. You know how
dangerous it is on them country roads at night. But to tell you
the truth, the next time anybody is off sick, they'll have to wait
until they get back to work to get their paycheck! My problem
is, I'm too nice, so folks take advantage of me—even when
they don't mean to."

Jessie let out a loud breath and patted my shoulder. "I'm
sorry for flying off the handle. I know how generous you are to
folks when they need something, no matter what it is. A lot of

men wouldn't be so accommodating. Folks couldn't have a better friend than you."

I beamed. "Thank you, baby. It runs in my family." I cleared my throat. "What all did you do while I was gone?"

"The usual. I ironed two baskets of clothes yesterday and darned some of your socks. When I finished doing all that, I visited that chicken-selling man down the street and bought a chicken to cook for this evening. I had planned on going to church when I got up this morning, but I got too lazy." She paused and stared at me with a frown on her face. "You still got on the same clothes you left here wearing Friday."

"I know. But I took a bath at my worker's house yesterday and this morning. He's a itty-bitty man, so he didn't have no clothes that would fit me."

"I declare, Hubert. Them clothes you got on must be musty and stiff enough to walk on their own by now. Go put on something fresh."

"All right, sugar."

I was in too good of a mood to get upset over the fuss Jessie was making. I had enjoyed my visit with Leroy so much, nothing could bring me down. Now that we had a plan, I felt much better.

Jessie had said she didn't want to do nothing special for her birthday. But when I offered to take her out to supper, she jumped at the chance. I took her to a place that specialized in neck bone stew. The headwaiter met us at the door and explained that they was about to close up for the evening because of a grease fire in the kitchen. Me and Jessie turned around and headed back to the car. "We'll go to the Seafood House," I told her. She stopped walking and grabbed my arm. There was a wild-eyed look on her face. "Jessie, what's the matter?"

"We ain't going there!" she snapped. Her reaction surprised me.

"That's one of your favorite places. You said that they serve the best fish-head soup in town. And we ain't been there in a while. Why don't you want to go now, since we planned to eat out this evening anyway?"

"Um, I'm just not in the mood for no kind of fish. Besides, we just ate red snapper for supper last Monday and catfish on Wednesday. It's a wonder we ain't grew gills and scales by now." She laughed. "Let's drive over to Branson and go to that place called Mozella's. They make the best macaroni and cheese I ever ate."

"That's in the next county!" I pointed out. "That's a long way to go for a meal, unless it's for a special occasion." I immediately wished I could take back my words.

Jessie whirled her head around and gave me a hot look. "Hubert, if my birthday ain't a 'special occasion,' what is?"

"I'm sorry, sugar." I gave her a quick peck on her jaw. "It *is* a special occasion. Wait until you see the two birthday presents I got for you."

"You always buy me more than one gift for my birthday. I feel bad because all I gave you for yours was them striped pajamas."

"It wouldn't bother me if you didn't give me nothing. I know what's in your heart."

I opened the door for her and she eased into the car. Before I started the motor, she rubbed my arm and told me, "I am so glad you are in much better spirits than you've been lately. I think it's wonderful."

"I think it's God." Leroy was the reason I was in a much better mood, but I didn't mind giving God the credit.

CHAPTER 15
Jessie

I couldn't believe how giddy Hubert had suddenly become. He gave me flowers the Saturday after my birthday and took me shopping the same day. He didn't even bat a eye when I picked out two new nightgowns. Both was low-cut and see-through. They didn't do me no good, though. He'd seen me near naked and all the way naked a heap of times, and still hadn't made love to me yet. But I wasn't going to get too upset about it. After all, his manhood was in God's hands.

But the more I thought about Hubert's condition, the stranger it sounded to me. According to Maggie, he had pestered her almost every night since their wedding day. And he hadn't let up until she was almost ready to deliver Claude. I'd been taught that too much of a good thing wasn't good for nobody, even sex. Too much sex was one thing. *No* sex was something else. Could losing a wife cause a man who had once been so frisky to shut down forever?

I eventually convinced myself that God had allowed Hubert to lose his manhood because He wanted him to become more spiritual, and not rely too much on pleasures of the flesh. The

Lord must have wanted me to become more spiritual too. But Him denying me sex didn't make no sense. I was already a very spiritual woman.

April was almost over, and I was so sexually frustrated, I was climbing the walls. The last Tuesday in the month, Hubert wolfed down so fast the collard greens, corn bread, and chicken gizzards I had cooked for supper, you would have thought it was the last meal he'd ever eat.

I gave him a stunned look. "My goodness, Hubert. How come you eating so fast?" We'd only sat down at the table six or seven minutes ago and he had almost finished everything on his plate.

"I have to drive over to Branson and see a man about a car he wants to sell," he blurted out. "He goes to bed with the chickens, so I need to leave soon."

"Why didn't you go right after you got off work instead of coming home first?"

"Um, I got the days mixed up and thought I'd told him I'd come tomorrow. I didn't realize my mistake until I got home today."

"Oh, Hubert. You are getting too forgetful for your own good. I told you, more than once, that I didn't want you spending no money on a car for me. I don't mind taking the bus to and from work. And another thing, how come you didn't talk to me about buying another car first?"

"The car ain't for you, sugar. I been driving the same old jalopy too long and it's costing a heap of money to keep it running. Last month, I had to have the brakes replaced. The month before that, it was the lights."

"Oh. Well, I ain't got nothing to do but drag around the house, so I'll go with you."

Hubert held up his hand. "Women and car buying don't mix. I don't want you to say something that'll make that man up his price or change his mind."

I couldn't believe the way men's minds worked. As smart as Hubert was, sometimes the things he did and said was so dumb. "If the man wants to sell the car, don't you think he'd be reasonable about it? What could I say to mess anything up?"

"Oh, there just ain't no telling. And another thing, completing the deal could take quite a while. That booger is so long-winded, he'll have me over there half the night. Why don't you go visit Yolinda or your mama? And I didn't want to bring it up, but my mama mentioned to me the other day how disappointed she is that you ain't been over to let her do your hair in two months."

"I don't mind doing my own hair, but I'll go visit Ma Wiggins in the next day or so. One thing I need to do is get my butt back to church soon. I don't want Pa Wiggins to accuse me of backsliding. Unless the world ends, I'm going to get my lazy tail out of bed and drag it to church this Sunday. I hope you'll go with me."

"I will. I declare, I could use some spiritual nourishment. We'll even stay for the afternoon service. I just want to make sure I'm doing my duty as a upstanding Christian husband, especially with a flawless wife like you."

"You boost my morale better than a elixir." I exhaled and looked at him in awe. I couldn't stop smiling. "Well, you'd better wipe your greasy mouth off and go meet with that car man."

Ten minutes after Hubert left, I decided to go back to Glenn's place. I didn't care if Amos was there or not, but I thought it would be nice to see him again.

When I got there, Carrie opened the door for me and looked surprised to see me. "Speak of the devil. We was just talking about you!" she hollered as she waved me in and led me to the back of the crowded living room.

My breath caught in my throat. "Who was just talking about me?"

"Me and a couple of the men you danced with the last time

you came over. I was wondering when and if you'd come visit us again. We ain't seen you in quite a while."

"I been real busy lately," I explained.

"So have we! We had a full house last night and some of the same folks swore they'd return tonight. Ever since Glenn hired a man to come play his guitar and sing the blues, business is booming. And we just got a mess of new records, so there'll be plenty of good music to dance to."

"I'm glad to hear that. Um . . . how is Amos doing these days?" I asked in a meek tone.

"Why don't you ask him yourself? He's in the kitchen frying some chicken gizzards."

"Did his wife come with him?"

Carrie snickered. "Pffftt! That gal is sanctified to the bone. She don't come to places like this. He just got here twenty minutes ago."

"Oh. Well, I'll go in the kitchen and say hi to him." I moved away fast so Carrie wouldn't have time to get too nosy about why I was so anxious to see her brother.

Amos was leaning over the stove with a long fork in his hand. He had on a beige shirt and a pair of brown corduroy pants. I'd had a crush on one of my teachers in high school who used to wear them same colors a lot. I didn't think women my age still got crushes. But that was exactly what I had on Amos.

When he looked up and seen me, he started grinning. "Hey now! I thought you had skipped town on me," he yelled as he rushed up to me. "Give me some sugar!" Before I could protest, his arms was around me and his lips was on mine. I didn't do nothing to end the long kiss because it felt so good; I was tingling all over. When he finally pulled away, he looked into my eyes and said, "You taste even sweeter than you look."

"What's wrong with you? I'm a married woman!" I hissed.

Amos snickered. "So what? I'm a married man. That makes us even."

"Besides, I'm in the Church."

He hunched his shoulders and snickered again. "Who ain't? I got baptized thirty-five years ago."

"Do you go around kissing other men's wives?"

"Nope. You are the first one I ever seen that I wanted to do it to." He put his arms around me and kissed me again. This time felt even better. We heard a loud thump coming from the living room and then loud laughter. "Let me set these gizzards aside so they can cool off. Then we'll go outside, where it ain't so noisy and we can talk in peace."

"Okay," I chirped. I didn't know why I was feeling so relaxed already. I hadn't even had anything to drink yet.

When Amos took me by the hand and led me out the back door, I followed him like a lost sheep. We stopped in front of Glenn's dusty old truck, which was parked right next to a walnut tree. "I got the keys. Let's take a ride, okay?"

"What about them gizzards you fried? Don't you have to serve them?"

"All I said I would do was cook them damn things. Let Carrie or Glenn worry about the rest. You want to take a ride with me, or not?"

"I guess. Where to and why? Amos, I know you ain't crazy enough to be using Glenn's truck to go to another moonshiner's house."

"Girl, Glenn would maul my head if I betrayed him like that. You'll see where I'm taking you in a few minutes. It's just down the road a piece."

"What if Glenn or Carrie come looking for us?"

"We'll tell them I drove you home to get your wallet that you forgot. You know they don't give no drinks on credit."

"Oh."

After we had been riding for about five minutes, I pinched

Amos's arm. "I thought you said the place was just down the road a piece."

"It is. I took a wrong turn back at that last crossing."

He stopped in front of a dreary-looking motel. It had a tin roof, one of the two front windows had been busted out and covered with cardboard, and the other window had a crack that ran from top to bottom. But it was one of the only three motels in the county that rented rooms to colored folks. "Why did you bring me to a motel?" I asked dumbly as I piled out of the truck.

Instead of answering my question, Amos pulled me into his arms and covered my mouth with his. No man had ever shown me so much passion before. It was a long kiss, but I wished it had lasted even longer. We was panting like big dogs when he reared his head back and stared into my eyes. "Jessie, I been thinking about you ever since the night I drove you home. And you can lie if you want to, but I know you been thinking about me, ain't you?"

I had to clear my throat before I could respond. "Uh . . . huh." I glanced at the motel's front door. "I can't stay here long. I'd like to make it home before my husband."

"Don't you worry your pretty little head about that. We'll be in and out before you know it."

Amos ushered me into the office, where a bored-looking white woman was sitting at the counter smacking on some chicken wings. She didn't say nothing as she wiped hot sauce and grease off her lips with a dingy rag. "Good evening, *young lady*," Amos said with a wall-to-wall smile on his face. One thing I knew about white folks was that if you wanted to start off on the right foot with them, pay them a compliment. This "young lady" was sixty-five if she was a day. I had to cover my mouth to keep from snickering. "We need a room, if you have one available to rent to colored folks."

I was surprised when the woman smiled. "Yeah, I got one.

It'll cost you half a dollar," she said with a belch. "Checkout time is noon."

Amos tapped my shoulder and said, "Baby, I'm as broke as a haint. Can you cover this?"

I was so taken aback, I didn't know if I was hearing right. What grown man didn't have half a dollar? Even the ones I knew who didn't have jobs had at least that much on them at all times. "No problem." I fished two quarters out of my coin purse and handed them to the woman.

CHAPTER 16
Jessie

While the desk clerk was taking her time getting the key and rambling off a bunch of room rules and regulations, I asked myself, *Girl, why in the world are you paying for a motel room to lay up with a man you barely know?* I was glad I didn't have time to think about what I was doing. Not that I would have changed my mind. If I was going to do that, I would have done it before now. After the woman handed Amos the key, he grabbed my hand and held on to it until we got inside the room.

The room had a musty smell, but it was a step up from the tacky places I used to go to with the man I'd fooled around with last year.

"Go ahead and get comfortable," Amos said while he turned down the stiff-looking bedspread and fluffed the flat pillows. "I got you a birthday present."

"My birthday was weeks ago." I eased down onto the bed and kicked off my shoes.

"I know that. Then it's a belated birthday present. I didn't know when I'd run into you again so every time I went to visit

Carrie, I brought it with me." He reached into his jacket pocket and pulled out a little pink box and handed it to me.

I opened it right away. When I seen what was inside, my eyes felt like they had slid down to the end of my nose. Amos had bought me one of the most expensive, rose-scented smell-goods available. "W-why did you spend so much money on me?"

He puffed out his chest and said in a loud voice, "Because I like to see you smile. If I had had more money, I would have bought you a bigger size. I could tell the first time I met you that you was a woman who appreciates decent smell-goods. I'm sure Hubert gave you something even more special for your birthday, but this was the best I could do."

I smiled, but I had to blink hard to hold back my tears. "My husband gave me a new frying pan and some hairnets." I didn't mention that Hubert had also took me shopping and gave me some flowers because I didn't want Amos to feel bad about not being able to afford to do more for me.

Amos's jaw dropped. "Great balls of fire! That's a damn shame. What could he have been thinking?"

"Hubert is a no-nonsense type of man. He don't believe in giving gifts like smell-goods. He ain't never said it, but I know he thinks it's frivolous. He only gives me gifts that I can use around the house. Last year, he gave me a washboard and a eggbeater."

Amos laughed. "Shoot! If you was my wife, I'd buy you diamonds and gold jewelry—if I had the money. That's what you deserve. You ain't no frump that's only got high status in the kitchen or at a clothes-washing tub."

I beamed like a headlight. Before I knew it, I puffed out my chest so far, I was surprised my brassiere didn't bust loose. "I appreciate all the compliments you give me. They make me feel so good about myself. And I love the perfume." The next thing I knew, Amos was all over me.

It was not going to be easy for us to get together again when we wanted to. He didn't have no telephone at his house, and even if he had one, I wouldn't try to call him. I still couldn't figure out who had made them calls to my house and hung up when I answered. I didn't want to put his wife through the same thing.

When I went back to Glenn's place three days later, Amos was there and we snuck off in Glenn's truck. We went to the same motel. When the desk clerk asked for the money to cover the room, Amos turned to me with his eyebrows raised until I pulled out my coin purse and counted out fifty cents and handed it to the clerk.

Making love with Amos was doing so much for my self-esteem, as well as my body. I wanted to see him as often as possible. I decided to visit Glenn's place again the week after our last rendezvous. It was a Thursday and Hubert was in Hart-ville. Amos wasn't there when I arrived, but just when I was about to leave a hour later, he swaggered in. The way he walked was one of the many things I liked about him. Despite the fact that he didn't even have a job, a vehicle, or any money to speak of, he walked like he had enough confidence for three men. This time, he had on a white shirt and a pair of green pants. After he greeted a few folks, he made his way across the room to where I was standing and got right up on me. "I was hoping I'd see you tonight," he whispered in my ear.

"I was hoping I'd see you too," I whispered back. I was glad I'd drunk a glass of the latest batch of moonshine Glenn had made. It was more potent than the last one, so I already had a strong buzz. That made it easier for me to talk to Amos without fidgeting around like a virgin. His shirt was unbuttoned all the way down the front. Seeing his firm chest and belly got my blood flowing faster right off the bat. I wanted to jump on him right where he stood. If we had been in the house alone, I might have done that. My sex life had been on hold for too long, and I intended to get caught up.

So far, nobody suspected we was fooling around, and I wanted to keep it that way. I didn't know how long I'd see Amos, but for the time being, I wasn't going to think about that too much. I didn't like betraying poor Hubert. But my desire to be with a man whose manhood was in working condition was stronger than my desire to be a faithful wife. I felt bad about what I was doing, but not bad enough to stop.

I talked with Amos for just a few minutes before I started up a conversation with a woman who had complimented me on the shade of rouge I had on. I didn't want nobody to notice me giving Amos too much attention.

When I stopped conversating with the woman, Carrie beckoned for me to join her in the back of the room. "My brother is so shy. I wish you'd spend a little more time talking to him tonight. There's a couple of hussies in here that have been trying to get his attention for weeks. I ain't about to stand by and let one of them get in his head. I trust you. And you ain't his type, so I ain't got to worry about him getting no ideas about you."

"All right." I glanced around the room. "He was just here a few minutes ago. Where is he at now?"

"Amos is so handy in the kitchen, he cooks up something every time he comes over here. He's in there frying some frog legs right now. I wish he would hurry up because we got some hungry guests up in here."

"Okay. I'll go and see when he'll be done cooking."

I was glad Amos was alone when I got to the kitchen. I coughed when I walked through the door, and he turned around.

"Hey, Amos. Um . . . Carrie sent me to see when them frog legs would be done."

"They'll be ready in a minute." Amos glanced at the door and beckoned for me to get closer to him. "I'm really glad you came tonight. I got something to tell you. I didn't tell you in the living room because I didn't want nobody to start gossiping about why I was spending so much time talking to you."

I held my breath. The first thing I thought he wanted to tell me was that he was going to move back to Montgomery, or someplace else. I would have been disappointed. "I hope you ain't going to give me no bad news."

"Nope. It's real good news," he told me in a proud tone. "I just got myself hired today at the Fourth Street Café! I'll be washing dishes there until I find something better. Now instead of us trying to meet up here at the same time to make plans to be together, you can come by the café whenever you can, and we can make plans there."

My mouth dropped open. "I used to work at that café years ago! I washed dishes too."

"See there. We got something in common. I start on Monday, and I'll work from noon to five thirty, Monday through Friday."

"O . . . kay. I get off at five. It'd take me about fifteen minutes to get to the café on the bus. That's if the bus is on time."

"Good, good. When you get there, just have one of my coworkers come get me, or you can come knock on the back door to the kitchen. That's where I will be most of the time. We can spend a little time together before we have to go home to our balls and chains."

The following week, I went to the café two evenings in a row. Amos couldn't spend time with me the first day, but he could on the next day. We took the bus to the same motel. And each time I paid for the room. I didn't mind paying because I knew he didn't make much money, and he had a wife and six kids to support.

The rest of May seemed like a long honeymoon to me. Amos couldn't get enough of me, and I couldn't get enough of him. One Monday when I showed up at the café, I was pleased to see that he had borrowed Glenn's truck so we didn't have to catch the bus to the motel. He borrowed the truck again when we got together two days later. I didn't see him buying a car anytime soon, so each time he borrowed Glenn's truck, I paid for the gas. I was having so much fun, I never complained to Amos about me spending money to be with him. Besides, I didn't want to scare him off.

The last Friday evening in May, while Hubert was in Hartville again, I started letting Amos come to the house. I had him park the truck two blocks away and come inside through the back door. I couldn't bring myself to make love with him in the same bed me and Hubert slept in, so we went at it on the couch. And I didn't let him stay long.

The second time I let him come over, Hubert pulled into our driveway *fifteen* minutes after Amos left. It was a few minutes past 10 p.m. I was still naked, so I ran into the bedroom, grabbed a gown, and put it on before Hubert came in the house. I was so nervous about almost getting caught, I pretended to be asleep when he walked into the bedroom. That was such a close call, I knew then that I couldn't let Amos come to the house again.

Chapter 17
Hubert

Even though me and Leroy had agreed to meet up every week on Tuesday and Thursday, and on weekends when we could, I wasn't going to count on that. All kinds of things could come up beyond our control that could mess things up for us. But I didn't expect Memorial Day to interfere with our arrangement. I left work early the Tuesday after the holiday so I could be at the motel when Leroy closed up the barbershop. When a hour went by and he hadn't shown up, I knew he wouldn't. He'd never been that late. I didn't get upset, though. I didn't want my emotions and anger to get out of control, so I gave him the benefit of the doubt. There had to be a good reason why he had stood me up. I had a feeling that damn Sadie had something to do with it! I went home, and when I went to bed, I didn't get much sleep.

When I got up Wednesday morning, I took a chance and called his apartment before I went to work. I was pleased as pie when he answered the telephone. "I can't talk but a hot minute," he whispered.

"You didn't show up last night," I said in a stiff tone.

"That's because Sadie decided at the last minute that she wanted me to take her and the boys to a second holiday barbecue at her mama's house. We ended up spending most of Tuesday over there. It was too late when we got back to my place last night to call you to let you know I couldn't make it. And while we're on the subject, I can't make it this Thursday neither. She's cooking supper for her mama and daddy's wedding anniversary and wants me to be there. Listen, I can't do nothing that'll upset Sadie enough to make her keep my boys from visiting me."

"How much longer do you think she's going to be with you?"

"I don't know exactly. But I can tell you that it'll be a while before things are back to normal between me and you."

I moaned and rubbed the back of my neck. "Why do you think that?"

"Well, the boys really like the school Sadie put them in over here and they done made some new friends. She got her mail coming to my address and she had me paint the boys' bedroom. Two days ago, her husband dropped off the rest of their things, even the boys' fishing poles."

Hearing that almost made me puke. "So it sounds like she is in Hartville to stay," I griped.

"I don't know. She's so fickle, anything is possible." Leroy mumbled something under his breath that sounded like gibberish.

"What did you just say?"

"I said, I know this is hard on you. But it's even harder on me. I don't like being with somebody I no longer love."

"Speaking of love, you still making *love* to her?"

"Come on now. Let's not go there." Leroy sounded bone-weary. I didn't care because I was just as weary as he was. I wanted to hear everything he had to say, until he said the *last* thing I wanted to hear: "If you want to end things—"

I didn't let him finish his sentence. "You done lost your

mind? You know I don't want to do that!" I calmed down immediately. My emotions was running amok. The last thing I
needed to do was get hysterical. I already felt like a madman, I
didn't want to sound like one too.

"Hubert, please cut me some slack. I'm going through hell
with Sadie, and I would appreciate getting some sympathy
from you." The pleading in Leroy's voice really got to me.

"Okay, okay. All right, then. I'm sorry. I'm going to check into
the motel room Thursday evening anyway. Maybe you can sneak
away after she goes to sleep and spend a little time with me."

"I'll do my best." The way his voice cracked I was beginning
to feel sorrier for him than I felt for myself.

Leroy didn't come to the motel on Thursday. All the way
back to Lexington, I cussed and called Sadie every nasty name
I could think of. By Friday, I was almost a basket case. When I
got off work, instead of going home, I headed back to Hartville. I just wanted to be *near* Leroy, and I couldn't wait until
next Tuesday. I didn't believe I'd see him tonight, but the way
I was feeling, just breathing the air close to him would work on
me like a tonic.

It was a long, painful drive because I didn't know what to
expect. The barbershop was closed when I got to Leroy's
street, but his car was sitting out front, where he always parked
it. I cruised to the end of the block, turned around, and drove
real slow back in the same direction I had come from. When I
approached the barbershop this time, what I seen next almost
scared me to death. Waddling from the back of the building
was a great big, high-yellow woman in a long blue tentlike
dress. She had a scowl on her face that was so extreme, it
looked like she was mad enough to cuss out the world. There
was a flowered scarf wrapped around her head.

Sadie must have been a decent-sized, good-looking woman
when she first landed Leroy because there was no way he

would have looked twice at a humongous frump like her. I understood why he didn't want to make her mad. A beast like her could whup a man his size to death with one hand tied behind her back. She abruptly stopped and looked out toward the street. Our eyes locked for a split second. I had been raised to be a gentleman, so I nodded and smiled at her. But that scowl stayed on her face. I didn't want Leroy to come out and see me, so I shot off down the street like a bullet.

Things was not looking good for me and Leroy. I was very upset and didn't feel like driving back to Lexington until I'd calmed down. So I decided to get a room and spend the night. I had already come up with a real good lie to tell Jessie when I got home. She knew how much my boss at the mill liked me. Mr. DeBow asked me to do favors for him every now and then. One day last month, he asked me to drive to Mobile and take some money to his elderly mama. I'd left work three hours early and he still paid me for the whole day. Mr. DeBow also paid for my gas and gave me a extra dollar, to boot. He'd asked me at the spur of the moment, so I hadn't been able to get in touch with Jessie before I got on the highway.

When I got back to my house and told Jessie why I hadn't come home the night before, she had been very understanding. "Hubert, I know how often you have to go outside of Lexington to pick up things you need at the funeral home. And that you like to stay overnight. When you didn't come home by suppertime or called, I figured that was the reason. I'm glad this time it was to do Mr. DeBow a favor. He's good to you. I advise you to accommodate him whenever he asks you to do him a favor."

Using Mr. DeBow's mama to explain another overnight trip was such a believable story, I planned to get as much mileage out of it as possible.

* * *

After I checked into the motel this evening, I got bored right away. There was nothing in the room I could use to kill time with. All I could think about was Leroy, and what the separation from him was doing to me, especially tonight.

I had never had a reason to have a backup plan, like a spare boyfriend. If I'd had one tonight, I would have been all over him like a cheap blanket. Maybe it was time for me to get one . . .

CHAPTER 18
Hubert

The motel was shabby and cheap, but the walls wasn't thin enough for me to hear folks in the other rooms on the sides of mine. I wished I'd brought a magazine to occupy myself with because I was going stir crazy.

I didn't want to find a boyfriend to replace Leroy, or even have as a spare. All I wanted to do tonight was take the edge off the frustration I was feeling. Without thinking about it too much, I decided to visit a dingy little restaurant where I knew men like me hung out. It was close enough for me to walk, but I decided to drive.

Within minutes after I got inside and sat down at a table, I noticed a handsome, friendly-looking man, who appeared to be in his early twenties. He was sitting by hisself a few feet from me. There was a shot glass in his hand. He smiled at me and that got my juices flowing.

I was so anxious to make a connection, my mind was not as sharp as it usually was, so I thought he was coming on to me. I decided to be bold and take him and run before I lost my nerve. "My, my, my. You looking nice tonight," I said with the biggest smile I could manage.

He looked me over before he said, "Thank you. That white shirt and them black britches make you look right dapper." His voice was so nice and husky, it made my temperature rise. He had on a short-sleeved plaid shirt, so I could see his big, firm muscles. Compared to his, my arms looked like bat wings, which was why I always wore long-sleeved shirts.

I took a deep breath and blurted out, "Do you mind if I join you? I don't like sitting alone . . ."

"Suit yourself." He shrugged and nodded at the chair across from him, but I plopped down in the one on the side so we could be closer.

There was only two waiters and a fairly big crowd, so I knew it would be a while before I could place my order. Me and the man chatted for a couple of minutes about how great the food at this place was, the change in the weather, and the mess the country was in. I was getting antsy, so I bit the bullet and made the first move toward us getting together. "You look mighty strapping with all of them muscles. You work at a lumber mill?"

The man's demeanor suddenly turned hostile. "Naw! I don't work for no lumber mill!"

I held my breath for a few seconds before I went on. "My name is Hubert." I didn't see no reason not to give my real name, because if we got together, it would only be for tonight. "What's your name?"

I wasn't prepared for his hostile response. "You don't need to know my name! And you can stop trying to get close to me, because I ain't never been with a man before in my life! Even if I wanted to, I wouldn't look twice at a geezer like you. Now get the hell away from my table, *Methuselah*."

I got up so fast, my chair fell over. While I was leaning down to pick it up, a great big woman with a red scarf tied around her head like a pirate approached the table. "Isabel, is this man bothering you?"

My jaw almost hit the floor. "Oh! I'm sorry!" I had never been more embarrassed in my life. I had approached a woman, thinking she was a man.

"You must be blind and dumb if you don't know a bulldagger when you see one, fool!" Isabel exploded.

I had never before in my life met a woman who was into women. I had probably been in the company of a few at some of the places I'd gone to and hadn't realized it. It made sense that women like Isabel would go to the same public places men like me went to.

I left that place in a hurry. After driving around for about fifteen minutes, I ended up at the Half Moon Diner. It was the same restaurant where I'd seen Leroy kissing a handsome young man, before me and him got together. When I seen that same man right after I walked through the door, I got excited. I knew what he was about, and he was sitting at a table by hisself. I smiled and approached him. I felt good when he smiled back and nodded. I stopped beside him and asked in a low tone, "Can you come outside with me so I can talk to you in private?"

He pursed his lips and gave me a sheepish look. "What about?"

"Well, I got a couple of hours to kill. I was wondering if you would like to help me kill them hours?"

He looked me up and down before he responded. "You got a car?"

"Yeah. It's right outside."

"You got a place we can go to?"

I nodded. It had been quite a while since I'd picked up a stranger. I'd never had no trouble, so I wasn't worried about that tonight. Especially since I knew that this stranger really was a man. "I got a motel room. It's paid for until tomorrow."

The man looked me up and down again. "All right, then. You kinda cute for a man your age." He abruptly stood up and motioned for me to follow him out the door. I attempted to conversate with him in the car, but he wasn't interested. "Do you mind if we keep quiet until we get to your room? I don't even want to tell you my name."

"No problem. We'll be at the motel in a couple of minutes. I guess you don't want to know my name neither, huh?"

"Naw."

Since this man knew Leroy, if I told him my name, there was a chance that he would tell Leroy about me and him someday. But at this point, I didn't care if he did. Shoot. Leroy was holed up in his apartment, sleeping with a sow, so he didn't have no room to get on me about being unfaithful. I wasn't angry with Leroy, because I knew Sadie being back in the picture wasn't his fault. I needed some affection, and I didn't know what else to do. But picking up this particular man would turn out to be one of the biggest mistakes I ever made in my life.

Less than a minute after we got in the motel room, my "date" said something I never expected to hear. "I charge two dollars."

I thought he was joking, so I laughed at first. "Two dollars for what?"

"For my services!" he boomed as he patted his crotch.

If he had clobbered me over the head with a dead bird, I wouldn't have been more surprised. What did I get myself into? I wondered. I got so light-headed, I thought I was going to faint. I wasn't about to let that happen. If this man was telling me I had to pay him for some pleasure, there was no telling what he'd do if I was unconscious. He might root through my wallet and take every dime I had, and maybe even rough me up. If he stole my keys and took off with my car, I couldn't even report it to the police without bringing down a world of shame on myself. It would be in the newspaper and somebody in Hartville who knew somebody in Lexington was bound to see it and blab. My life wouldn't be worth half a penny if that happened.

When I realized I'd picked up a male prostitute, I was mortified. "No, no, no," I said as I shook my head. "I declare, you got the wrong idea! I ain't never been asked to pay for sex, especially not a whopping two dollars. I could treat myself to a feast at the best restaurant in Hartville for two dollars. Shoot!"

The prostitute rolled his eyes and wagged his finger at me. "I know you didn't think a handsome young man like me was going to spend time with your flabby old self for *free*. I don't do charity work!"

"Humph! I advise you to drag your tail back to that restaurant and find a sucker who will pay you for some pleasure! I sure ain't going to."

"That's fine with me, and probably better for your health. A old goat like you might up and have a heart attack and die on me. But I ain't going no place until I get *my* money."

My brain felt so scrambled, I had to shake my head to put my thoughts in order. "You ain't getting no money from me. And you done got on my nerves so bad, I'll give you half a dollar to get up out of here lickety-split."

"Half a dollar, my foot. I ain't going to settle for nothing but what I would have made if we'd actually had sex, and that's two dollars! Otherwise, your butt is mine—and not the way you want it to be. I'm a devout Pentecostal and a usher in my church, so I'm against violence. But I will kick your ass to kingdom come if you don't pay me!"

I hadn't seen eyes as menacing as his since the ones I seen on a mad dog that chased me home from school one day thirty-five years ago. When the prostitute started to inch closer to me, I backed away and held up my hand. "All right, then. It'll be worth two dollars just to get rid of you." I reached in my pocket and pulled out some loose change, mostly nickels and dimes. I couldn't count out two dollars fast enough.

After he stormed out the door, I was so hot with anger, I had to wet a bath rag and hold it against my face for five minutes before I cooled off.

CHAPTER 19
Hubert

The two incidents I'd gone through tonight had riled me up so bad, I decided to check out of the room and head home as soon as I could.

I had only been driving for about fifteen minutes when a noisy pickup truck approached me, coming from the opposite direction. There was enough light coming from the moon and my headlights for me to see four angry-looking white teenage boys in the bed of the truck. Each one was holding a shotgun. The driver, another teenager, slowed down as they drove past me, and they all gave me threatening looks. I drove faster and prayed that they wouldn't turn around and follow me. They didn't, and I breathed a sigh of relief. The rest of the way, I didn't see nobody else that looked like a threat. But I wouldn't feel safe until I was in my own neighborhood.

This was a night I'd never forget.

I was glad Jessie was in bed asleep when I got home about a hour before midnight. I didn't want to answer no questions, so I stayed as quiet as I could and crawled into bed like a scolded child.

I realized how close I'd come to getting beat up, robbed, or even killed. I had never fought another person before in my life and wouldn't even know how to defend myself. If I didn't get back together with Leroy, I'd be a fool to keep living the same lifestyle. If something bad happened to me, I couldn't blame nobody but myself. As much as I hated to admit to myself, I was prepared to spend the rest of my life without sex. Just like Jessie.

After I'd been in the bed about a hour, she woke up, clicked on the lamp, and went to use the bathroom. When she came back, she looked surprised to see me sitting up in the bed. "Hubert, I didn't hear you come in. Where you been? When you didn't come home before I went to bed, I got worried."

I told her a story about my boss suddenly asking me to go to Mobile to take money to his mama again. "Her neighborhood is full of dead-end streets. I get confused every time I go over there. This time, I got lost and didn't see no colored people out and about to ask for directions. I drove around until I figured out how to get back to the highway."

"I'm just glad you made it back home safe and sound. That's a hour-long drive each way and Mobile is a big city. I can see you getting lost in the white folks' part of town. But Mr. DeBow is such a good man, you can't turn him down."

"Oh, he's more than just a good man. He's the salt of the earth."

Jessie sucked on her teeth. "Bless his soul. A heap of white folks, especially as well-off as he is, wouldn't hesitate to dump their elderly mama or daddy off at a nursing home. You wouldn't believe how many patients I work with that ain't seen none of their relatives in weeks."

"Mr. DeBow told me that so long as there is a breath in his body, his mama wasn't going to no nursing home."

Jessie gave me a curious look. "Why don't he move her in with him and his wife? Why is she in Mobile in the first place?"

"See, his wife's mama and daddy lives with them, so they ain't got enough room for another person."

"Do you mean to tell me his mama lives by herself?"

"No, Mr. DeBow's old-maid niece lives with her. She quit her job at a feedstore to move in and take care of the old woman. Some of the money I take to Mobile goes into her pocketbook."

"Mr. DeBow can't find nobody else to take money to his mama? A rich man like him must have a heap of friends and other relatives. And why can't he take the money to her hisself? Or send it through the mail or wire it to her bank?"

"He don't trust too many folks. And he don't do much driving since he had to have his knee operated on last year. The mail and the wire service ain't reliable, and he sure don't trust no bank. One of the ones he had part of his money in fell when the Depression first hit and Mr. DeBow lost oodles of money."

"That poor man. I'm glad he still got some money left."

"Yeah, but Mr. DeBow's life still ain't peachy keen. He got more problems with his family than you can shake a stick at. He used to have his oldest boy take the money to his mama until he found out that trifling sucker was shortchanging that old woman. He was keeping part of that money to go gamble with and spend on fast women."

"Mr. DeBow got two grown sons. What about the other one? And why can't Mrs. DeBow take the money to Mobile?"

"Pffftt. The other boy drinks like a whale, so he ain't no option. And Mr. DeBow's wife never learned how to drive. I promised I'd help him out until he felt comfortable enough to drive that far again."

"Hubert, you are so nice to folks. God's got his eye on you. He's going to bless you even more." Jessie gave me a wistful look before she went on. "Hmmm. How come you didn't get a motel room this evening like you usually do when you stay overnight in Hartville? Mobile is about the same distance from here, maybe even farther."

"I tried. But none of the motels that rent to colored folks had any rooms available. Besides that, I didn't really want to stay. I'd rather be with you tonight." Jessie must have misinterpreted my comment, because she slid under the covers and scooted so close to me, her bosom was pressed up against my back. "You trying to push me off the bed?" I teased.

"No. I just want to sleep closer to you."

"Why?"

"Because I'm your wife."

"Oh. Well, try not to grind your teeth in my ear."

Jessie didn't say nothing else. When I woke up during the night, she was on her side of the bed with her back to me.

I didn't know what Jessie had tried to pull by snuggling up to me tonight. I wasn't blind or dim-witted, so I knew she was frustrated, probably more than I was. I felt sorry for her and wished there was something I could do about it. But I was doing the best I could do for her by giving her a good home and financial security. A lot of married women didn't even have that. Besides, I thought Jessie was a little long in the tooth for sex to still be that important. I was too, for that matter. Despite how active me and Leroy still was in the bedroom, I knew it wouldn't be too long before our desires fizzled out. That was Mother Nature's plan for humans.

When sex was no longer part of my relationship with Leroy, I'd still want to be with him. The emotional support I felt when we was together did a lot for my morale. And if Jessie could go without sex and still live a meaningful life, I knew I could too.

CHAPTER 20
Jessie

When I woke up at daybreak, Hubert was still snoring like a moose. I usually got up around this time every Saturday. I decided to get a later start this morning because I had to lay in bed and think about what Hubert had told me before he went to sleep. If he didn't want me to sleep too close to him because I might grind my teeth, he'd never let me get close enough to him for us to have sex. Until then, I'd keep on seeing Amos. Even though it was costing me a pretty penny.

Amos was broke most of the time and didn't hesitate to ask me for loans. Out of all the times I'd been with him since we first got together, he'd only paid for the motel room two times. Another time when he'd paid for the room, he'd "borrowed" the same amount of money from me that the room had cost. I kept telling myself that eventually I'd stop lending to him, but I didn't know when or how I'd do that. In the meantime, I was having too much fun to make a fuss over a few dollars.

There was so many things I loved about Amos. One was the compliments he gave me. "I declare, Jessie. You are the most easygoing woman I ever met. You never complain about nothing, and you do everything I ask you to do in and out of the bed. And you ain't ugly. What more could a man ask for?" He'd said all that to me on our last date. I'd beamed like a flashlight.

Another thing I loved about Amos was the fact that he was so considerate in bed. If he finished before me, he would keep going at it until I was satisfied too. According to Maggie's brags, Hubert had been the same way with her. There was no telling when, and if, I'd ever find out for myself. Amos was also smart, so he was a good person to conversate with. He didn't mind listening to me gripe about the duties at the nursing home I had to perform that made me squeamish.

When me and Hubert ate breakfast this morning, one of the first things he did was grab my hand and squeeze it. "How are you doing this morning, sugar? Yesterday must have been good to you, because your eyes is sparkling like diamonds."

I didn't know that good sex could affect a woman's eyes. I would have gave anything in the world if Hubert had been the man making me experience so much pleasure Friday night instead of Amos. I swallowed the chunk of biscuit I had just chewed and blinked hard to squash the sparkle in my eyes. I played it off the best way I could. "Well, I'm feeling blessed because we only lost one patient in the last week. That's why my eyes is shining so bright. But don't let that fool you, because I've had better days . . . and nights." I raised my coffee cup up to my lips and took my time sipping.

"Better how?" he asked with his eyebrows raised. He didn't give me time to answer. "Jessie, I know you been praying that me and you would get closer in the biblical sense someday, and I hope you're right. I . . . I miss being intimate. But everything is in God's hands. You just have to be patient."

I rolled my neck and gave him a stupefied look. "If I ain't being patient, Job wasn't neither when he had to wait for God to give back everything he'd lost."

Hubert held up both of his hands. "You hold on, Jessie. Don't go comparing yourself to men in high positions with the Lord, like Job was. God had a purpose for him—"

I cut him off before he could say something else stupid. "According to your daddy and every other preacher I know, God's got a purpose for all of us. I wish you could put yourself in my place. Then you would really know how I feel about our situation. I get tired of listening to Yolinda and my sisters and a few other women brag about all the affection they get from their men. I'd like to tell them something other than the lies I been telling them about what a great lover you are."

Hubert gasped. "Why, Jessie Wiggins, I'm scandalized! Bite your tongue."

"I ain't biting nothing. I can say whatever I want to say to my friends."

"Yeah, so long as it don't include sex. In the first place, that ain't nothing to be bragging about. Besides, a godly woman should only discuss her intimate body functions in the bedroom with her doctor and her husband."

"My doctor don't care nothing about my 'intimate body functions' in the bedroom. And I do discuss it with you. You keep telling me the same thing: Losing Maggie made you lose your ability to make love. When you first told me, I was very sympathetic and I still am. But I still believe it's a temporary affliction. I don't know how I'll act when you make love to me for the first time."

"When I do, it won't be the first time we had sex together, Jessie." Hubert's lips quivered and his jaw twitched. "I don't like to bring it up again, but I *raped* you last year."

"Huh? Oh!" The lie I had him believing was the foundation of my marriage. I wouldn't undo it, even if I could. If I hadn't come up with it, I'd still be a miserable widow woman with nothing but a bleak future to look forward to. "That don't count because we was both too drunk to realize what we was doing. I don't remember a thing about it. Do you?"

"Not a bit."

I coughed to clear my throat. "Then we can forget about that. Besides, I'd like to talk about something else this morning. The subject of sex is too frustrating." I cleared my throat some more and steered the conversation in a direction as far away from the "rape" as I could get. "You might want to speak to Tyrone and Floyd about the way they dress these days. One of their cousins went on a vacation to New Orleans and brought them back all kinds of flashy shirts, caps, and whatnot. At least them overalls they used to wear all the time didn't make them look like peacocks. A couple of weeks ago, Floyd had the nerve to show up at church in a *red* suit!"

From the look of relief on Hubert's face now, I could tell that he was glad I'd changed the subject. "What's wrong with a man wearing a red suit?"

"Nothing if his name is Santa Claus."

Hubert gave me a pensive look. "Yeah, a red suit is kind of gaudy for church. Other than that, what's wrong with the way they dress? You can't expect two countrified bumpkins like them to be as dapper as me."

"No, I don't. But Yolinda mentioned to me the other day that she seen them coming out of the funeral home a couple of times wearing them flowered shirts their cousin gave them."

"So?"

"Yolinda said, and I agreed with her, that flowered shirts don't belong in a funeral home. At least not on the folks who work there. If you don't put your foot down now, Floyd will be wearing that red suit to work. Being a undertaker, you have to maintain a high level of dignity. Flowered shirts, red suits, and pastel-colored neckties are for parties, Mardi Gras parades, and juke joints. If I was somebody else and came to you for service for a deceased loved one and you was dressed in such a flashy way, I'd think twice about using your services. As tacky as the Fuller Brothers are, every time I see one of them in public, they are dressed in their Sunday best."

"I see your point. I'll have a talk with Tyrone and Floyd."

"Be nice about it. Don't fuss at them. I don't know what you would do without them. And I advise you to keep giving them nice bonuses from time to time. Ain't too many men brave enough to work at a funeral home. I'd hate for you to make them mad enough to up and quit and go work for somebody else."

Hubert took a long pull from his coffee cup before he continued. "Can we change the subject again? This one is making me weary."

I shrugged. "Okay. What else do you want to conversate about?"

"Anything that ain't too serious." Hubert snorted and gave me a weak smile. "What did you do while I was gone last night? The front door was ajar when I came home, and I know you leave it that way sometimes after you been out."

"I did go out for a little while. I'll be more careful about making sure I shut the door all the way when I come in. Anyway, I went to visit a lady who used to work at the nursing home. She's got family coming to visit her in a few days and needed somebody to help her clean some chitlins. Her kids and husband are all useless when it comes to things like that." I laughed and was glad Hubert did too.

"Did you have something to drink at that woman's house?"

I gulped. "Why do you ask that?" I asked stupidly.

"I smelled it when you snuggled up to me in bed last night."

"Yup, I did drink something. Only half a glass of moonshine, though. And only because it was her husband's birthday."

"Uh-huh. I hope you don't get back in the habit of drinking. There ain't no telling what kind of mess you could end up in the next time. There is a heap of frisky men out there who would love to pester a woman like you."

Poor Hubert. There was no telling what he would say or do if he knew I was going at it, left and right, with one of them frisky men. "I know how to spot them kind of men."

"Jessie, you are only human, so you could slip up and get weak. You might even stumble into somebody you'd rather be with instead of me."

Hubert had a mournful expression on his face, but I still gave him the most exasperated look I could manage. "Hush up! You know I love you to death and I'm very happy being married to you. No matter what happens, or don't happen, I still wouldn't leave you for another man."

He looked confused. He was the one who had brought up this subject, so now I was confused. "Jessie, where are you going with this conversation?"

"Nowhere, I guess. I just want you to know how I feel."

"I already know that."

I smiled. "Then there ain't nothing else to say about it." I stood up and started clearing the table before he had time to say anything else.

Sometimes if I was ready to leave for work when Hubert was, he would drop me off at the nursing home. I wasn't ready Monday morning, but I didn't mind the short walk to my bus stop. I was still feeling so good because of my date with Amos on Friday evening, walking past Blondeen's old house didn't bother me half as much as it usually did. Besides, I liked to breathe in the fresh air and get a little exercise at the same time. I had been eating more and exercising less lately so I was gaining weight faster than I wanted to and I didn't like that. Amos had told me more than once that one of the things he liked about me was my petite body. The extra weight didn't faze him. He even complimented me on that. "Jessie, I noticed how plump you been looking these days. But I don't care if you put on a hundred pounds. That would be more of you for me to love. I bet your husband feels the same way."

"He told me he didn't care how fat I got; he would still love me." Hubert hadn't said that, but I knew my size didn't matter to him. At the end of the day, no matter how big I was, I had a feeling he still wouldn't touch me with a stick.

CHAPTER 21
Hubert

June was a bad month for me. During the first two weeks, I'd gone to the motel in Hartville every Tuesday and Thursday, and Leroy had only joined me two times. As much as I'd wanted some pleasure the nights he didn't show up, I didn't even think about trying to find another man. What had happened to me the last time I did was still fresh on my mind; I cringed every time I thought about it.

July wasn't much better. The Tuesday evening before the Fourth of July, Leroy came to the motel. I had been in the room twiddling my thumbs for over a hour wondering if he was going to join me. When he came twenty minutes later, I acted like I didn't notice the glum look on his face. He gave me a quick kiss, but it was missing most of the passion I was used to. While I was taking off my clothes, he blew out a loud breath. "I'm glad I was able to make it," he mumbled.

"I'm glad too. Ain't you going to take off your clothes?" I had already stretched out in the bed.

Leroy sighed and unzipped his pants real slow before he dropped down on the side of the bed. That glum expression was still on his face. "I can't take everything off." This would be the first time he hadn't got completely naked.

"You in a hurry?"

He raked his fingers through his hair and scooted closer to me. "I can't stay but a few minutes this time. I'm so sorry." I knew he really meant it because of the sad look in his eyes and the way his lips was trembling. But that didn't make me feel no better.

"*A few minutes?* What can we do in a *few minutes?* Can't you stay at least a hour?"

I could tell he was agitated by the way he kept fiddling around with his hair and wringing his hands. He didn't look like a man who wanted to make passionate love. That bothered me so much, I couldn't get aroused. And my voice got snippy. "Maybe you shouldn't have came at all."

Leroy sighed again, louder and stronger this time. He looked so hopeless now, I felt bad about what I'd just said.

"Hubert, I'm in a crazy situation right now. I need your support more than ever. Sadie done practically took over my place. Her rowdy friends drop in all hours of the day and night, she drinks moonshine like it's going out of style, and she's about to send me to the poorhouse. I don't mind giving the boys some loose change to spend each week, but Sadie is going through my money like I'm growing it in a garden. No matter how much I give her, it ain't never enough. One day, she went behind my back and almost cleaned out my wallet while I was taking a bath. Now I don't let it out of my sight. At the rate things are going, I'll probably end up in the crazy house too. I even had to borrow money to pay rent this month."

I was dumbfounded. "I had no idea things had got that bad. I can't do nothing about you going crazy, but I can give you some money every time we get together."

Leroy shook his head. "No, I don't want your money. Don't worry about me. I'll get by. I got ways to increase my income.

Last week, I sold a few pieces of the jewelry my grandmamma left me. And I recently raised the prices at the shop—something I hadn't done in four years. Three of my regular customers, who had been with me since I opened my shop, didn't like that. They done already switched to another barber."

I stared at the wall in front of me for a few seconds. Leroy stood up and got out of the rest of his clothes. "What you doing that for?" I asked. "I thought you was only going to stay a few minutes."

"Aw shuck it! I'm going to stay as long as you want me to." Leroy gave me the most defiant look I'd ever seen on his face. "I might even spend the whole damn night!"

I was shocked at the way he was behaving now. But I was glad he was finally showing some moxie. "What about Sadie? If you stay out all night, she'll be mad as a hornet."

"She is always mad as a hornet. I am too, but I been able to hold it in." Leroy was such a gentle man, hearing him say something so harsh made me realize Sadie had pushed him close to the edge. I hoped she would haul her big ass back to her husband before Leroy fell or jumped off. "It's getting harder and harder for me to put up with that cow!"

I gently patted Leroy's shoulder. "Don't let her get to you. Just think about how hard and long we'll celebrate when she leaves."

Leroy's eyes lit up and he smiled and told me, "We'll celebrate every single day."

We made love off and on for the next two hours.

When we finally took a break, we went out and picked up some pig feet, crackers, and Dr Pepper. "This is like old times, ain't it?" Leroy said as we sat on the bed enjoying our snacks.

"Sure enough." We laughed.

He decided to go home a few minutes before 11 p.m. "I hope Sadie don't jump on you for staying out so late," I told him just as he was about to leave.

"No matter what I do, she'll find a reason to 'jump on' me."

Right after he closed the door behind him, I washed up in the sink and put my clothes back on.

It was going to take me a hour to get back to Lexington, so I knew I'd be gone way beyond the time I'd told Jessie. The story I'd gave her this time was that I had to go to Toxey this evening to let a new mechanic I'd heard about check out a noise under my hood.

I got home at midnight. Jessie was frantic when I walked through the door. "Hubert, thank God you're all right!" she hollered as she ushered me to the couch.

"What's the matter? I told you I had to go to Toxey after work to meet with that mechanic."

"I didn't think it would take this long for you to get your car checked out."

"I keep telling you to let me teach you a few things about the car in case you're in it by yourself one day and have problems." Despite everything that was happening because of Sadie, and Jessie getting in my face now, I felt like a new man after seeing Leroy tonight.

"Forget about cars and mechanics!" she screamed. "It done happened again!"

My eyes got big and I held my breath. It was several seconds before I could talk again. "What done happened again?"

"The Klan done lynched another colored man! This time, they got Victor Freeman."

CHAPTER 22
Jessie

Nobody I knew was in a holiday mood, so there wouldn't be much of a celebration on the Fourth of July tomorrow. Victor's lynching was too fresh on our minds. Not only was he the twenty-three-year-old son of Pa Wiggins's main soloist, but he was also one of the sweetest, most promising colored men in town. A heap of unmarried young women had been competing for his affection for years. He was the only member of his family to finish high school and he had a good job at the farm where they slaughtered chickens, so his folks depended on the money he contributed to the household.

Me and Hubert was sitting at the kitchen table, but neither one of us was paying much attention to the bacon, eggs, and grits on our plates. We felt bad for the murdered man's family, but we couldn't let grief interfere with our daily plans too much. If we did, we would be walking around with long faces almost every day. "I have to go somewhere this evening, so I'll be home late," he told me.

"You going to meet with the Freeman family and iron out the rest of the funeral arrangements?"

"No, we got everything situated last night. You can go ahead and eat supper and keep mine warming over in the oven this evening," he said as he slowly bit into a piece of bacon.

I took a sip of my coffee before I responded. "Don't tell me you going to Hartville again already. I thought you bought enough embalming fluid and other stuff to last awhile when you went over there last week."

"I ain't going to Hartville this time. I can hold off on that until next week." Hubert cleared his throat and continued. "Mr. DeBow wants me to do him another favor this evening. This time, he not only wants me to deliver more money to his mama, he wants me to prune her walnut tree. She's having a big cookout in her backyard to celebrate the holiday tomorrow, and she's real persnickety when it comes to things like her yard. The inside of her house looks like it belongs to a film star. I ain't never seen so many expensive vases, lamps, plush couches, and whatnot."

I chuckled. "You know how white folks with money like to show off. I used to work for a lady who was so particular, she would make everybody take off their shoes before they came into her house."

"I just wish Old Lady DeBow didn't live in such a *white* neighborhood. I feel like a fly in a bowl of buttermilk every time I go over there."

"Hubert, what do you expect? Only white folks live in white neighborhoods. Even if me and you could afford to buy a house close to somebody like Mr. DeBow's mama, it wouldn't take long before some of them devils burned it to the ground with us in it."

"I know that, sugar. You ain't got to run on about it. I know how to stay in my place when it comes to dealing with them folks."

"I worry myself sick thinking about you being somewhere you don't belong. Especially lately." I sucked in a deep breath and gave Hubert a pitiful look. "Oh, Lord, I just wish you didn't have to get on the highway so soon after the lynching."

Every time there was a lynching, or if a colored person just got chased or beat up by white folks, we all got real careful about leaving our houses for a while. After the Puckett boy's murder, a few colored men and women I knew didn't feel safe enough to continue working in white neighborhoods. They had quit their jobs and went to work at places like the farms and restaurants. That didn't make no sense to me because some of them jobs wasn't no safer. Three farmworkers had been attacked in the last six months while they was plowing fields and tending livestock.

"I doubt if they'll lynch somebody else for a while. The last one was around five months ago."

"And that's when you almost had a run-in with them Klan devils on your way home from out of town. If they had caught you, there ain't no doubt in my mind that they would have strung you up!"

"Jessie, I feel bad enough. Please don't make me feel no worse."

"All right, then. You just be careful. Um . . . what time do you think you'll be back home?"

"Oh, it'll be way before you get ready for bed. Why?"

"Um . . . I wanted to know if you'd be back before that fish place closed so you could pick me up some fish-head soup."

"I might be back before they close, and I might not. If I do get back in time, I'll swing by and get you some soup."

I was glad when Hubert left. The reason I'd asked what time he'd be back home was because I wanted to be with Amos this evening. I needed to know if I'd have time to go by his work after I got off and set up a date with him. I thought it would do me a world of good to do something that would take my mind off the lynching.

Lexington was such a small town, I was familiar with most

of the colored folks. Even the ones I didn't know knew who Hubert was and that I was his wife. That was the reason me and Amos decided to stop riding on the same bus at the same time. We'd been lucky so far. "What if somebody already seen us together?" he asked during our most recent bus ride to the motel. It had been a week since he'd been able to borrow Glenn's truck for us to ride in.

I sucked on my teeth and gave him a thoughtful look. "Well, everybody knows my father-in-law is a preacher. If somebody done already seen us together on the bus and asks me about it someday, I got a good story ready. I'll tell them that Reverend Wiggins is so busy, he ain't got time to give all of his flock the spiritual guidance they need. So he asked me to do it when I ain't too busy and we took the bus to a nice quiet spot in the colored section at the park."

There was a thoughtful look on Amos's face. "I declare, that story makes sense to me, but my wife might not believe it. I think we need to start being more careful—just to be on the safe side."

"All right, then. We'll change our routine."

We came up with a good plan. I would go to the café when I got off work, like I always did, and peep in the café's back window until Amos seen me. He'd come outside and tell me if he could spend some time with me or not that evening. If he could, I'd get on another bus and go to the motel. He'd take a later one and meet me in the alley between the motel and a shoe store that had went out of business. The desk clerks at the motel didn't know us from Adam and Eve, we didn't have to worry about one of them tattling on us, so we always checked in together. But we always used fake names in case one of the clerks ran into somebody who knew our names and started gossiping. Even though the segregation laws was very strict, a few white folks associated with some of the most meddlesome colored folks in town.

* * *

"I am so glad you came by today. I been feeling real low because of that lynching," Amos told me as soon as we got to the motel Thursday evening.

"Me too. Let's not even talk about that. It'll be on everybody's lips enough for a while."

"All right, sugar." Amos rubbed his hands together and grinned. "I been thinking about you ever since the last time I seen you." He was so giddy, he started taking off his clothes right after we got inside our room.

"Slow down!" I slapped his hand as he lifted the tail of my dress. "You just seen me last week."

"I don't care if I seen you last night!" he growled.

We was both naked when we eased down onto the bed a few moments later. His eyes was roaming all over me like I was something good to eat. The next thing I knew, he hauled off and kissed me long and hard. Since Hubert didn't believe in kissing, at least not with me, I really enjoyed feeling Amos's lips on mine. I wished he had kissed me longer. When he moved his lips away, he stared into my eyes for several seconds without even blinking. "Baby, I just love looking at you."

"I love looking at you too, but I wish we didn't have to drag around on buses when we wanted to spend some time together," I whined.

"Aw, come on now, sugar pie. You know I can't afford no wheels right now, and I can't always borrow Glenn's truck when I need it. If you could chip in and help me with a down payment, I could get a decent car."

One thing I didn't like about my trysts with Amos was that the subject of money always came up, and it was always *my* money. I paid for our bus fare, gas for when he borrowed Glenn's truck, the motel room, and he asked me to lend him a few dollars from time to time. "I can't help you get no car," I said in a firm tone. "If I had that kind of money, I'd have a car of my own."

"Oh, well." Amos hunched his shoulders and pulled me into his arms. "I didn't think it would hurt to ask. Especially since you so nice and generous . . ."

"Yeah, I am, ain't I?" I didn't know what was wrong with me. I had the most wonderful husband in the world, I was in the Church, and here I was acting like one of them worldly wenches Pa Wiggins criticized in his fiery sermons. The way I was behaving with Amos, and the way I had carried on with that handyman at the nursing home, was how I used to act when I was still in my teens. All I'd cared about back then was having a good time. I decided that the reason I had lost my common sense was because I was having a good time again. I wasn't proud of what I was doing. But if Hubert was doing what a real husband was supposed to in the bedroom, I wouldn't give another man the time of day.

After me and Amos had had our fun, I washed up in the sink, but I didn't feel clean. The first thing I planned to do when I got home was take a hot bath. Amos had been friskier than usual this time and had sweated the whole time he was on top of me.

We always took the same bus to go home, because it was the last one of the evening, but we never sat together if there was enough empty seats available. This time, Amos sat two seats behind me and got off at the first stop near his neighborhood.

I made it into the house five minutes before Hubert pulled into our driveway, so I didn't have time to take a bath. I still had on my work uniform when I plonked down on the couch. It was a quarter to eight.

"See, I made it back safe and sound," he chuckled as he dropped down onto the couch, all the way at the opposite end as usual.

"Praise God for that. I hope you got something to eat along

the way because I didn't cook no supper." Amos had swiped some baloney sandwiches and Dr Pepper from the café this evening for us to eat, so I wasn't hungry.

Hubert waved his hand. "Don't worry about it. Old Lady DeBow insisted on giving me some fresh baked tea cakes and black-eyed peas." He paused and glanced around the room. "What you been doing? Working on another quilt?"

"Yup. As soon as I finish the one I worked on this evening, I got a itching to start on a new one."

"Good! I like knowing you got plenty to keep yourself busy when I ain't home. I just hope you don't get bored with quilt-making, cooking, and housework and start doing activities you'll regret. Don't you never forget that you are a preacher's daughter-in-law and duty-bound to behave like one at all times. The bottom line is, you can always find something to do to content yourself when I ain't with you. Am I right?"

I cleared my throat and answered, "Right." I had been "contenting" myself so well these days; just thinking about all the things me and Amos had done when we was in that motel bed made me smile.

"I love it when you smile!" Hubert hollered. "A happy woman is a happy wife."

"Right again. Um . . . do you need to use the bathroom? I'd like to take a bath."

"Mrs. DeBow served me four cups of tea, so she advised me to use her toilet before I made the long drive back home. But it's time for me to go again." Hubert stood up and started unzipping his pants. He suddenly gave me a puzzled look. "How come you ain't took a bath before now? You got off work hours ago."

"Huh? Oh! I was going to, but I was so tired, I took a nap right after I got home. And then I got so busy on my sewing machine, I didn't realize how late it was until you walked in the door."

When I finished scrubbing myself off, I splashed on two different smell-goods before I went into the bedroom, where Hubert was now. He had already put on his pajamas. "You going to bed now?"

"Yeah. Them long drives to and from Mobile wear me out."

"I bet they do. But Mr. DeBow is so nice, I hope you will always accommodate him. We might need his help someday."

CHAPTER 23
Jessie

With Victor's funeral coming up on Monday, Friday was the saddest Fourth of July I'd ever experienced. A lot of us cooked anyway, but most of the ribs, chicken, links, and all the fixings was donated to the grieving family. I even made twice as much potato salad as I had planned to make.

Most of the funerals Hubert organized was open casket, unless the body had been mutilated or disfigured in some unholy way. Like if they'd burned to death or got mangled in a car wreck. But every victim of a lynching *had* to have a closed-casket service because nobody wanted to see the mark the noose left around their neck. We was all surprised that the Freeman family insisted on a open casket. Victor's mama had told Hubert to use all of his expertise to make her baby boy look good so everybody could get one last look at him.

Hubert had tied one of my bright green scarves around Victor's neck so nobody could see the noose mark. "I wish it wasn't going to be no open casket," I complained to Hubert on the way to the church. "I'll probably have nightmares for days. And there ain't no telling how long his family will have them."

"I wish it wasn't going to be no open casket, but I have to do what the Freeman family told me to do. Tyrone and Floyd used face powder to cover the black-and-blue bruises on Victor's face, so he looks pretty good."

"I don't care how good he looks. The bottom line is, he's still dead," I choked. I was glad the funeral was early in the day so we could get it over with. "And to think that the men who killed him ain't going to pay for it."

"Don't you fret none, sugar. What goes around, comes around. The devils that lynched Victor will be punished for it someday."

It was such a heart-wrenching funeral, I wished I had stayed home. Two colored men had been lynched in less than six months! Our newspaper had reported the first one at the bottom of page four in three sentences: *A colored field hand was found hanging from a tree near Burberry Road. He had many friends and relatives. A police investigation is under way.* They didn't even give Victor's that much space: *Another colored man was found hanging from a tree near a cotton field. Police have a few leads.*

A "few leads," my tail! We knew nobody would ever go to jail for killing Victor, or any of the other colored murder victims. As far as I knew, no white person had ever been prosecuted for killing somebody colored in the South. When I was fourteen, two white men stormed a colored man's house because he had been seen talking to the wife of one of the men. They beat him to death with bricks right in front of his wife and kids and claimed they'd acted in self-defense. The family's testimony as eyewitnesses hadn't made no difference. The judge referred to them as being unreliable, so the jury had acquitted the men.

The woman Victor had spent the most time with was so distraught, she had to be carried into the church before the service started. One of the pallbearers had been Victor's best friend. He got so overcome when they was carrying the casket in, he fainted and fell flat on his face. I was glad the other pall-bearers was able to keep the casket from hitting the floor. Two ushers ran up to the unconscious man and carried him out of the church.

The Freeman family was so huge, they filled up half of the pews on one side of the church. Me and Hubert occupied one close to the exit, with Tyrone and Floyd. Most of their kinfolks was present too.

Pa Wiggins preached like he had never preached before. I could tell he was as angry and frustrated as the rest of us. "Behold, I can smell the brimstone! It's oozing throughout like a cloud of deadly smoke. That's a sign that Satan is working overtime again! But we shall not be defeated! I don't care how many of us his minions strike down, we won't stay down!" There was so much sweat dripping off Pa Wiggins's face, the front of his robe was soaking wet. Ma Wiggins waddled up to the pulpit and mopped his face with a large white handkerchief.

The congregation was egging Pa Wiggins on by clapping and shouting all kinds of praises. That made him preach harder and louder. "I baptized Victor when he was just a young'un, and from that day on, he walked the path of a righteous man. The law ain't going to do nothing to identify the people who took his life. But we all know who is responsible. Victor is in a place where he won't never feel pain again, at the feet of the lamb in heaven. That's where every last one of us here today will end up, some of us sooner than others." The church got so quiet, you could have heard a pin drop. And then folks started weeping and wailing and praying some more.

When the service ended, Tyrone and Floyd went up to Victor's family and shook hands and hugged necks. I was glad to see that Hubert had talked to Tyrone and Floyd about the clothes they'd been wearing. They had started back to wearing overalls and plain shirts and pants. Today they had on black suits.

Victor Sr. clapped Hubert on the back, shook his hand, and said, "Thank you for all the work you done to make my boy look so good. His mama is real pleased. God is going to bless you."

"He done blessed me and my family so much already," Hubert choked.

The rest of the Freeman family went up to Hubert and hugged and thanked him. "I don't deserve all the praise," he said, beckoning for Floyd and Tyrone to join him. They shuffled over, sniffling and wiping tears and snot off their faces with napkins they'd plucked from the dining area. "I am so blessed to have such wonderful assistants. I don't know what I'd do without them."

Even though Tyrone and Floyd still had tears rolling down their faces, they smiled, puffed out their chests, and beamed like the sun at high noon. "I c-can feel Victor's presence as w-we speak," Tyrone stammered.

"Him and my sons used to go fishing together," Floyd added. "He was a fine specimen of a man."

I didn't want to stay and eat with the rest of the congregation, and I sure didn't want to go to the graveyard for the burial. Hubert didn't go to all of the burials, but he always went when the deceased was the victim of a crime. Tyrone and Floyd dug all the graves for the colored folks in Lexington, even when the Fuller Brothers handled the final arrangements, so they had to attend every burial.

I wanted to get out of the church as fast as I could. Just before I reached the door, Glenn and Carrie came out of nowhere. They had on the same stiff, drab black frocks they wore to every funeral I'd seen them at. "Jessie, you ain't going to stay to eat nothing?" Glenn asked. He must have coated his bald head with three coats of the oil he used as a moisturizer, because it was shining like a new penny.

"I can't eat nothing right now. I used to babysit Victor and his brothers and sisters when they was growing up. This home-going is real hard on me," I explained.

"It's hard on all of us." Carrie abruptly stopped talking and looked around. "Amos and Nita must be close by. You want me to find them so you can meet her?"

Just the mention of Amos's wife made my stomach feel like I had knots in it. I didn't want to conversate with his wife, or him either, for that matter. "Not today. I got a bad headache, so I need to get home and take a pill."

"Aw, come on. It won't take but a minute," Carrie insisted. She clamped her hand down on my shoulder like she was trying to hold me in place.

I moved away from her, and shook my head. "My head feels like it's about to split in two. I'll meet her some other time."

"All right, then. Go home and take care of yourself. I sure wanted you to meet Nita today," Carried whined.

"I'm sorry." I spun around and started to walk toward the door. From the corner of my eye, I seen Amos and a very pretty, dark-skinned woman heading toward the dining area. I practically ran out the door.

CHAPTER 24
Jessie

I walked home from the church with Yolinda and invited her to come in and have a glass of cider. She dropped down onto my couch with a groan. I sat in the chair facing her. "I'm so glad that funeral is over. My tailbone is throbbing from sitting on that hard pew so long," Yolinda complained.

"Hubert appreciates the business, but I hope we don't have another funeral anytime soon." My words made me shudder.

We both took big gulps from our glasses. "My Lord in heaven. Some folks make a sport out of killing, so things will get worse before they get better," Yolinda said before she let out a mighty burp and went on. "What's going to become of us colored folks with all these white beasts on the loose? Not to mention, whoever it is that's running around killing colored women."

"I worry about that all the time. Even though Pa Wiggins tells us that Satan is working in three shifts, I still believe God is in charge. But I decided a long time ago to live every day like it's my last."

"Well, one day it will be." Yolinda shook her head. "Let's

lighten up the conversation. Things will be gloomy enough around here again for a while, and I ain't looking forward to it."

"Neither am I." I finished my cider and gave her a thoughtful look. "What would you rather conversate about?"

"Anything but funerals, lynchings, and murdered colored women. Let's move as far away from them depressing subjects as possible."

"That's fine with me. I would have brought that up myself if you hadn't. Why don't we discuss quilt-making, new recipes, or shopping? That store on Third Street is having a big sale on brassieres and bloomers next week. We can talk about either one, or all three."

Yolinda set her glass on the coffee table, clucked her tongue, and rubbed her hands together. "To hell with all that! Let's talk about men. Them dogs is so complicated; we can have more fun conversating about them."

I raised my eyebrows and swallowed hard. I was disappointed that she hadn't chose one of my other suggestions. "All right, then. I guess that subject is as good as any." I reared back in my seat and gazed at Yolinda with my eyes squinted. "Speaking of men . . . you ain't mentioned yours in a while. Y'all still together?"

"Yeah, and I'm going to hang on to him as long as I can. Finding a good quality one ain't easy these days, especially for women our ages. Praise God I ain't at the point where I believe a piece of a man is better than none."

"Well, I don't want no piece of nothing. I had enough of that with my first husband." The truth was, so long as Hubert wasn't able to perform in bed, he was a "piece of a man" to me too. Amos made up for him, though.

"The only problem with my man is, he can't keep his tally-whacker in gear long enough for me. And I don't like it. I got too much juice left in me to go without some serious hanky-panky." Yolinda sucked on her teeth and gave me a mysterious wink.

"Well, your man is in his sixties. Tallywhackers is like cars and tractors, they ain't built to last forever. I don't care how robust a man is, his pleasuring piece will fizzle out eventually. Some sooner than others . . ."

Yolinda gave me a dismissive wave. "Pffftt. Four years after my husband died and before I met the boyfriend I'm with now, I got involved with a man who was in his *seventies*. I had just turned fifty but I was still real frisky. I met him over in Branson and we hit it off lickety-split. His pecker was always in good working condition, from the first night he mounted me to the last."

I was sorry I had agreed to discuss men. I didn't need to be reminded about me and Hubert's problem. "Maybe you should have kept him."

A sad look crossed Yolinda's face. She fished a handkerchief out of her brassiere and dabbed her eyes before she honked into it. "I would have, if that sweet man hadn't died a week after the last time we was together. Bless his heart. I hope him and his pecker is resting in peace." She sniffled and dabbed her eyes some more. "I lost a useful man."

"I'm sorry for your loss. It's too bad the boyfriend you got now ain't always in the mood when you are."

Yolinda gulped some more cider before she responded. "Well, if he can't get in the mood more often, soon enough, I'm going to find a man who can. But I'd have to let him go first. Now that I have a stronger relationship with God, I don't believe in cheating no more."

Yolinda's words shocked me. I never expected to hear something like that from her. "If your man can't never perform again, you going to break up with him?"

"I don't know if I will or not. I really love him and he's good to me in every other way. I don't think I'd be happy with a man who could perform, but didn't treat me good." Yolinda chuckled. "I do get jealous when I think about some of the things other women have told me about their men. You are one of the women I'm jealous of."

Her last statement surprised me more than the one she'd said a few moments ago. "Me? Why?"

"You ain't never said nothing about Hubert, but Maggie told me that he was a pistol between the sheets." Yolinda snickered and gave me a side-eyed glance. "True or false?"

"Hush up. I ain't going to talk about something that personal about my husband. That's being too nosy, even for you!" I scolded as I wagged my finger in her direction.

"You ain't got to tell me nothing. I ain't blind. You been walking right funny lately and smiling more than usual. That's what a woman does when her man is taking care of business. I noticed the change in you for the first time a month or so ago. You acting the same way Maggie used to. I don't know what y'all do in the bedroom to make Hubert so frisky, but keep doing it."

My stomach churned when I tried to imagine what Yolinda would say if she knew Hubert had never made love to me and that I was going at it with another woman's husband. She drank some more and burped again. "Dagnabbit! I wish you had something stronger to drink. I sure could use a buzz."

"You know we don't keep nothing else in the house to drink but water and buttermilk. Hubert stopped drinking last year and I only take a few sips when I visit my mama's house. She keeps two or three bottles of moonshine in her cupboard at all times."

"Oh, well. I know people don't like to talk about certain things, but with all that's happened lately in Lexington, I realize we could be here today and gone tomorrow. I don't want to die and leave no stones unturned. I know you changed the subject before, but that maniac who is going around killing colored women is still on the loose, and now the Ku Klux Klan is on our case. Me or you could be the next victim! And you are the only person I feel comfortable enough with to tell certain things."

"I'm glad you think that about me, but I'm sorry you have such a grim outlook on the future, Yolinda. Us getting murdered ain't the only thing that could take us out. We can't hide from cancer or some other deadly disease. When it's our time to go, it's our time to go. Now, what stones is it you don't want to leave unturned?"

Yolinda hesitated. And then she started to talk in a low, controlled manner, like she was reading a book to me. "What I'm fixing to share with you is some stuff about myself that I ain't never told nobody. I might not never have the nerve to do it again. I'd hate to take it to my grave, like I had planned to."

My chest tightened. Even if Yolinda told me she had something to do with a killing, I was not about to tell her we was in the same boat. Or about the double life I was living. I was taking all of my secrets to my grave. "Um, if you done something bad, maybe you shouldn't tell nobody, not even me."

"Some folks might call it *bad*, I wouldn't. You want to hear it or not?"

"Well, since you already brought it up, you might as well get it all out."

Yolinda cleared her throat and started talking with a blank expression on her face. "Twenty years ago, when I had my seventh and last baby, my husband stopped pleasuring me. He blamed it on a weak spell due to his age. I was thirty-six at the time, he was sixty-two." She paused and wiped a tear from her eye. "But I knew age couldn't stop a man from performing—if he really wanted to." Yolinda fanned her face with her hand and gave me a wistful look.

"Uh, I can see this ain't easy for you to talk about. You don't have to go on."

Yolinda shook her head. "I need to talk about it. It keeps my mind off the funeral and the lynching, and I got a point I want to make to you." She fanned her face again and went on. "My husband had had three wives before me. Not only was he left-overs, but he was also a 'piece of a man,' if ever there was one. He'd abused his body for years with so much unhealthy food and alcohol, he didn't have but eight teeth left when we got married. He had a lazy eye, a gimpy leg, and a long scar on the side of his face, where one of his wives had sliced him." I cringed as I pictured in my mind the gargoyle Yolinda described. I was so happy I had a handsome husband.

"But"—she paused and raised her hand in the air—"he was also a gold mine and I wasn't about to let some other woman get her paws on nothing. He had worked hard all his life and saved up a heap of money. On top of that, the white man who had owned his family during slavery was his daddy, and he hadn't had no other kids. Most of the master's other kinfolks had died in the war between the North and the South. So he'd left my husband a little piece of land and part of the money he'd hid to keep the Yankees from taking, like they'd done with so many other slave owners. I knew that if he died before me, I'd be sitting pretty financially. Naturally, I figured I could live without sex. After having more than half-a-dozen babies, I decided I'd had enough sex anyway—at least with him." She laughed and finished her cider.

I shook my head. "Did you still love your husband?"

Yolinda waved her hand and gave me a pensive look. "Not as much as I used to, but he was the daddy of my kids, so I still had some feelings for him. With all that money and property at stake, I was more interested in the financial details of our marriage. Anyway, I never badgered him about sex. Back in them days, that was a subject married couples avoided talking about. After a while, there came a point in time when I wanted to enjoy some physical pleasure with a man again. I had gone without for five long years. When I got sick and tired of not being satisfied, I did something about it. Every time he went fishing or hunting, or to hang out with his friends, I went to blues clubs and moon-shiners' houses. I would flirt up a storm with every available man in sight. Before I knew it, I had so many trying to get into my bloomers, I had to beat them suckers off with a stick."

I was so relieved that Yolinda hadn't told me she'd done something that could send her to prison, like me and Hubert. If we hadn't just come from a funeral, I would have laughed. I gawked at her like I was seeing her for the first time. "Oomph, oomph, oomph. Ain't you a dark horse!"

Yolinda sniffed. "Make that a *satisfied* dark horse."

It was getting harder for me not to laugh, but I wanted to hear more. "How long did you fool around like that?"

"Until my husband died."

I didn't know what to say or think about a woman I thought I knew. But she really had my attention, so I wanted to hear her whole story. "Did he find out what you'd been up to before he died?"

"If he did, he didn't say nothing about it."

"Did you ever feel any guilt?"

"I did for a little while. But the day after his funeral, three different women came to my house and claimed that he was the father of their children. One even brought her three sons to my house and asked for money she swore he had promised to leave them. Every single one of them kids was younger than my last baby, so he had to have made them during his so-called weak spell."

"Oh, my God. Did you believe them women? Maybe they was just after his money."

"Hell yeah, I believed them. All five of them kids looked more like my husband than the ones he had with me."

"That must have made you even madder. Did you give any of them women part of your dead husband's money?"

"I didn't want to! Their young'uns wasn't my responsibility, and besides, two of them hussies had husbands at the same time they was messing around with mine. I used the money I got from selling that scoundrel's land and bought a house for me and my kids." Yolinda sniffed and got quiet for a few seconds before she continued. "As time went on, I thought about his other kids a lot. When I'd run into them in public and see them dressed in shabby clothes and looking underfed, I felt bad about the way I had behaved toward them. I felt bad for three long years. To make myself feel better, I decided to help them kids out a little. The woman with the three boys was married to a man from one of them islands—Jamaica, I think. When I went to her house, she had moved. Her neighbor told me that she and her husband and the boys had moved to that island he was from to be closer to his family. I didn't want to reach out that far to her, so I decided to concentrate on them other two women. Before I could go see the youngest one, I heard she and her child had died in a car wreck in Atlanta a few days before I went to her house." Yolinda blinked hard, but I'd already seen a tear roll down her cheek.

"Yolinda, don't tell me no more—"

"Please let me finish. I ain't never going to have enough nerve to talk about this again. And if I don't, it'll keep eating away at me like it's been doing all these years. Believe me, it goes against human nature for anybody to hold on to secrets too long." Yolinda pressed her lips together and gave me a pleading look.

"All right. Go on and finish."

"The third woman was living with her mama in a shack out by that cornfield near the county line. Her husband had left her, and she was struggling just to feed herself and her little girl. I didn't know how she'd react if I knocked on her door, so I didn't. But that weekend, I took a bunch of clothes and money for her and her daughter to the church they belonged to. I told the preacher to give them to the woman, but not to tell her who had donated it. Every Christmas after that, and on the child's birthday, I took money and clothes to that preacher and told him to make sure she got them. I did that until the girl grew up, got married, and moved away. By then, her mama had passed."

I had to blink hard to hold back a few tears of my own. I was glad Yolinda had shared her story with me. We didn't get close until last year when we worked together on a bunch of church events. Before me and Hubert got married, I had heard gossip about her late husband having kids with other women. But in them days, I was more interested in keeping up with gossip that involved my family and close friends. Once me and Yolinda became friends, she never told me a lot of details about her past and I never asked.

"Girl, that is some story. I'm glad you shared it with me, and you ain't got to worry about me telling nobody."

"I know you won't, Jessie. I feel so much better, now that I finally told somebody. One thing I still regret is that I never told my kids they had other siblings. I don't see no reason to tell now, because them kids ain't around no more. I don't want my kids to judge me or their dead daddy." Yolinda exhaled and gave me another pensive look. "Another reason I told you all this is because you are the best friend I got, and the only one I can trust. I was bitter for so many years. Not just because of what my husband had done to me, but because of what I had done to myself. I wish I had told my family everything when it was going on. Instead, I held in secrets that almost destroyed me. I hated the taste of alcohol, but it was the only way I could numb all the pain I was in."

"But you still drink," I pointed out.

Yolinda laughed. "I still hate the way it tastes, but now I drink it because I like the way it makes me feel. Hubert is your family. Keep praying that your marriage will stay as strong as it is now. You and him ain't perfect, but y'all perfect for each other. I wish I could have been as lucky as you."

"Thank you for saying that. You just made my day." I was touched by her words. Nobody else had ever gave me such a glowing compliment. I didn't feel half as bad as I had felt at the funeral.

"I truly regretted how I'd treated them kids my husband had with other women. And I was also ashamed of the way I had fooled around with so many men while I was still married. In the long run, I ended up feeling worse; because at the end of the day, my situation with my husband didn't change for the better because I went with other men. Once all the fun was over, I always ended up right back where I started. But now that I got a good man and a friend like you, I feel better about my past."

Yolinda stared at me for so long, I got self-conscious. "Why are you staring at me like that?"

"Jessie, I know you had problems with your first husband, but if things hadn't turned out the way they did, you wouldn't be with Hubert. Don't you never leave him. And don't do nothing that'll make him mad enough to leave you."

"I won't," I mumbled. This conversation was making me very uncomfortable now and I was anxious to end it. "Uh, thanks for coming over. That funeral wore me out, so I think I'll go take a nap."

Yolinda must have been ready to leave anyway. She stood up before I did. "I'll see you in a day or two. I promise I won't talk about my past no more. Next time, we'll conversate about quilt-making, new recipes, and shopping."

After Yolinda left, I thought about everything she'd told me. There was times when I felt guilty about what I was doing behind Hubert's back. But I didn't feel guilty enough to stop seeing Amos just yet. I hoped that things would improve between me and Hubert before I started feeling as guilty as Yolinda must have felt before she seen the light. But I wasn't as strong as she was, and I knew that I wouldn't behave myself until something happened that would make me want to give up Amos.

CHAPTER 25
Hubert

I lied to Jessie so much now, I couldn't tell the complete truth if she held a butcher knife to my throat. I hadn't took no money to Mr. DeBow's mama like I'd told her I had the day after the funeral. His alcoholic son had stopped drinking and was going to be delivering the money—unless he started drinking again. I'd spent that Tuesday evening with Leroy. He had picked up some rib sandwiches and Nehi soda pop for us to snack on. Sadie had planned to play bingo longer than she usually did with her church friends that night, so we took our time enjoying each other's company.

I still had to go to Hartville to pick up products for my undertaking business, but it didn't make sense for me to spend money on motel rooms and stay overnight when I didn't have to, especially if I couldn't see Leroy. Whenever I could, I picked up things for work on the days I was able to see him. But I didn't stay overnight as often as I used to.

Mr. DeBow's alcoholic son had backslid before, and I knew he probably would do it again. When that happened, Mr. DeBow would start sending me to take money to his mama and I would tell Jessie I was going to stay overnight in Mobile. But after I dropped off the money, I'd swing over to Hartville, slip a note to Leroy, if I could, to see if he'd come visit me at the motel. I would stay overnight on them nights.

Living a double life was hard work. I wondered how so many people was able to pull it off for years on end. Especially folks like me. Sometimes when I thought about how devoted Jessie was to me, tears flooded my eyes. She deserved more than I had to give. But I felt that as long as she put up with me, I didn't have no reason to change.

I had got a little more used to me and Leroy's current arrangement, but I didn't like it. Since it didn't seem like that damn Sadie was ever going to get her lard ass up out of Leroy's apartment, I was prepared to go along with the arrangement as long as I had to. When I asked him if he'd made Sadie mad that night last month when he stayed with me longer than he should have, he just gave me a tight look and I left it at that.

The next few weeks seemed to drag by, slow as molasses. I couldn't wait for July to be over.

The first Monday in August, Leroy called me up at home before I left for work. He called at the right time, because Jessie was still primping in the bathroom. I was in the kitchen finishing up my second cup of coffee. When I heard his voice, I got so excited, I could hardly contain myself. I started grinning right away. "It's so nice to hear from you!" I gushed.

"Is Jessie close by?" he asked.

"Uh-uh. She'll be in the bathroom for a few more minutes. I know Sadie is probably nearby and I don't want her to sneak up on you, so talk fast."

"Pffftt! I ain't got to 'talk fast' to you no more."

"Huh? What's going on?"

"Good news! Sadie decided to go back to her husband. He came with his truck last night and loaded up all their stuff and they took off. I would have called you last night, but it was too late when they left."

I was speechless. I tried to talk but my tongue felt like it had froze up.

"Hubert? You still there?"

"Um . . . yeah, I'm here. You ain't kidding?"

Leroy laughed. "I wouldn't kid about this."

"I . . . I'm so happy I could wrap it in a gift box! Great day in the morning! This is the best news I've heard this year!" I didn't realize I was talking too loud until Jessie ran into the kitchen.

"My goodness, Hubert. Who is that on the phone?" She stopped next to me and gawked at the telephone in my hand. She didn't have on nothing but her brassiere and bloomers.

I could have kicked my own butt for being so careless. "Huh? Oh! It's the man who is going to sell me some new car tires. He ordered them two weeks ago and they finally came in. I wasn't expecting them for several weeks."

Jessie gave me a side-eyed look. "How come you ain't mentioned buying new tires to me before now?"

I waved my hand at her. "You know you women don't care about nothing but quilt-making, smell-goods, pie baking, and all of them other frivolous activities y'all known for. And for your information, I did mention it to you last month."

"Hmmm. I guess I forgot about it."

"You must have! That's what I mean. Women don't care nothing about things like car tires. No wonder you forgot I told you."

Jessie rolled her eyes. "You get that excited about some tires?"

"Yup. Just like you get when you find new brassieres and bloomers on sale," I said, giving her a stern look. "I'm getting them for a lot less than the first man I talked to, so I'm real happy about it."

Jessie gave me a dismissive wave and left the kitchen. "Sorry about that, Leroy. Jessie went back to the bathroom, so I can talk again now," I whispered. "Um . . . what if Sadie comes back?"

"I doubt that. She told me she wasn't surprised that I was still a boring so and so that she couldn't stand to be around another day longer. That miserable heifer cussed at me, and in the next breath, she admitted that I had the best tallywhacker between my legs she ever had." Leroy laughed.

"I'll vouch for that." I laughed too, but inside I was burning with rage about him having sex with her. "She said that in front of the kids?"

"No, they had already got in the truck. But our arrangement for me to have the boys on some weekends is still the same."

"What makes you so sure she won't come back?" The thought of that woman returning made my chest tighten up.

"Because I said so! I told her that if she decides to leave her husband again, she'd better go to her family, friends, or in-laws for help because she can't come to me again. She was so surprised that I stood up to her, she cried and told me she'd go live in a cave before she came to stay with me again. One thing is for sure, I will lock my front door from now on so she won't be able to let herself in, like she did this time."

"That sounds pretty final to me."

"Believe me, it is. If you can get away this evening, come over and we'll celebrate. If you can't make it, we'll do it when you can."

"I'll be there this evening with bells on."

I was glad I hung up when I did, because a second later, Jessie came back into the kitchen. "Um . . . Hubert, I might get home late today." She seemed a little nervous. She was smoothing her hair back and didn't make eye contact with me while she was speaking. "I'm going to pay a visit to a lady that used to work with me. She's sick with the lumbago and could use some cheering up." I thought her behavior was odd, but I'd seen her this way before, so I didn't think that much of it. I assumed she was having a female moment, like cramps or menopause.

"That's wonderful, baby. The man with the tires wants me to come to Toxey and look at them this evening. I'll probably be gone for two or three hours . . ."

"You just going to 'look' at them tires? You ain't going to buy them today?" She looked me straight in the eyes this time.

"Well, I will after I inspect them, and if he does give me that good price he promised. I don't want him to think he's dealing with a fool."

Jessie gasped. "It sounds like he done already done that! What was you thinking by having him order tires before y'all firmly agreed on a price?"

"Jessie, I know the way men do business seems ridiculous to women, but that's the way it is."

She shook her head and clucked her tongue. "Humph. I'll never figure men out."

"I can give you a ride to the bus stop this morning if you want me to."

"That's all right. I been gaining weight, so I need to walk every chance I get."

I was downright giddy when I got to the mill. The day went by fast, but I still left early so I could spend at least two or three hours with Leroy. The only reason I didn't plan on staying with him all night this time was because I had already told Jessie how long I'd be gone. I had also decided to tell her that me and the tire man couldn't agree on a price, so I'd canceled the deal. He had lied to me about selling them at a discount. That would explain me coming home with the same tires on my car.

When me and Leroy got back into the swing of things, I'd use the same excuses I'd used before to keep Jessie in the dark. Them excuses had kept her at bay since me and her got together. I didn't see no reason why they wouldn't work on her now. But whenever I could, I'd add some new ones.

* * *

I was just about to tell Jessie over breakfast Friday morning that I had to take Mrs. DeBow some more money this evening and planned on spending tonight, and maybe Saturday night too, in Mobile. Before I could get the words out, she told me, "Hubert, uh, when I get off work today, I might go visit a lady I promised to help work on a quilt that she's making for her bed-ridden mama. She's new at it and needs help getting her quilt started. I'll probably stay at her house at least a couple of hours. Can you start supper?"

"Oh, didn't I tell you?"

Jessie's eyebrows shot up. "Tell me what?"

"I'm going to Mobile after work to take Old Lady DeBow some more money."

"Again already? I can't believe that old woman spends up all her money so fast. She must be misplacing it."

"Humph. That ain't hardly the case. That old woman's mind is still as sharp as a serpent's tooth. See, Mrs. DeBow is like every other woman. She loves to go shopping."

"*Shopping?* For somebody who needs round-the-clock care, she sure gets around a lot. Anyway, a woman her age should have everything she needs. What do she go shopping for?"

Hubert snickered. "She likes to buy knickknacks for her house, smell-goods, and frocks fit for a film star, just like you. Her niece told me that she don't like to wear the same piece of clothing more than two or three times—including bloomers and brassieres. And she loves to eat in fancy restaurants."

Jessie rolled her eyes and chuckled. "I feel so sorry for Mr. DeBow. He done spoiled his mama and now he got to keep giving her more and more money to keep her contented."

"It's his money. He can do whatever he wants with it. I wish I had enough so me and you could spoil our mamas more."

"Bless your soul for saying that. I wish the same thing. All right, then. You be careful driving on that highway."

CHAPTER 26
Hubert

The minute I walked through Leroy's front door, he was on me like white on rice. Even though I weighed about twenty pounds more than him, he picked me up and carried me to the bedroom. We stayed there for the next hour. Words could not describe how happy I was.

"Hubert, I can't tell you how many times I dreamed about this moment."

"Well, you don't have to dream about it no more."

"It seems like it's been years since we was able to cuddle in this bed," he said as he nuzzled my ear.

"Tell me about it." Being naked brought back the painful memory of me hiding naked under the same bed I was in now. "It's a good thing Sadie left before I reached my breaking point. And I was *real* close to it." I didn't think it would do no good to tell Leroy how I'd come all the way to Hartville that day and drove past his shop just to get a glimpse of him. After all I'd been through already, I didn't want to put the idea in his head that I was desperate or obsessed. It would have scared me if he had come all the way to Lexington just to get a glimpse of me.

Leroy sat up and gave me a distressed look. "I am so sorry I put you through this mess," he said with his voice cracking.

I squeezed his hand. "You ain't got nothing to be sorry about. You didn't have no control over Sadie's actions."

A pensive look crossed his face. "I could have turned her away."

"We done already been over that. You couldn't let her and them boys end up on the street. What I don't understand is if she thought you was such a jackass, why she didn't go to her kinfolks or some of them bingo-playing friends she reconnected with so soon."

"For one thing, her kinfolks can barely feed themselves. Sadie is the kind of woman who could eat anybody out of house and home. I told her that if she went to stay with them, I'd give her money whenever she needed it, but she wasn't interested in that. She was determined to stay at my place, no matter what. And the main reason was because her kinfolks wouldn't have put up with her mean mouth the way I always did."

I shook my head and sighed. "I been so miserable and lonesome, I had a hard time functioning."

"I figured that." Leroy paused and cleared his throat. "Did you consider cheating on me?"

I was taking so long to answer, he said, "Never mind. You just *answered* my question. I'm disappointed . . ."

I threw up my hands. "You ain't got nothing to be disappointed about. Before you get upset, let me explain." I had to swallow the lump in my throat before I could go on. "Yeah, I did consider cheating on you, but I didn't."

Leroy gave me a side-eyed look. "Oh? What stopped you?"

I reluctantly told him about my encounter at that restaurant with a woman I'd mistook for a man. He laughed about it. But he bristled when I told him I had gone to a different place the same night and picked up a man and didn't find out he was a prostitute until we got to my motel room. Leroy was pleased to hear that I didn't do nothing with that man and had only gave him some money because he threatened to beat my tail if I didn't. What I didn't tell him was that the prostitute was the same man I'd seen him kiss at that New Year's Eve event before me and him got together. If he had paid that prostitute for his services, I didn't want to know.

Leroy laid back down and squeezed my hand. "Hubert, I am so pleased you waited for me to get things straightened out with Sadie. Most men probably would have wrote me off."

"I'm just glad she's gone." I glanced toward the door. "I didn't eat nothing before I came over here."

"I tried to cook supper for us, but I was so excited about you coming, I got careless."

"You didn't cook nothing?"

"Yeah, I did. But I burned the coon. And it was one of the biggest, juiciest critters I ever seen."

"Where did you get a coon from? You don't hunt."

"One of my customers hunts up a storm and keeps a mess of meat in his smokehouse. He didn't have enough to pay for his haircut the day before yesterday, so I took the coon instead. I do trades with a heap of my customers."

"That's mighty generous of you. Money is still so tight for some folks these days. Well, I'll eat whatever you didn't burn."

After we piled out of bed, got dressed, gobbled up some turnip greens, potato salad, and hot-water corn bread, we cuddled up on the couch. "Hubert, I hope we can always be this close and happy."

"I don't know why we won't be."

I didn't like the way Leroy's face was scrunched up. "What about your wife? She still ain't suspicious?"

I gave him a dismissive wave. "Pffftt! Jessie was born with a blind eye. She could gaze at the blue sky and believe it was purple if I say it is. She believes *everything* I tell her, so she ain't got no reason to be suspicious."

Leroy snorted and took a deep breath before he asked the next question. "What about you?"

"What about me?"

"You ain't suspicious of her?"

That question made me wheeze. "Let me tell you one thing, Jessie ain't got eyes for no man but me. She's a good-looking, well-built woman, so I know other men look at her. They could parade around in front of her naked and it wouldn't faze her one bit. And another thing, any woman who would marry a man who admitted to her that he had lost his manhood would be happy married to a gelding."

Leroy snickered. "I couldn't imagine no woman who would be happy married to a castrated man. Or 'a gelding,' as you called it."

"Humph! My first wife was as happy as a fox in a henhouse. Me and Maggie slept in the same bed for over twenty-two years and never did nothing intimate. Sex was the last thing on her mind. All she cared about was the four *c*'s."

"What's the four *c*'s?"

"Children, cooking, cleaning, and church."

"I know my Bible, so I know that's what God created women for. But I'm surprised you was able to find a second wife who could live without sex. That's like lightning striking twice in the same place. It's damn near *umpossible*."

"Well, it wasn't 'umpossible' in my case. I got a good thing going with Jessie. So long as she believes I done lost my manhood, I can hold her off forever."

I didn't see no reason to tell Leroy that Jessie did care about sex and that she had cheated on me. Especially since she'd only done it one time. And since the man had took advantage of her, I couldn't hold her responsible for her actions.

CHAPTER 27
Jessie

It had been a month since Yolinda had told me about her past. She hadn't mentioned it since, and I didn't want her to. Even though I agreed that keeping secrets bottled up could do a lot of damage to a person, I had to keep mine. I would have suffered a lot more than she had if somebody found out the truth about my past. I didn't think I had to worry about nobody finding out what had really happened to Blondeen, or how I had tricked Hubert into marrying me. And so long as I was careful with Amos, nobody would ever find out about that secret neither. As far as I was concerned, it was business as usual for me.

The nursing home admitted a bunch of new patients in August that was so cranky they required a lot of extra attention. I'd had to come in a hour earlier and work some overtime almost every other day.

In September, I even worked on Labor Day. Hubert had to go to Mobile that Monday to take the DeBow woman some more money and I didn't want to celebrate the holiday with my in-laws or anybody else. But I was with Amos the day after the holiday and a couple of times each week the rest of the month. I never thought I could experience so much pleasure. It was a shame I had to get it all from a outside man.

As much as I enjoyed spending time with Amos, I wouldn't have married him if I was still single. For one thing, he reminded me of that footloose handyman I fooled around with last year. Both men was handsome, overconfident, and they knew how to sweet talk vulnerable older women like me. They was both in serious relationships with other women, but that didn't stop them from messing around with me. The main differences between them was that the handyman was younger and had a steady job, so he never asked me for money. Amos made me feel like his personal piggy bank.

On top of all the other things I had going on, Ma Wiggins had talked me into volunteering *again* to make three new quilts that the church would donate to poor folks. They needed them by the end of the month, so I had to get busy right away on that. But I always found time to spend with Amos. On the days Hubert had to go out of town, I was able to stay longer at the motel.

October looked like it was going to be just as busy as September had been for me. I had completed the latest request for handmade quilts, and that pleased my mother-in-law. "Jessie, I declare you are a godsend. Them quilts is so nice, I want you to make a couple more, and I'd like to have them by the end of this month." By now, I *hated* making quilts. But it was better to make them, and get praised, than to disappoint Ma Wiggins. Besides, it was a way for me to kill time between my trysts with Amos.

One day halfway into the month, me and Amos took a day off from work so we could spend the whole day at the motel. I left my house that Thursday morning dressed for work. I took the bus to the motel and got our room. Amos showed up about twenty minutes later.

He was still asking me to lend him money, and I was still giving it to him without hesitation. But he had gone from borrowing every now and then, to almost every time we got together. I couldn't tell him I couldn't afford to give him money, because I'd been stupid enough to brag about the big raise Hubert had recently got at the mill, and that he got more business than the only other colored funeral home in Lexington.

The last Monday in October, Floyd came to the house that morning to pick up his paycheck and he stayed for breakfast. He seemed fine sitting at the table smacking on the sausages and grits I had cooked. He abruptly stopped eating when Hubert started complaining about how slow business was lately. The Fuller Brothers had handled the last three funerals this month. "I better get a body soon or we will be in big trouble," he griped.

There was a frightened look on Floyd's face when he spoke. "You ain't thinking about laying me and Tyrone off, I hope. I got a family and a mountain of bills, so I *can't* afford to be out of work."

I liked Hubert's response because it was gentle and the most appropriate one he could give. "I'm sorry. But when there ain't no business coming in, there ain't no money coming in."

Hubert had sung the same song a few times before in the past year or so. But he cared so much about his assistants, one month when business was slow, he paid Tyrone's and Floyd's salary out of his own pocket. They was as happy as fleas on a dog, but they couldn't believe Hubert had made such a sacrifice for their benefit. A week later was when that maniac murdered the first colored woman. The money her family spent on her lavish funeral made up for the money Hubert had paid Floyd and Tyrone out of his pocket, and there was a lot left over.

I returned my attention back to Floyd. "You want some more coffee?"

"Naw. Hearing I might get laid off made me lose my appetite," he whined.

Hubert's tone turned real firm. "Floyd, I hope I don't have to lay y'all off. But if I have to, I will. Pass the biscuits, please."

I liked Floyd and Tyrone and didn't want to see them out of work, not even temporarily. Hubert's late uncle had never laid them off when he was still running the show. But I would support whatever decision Hubert had to make. The bright side was, even if he had to lay them off, sooner or later, he'd get another body. There was way more colored folks connected to Hubert than the Fuller Brothers, so naturally he'd still get more business. There was currently half-a-dozen old folks at death's door and five of them belonged to Pa Wiggins's congregation.

"Do we have to talk about dead folks?" I asked as I passed the bowl with the biscuits to Hubert.

"Dead folks is our business," he reminded.

"Thanks for breakfast, y'all. I better get up out of here and make tracks." Floyd abruptly pushed his plate to the side, let out a mighty belch, and left. I was glad, because I didn't want to hear nothing else about dead folks this morning.

One of the things I enjoyed about being with Amos was that we never discussed gloomy subjects. And every time I brought up his wife or my husband, he changed the subject, so I stopped doing that. When we took breaks from making love, we talked about things like my quilt-making and church matters. He loved talking about his kids. He didn't have no pictures of them, but according to him, they was the best-looking, smartest young'uns in Lexington. I didn't like talking about my son, so whenever that subject came up, I didn't have much to say.

The more I seen Amos, the more I wanted to see him. I had planned to go by the café after work today to see if we could get together this evening. I had to squash them plans when Hubert told me when we was eating breakfast that he was going to pick up some pig feet for supper on his way home from the mill.

"What if Mr. DeBow asks you to take his mama some money this evening?"

Hubert gave me a dry look. "Then I'll drive over to Mobile this evening. And it's a strong possibility that's something I might have to do today. See, Mr. DeBow's son is back to drinking, so I'm sure he'll expect me to take money over there until that fool gets back on the right track."

"If you do have to go, before you leave, could you come by the nursing home to let me know?"

"Well, I will if I can. But I don't know if I'd have time to do that. It's a long drive to Mobile, and I always like to leave work early and get on the road as soon as I can. Besides, Mr. DeBow wants me to get there before it gets too late, because his mama gets real cranky toward the evening." Hubert scratched the top of his head and gazed at me with a puzzled expression on his face. "Is there something you wanted us to do this evening?"

I blinked and hunched my shoulders. "Not really. But it would be nice to go see a movie. We ain't been since we seen that popular movie that our rinky-dink movie theater finally ran back in September last year."

"And I didn't like that flick one bit! Humph! What kind of name is *Gone with the Wind* for a movie? And they made slavery look like a picnic."

"At least them white women wore pretty clothes. That, and that handsome Rhett Butler, was the best things about that movie." I laughed.

"If you feel like going to the movies this evening, you go on without me. I'd rather wait until they show better-quality stuff, like the next Tarzan movie, or something funny with Groucho Marx and his brothers." A frightened look suddenly crossed Hubert's face. "Jessie, I just thought of something. Halloween is this coming Friday. Some folks done already started pulling pranks and acting like fools. Not to mention that the killer is still on the loose. If I don't have to go to Mobile this evening, we can play checkers for a few hours after we eat them pig feet I'm going to pick up."

I stifled a groan. "I don't want to play checkers, and I don't want to go see no movie by myself. I'd rather work on some new pillowcases."

"All right, then. If you going to be in a sewing mood, I got a couple of shirts that need new buttons, and a heap of socks that need to be darned."

When I got to work, I told my supervisor I had a doctor's appointment. I explained to her that I needed to get on the bus in a couple of hours so I could make it to the clinic and be back by noon. I rarely missed work, all the patients and most of the staff liked me, and I always did a good job. That was why I never had a problem taking off when I needed to. I didn't have no appointment. I wanted to go see Amos.

I left the nursing home at exactly 10:30 a.m. and rushed to the bus stop. I got off the bus a block from where Amos worked. I trotted all the way to the café's back window, which was right over the sink, where the dishwashing was done. Amos seen me right away. He immediately came out the back door, wiping his wet, soapy hands on the black rubber apron he had to wear. "Jessie, what you doing here this time of day? You didn't go to work?"

"Yeah, I went. I told my supervisor a fib about a appointment at the clinic. You was on my mind, so I thought I'd come see you," I said in a meek tone. "I hope you can get away so we could take a little walk. Could you take your lunch break early?"

Amos frowned and shook his head. "I wish I could, sugar. But the other dishwasher didn't come in today, so I'm real busy. Why didn't you come over here when you got off work, like you always do? We could get the motel room and have some fun then." Amos stroked my rump and chuckled. "I don't want to waste time just taking a walk with a juicy-butt woman like you."

"I have to go straight home when I get off today. I don't know if my husband is going anywhere. He said he might, but he was real iffy about it."

"Shoot! Hauling piles of them damn dishes all by myself today and getting my hands all pruned up in that hot, soapy water got me tensed up. I really would like to get loose with you when I get off." Amos licked his bottom lip and suddenly looked around. And then he looked at me like I was a entrée on one of them dishes he had to wash. "Baby, how long can you be away from work?"

"The bus was slow getting over here, and it'll probably be late and slow when I go back. I told my supervisor I'd be back before noon, so I can only be with you for ten or fifteen more minutes."

"What I got in mind won't take that long."

Amos had such a bold imagination when it came to sex, I couldn't wait to see what he wanted to do now. "What do you have in mind?"

"You'll see," he said in a growly tone.

He looked around again, got up real close to me, and stared into my eyes for so long, I got fidgety and snapped my fingers in his face. "That gazing ain't doing neither one of us no good. You better hurry up and do something so I can get back to work."

Amos didn't say nothing else, but he stopped staring at my eyes. The next thing I knew, he led me to the side of the café. There was a tall fence, so nobody could see us. Other than on the ground in a cornfield when I was a teenager, I had never made love in such a crude location. "You better make this quick," I advised. He gently pushed me up against the wall, unzipped his pants, and lifted up the tail of my drab gray uniform. I was glad he finished doing his business in less than five minutes.

CHAPTER 28
Jessie

I got back to work one minute before noon. My body was still tingling after my makeshift rendezvous with Amos. I was in such a good mood the rest of the day, I didn't even mind emptying and cleaning out a dozen stinky bedpans.

When I got off work, I stopped at the market to buy a few things to go with the pig feet Hubert told me he was going to bring home, if he didn't have to go to Mobile. I was on my way to the cashier to pay for my vinegar, yams, and corn pone when somebody tapped me on the shoulder. I whirled around and was surprised to see Glenn and Carrie standing behind me, dressed like they was going to a real fancy event. Glenn had on a starchy-looking white shirt, brown britches with a matching jacket, and a wide-brimmed white hat with a brown feather on the side. Carrie had on a bright green cotton dress and a white silk shawl. Next to them, I felt like a hobo in my plain gray work dress and flat brown moccasins.

"How you doing, Jessie?" Glenn asked.

"You ain't been to the house lately," Carrie said.

"You been going to one of them other moonshiners' houses," Glenn accused.

"No, I ain't!" I hollered. "I wouldn't be caught dead in one of them other places. I heard a man punched a woman in the nose at that place down the street from y'all."

"One thing is for sure, nobody would ever get beat up at our place, especially a woman. I won't stand for it. I keep my shotgun close by at all times to let folks know I mean business," Glenn told me with a firm nod.

"I ain't been to visit y'all because I been real busy working on quilts for the church, and doing a slew of other things around the house. And Hubert keeps me running around like a chicken with its head cut off, shopping and going to pay bills and whatnot. Some evenings, I'm so tired, I go straight to bed after I eat supper."

Carrie gave me a pitiful look and shook her head. "That's a shame. Well, you married a man with a very active life. What did you expect?"

"That's all the more reason why you should come visit us and have a few drinks. That way, all of them other things won't feel like such a load," Glenn tossed in.

"I know. I was planning to swing by real soon. Maybe even tonight. It all depends on whether or not Hubert has to go somewhere." I cleared my throat and lowered my voice. "Um . . . I don't want him to know I been coming to visit y'all." I sniffed and looked from Glenn to Carrie. "Y'all ain't got to mention my visits to nobody."

"Girl, we don't broadcast nobody's business. But I can't vouch for none of our guests."

"Pffftt! I ain't worried about them. The folks I've seen there so far don't know me that well, and they are usually so drunk by the time I get there, they wouldn't remember me long enough to tell nobody they seen me." I laughed.

"I hope you can make it tonight because we'll be hosting a really big party," Glenn announced.

I rolled my eyes and snickered. "I thought y'all hosted a big party every night. Just like all the rest of them moonshiners," I teased.

Carrie nodded. "True, true. But this one is special."

"Is that why y'all so dressed up?"

"Yeah, we wanted to get a early start. Some folks said they'd be coming over right after they got off work. We needed a few items, so we decided to come finish up some last-minute shopping. We didn't want to waste time changing back into our regular clothes."

"Hmmm. The party is going to be that fancy, huh?"

Glenn was beaming. "Sure enough. Even some of the other moonshiners will be joining us. It's invitation only."

Moonshiners made their money by luring as many folks as possible to their places. They depended on their customers to make money. And the more customers, the more money. This was the first time I'd heard of one having a "invitation-only" event. "I'm curious now. What's the occasion?"

"We'll be celebrating Amos's wedding anniversary!" Carrie hollered.

I swallowed a huge lump that had suddenly eased into my throat. "Oh," was all I could say.

"After all the years Amos and Nita been married, they still behave like newlyweds. I'm embarrassed to admit it, but sometimes seeing them two lovebirds holding hands and kissing up a storm gets on my nerves."

"Hush up, Carrie. You ain't got nothing to be jealous about," Glenn scolded. "When you want more attention, all you got to do is let me know."

My heart felt like it was going to slide down to my feet. If that wasn't bad enough, it felt like a hammer had slammed into the side of my head, trying to knock some sense into it. I could barely move my lips. My words came out sounding like a croak. "Carrie, your brother is so very blessed." Even though me and Amos had only spent a short time together today, I couldn't believe he didn't bother to mention nothing about a invitation-only party tonight in his honor. I knew I didn't have no right to be jealous, but I was.

"I hope you can come so you can meet Nita. You'll love her to death," Carrie added. "She'll be right skittish tonight being a churchwoman in a place where everybody is drinking. You being a churchwoman too, she'll feel more at ease if you was there. Maybe you can introduce her to some of your church friends. Most of the other women we know is so fast and worldly, we don't want more than a few of them loose booties at the house tonight. Even with his wife there, they might try to make moves on poor Amos, like they always do. But can't no other women tempt my brother, so we ain't too worried about them causing a ruckus. He would *never* cheat. Nita wouldn't have to worry about you eyeballing her property and making her uncomfortable."

"I'm sure the party will be a lot of fun. I'll try to make it," I mumbled.

"Amos is trying to scrape up enough money to go on the honeymoon they didn't get to take when they got married," Glenn said with a wishful look in his eyes. "They got a itching to spend three days in New Orleans. I know that ain't a lot of time for a honeymoon, but it's better than nothing. And after waiting all these years and having six kids, they deserve a nice little getaway. They'll get on the train Friday evening when he gets off work. He's even going to take off the following Monday. That way they'll have enough time to rest up after that train ride back from New Orleans. Me and Carrie done chipped in as much money as we could afford to help him pay for everything. He's still ten dollars short, though."

"Times is still hard. Ten bucks is a heap of money for colored folks to scrape up," I pointed out.

"Amos is so likeable. He done made a lot of new friends since he moved back here, so I know he'll be able to borrow the rest of the money from them in time," Carrie chirped.

"I hope so. It'd be nice if him and Nita could finally go on a honeymoon. Um, I hate to run, but I need to check out and get on home."

I paid for my groceries and rushed to catch the bus. I was too antsy to wait for it, so I walked the five blocks home. I cussed almost all the way. There was no way in the world I was going to attend a celebration for Amos and his wife! I scolded myself for feeling animosity toward a woman I'd never met.

Hubert didn't have to go to Mobile. He had already started cooking the pig feet he'd picked up. After we ate supper, I went into the bedroom to mend a few items on my sewing machine. That was what I did until we went to bed.

When I got off work on Wednesday, I headed to the café to see if Amos wanted to go to the motel. If he was going to go out of town soon, I wanted to see him before he left. I wasn't going to mention that Glenn and Carrie had told me about his anniversary party and his upcoming honeymoon trip to New Orleans. But I was still disappointed that he hadn't mentioned them two events to me when I seen him on Monday. I knew where I stood with him, so I didn't have no right to get in his face about nothing. And so long as I didn't have to see him with his wife, I figured I could put up with our flimsy relationship until Hubert got back on track in the bedroom.

I had told Hubert this morning that I would be coming home late this evening because I was going to visit one of my friends that he'd never met. I wanted to meet the new grandson that her daughter had recently given birth to. I told him the woman's husband would drive me home, so Hubert didn't have to worry about me being by myself on the bus at night. That excuse would give me a hour or more to spend with Amos.

He wasn't surprised when I pecked on the café's back window. He ran to the door right away and stuck his head out. "I'm so glad you came by. I prayed all day you would."

"I can't stay long this evening. I told my husband—"

Amos held up his hand and cut me off. "You don't owe me no explanations about nothing that involves your husband. I done told you that before."

"I told you the same thing about your wife," I reminded.

"Good. Let's keep it that way. Go on and get on the bus. I'll meet you by the side of the motel in about twenty minutes."

Amos was right on time. He seemed even more anxious to spend time with me than he usually was. When we got to the motel lobby, I was pleased when he pulled out his wallet and paid for the room. But I always made sure I had enough money on me anyway, just in case.

We didn't waste no time taking off our clothes and jumping into the bed. After we'd made love twice, Amos sat up and gave me a serious look. "Is something the matter?" I asked.

He nodded. "See . . . uh . . ." He stopped and started to wring his hands. Amos was not a shy man, so I couldn't understand why he was having a hard time answering my question. I had never seen such a sad look on his face before. The way his eyes was watering, you would have thought somebody close to him had died. "Sugar, I got a mess on my hands that I need to figure out."

I didn't have to read his mind to know he was about to tell me something I didn't want to hear. "Oh. Is there anything I can do to help?"

He nodded again and tickled my chin. "Yup, you can help . . . if you want to." His eyes suddenly looked fine. "Uh, baby, I hate to ask you for more money, but I *really* need your help this time."

I sat up. "How much do you need?"

"Ten dollars."

I gasped so hard I almost choked on some air. "Ten . . . dollars? *Ten dollars?*" I repeated with my lips quivering. It was the same amount Glenn and Carrie had told me Amos needed to take his wife on their belated honeymoon. "What do you need that kind of money for?" I didn't know what made me think he'd tell me the truth.

He suddenly looked sad again. "See, my godmother recently died in Huntsville. Bless her soul. I'd like to do the Christian thing and help her family pay for the funeral."

"Oh, I'm sorry to hear that. You must have been real close to her."

"I was. She treated me like I was one of her kids. Bless her heart."

"When do you need the ten dollars?"

"She died last week, but I wasn't able to take off work and go to pay my respects. I figured the least I could do was help the family pay off the undertaker. I need the money by this Friday, as early in the day as possible, because my train leaves at noon. It would be even better if you could give it to me later today or tomorrow. My boss said I could take off Friday and come back on Tuesday, so don't come to the café looking for me until after Tuesday. I'll pay you back, if you want me to . . ."

I didn't know what to say next. The godmother—if he had one—was probably sitting on her front porch gossiping with her friends or working on a quilt. I didn't know what Amos had done with all the money I'd already gave him. But I drew the line when it came to me helping finance his honeymoon!

I wanted to bust him and let him know what Carrie and Glenn had told me. But instead of doing that, I said what I should have said a long time ago. "Amos, I ran into you at a time when I really needed some attention. You gave me that, right off the bat. I done had a lot of fun with you, but I can't see you no more after today."

He grabbed me by the shoulders so hard, my head started swimming. "W-what? How come? You done met somebody that suits you better?"

"Something like that."

"Something like what? Jessie, this better be a joke!"

I pried his hands off me and stood up. "You think this is a joke? Do you see me laughing?"

Amos leaped off the bed, got smack-dab in front of me, and

wrapped his arms around my waist. I turned my head when he tried to kiss me. He sucked on his teeth and said in a gruff tone, "What's wrong with you, girl? This ain't the way to end a relationship!"

"It is for me. Now, if you don't turn me loose, I'm going to scream bloody murder."

He moved back a few steps, rubbed the side of his head, and gave me a puzzled look. "What about the ten dollars I need to borrow?"

I looked at him like he'd lost his mind. I must have lost mine too, because I'd let this man play me for a fool. "You got some nerve, Amos Meacham! You *can't* 'borrow' no more money from me," I hissed with my jaw twitching.

He looked at me like I was threatening to tell his wife about us. "Woman, let me tell you one thing. You ain't never going to find another man like me!"

I laughed long and loud. "I hope I don't find another man like *you*," I said with a smirk.

He stared at me for a long time, but he didn't say nothing else. I was in such a hurry to leave, I didn't even wash off like I usually did. While I was putting my clothes back on, Amos said, "Jessie, I can't believe you playing with my emotions like I ain't got no feelings. And you call yourself a Christian. You ought to be ashamed of yourself!"

I looked him straight in his eyes and said, "I am ashamed, but not for the reason you think."

CHAPTER 29
Hubert

We had another tragedy on Halloween. It wasn't another murder, praise the Lord, but it caused just as much pain. We lost a middle-aged man and a woman in her late twenties. They was guests at Yolinda's annual Halloween party. They had left together to go pick up some more alcohol for her from one of the moonshiners. They never returned.

They was found dead in the man's car on Sunday morning by a fisherman. It had got too close to the edge and slid into Carson Lake and the couple had drowned.

The man and woman was married, but not to each other. Right after the newspaper reported the story, a motel clerk went to the police and said he had rented a room to the couple on Halloween night. That was when folks figured the couple had been involved in some serious hanky-panky. What nobody could figure out was: If they'd already fooled around at the motel, why was they at the lake in the first place?

Both of the victims had belonged to my daddy's church. There was no doubt in anybody's mind that I would handle their final arrangements. They was from large, hardworking families, so I was fixing to make a heap of money. When me and Floyd and Tyrone collected the bodies and took them to my funeral home, I found the woman's bloomers in the man's coat pocket. That was more proof that they had been up to no good.

"If it ain't one thing, it's another," Mama groaned. She called me up on Monday morning, three days before the woman's service, set for Thursday. The man's was going to be on Friday. With so much going on, I had to put my next visit to Leroy on hold. I didn't mind because I knew that when we got together again, we'd make up for lost time. "It's a shame the families want the caskets closed. I been doing that gal's hair for years and I sure would like to see her face one more time," Mama added.

"I don't think nobody should view the bodies in this case, Mama. Not even the families. This scandal is already hard enough on the other wife and the other husband, knowing they was being cheated on. They'd only be more upset if they seen how much damage that mossy, murky water in the lake done to the bodies. Me and Floyd and Tyrone really got our work cut out for us this time."

"The bodies must be pretty well-bloated from being in that water, huh?"

"No, they ain't bloated. They wasn't in the water long enough for that to happen. But them leeches, crayfish, and God only knows what other creatures done a heap of nibbling from their faces on down."

"Oomph, oomph, oomph. I heard the car had weak brakes. And as drunk as they say the man was, he shouldn't have been driving at all, especially with somebody else's wife in the car with him. Why can't married folks be satisfied with the spouse God chose for them? I never could understand why anybody would want to go outside of their marriage. Sex is sex! In the dark, everybody feels the same. So, what's the point in trying it with somebody you ain't married to?"

"Mama, I don't know why people cheat. But even God sending His only son down here to straighten out the mess mankind was in didn't stop folks from cheating. And if He came back today, folks wouldn't stop cheating."

"Oh, well. I just hope that things get better before the Rapture."

"I hope so too, Mama. I have to hang up and get ready for work. I'm going to be busy for the next few days, so please pray for me."

"Sugar, I pray for you every day. I been one of God's most determined warriors all my life. That's one of the reasons you and Jessie have such a solid marriage. I won't allow y'all to go through no pain without some spiritual backup."

The dead woman's husband seemed to be more upset to find out she'd been cheating on him than he was about her death. He didn't even try to hide his anger. "If I wasn't a Christian, I'd chop that damn floozy up and chuck her pieces into the swamp!" he blasted when I met with him. He picked out the cheapest, plainest casket I had.

The philandering man's wife was so angry, she brought over his shabbiest suit for him to be buried in, and she didn't even want to spend no money on flowers. She also picked out a cheap casket. The man's grief-stricken family told me they would pay for some flowers and a soloist, but they couldn't agree on how many flowers or which soloist.

Daddy was uncomfortable about preaching funerals for two adulterers. He promised me he'd do a honorable job with each one, but he was anxious to get everything over with.

Overseeing two funerals in the same week was heart-wrenching for me. It was only because I had been through so much personal trauma myself that I was able to keep my emotions under control. But even after all the misery I had suffered, I was still a happy man. Mr. DeBow had promoted me to senior supervisor last month. Now I had a couple of white men reporting to me, which was almost unheard of in the South. I could tell from the looks on their faces when I told them to do something that they didn't like being told what to do by a colored man. Other than that, they didn't give me no trouble. Folks had suddenly started to die, left and right, so my undertaking business was steady. I couldn't think of nothing that could happen that would mess things up for me and Jessie.

I was wrong.

Me and Jessie went to the market when we got off work Tuesday evening. She wanted to bake a bunch of pies and casseroles to donate to the families of the two deceased folks. "I need to stop by the funeral home so I can check in with Tyrone and Floyd," I told her on the way back to our house.

"Aw, shuck, Hubert. Can't you just call them up when we get home? We need to get all this meat we just bought in the ice box before it spoils," she said sharply.

"You don't have to wait for me. Take the car and go on home. I'll have Tyrone drive me home, or I'll walk them few blocks." I stopped the car and piled out.

The front entrance to the small red brick building I owned was for the public to use. Right inside was a lobby with a couch, where we sat down to talk with bereaved family members. There was also a stand with some checkers and dominoes that Tyrone and Floyd played with when they wasn't busy. Me and them entered the building through a door on the side. I eased it open and headed to the main room, where Tyrone and Floyd usually was. They was nowhere in sight. I knew they was on the premises because Tyrone's raggedy-old Buick was parked right next to the hearse on the side of the building. I strolled up to the door of the room in the back, next to the toilet, where we did the embalming. It was closed, but I could hear voices. I couldn't make out what was being said, though. I put my ear up against the door. What I heard in the next few minutes would haunt me until the day I died.

Tyrone said to Floyd, "I'm glad you could meet me here so

we could talk in private. Did you move everything to a safer place?"

"I done told you that I put everything we collected from them bodies in a crocus sack and buried it under the pecan tree in my backyard."

I was confused, to say the least. It sounded like Tyrone and Floyd had been robbing dead folks!

"Good!" Tyrone boomed. "I would have kept everything myself if that woman of mine hadn't been snooping in them barrels I keep in my shed. It's a good thing I found out what she was doing before she got to that last barrel, where I had stashed that stuff. We'll wait a few more months and then I'll take everything with me when I go visit my mama in Atlanta. I won't have no trouble selling none of it. Especially that necklace and ring we took off that first woman. I know a lot of shady people over there that won't ask no questions about where I got the stuff from. Oh! Before I forget, what did you do with the gun? You got it hid good until we need it again?"

"It's in the same sack with the rest of that stuff. I figured it made more sense to keep everything together in the same place."

"Sure enough."

"Ooh-wee, cuz!" Floyd squealed. "Our plan turned out better than I thought it would! We'll be rich when we retire!" He sounded giddy with excitement.

My ears was ringing, my head was spinning, and my stomach felt like somebody had punched it with all of their might. If I was going to drop dead, I couldn't have been in a better place.

They didn't say nothing else for a few seconds. Then Floyd said in a nervous tone, "Hush up and listen. I heard something."

"You hush up!" Tyrone blasted. "I didn't hear nothing. Stop being so paranoid. We ain't got nothing to worry about. As long as we watch our step and keep killing folks connected to Hubert so the families will have him handle the final arrangements, he won't have no reason to lay us off. He is way too stupid to ever suspect anything." Tyrone and Floyd laughed long and loud.

"You got that right, Tyrone. I declare that fool is so wrapped up in Jessie, he don't pay too much attention to nothing else."

"Tell me about it. She could build a nest up in his butt and he'd never know it." They laughed some more.

"You know something, I am so glad you suggested we stop doing women and concentrate on men," Floyd told Tyrone.

"Me too. But I don't like lynching colored men. Killing somebody like that is a little too cruel." I could actually hear some remorse in Tyrone's voice.

"That's so true. I been having nightmares about that," Floyd replied. "I'll never forget how hard Victor Freeman cried and begged us to let him live. And I can still see that Puckett boy's eyes staring into mine when I put that noose around his neck. Two lynchings is enough. And maybe leaving a half-burned cross under each tree was a little too much."

"If we hadn't burned them crosses, how else would they have pinned them lynchings on the Klan?" Tyrone asked.

"That's a good point. Nobody in the world would suspect colored men of lynching colored men and leaving burned crosses under the hanging trees. Who else but the Klan would do something that heinous?" There was a long moment of silence. And then Floyd added in a casual tone, "We'll coldcock the next one over the head with a rock or something and crack his skull open."

"It'll be easy to sneak up on one of them drunk fools coming from a moonshiner's house. But since business is good for now, we need to cool it until it slows down again. Then we'll decide who goes next."

"Oh! I already got somebody in mind—that skinflint that sells them live chickens and won't give me and you nary one on credit!" Floyd snickered. "What do you think?"

Tyrone belched before he answered. "I think he's a good choice. I never liked him. Jessie buys a lot of chickens from him, but how else is he connected to Hubert? We have to make sure he'll get the body."

"He joined Hubert's daddy's church last month. Besides that, the chicken man's daddy is one of the biggest moonshiners in town and he likes to show off. I know he'll pay for a real fancy funeral. He went all out when his wife died a couple of years ago." Floyd snickered again.

"Praise the Lord! He'll be the perfect next victim. Since we got the cheating man and woman that kicked the bucket last week, we don't need to rush our next project. But let's get rid of the chicken man before the holidays. I want to celebrate the Lord's birthday with clean hands. Besides, if his family pays Hubert right away, he'll give us another bonus in time for us to buy a heap of Christmas presents. Yippee!"

I couldn't believe the glee in Tyrone's voice! My ears felt like they wanted to shrivel up and fall off. I didn't think I could stand to hear nothing else. I'd heard enough.

I couldn't push open the door and let them know what I'd heard. I knew that if I did, all hell would break loose. They had proved to me that they didn't have no problem doing away with somebody. The thought of being killed in my own funeral home—by people I'd trusted and cared about for so many years—sent a chill up my spine that almost paralyzed me.

I tiptoed back outside and hid behind my hearse so they wouldn't see me if they happened to look out the window before I could make it to the street. If they seen me, they'd know I heard them. When I raised my head high enough to see the window, I didn't see them. I took off running and didn't stop until I made it to my house.

I had to do something, and I had to do it fast. I wouldn't be able to live with myself if I didn't stop them before they killed again.

CHAPTER 30
Jessie

I had been thinking about Amos a lot since I cut him loose. I was still mad at him for playing me for a fool. But I was also mad at myself for letting him.

I should have ended things with him long before I did. If and when I bumped into him on the street or anywhere else, I'd run in the opposite direction. If I couldn't get away from him in time and he tried to talk to me, I'd let him know up front that there was nothing he had to say that I wanted to hear. I was sorry I hadn't told him I knew why he needed the ten dollars he tried to borrow from me.

As much as I liked Glenn and Carrie, I decided I would never go back to their house as long as there was a chance I'd run into Amos there. If I wanted to have a drink, I'd either buy myself a bottle, go to another moonshiner's house, or go to my mama's house and drink some of hers.

I wasn't worried about Amos blabbing to somebody about me and him. He had as much to lose as I did. I had enjoyed all the pleasure he'd gave me, and I would miss that. I'd think twice about getting involved with another man, though.

Poor Hubert. I felt sorrier for him than I felt for myself. But at least my female equipment still worked. I couldn't imagine how bad it was for him not to be able to perform. The thought of how tortured he must feel now—with a useless pecker—brought tears to my eyes. I went in the bathroom to dab my eyes and splash some cold water on my face. While I was still bent over the sink, Hubert came home. "Jessie, where you at? Get out here. I need to talk to you!" The frantic tone of his voice scared the daylights out of me.

I panicked right away. The first thing that came to my mind was that Hubert had found out about me and Amos. If that sucker had blew the whistle, I was going to make his life a living hell! I didn't know how, but I was going to find a way. And, if Hubert got ugly with me, the same went for him. My heart started to beat so hard, I was afraid I would have a heart attack and keel over and die before I found out what Hubert wanted. "I'm in the bathroom. I'll be right there," I yelled back, with my knees knocking together.

"Hurry up and finish your business, because I need to talk to you! We got a serious problem!"

Somehow I managed to make it to the living room without collapsing. My heart was beating even harder now, and rubbing my bosom didn't help none. Hubert was standing in the middle of the floor. He looked like he'd seen the devil. His eyeballs looked like they was trying to escape, his mouth was hanging open, sweat was all over his face, and he was shifting his weight from one foot to the other. I felt the same way I did when Mama caught me and my first boyfriend going at it in our pantry thirty years ago. I made a snap decision to say the same thing to Hubert that I'd said to her that day, "I can explain—"

He waved both of his hands and cut me off. "You ain't got nothing to explain! This ain't about you! We got trouble!"

I was so relieved, my heart immediately slowed down to its

normal speed. I didn't want to get too excited too soon, though. "Oh? W-what is it?" And then another thought crossed my mind: Blondeen's killing. My mouth dropped open, and my heart started to beat hard again. "Somebody found out the truth about Blondeen?"

"No, that ain't it. It's much worse."

I wondered, what could be worse than Blondeen getting shot in our bedroom, and us covering it up and letting somebody else get blamed for it? "Hubert, what's going on?"

Nothing could have prepared me for what he told me he'd heard at the funeral home. When he finished repeating the conversation between Tyrone and Floyd, my eyes was bugged out and my stomach felt like it was on fire. I was relieved that he hadn't killed nobody else, and that he hadn't found out about me and Amos.

"We need to call the police!" I was wringing my hands and pacing the floor like a caged animal.

"You want to call the *police*? You must be kidding! What's wrong with you, Jessie?"

"There ain't nothing wrong with me. I'm just trying to make sure we do the right thing."

"Calling the police ain't the right thing in this case. You forgetting about the color of our skin? *We* might be the ones to end up in jail!"

"But we didn't kill nobody!" As soon as them words left my mouth, I wished I could have pushed them back in. "Um . . . we didn't kill none of them *innocent* folks Floyd and Tyrone killed."

Hubert rubbed the back of his head and scrunched up his face. "Jessie, my noggin feels like it's going to bust wide open. I don't know what to do!"

"Hubert, if you don't want to involve the police, then we have to figure out a way to chastise Tyrone and Floyd ourselves. If we don't, they will keep killing folks. You said they was already planning to kill the chicken man. Them *lynching* two colored men, and letting folks think the Klan done it, is about as unholy as you can get. They'll burn in hell for sure."

Hubert looked at me with his eyes blinking. "What about us? We let everybody think the same man who killed all of them other women killed Blondeen."

I threw up my hands. "That's a horse of a different color. What we done ain't nothing compared to what Tyrone and Floyd done. Let's go tell Pa Wiggins! He can help us figure out how to handle this."

"Good God no! We can't tell him yet. He'll tell Mama and she'll get hysterical and blab to one of her friends. Tyrone and Floyd could find out what we know and skip town."

"If we don't get the police involved, how else can we get justice for the folks they killed?"

"From what they said, it didn't sound like they was going to go after the chicken man right away. But they talked about killing him before the holidays."

"How soon before the holidays? They could change their minds today and go after him tomorrow. If we don't stop them in time, we'll have blood on our hands. Let's sit down so we can compose ourselves and think everything through. But first, I need to go back to the bathroom. The way my stomach is churning, I'm about to get real sick." The news I'd just heard made me feel like I'd been kicked in the gut.

CHAPTER 31
Hubert

While Jessie was in the bathroom puking, I ran into the kitchen and dialed Leroy's number. "Don't say nothing, just listen," I told him in a low tone. "I know who killed all of them colored women."

"Huh? What in the world are you talking about? What colored women?"

"The ones I told you about being killed over here by a unknown maniac, remember? You told me you read about them cases in the Hartville newspaper last year." The Hartville newspaper and ours had only mentioned each murder in a few sentences, and buried so far back in the newspaper a lot of folks had missed every single one. News about one of the murders had been put at the bottom of the last page right below a ad for wig-hats.

"Oh yeah! We ain't talked about them cases in a while. How did you find out who killed them women, and when did you find out?"

"I just found out today. I can't go into all the details right now, because I need to spring into action as soon as I can."

"What are you going to do?"

"I don't know yet. Me and Jessie don't know how to get the police involved. If we go tell them what I found out and they don't do nothing, they could tell somebody. The news could get back to Tyrone and Floyd. If that was to happen, my goose would be cooked. And Jessie's probably would be too."

Leroy gasped so loud, it sounded like he was standing right next to me. "Tyrone and Floyd? *Your assistants?* Is the killer one of their kinfolks or friends?"

"Leroy . . ." I had to pause and take a real deep breath before I could get the rest of my sentence out. "It was Tyrone and Floyd that done them killings. And they ain't done yet."

Leroy gasped again. "Hang up this telephone and get to the police station right now!"

"The colored folks over here have been trying to get them to do more about finding the killer. They ain't done nothing so far. Our sheriff threatened to arrest the next one of us that tried to tell him how to do his job."

"I just got a idea!" Leroy yelled.

"It better be a good one, because I can't come up with nary one."

"White folks listen to other white folks, especially if they got money."

"That's for damn sure."

"Ask that nice Mr. DeBow to go with you to talk to the sheriff. Him being the owner of the turpentine mill and liking you so much, I'm sure he'd speak up for you. That goofy sheriff y'all got would have to take him serious."

I suddenly felt a little better. Leroy was right. Mr. DeBow was one of the most well-respected men in Lexington. He had a lot of friends in high places. If he couldn't get the sheriff to listen to me, nobody could.

Just as I was about to end the call, Jessie shuffled into the kitchen and stood next to me. The telephone was still in my hand. "Who's that on the phone, Hubert?"

"Jessie, I thought you was still in the bathroom," I said in a sharp tone. "I was fixing to call up my boss." Leroy took the hint, so he abruptly hung up.

"Mr. DeBow? What do you need to talk to him about? He done already gave you the okay to take off time this week for them two funerals."

"If I could get a highfalutin man like him to go with us to talk to the sheriff, I'm sure we'd get somewhere."

Jessie gave me a hopeful look. "That should work. At least they wouldn't shoo him away the way they do colored folks when they try to get some assistance. Call him up."

I immediately dialed Mr. DeBow's number. His wife answered and called him to the phone right away. "Who's calling?" he asked.

"Mr. DeBow, this is Hubert. I need to talk to you right now!"

"Now, now, Hubert. I already told you not to worry about taking all the time you need for those funerals."

"I ain't calling about that."

Mr. DeBow took his time responding. That made me more nervous than I already was. "Oh. Then this is a work-related issue. Well, what's it about?"

"This ain't got nothing to do with work, sir. I'm calling about a criminal matter. A mess of murders!"

"M-murders? Great balls of fire!" he boomed. "Did you kill somebody, Hubert?"

"No, I didn't. But somebody close to me did."

Mr. DeBow drew in his breath. "O Lord, have mercy! Please don't tell me that sweet little wife of yours has harmed somebody—"

It was against Southern protocol for a colored person to interrupt a white man, but I made a exception this time. Besides, Mr. DeBow wasn't nothing like most of the other white folks in Lexington. "No, that ain't it." I was talking so fast, I had to stop and catch my breath. "I know this is a lot to ask a busy man like you, but can we talk in person? I swear to God, I won't take up much of your time."

"If this is as serious as you seem to think it is, don't worry about how busy I might be. I advise you to get over here lickety-split."

"Do you mind if I bring Jessie?" She was breathing through her mouth, and so was I.

"No, I don't mind one bit. I'll see y'all when you get here."

"Thank you, Mr. DeBow. We'll leave here right now." I hung up and looked at Jessie. "Go put on your shoes so we can get going." Before she could leave the kitchen, the telephone rang. I thought it was Mr. DeBow calling. My heart skipped a beat. My first thought was that he was calling to tell me to come later, or not at all because he didn't want to get involved in colored folks' business. My heart skipped two beats and I almost collapsed when I heard Floyd's voice on the other end of the line.

Jessie seen the new panic on my face and gripped my arm so tight, I was afraid she'd stop my blood from circulating. "Who is it?" she whispered, looking at the phone like it was a snake's head.

"Floyd," I mouthed. She stumbled back a few steps and covered her mouth with her hand. I hadn't seen her look so scared since the night I shot Blondeen.

I don't know how I was able to talk in my normal tone to a cold-blooded killer. "What is it, Floyd?"

"I hate to bother you at home, boss. I just wanted to let you know we done almost finished getting them two bodies ready. We'll be done directly so you don't need to come over here this evening to help with that."

"T-that's good. Good work."

"Well, you know you can always count on me and Tyrone to get the job done. I just feel so bad for these folks dying the way they did in the lake."

"Drowning is a awful way to die." I was surprised that I was able to speak in such a calm manner. "But at least nobody killed them . . ."

"Well, that man's wife came by earlier today to drop off some insurance papers. She is still madder than a hornet. She said that if she had caught her husband with that woman, she would have killed him herself. I hugged her neck and told her that killing is a deadly sin and to put it out of her mind."

I couldn't believe my ears! "You told her right, Floyd. Killing folks is a deadly sin. But I believe *all* killers get their comeuppance sooner or later . . ."

"Never soon enough, though!" Floyd snorted before he went on. "By the way, do you know when Jessie is going to cook another mess of turnip greens? My wife don't like greens and will only cook some when me and the kids beg her to. Can you believe a *colored* woman don't like greens? Greens is like air and water to us." Floyd guffawed like a hyena. I couldn't have laughed if I wanted to.

"Um . . . I'm sure she'll be cooking some in the next few days. I'll let you know." After today, Floyd wouldn't be eating no more turnip greens, or none of the other delicacies he'd been gobbling up all his life. I heard that the food they served in prison wasn't even fit for hogs. "I have to hang up now. Jessie needs to use the phone to call her mama."

"Okay, boss man. Tell her I said hi and don't forget to ask her about them greens. Y'all have a blessed evening."

I hung up and looked at Jessie with my mouth hanging open. "You wouldn't believe what that devil just had the nerve to say to me!"

"Whatever he said, I don't want to hear it. Let's get over to Mr. DeBow's house right now!"

CHAPTER 32
Jessie

I was having a hard time breathing on the way to Mr. DeBow's house. I was so nervous, my knees was knocking together. And even though the weather was chilly, I was sweating up a storm.

Mr. DeBow lived on the other side of town, where all the rest of the well-to-do white folks lived. The way I was feeling, I wasn't sure I'd still be in my right mind by the time we got to his house.

Hubert was such a wreck, driving like a bat flying out of hell. "You need to slow down," I advised. "I don't want us to get hurt or killed before we stop them two devils. What would happen if we ended up in comas for five or six months? Tyrone and Floyd would probably go hog wild and kill a heap more folks before they got through."

"Mr. DeBow wants us to get to his place as fast as possible." Hubert wiped sweat off his face and didn't slow down. By the time we reached Mr. DeBow's street, he was sweating twice as much as I was.

The houses in this neighborhood was big and well-tended, and they had nice cars sitting in the driveways. We was less than half a block from Mr. DeBow's stately white house. It was so breathtaking, it made our house look like a shanty. There was a spacious wraparound front porch with a swing, a glider, and rocking chairs on both sides, and two huge, beautiful magnolia trees stood in the yard. While Hubert was looking for a place to park, a police car pulled up along beside us. Sheriff Zachary was behind the wheel, pointing to the side of the street.

"Hubert, he's telling you to stop," I said with my voice cracking.

"Oh, Lord. He's the last person in the whole wide world we need to see before we talk to Mr. DeBow," Hubert said in a shaky tone. He pulled to the curb and turned off the motor.

Sheriff Zachary jumped out of his car with his gun in his hand and ran up to our car. He was a short, homely man with a huge potbelly and thin black-and-gray hair. I'd only seen him up close a few times, and each time he'd had a mean look on his face and a jaw full of chewing tobacco. Today he looked even meaner. "Get your black ass out of this damn car and put your hands in the air!" Sheriff Zachary didn't wait for Hubert to open the door. He snatched it open, pulled him out by his arm, and immediately pressed the gun against Hubert's jaw. Then he glared at me and barked, "Didn't you hear what I just said, gal?"

I got out as fast as I could and stumbled around to the driver's side with my hands raised. Smart colored folks never sassed or talked back to white men or women, especially a gun-happy oaf like Sheriff Zachary. We knew better. He'd already shot and killed a bunch of colored men, and a few white ones. "Is there a problem, Sheriff?" Hubert asked in a gentle tone.

"Yeah, there's a problem! Who the hell do you think you are coming to *this* neighborhood driving like a maniac? And unless you work for somebody over here, you ain't got no business in this side of town! Thank God there ain't no white gal in the street for you to rip her clothes off and pester against her will!" I couldn't believe what I was hearing. How could even a buffoon like Sheriff Zachary believe that a white woman was in danger of being raped by Hubert, especially with me sitting in the same car with him? But that was the way racist people's minds worked. It was hard to believe that the same God who had created us and the rest of the fair-minded folks in the world had created so many monsters who thought they was better than everybody else just because they had white skin.

Sheriff Zachary hawked a big wad of spit on the ground, missing Hubert's foot by inches. The hand with the gun in it was shaking so hard, I was scared that it would go off by accident and fatally shoot Hubert. If that happened, I would have to do something to make this demon shoot me too, because I would have never got over seeing my husband shot down like a dog.

"Um . . . I was coming to see my boss about a real important matter. He told me to get over here as fast as I could. I didn't realize I was going so fast."

"That ain't no excuse! I ought to blow your damn brains out where you stand!" Sheriff Zachary threatened. "You niggers done got right uppity, and we ain't going to stand for it. Whose car is this you're driving, boy?"

"It's our car," I answered as meekly as I could. The last thing I wanted this jackass to accuse me of was sassing him or being disrespectful. "It's paid off in full and we got the papers to prove it."

"Paid off in full, huh? Humph. I declare, that's a blip. How can *niggers* afford a sharp car like this?"

Hubert opened his mouth to speak, but I didn't give him a chance to answer that question neither. "My husband is a undertaker and he works at the turpentine mill for Mr. DeBow, so we are pretty well-off."

"Well, none of that cuts no mustard with me. A 'well-off' nigger is still a nigger."

When I was still in my teens, I worked for a year and a half for women in this very same neighborhood. A few folks had gave me mean looks, and one time a teenage boy called me names and threw rocks at me. Other than that, I had never had a serious problem in this location. I didn't know what to expect now, because times had changed, and some white folks had got meaner.

I glanced around and seen a great big, fat, blond-haired man standing on the front porch of the house next to Mr. DeBow's. He was holding a shotgun. The man fished a pair of glasses out of his shirt pocket and glared at us like he was itching to shoot us. I started praying under my breath, begging God to let us get out of this mess alive.

It was hard to believe that the day had started out on such a good note. Me and Hubert had gone from shopping and having a good time together, to a multiple-murder situation and a run-in with the police all within the same hour. The issue involving Tyrone and Floyd was going to change our lives and the lives of every other colored person in Lexington. That was bad enough. But me and Hubert getting shot and killed by the sheriff would have caused the kind of pain to the colored folks in town that I couldn't begin to imagine.

Before Sheriff Zachary could say anything else, Mr. DeBow skittered off his front porch and trotted in our direction in his bare feet. He was a stout, bald, plain-looking man in his sixties; but I was so glad to see him, I could have kissed him on his lips. "What the devil is going on here, Zachary?" Mr. DeBow stopped in front of the sheriff, who still had his gun pressed against Hubert's jaw. I looked up at the sky and silently thanked God.

Sheriff Zachary tipped his hat and smiled. "Good evening, DeBow. Ain't seen you and your lovely wife at church lately."

I was stupefied that this devil was standing here smiling and talking about *church* with a gun in his hand threatening somebody whose only crime was speeding. And being colored.

"My wife claims she's been feeling poorly. But you know how women like to exaggerate when it comes to their health."

"I'm going to pray for her," Sheriff Zachary said in a concerned tone.

Mr. DeBow looked at me and Hubert and folded his arms. "Now, what's going on here?"

"I just caught these niggers breaking the law," Sheriff Zachary answered. He spewed out some more spit. This time, big gobs landed on both of Hubert's feet. It was a shame to see such a mess on a pair of shoes I had helped him pick out just last week.

"How were they breaking the law?" Mr. DeBow asked.

Sheriff Zachary snorted and stomped his foot. "Speeding and no telling what else. They look mighty suspicious to me. We never caught the culprit that run up behind the mayor last month on this very same street, knocked him out, and took off with his wallet."

"Well, other than speeding, I can assure you that these folks haven't done anything else criminal over here. I was expecting them and we were all going to come see you."

Sheriff Zachary whirled around to face Hubert directly before he returned his attention to Mr. DeBow. "This nigger is coming to see *me*? What about?"

"Well, I don't know all the details. That's what Hubert came over here to tell me. Ain't that right, Hubert?"

"Yes, Mr. DeBow." Hubert's voice was low and weak. I felt so sorry for him, I wanted to cry. But I was holding all my tears until we got back home—if we did.

"You have always been a good ol' boy, Mr. DeBow, so I'll let them be on their way and finish their business with you." Sheriff Zachary finally put his gun back in his holster. "Whatever it is y'all need to discuss with me, it better be worth my time. I'll stay in my office another hour, so y'all better get there soon. I got choir practice tonight and I don't want to be late." He got back in his car and sped off, going even faster than Hubert had been.

"I'm sorry y'all had to go through this unpleasant mishap. I hope it didn't cause no more distress than y'all already feeling," Mr. DeBow said, looking from Hubert to me.

"We're fine," Hubert mumbled.

The man with the shotgun marched out onto the sidewalk and stopped just a few feet from us. He was still looking at us like he wanted to blow our heads off. Mr. DeBow glanced at his neighbor and shook his head. "Go back in the house, Skeeter. Everything's under control." The man grunted and went back into his own house. Mr. DeBow gave us a apologetic look. "I apologize for my neighbors. The folks over here are really nice, peaceful Christians. Even Sheriff Zachary is a pretty good egg, once you get to know him. But a few of my neighbors tend to get a might fretful when they see unfamiliar colored folks. Let's get in the house, where it's safe, before one of these looky-loos start up something. I want y'all to tell me everything."

CHAPTER 33
Hubert

After I had told Mr. DeBow everything in the privacy of his parlor, he followed us to the police station in his shiny black LaSalle.

The police station was on the corner of Main Street right next door to one of the banks that had failed during the Depression. Two slovenly deputies was hanging around outside when we parked in front, right smack-dab behind the sheriff's patrol car. The deputies glared at us when we started walking toward the entrance behind Mr. DeBow. I shuddered when I thought about all the nasty things that was probably going through their minds about us.

Once we got inside, a young woman, with bright green eyes and red hair, sitting behind a scarred-up counter, actually smiled at us. "Hello. How are you folks doing?" I never expected anybody associated with the jailhouse to be friendly to us. I actually turned around to see if some white folks had come in behind us and that the woman was talking to them. I wanted to smile back at her and say something, but it felt like my tongue had froze up on me.

"Um . . . we're doing just fine, ma'am. Thank you for asking," Jessie replied.

"Evening, ma'am." Mr. DeBow smiled at the woman and tipped his hat. "The sheriff is expecting us."

"Then y'all go right in. And enjoy the rest of your day."

Me and Jessie stumbled along behind Mr. DeBow. I didn't know about her, but I was holding my breath and didn't let it out until we got inside.

Sheriff Zachary was slumped in a chair behind his cluttered desk, with his feet up on top. He was smoking a corncob pipe. He waved Mr. DeBow to the chair facing him, and he didn't even acknowledge me and Jessie. There was two other chairs, but we didn't sit down.

"Who is going to do the talking?" Sheriff Zachary asked, looking directly at Mr. DeBow.

"If you don't mind, I'd like to do that," I volunteered.

Sheriff Zachary slammed his fist down on his desk. "How can you tune up your mouth to be so disrespectful, boy? Didn't your mama teach you how to address a white man at all times? I let it slide when I stopped y'all a little while ago, but I ain't letting it slide this time."

I didn't know how I was able to keep my lips from quivering. It was probably because I was angrier than I was scared. "Yes, she did, *sir.* I'm sorry, sir."

"That's better. Now get on with your story."

"Um, I'd like to tell you what I found out about them six murdered colored women, and the recent lynchings of two colored men, sir," I said with my head bowed mighty low. I had never wanted my wife to see me cowering like a scared puppy in front of nobody, not even a white man. But under the circumstances, I didn't mind this time.

"Start talking then, boy! I ain't got all day!" Sheriff Zachary barked as he blew smoke in me and Jessie's direction. The smoke was strong, but she didn't flinch. It burned my eyes and nose, but I didn't flinch neither.

When I finished telling the sheriff about Tyrone and Floyd's conversation, he sat there with his eyes big and his jaw twitching. "And you believe this nigger's story?" he asked Mr. DeBow.

I was glad Mr. DeBow answered real quick and in a firm tone. "Yes, I do. Hubert has been working for me for almost twenty-five years and has never lied to me, or even stretched the truth. Next to his daddy, Reverend Wiggins, he's the most highly regarded colored resident in Lexington. Therefore, I advise you to take some action on his behalf *today*. Otherwise, this story *might* get leaked, and the newspapers will be all over it. Before we know it, crybaby agitators in every northern state will be down here on our tails." I didn't know if the dim-witted sheriff had enough sense to realize that Mr. DeBow had just waved a threat in front of his face. I was proud of my boss and glad we hadn't wasted no time asking him for his assistance.

I was also pleased to see a worried look finally on Sheriff Zachary's face. "That's for sure. And can't nobody stir up a mess like them Yankees. As if we don't have enough trouble trying to keep these darkies under control." He stood up, laid his pipe on a upside-down jar lid, and tapped his gun. "Let me round up my deputies so we can pay a visit to them two murdering coons."

Mr. DeBow raised his finger in the air and let out a mighty snort. "I got one more thing. I don't like to tell you how to do your job, but I advise you to check under that pecan tree in Floyd's backyard. If the things they took from some of the victims are really buried there, like Hubert heard them mention, you'll have an airtight case."

"Hmmm. I guess you got a point there, Mr. DeBow. If we mess this up, I'll have the mayor on my ass, day and night. Not to mention them busybody boogers in the state capital." Sheriff Zachary lifted his hat and scratched his head. "Don't you worry about nothing! I got everything under control." He reached out and shook Mr. DeBow's hand and escorted him to the door. What got my goat was the way he was ignoring me and Jessie. You would have thought we had already left the room. But I didn't care. All I cared about now was that I'd done all I could do. I just hoped it was enough.

Before we got in our car, Mr. DeBow shook my hand and hugged both me and Jessie's necks. "Now y'all go on home and get some rest. Things are about to get real testy in the next few days." He looked at the two deputies still scowling at me and Jessie and shook his head. "Those two are a fine example of pure white trash," he said before he glared at them and spit on the ground.

"Mr. DeBow, we can't thank you enough for helping us," Jessie said. "I'm going to bake you a pie, and Hubert will bring it with him when he returns to work."

"I'd appreciate that, Mrs. Wiggins." Mr. DeBow looked at the deputies again. "Um . . . I'll escort y'all back to your own neighborhood so nobody will accost y'all."

A hour after me and Jessie got back home, Mr. DeBow called me up. "Hubert, it's over. The sheriff found Tyrone and Floyd together, holed up at one of the moonshiners' houses, drinking like they didn't have a care in the world. Oomph, oomph, oomph! Him and his deputies dragged them out and hauled their tails to the station. They both confessed to every single thing you overheard."

"Sure enough? Thank you, Mr. DeBow, sir." Words couldn't describe how happy his words made me. "I can't tell you how much we appreciate your help. I'll have Jessie bake you two pies."

"And I do thank you in advance." He paused and then whispered, "If it's not asking too much, throw in a mess of Jessie's gourmet pig ears, like the ones you occasionally bring to work in your lunch bag and share with me. That's the one thing my wife can't cook worth a damn." I couldn't tell who laughed the loudest, him or me.

When I hung up, Jessie came up to me. "What did Mr. DeBow say?"

"Everything I needed to hear." I had to pause because I was grinning so hard and I couldn't speak for a few moments. "Baby, it's over." When I told her what Mr. DeBow had told me, she hugged my neck. And then she steered me to the living-room couch and gently pushed me down. I was so light-headed that I could barely talk. "G-go make us some tea. It'll help calm my nerves and soothe my throat," I said in a hoarse tone. I didn't realize it until now that the inside of my throat was almost as dry as an old bone.

The tea did help, but only a little. Now that a few hours had passed, I'd had time to really process what was going on. I was so overwhelmed by the time we went to bed; I didn't sleep no more than two or three hours. And neither did Jessie.

CHAPTER 34
Jessie

Tyrone and Floyd had caused so much pain to the colored folks in Lexington, I knew I could never forgive them two idiots. But we all felt sorry for their families. Some of the victims' loved ones was so mad, they wanted to storm the jailhouse and handle Tyrone and Floyd themselves. They wasn't that crazy, though. Sheriff Zachary and his deputies wouldn't have wasted no time shooting them down like they was mad dogs.

What we read in the newspaper on Wednesday about the crimes made us even angrier. It was such a big story, complete with pictures, it took up half of the whole front page. In the first picture, Sheriff Zachary and two of his deputies was grinning and holding their shotguns. Tyrone and Floyd, looking like dazed rabbits, was sitting on the ground in front of them in handcuffs. They both had black eyes and other bruises on their faces. We all knew that one of the first things Sheriff Zachary and his deputies did when they arrested somebody colored was to beat them up, men and women. But they only beat the ugly women. The pretty ones was forced to do sex acts with the deputies, and sometimes with Sheriff Zachary.

The newspaper headline screamed: SHERIFF ZACHARY SOLVES MULTIPLE-MURDER CASE. There was nothing about the fact that Hubert had been the one who had cracked the case. The sheriff's quotes made me sick, especially the first one: *"I am so pleased that all the time and hard work I devoted to these murders finally paid off."* In the middle of the page, there was another picture of the sheriff, being patted on the back by our mayor, right next to another one of his quotes: *"I am pleased that a reliable source did the Christian thing by coming forward with some very important information. I immediately followed up. The information that was revealed to me helped me solve these murders that my associates and I have been investigating for many months. I feel for the families of the victims, as well as the rest of our colored folks. It's a shame that the vicious killers blamed the two colored men they lynched on the Klan!"* He went on and on about his "investigation" and how several leads had not panned out.

The only reference to Hubert was made in the last paragraph. It was stated that Tyrone and Floyd worked at the Wiggins Funeral Home and had never been arrested before. Sheriff Zachary didn't even mention Mr. DeBow, and he didn't like that. "It would have been nice if that sucker had mentioned me as his 'reliable source' and told the whole story," he griped to Hubert on the telephone after he'd read the newspaper.

This was one time I was glad news traveled as fast as it did among the colored folks. Within hours after the arrests, everybody knew it was Hubert who had overheard Tyrone and Floyd bragging about the killings. And that he had asked Mr. DeBow to go with us to the police so he could report what he'd heard. "The least they could have done was give you a reward for identifying the killers," one of our neighbors told Hubert.

"I don't need no reward for doing the right thing," Hubert replied.

Everybody was still overwhelmed about the man and woman

who had drowned. But because of what was happening with Floyd and Tyrone, a lot of folks didn't attend the funerals. Some didn't even want to leave their houses because a white employer had told a colored man who worked on his farm that he'd heard a rumor that the sheriff and his deputies was itching to arrest more colored men.

One of the colored women who worked with me at the nursing home was so distressed, she took a day off without letting our supervisor know. When she returned to work, she didn't have no job. I showed up like I always did, because I didn't want the same thing to happen to me.

My older brother, Karl, and a couple of his friends helped Hubert finish organizing everything for the drowned couple's funerals on Thursday and Friday. Tyrone and Floyd had already dug the graves. And from what folks was predicting, somebody would be digging graves for them soon because the state was going to put them to death for sure.

Hubert was so amazing. He bounced back like nothing had happened. At least that was how it looked to me. But I had a feeling he was feeling pretty bad about everything, especially having two killers in plain view all this time. He hired Karl to be his new assistant, so it was business as usual at the funeral home.

My brother had been between jobs for so long, he was glad to be working again. His wife had took off with another man eight years ago. A month later, our daddy died. Karl had moved in with Mama so she wouldn't be by herself. He didn't have no kids to support, and when he did work, he helped Mama pay her bills. She was still healthy enough to do rich women's laundry and housekeeping, but because there was so many women competing for the same jobs, she could only find work two or three days a week, and some weeks she couldn't find nothing at all. She was so pleased Karl finally had a full-time job that paid well. And so was I. I had been helping Mama as much as I could since Daddy died.

It had been a week since Tyrone and Floyd had been arrested. But a lot of the colored folks was still in a state of shock. I hadn't seen so many long, sad faces since Victor Freeman got lynched. A hushed quiet was hanging over the colored part of town. Everything had slowed down. The moonshiners wasn't entertaining the huge crowds as much as they usually did, not too many kids was playing outside.

The mama of the second woman Tyrone and Floyd had killed was still grieving. She went to the graveyard to put flowers on her daughter's grave once a week. When she went last Friday, she never came home. Her brother went to look for her that evening and found her laying facedown on top of her daughter's grave. When Hubert and Karl picked up her body and brought her to the funeral home, Hubert found a note in her brassiere instructing him to bury her as close to her daughter as possible.

Other than Mr. DeBow, the crimes Tyrone and Floyd had committed didn't faze most of the other white folks in Lexington. One housekeeper told me that the man she worked for had said, "It's a good thing for you people that Sheriff Zachary caught them rascals before they done any more killing. Now, if you want to keep your job, you better stop moping around with that puppy-dog expression on your face, upsetting my family."

Two things really bothered the colored folks. One was why Tyrone and Floyd had admitted to killing them five women and two men, but swore they hadn't killed Blondeen. It didn't matter what they said at this point. Everybody thought they had killed her, and that was all that mattered. Folks didn't dwell on that too much, because the idea that another killer was on the loose was too painful to even think about.

The main thing bothering folks was that Tyrone and Floyd had *lynched* two colored men, knowing how painful such a heinous act of violence was to every colored person in America.

The families of Tyrone and Floyd was laying real low. Nobody had seen Tyrone's girlfriend and Floyd's wife in public since the arrests. None of their kids had been to school since. Most of them was teenagers, so nobody expected them to return. Besides, half of the colored kids in Lexington never finished high school anyway. They had to get jobs and help out at home.

When me and Hubert drove past Floyd's house this evening on the way home from the market, his mousy little wife was sitting on the front porch, crying. I felt so sorry for that poor woman. "Hubert, do you think we should stop and say something to her?"

He almost lost control of the car when he whirled around to face me. "Jessie, w-what in the world do you think we could say to the wife of a man who done caused so much sorrow? What could you say to make her feel better?"

I shrugged. "I don't know. I just thought it'd be a nice thing to do if we let her know we ain't mad at her."

"The 'nice thing to do' is let that woman and the rest of Floyd's and Tyrone's families alone so they can get over this mess and move on. We can't change what done happened. Besides, I'm the last person Floyd's wife wants in her face. If I hadn't done what I done, he wouldn't be in jail. You need to think about that."

"And you need to think about the fact that if you hadn't turned him and Tyrone in, they would have kept killing folks. And since you told them that you was going to leave them your business if you died before they did, *you* could have been one of their next victims."

CHAPTER 35
Hubert

I hadn't visited Leroy or talked to him since Tyrone's and Floyd's arrests last week. I called him this morning while Jessie was still in the bathroom getting ready for work.

He let out a yelp when he heard my voice. "Hubert, I declare, I'm so glad to finally hear from you again. I was getting worried."

"I been so busy, but you was on my mind." I drew in a deep breath and told him, as much as I could, about everything that was going on. I'd tell him the whole story when I seen him. Leroy was just as shocked as me and everybody else.

"My Lord, Hubert! I can't imagine how betrayed you must be feeling, not to mention the victims' families. You gave Tyrone and Floyd good jobs and damn near treated them as good as kinfolk. The story ran on our newspaper's front page, and family and friends as far away as Texas done called to tell me they read about it. Not one time was your name mentioned."

"I don't care about me not getting no credit. I'm just glad it's over. Knowing that I had two devils working for me for so many years is a mighty heavy load to carry. All this time they was betraying every colored person in town in the worst possible way, right up under my nose. I feel so guilty."

"You stop talking like that. You ain't got no reason to feel guilty. You didn't do nothing wrong. Please don't be beating yourself up over something you couldn't control. It could have happened to anybody."

"I know, I'm just sorry it had to be me. I don't know who I can trust no more."

"I hope you still trust me . . ."

"I do, and I always will."

"It's so hard to believe that *nobody* suspected what Tyrone and Floyd was doing. From what you told me about them, it sounded like they didn't have a lick of sense. But even the smartest criminals do stupid things that gets them caught. I can't believe numbskulls like them two could kill so many folks and get away with it for so long. I'm sure they made a lot of mistakes along the way."

"They made their biggest one last week by discussing their crimes where they could be heard. They had me just as fooled as they had everybody else. Floyd even taught Sunday school at my daddy's church, helped organize church events, and both him and Tyrone sang in the choir!"

"None of that matters now, Hubert. They was nothing but wolves in sheep's clothing."

"Thank you! One good thing is that they pleaded guilty, so there won't be no trials. They was sentenced to die in Yellow Mama's lap." That was the nickname for Alabama's electric chair.

"Oh, my God! Getting fried is a messy and gruesome way for somebody to die. Just thinking about it sends shivers up my spine. I thought they hung criminals in this state."

"Leroy, don't you keep up with the news? Alabama stopped hanging folks about thirteen or fourteen years ago."

"Oh yeah. I do remember hearing about that on the radio a few years ago. I try not to think about things like that too often. It's way too depressing. When do you think they'll be executed? I know the state is just itching to pull the switch."

"You're right about that. Them being colored—they'll die much sooner than white men. I read somewhere that one white man had to wait six years before his date with Yellow Mama. I suspect Tyrone and Floyd will be gone within two or three years, maybe even sooner. A swift execution would be better for them and their families. The prison conditions are so bad, they'll suffer a lot before they die. I think the white folks want them to suffer first anyway. Daddy's head usher's son was locked up for five years for stealing a car. We barely recognized him when he got out. He told me that them evil guards beat the prisoners on a regular basis just for sport, fed them food I wouldn't give to a hog I didn't like, and the men never got medical help when they needed it. The last beating that boy got from them guards left him paralyzed on one side for life. That's the worst kind of suffering, even for a prisoner. I know what Tyrone and Floyd did was despicable, but I do feel sorry for them in a way. It would be better for everybody if they was to die before they can be executed."

"You hoping that some of the other prisoners or them evil guards will beat them to death instead?"

"That could happen, but I hope they die of natural causes, for the sake of their families. Floyd started having pains in his belly a few weeks ago. The same kind that killed his grandpa and one of his brothers a couple of years ago. It turned out they had stomach cancer. That's a bad way to go, but it'd be better than going out in the electric chair."

"Dying of cancer would be the lesser of two evils, I guess."

We got silent for a few seconds. "Hold on. Let me check to make sure I ain't got to worry about Jessie sneaking up on me." I laid the phone down and trotted to the bathroom and knocked on the door. "Sugar, how much longer are you going to be in there?"

"Hell's bells, Hubert. I just got in here. I'll be out directly. If you need to use the toilet, come on in. Don't be scared. I ain't going to bite you."

"Um, I ain't got to do nothing."

"Then how come you want to know how much longer I'm going to be in here?"

"Well, I wanted you to have time to eat breakfast before you go to work. You ain't been eating much lately."

"I'll be out in time to fix breakfast. If you can't wait, go ahead and cook. I should be out by the time it's done. And listen here, you make sure them grits ain't as overcooked as they was the last time you cooked breakfast."

"All right, baby." I skittered back to the kitchen and picked up the phone. "Sorry, Leroy. Jessie is still in the bathroom, so I can talk for a few more minutes."

"Good." Leroy sucked in a loud breath. "I just wanted to ask you something."

"Like what?"

"Um . . . I don't know if I should even bring this up now, but after Tyrone and Floyd die, will you handle their burials? After all, they was members of your daddy's church and they worked for you."

"Good God! Me handle their final arrangements? I hadn't even thought about that detail! Just the thought of driving my hearse to the prison to collect their bodies gives me the heebie-jeebies."

"Well, the subject is bound to come up sooner or later. I'm surprised it ain't already."

I swallowed the lump that had suddenly swole up in my throat. I rubbed my chest because it felt like it was getting tighter by the second. "No, I ain't going to get involved. It wouldn't be fitting. Besides, Jessie, my mama and daddy, and everybody else would think I'd lost my mind. This is one time I'd be glad for the Fuller Brothers to take some business away from me. But I wouldn't blame Ned and Percy if they didn't want to do it neither. Everybody is so angry—they'd probably lose a lot of business if they was to handle the final arrangements. And I don't think there is a preacher in Lexington that'd be willing to preach their funerals. There's a undertaker in Meridian, Mississippi, just a hop, skip, and a jump from here, that some folks in Lexington use when me and the Fuller Brothers ain't available."

"I feel the same way you do."

"You know what, I been scolding myself for ignoring all of them red flags Tyrone and Floyd waved in my face."

"What kind of red flags? You mean you *did* suspect something was amiss?"

"Something like that. The first time I mentioned laying them off because business was slow, they both assured me that we'd get a body soon. That first woman was murdered a week later. I thought that was a strange coincidence, but I didn't say nothing to nobody about it. After that, whenever I mentioned business being slow and possibly laying them off, each time within a week or two, another woman turned up murdered. And it was *always* somebody connected to me or my daddy's church. Why—oh, why—didn't I put two and two together and realize what they was up to?" I groaned and rubbed my chest some more. It felt as tight as a drum.

"Hubert, there was no way you could have known what them devils was up to. If you hadn't heard them discussing it that day, you probably would have never known, and there'd be God only knows how many more murders."

"I'm still having a hard time believing it all. It's going to be quite a while before I get over this."

"I'll help you get over it as much as I can," Leroy said in a somber tone. Then his voice suddenly perked up. "Let's change the subject and discuss something more pleasant."

"You took the words right out of my mouth."

"Could you get away long enough to come spend some time with me this coming weekend? I'm sure a good home-cooked meal and a little pampering would do you a world of good."

"I'll be there," I said.

CHAPTER 36
Jessie

The second anniversary of Maggie's and Claude's deaths was coming up in less than a week. It was a bad time because we was still reeling from what Tyrone and Floyd had done, and that man and woman who had recently drowned.

My brother loved having Hubert for a boss. Working at a funeral home didn't seem to bother Karl at all. He was out of work so often and for so long, he told me he was so desperate that he'd shovel shit for a paycheck if he had to.

The week before Thanksgiving, I found out something from Mr. DeBow that threw me for a loop. I bumped into him at the grocery store on my way home from work that Thursday evening. Even though the white customers and colored ones didn't mix while shopping, he rushed over as soon as he spotted me rooting through the bin that contained the collard greens. I always took my time because I wanted to buy the biggest, freshest bunches. "Hello, Jessie." There was a big smile on his face as he looked me up and down before he added, "My, my, my, you're looking mighty spruced up today."

I had on one of the same drab gray uniforms I wore to work

every day. The only thing "spruced up" about me today was the new shade of rouge I had on. I looked around before I responded. I didn't want none of the other white customers to see me being too friendly with a white man and get the wrong idea. "Hello, Mr. DeBow," I said in a shy tone.

"What a day this has been! I had three meetings, back-to-back, with merchants and each one spent the whole time complaining about late orders and trying to get me to lower my prices. By the end of the last meeting, I was so beaten down, I had to stretch out on the davenport I keep in my office until I got my bearings back." He mopped sweat off his face with the sleeve of his shirt. "Just when I thought I could get up and go home to relax, my wife calls me as I'm about to walk out the door. She tells me to stop at the market on my way home and pick up a few items." Mr. DeBow was talking so fast, he had to stop and catch his breath. "By the way, I hope Hubert got his business taken care of this afternoon."

"What business?"

Mr. DeBow looked confused. "Well, today he asked to take off a extra two hours for lunch. He got back about a hour before we shut down the mill for the day."

Now I was the confused one. "I didn't know he had any business to take care of. Did he say what it was?"

Mr. DeBow hunched his shoulders. "Hubert never tells me why he needs to take frequent extended lunches."

"Oh? And how long has he been taking extended lunch hours?"

"Let me see now." Mr. DeBow scratched the side of his jowly face and gave me a thoughtful look. "He's been doing it for a heap of months now." He suddenly looked embarrassed. "Uh-oh! I hope I didn't spill the beans about something."

I laughed and waved my hand. "You ain't got to worry about nothing like that. Hubert don't have to tell me everything." I leaned closer to Mr. DeBow and added in a low tone, "There is a heap of things I do that I don't tell him about."

Mr. DeBow responded in a tone lower than mine, "I declare, I'm sure most folks could say the same thing. And it is no wonder. Marriage is such a complicated and risky venture. My wife would skin me alive if she knew all the things I've done since we got married." His tone got even lower. "Lord knows, I'm no angel. However, so long as everybody is happy, that's all that really matters."

"I agree. But being married is much better than being single." My mind was all over the place. Where could my husband be going during the middle of the day and why? "Thank you again for helping us out with them murders. There ain't no telling what would have happened if you hadn't gone with us to tell Sheriff Zachary."

"Don't I know it! Y'all coming to me was a wise decision. I know what a scoundrel Zachary can be when he has to deal with colored folks. I'm glad I was able to be of some assistance. Well, it was nice seeing you again, Jessie. I best be on my way now before these red snappers I just picked up start to smell." Mr. DeBow tipped his hat and whirled around so fast, I didn't have time to say nothing else. I left the market without buying nothing.

Hubert's car was in the driveway when I got home. He was sitting on the couch reading the newspaper when I walked into the living room. He glanced at me, but kept reading. I took off my coat and dropped it and my purse into the wing chair before I eased down at the other end of the couch. "Hi, baby. How was work?" he asked with his eyes still on the newspaper.

"Same as always. I stopped at that market on Third Street on my way home."

He looked up from his newspaper and frowned when he seen my empty hands. "Oh? Didn't nothing suit you today, huh?"

"I went to get some chicken feet, but they had just ran out,"

I explained. "I wanted to cook them to go with the beans I'm going to cook for supper this evening. And I needed to put in my order for our Thanksgiving turkey."

Hubert chuckled. "Well, next to the pig ears, chicken feet is their most popular meat. The last two times I went there to buy some, they had just run out too. Oh, well. We can't eat like kings all the time. You can cook them gizzards for supper. The next time, you should go to that market on Pike Street."

"Colored folks can only shop there on weekends, remember?"

"Oh, I forgot. Damn these Jim Crow laws!"

"Hubert, we been living with segregation all of our lives and ain't nothing being done to change it."

"I hope me and you live long enough to see things change for the better for colored folks in the South. I declare, it's almost like being in prison with all these laws telling us what we can and can't do. It's a shame we can't do the same simple little things folks in the rest of the country, and the world, do without worrying about getting arrested, beat up, or lynched."

"I hope we live that long too, but we still manage to find ways to be happy. Besides, it could be worse." I sucked on my teeth for a few seconds and forced the painful subject of our oppression out of my head. "By the way, guess who I seen at the market?"

Hubert gave me a tight look. "Who?"

"Mr. DeBow. All the years I been shopping at that place, I ain't never bumped into him there until today."

Hubert immediately started to fidget in his seat. "Oh? Did he see you?" He abruptly folded the newspaper and set it on the coffee table.

"Uh-huh. He told me you took a real long lunch break today. Where did you go?"

"Well, I'm still in shock over what Tyrone and Floyd done. I took a drive to clear my head. I'm able to organize my thoughts better when I'm alone."

"What about all of them other times you took long lunches? Mr. DeBow told me you been doing it for quite a while."

"Jessie, you of all people know how bad I was hurt when Maggie and Claude died. Going off somewhere by myself so I could grieve and think helped. When that incident with Blondeen happened, I really needed to go off and be alone. Now this mess with Tyrone and Floyd . . ."

"Hubert, you can always talk to me. I been in pain since Maggie and Claude died too. And I was just as affected by Blondeen's death, and what Tyrone and Floyd done, as you was. But I felt better when I had folks who cared about me around. And I think you would too."

"That's debatable. Everybody don't react the same way to a tragedy."

I sighed and gave Hubert a hopeless look. I didn't care how honest I believed he was, all human beings made mistakes. I was a good example. It was because I had not been truthful with him that I had to consider the possibility that he had told me a few fibs. "If there is another woman in the picture, you need to come clean. The last thing I want to do is stand in your way if you would rather be with somebody else."

Hubert gasped and leaped up off the couch so fast, he almost fell. "What? What possessed you to say such a thing?" The way he was waving his arms, you would have thought he was trying to fly. Before I could reply, he marched over to me, leaned down, and wrapped his arm around my shoulder. What he did next almost made me faint: He hauled off and kissed me on my lips. This was only the second or third time he kissed me on the lips since we got married. Every other time, he'd kissed me on my jaw or forehead. He was such a good kisser, I hoped he would show me this kind of affection more often.

"I don't know what made me say what I said," I mumbled. "I ain't been reading Scripture like I should be, so I guess I had a weak moment."

"That happens to all of us from time to time. Even spiritual warriors like me. Well, I ain't going to hold it against you then."

"Thank you."

"You ain't got to thank me for nothing. You are my wife. I done told you before that I would *never* cheat on you with another woman." He looked so sad, I immediately wished I hadn't said nothing about what Mr. DeBow had told me. "You know that I *couldn't* go at it with another woman, even if I wanted to. My pecker is as limp as a wet dishrag. And it seems to be getting limper by the day."

I grabbed Hubert's hands and gave him the most sympathetic look I could manage. "I'm sorry. I shouldn't be putting no pressure on you. I know you can't have sex again yet. But since you brought up your condition, do you still not feel *any* desire for me? Not even a smidgen?"

"Not even a smidgen."

CHAPTER 37
Jessie

I was so glad I had broke things off with Amos last month. I didn't even miss the pleasure he had gave me. Yolinda said she regretted having them affairs when her husband stopped making love to her, because once them men was done with her, she always ended back at square one. And she had the guilt to deal with. That's how I felt now. On top of the sexual frustration and guilt, I had to worry about somebody finding out about me and Amos and blabbing. In the meantime, I would go on about my life and hope and pray for the best.

Even with all the perks I had by being married to Hubert, the idea of him never being able to consummate our marriage was a grim reality, and I had to live with it. But when I started feeling tense again, I would release that tension by letting Hubert know how I felt. I had already made that clear to him, but I didn't think it would hurt to remind him of it from time to time. And not just for my sake, but his as well. I didn't want him to get too comfortable in this situation. If I let that happen, the likelihood of us having a healthy, intimate relationship would get even slimmer. If such a thing was possible.

In the meantime, I had so many other things to round out my life, especially right before Thanksgiving. When I got home from work on Friday, I spent several hours at my sewing machine making more pot holders and pillowcases. On Saturday, I went shopping with Yolinda. After we had lunch at a rib joint, we spent a couple of hours at my house, getting caught up on our gossip. We didn't have too much juicy stuff to share with each other, so she started bragging about how passionate her boyfriend had been in the past couple of months. "I don't know what my man did to get more get-up-and-go in the bedroom after that dry spell I told you about back in July. His pecker is working better than it was when we first got together. He claims he ain't been this robust since he was in his thirties!" Yolinda getting sexed properly again was the last thing I wanted to discuss. I didn't think I'd be able to hide my jealousy. So I abruptly cut her visit short by telling her I had a lot of chores I needed to get done. When she left, I washed clothes and mopped all of my floors.

Hubert had gone to Hartville after work on Friday to settle a dispute with a vendor who he thought had overcharged him for the last batch of embalming fluid he had purchased. He had scheduled his meeting for Saturday afternoon, so I had no idea when he'd come home. But when I got up Sunday morning, I decided to cook enough breakfast for both of us anyway.

Hubert strolled into the kitchen just as I was taking the biscuits out of the oven. "Baby, them biscuits sure do smell good. I declare, your home-cooked meals work on me like a tonic." He pulled out a chair and flopped down at the table. "Lord, I swear, I'm glad to be home. Traffic was so heavy and the motel room they put me in this time had a foul odor," he complained.

"Stop complaining because every job got some ups and downs. At least your work is steady, and you make good money. Be grateful for that."

"I am. And no matter how much I gripe about it, there ain't no other job I'd rather be doing."

I walked up to him and wiped a dark smudge off his fore-head with the tip of my finger. He flinched the same way my son did when I wiped his face. Even though Hubert was a grown man and head of the household, sometimes I felt more like a mother to him than a wife. Since I was getting no sex from him, I figured that a motherly position was the next best thing. "I hope that vendor didn't upset you. Did y'all settle that billing dispute?" He flinched again when I straightened his collar.

"Huh? Oh yeah! It was a honest mistake. His bookkeeper got married last month and her mind ain't been on her work lately. Not only did she overcharge me, she done it to several other customers."

"I hope she don't let it happen again. It must have been a long meeting for you to spend Saturday night too."

"Well, you know almost every time I have business out of town, I leave the night before and usually spend a extra night. I like to be nice and relaxed before I start that long drive back to Lexington. Anyway, the meeting got off to a late start and then the man's wife and kids kept interrupting us. By the time we finally got everything sorted out, it was late. The vendor felt so bad about the billing mix-up and taking up so much of my time, he insisted on taking me out to supper."

"I'm glad. You know how I hate for you to be driving on that highway after dark. You want some coffee?"

"Yup. And some of that blackberry jelly you canned last year."

I grabbed a jar of jelly from the cupboard and set it in front of Hubert. My face was burning while I watched him pile sausages, eggs, grits, and biscuits onto his plate. With a loud sigh, I wiped my hands on my apron and sat down in the chair across from him. I sighed again, longer and louder.

Hubert stopped chewing and gawked at me with a con-cerned look on his face. "Jessie, is everything all right?"

I bit off a hefty chunk of my sausage and chewed and swallowed it before I answered. "Why wouldn't it be?"

"Well, I thought I'd ask, because you suddenly seem distracted. If I said or did something to upset you, you need to let me know so I can fix it."

"There ain't nothing wrong. I was just thinking about all the canning I need to get done." I had no idea what came over me all of a sudden. Even though I had accepted the fact that there might never be any sex in our marriage, the next thing I knew, I slammed my fist down on the table. Words started shooting out of my mouth like buckshot. "I don't know how much longer I can go on like this!"

Hubert's eyes got as big as saucers, and he stared at me like I had lost my mind. And maybe I had. "Go on like what, Jessie?"

"You know damn well what I'm talking about!" I snarled. I stood up so fast, my chair fell over. Hubert picked it up and was still staring at me when I started pacing the floor. "I'm a healthy woman, with healthy needs!"

"Oh, you talking about my . . . uh . . . man problem." I was surprised at how calm he sounded. "Jessie, you ain't being fair to me. I know you want some intimate physical attention, but you knew what you was signing up for when you married me. I guess me being honest with you about it didn't mean nothing." The pout on his face didn't faze me. I was hurting as much as he was, probably more.

I got close up to his face and whispered, "Why don't you at least try to do something about it? I never thought it would go on for so long." The kitchen got so quiet, you could have heard a tick sneeze. "When my sister Minnie's husband had the same problem you got, it didn't last as long as yours."

"Aw, sugar. I would do something to get out of this mess if I knew what." There was a hangdog look on his face. "I . . . I didn't tell you because I didn't want to get your hopes up, but last month, I went to see a doctor at the clinic. He told me there wasn't nothing medical he could do to help me, which is the same thing another doctor had already told me. This particular doctor grew up in the backwoods, where the folks got some real old-fashioned ideas. He suggested I go see a hoodoo woman operating out there and get a potion or pay her to cast a spell. He was laughing when he said it, but I think he was serious."

I rolled my eyes, shook my head, and gave Hubert the most incredulous look I could manage. "Hubert, I am too scientific to even think about you going to see a *witch doctor*. You know how your daddy warns folks in his sermons about anything the Bible condemns."

He sat back down, pulled me into to his lap, and started caressing the side of my face. "Like I said, I told you from the start what was going on with my body. It didn't bother you then."

"It's bothering me now!" I shrieked.

"Do you want a divorce?" he asked with his voice cracking. "I hope you don't, because I love you to pieces and I *need* you, Jessie. I don't think I could go on if I was to lose another wife. My house ain't been as clean as you keep it since Maggie died, and you know how much I appreciate your cooking talents." I was tempted to tell him that he was making me sound more like a maid than a wife. But that would open up another can of worms, so I didn't. He rubbed the side of his face so long, and looked so pitiful, I thought he was about to cry. I was glad he didn't, because it would have made me cry too. "If you decide to go back on the commitment you made, I'll have to live with that grief too. And if you want to leave me and get your own place, I can't stop you. But I think it would be a big mistake. You got just as much to lose as I got."

"I think I got *more* to lose than you. It'd be easier for you to find another wife than it would be for me to find another husband."

"That's debatable," he said with his finger pointed up in the air. "But I'll tell you why you'd be making a mistake if you took off. If we lived in separate locations, one of us might break down and blab to somebody what really happened to Blondeen. We could end up in prison. Not to mention what a ugly impact our fall from grace would have on our families and friends."

I almost laughed out loud. "You can't be serious. *You* killed her. I was only a witness. I done told you this already."

"And I told you that since you helped me cover it up, that made you my accomplice. The law would be as hard on you as they would be on me. We could end up where Tyrone and Floyd are at right now."

"What makes you think I'd be the one to blab?"

"I didn't say you'd be the one. I said one of us, so it could be me."

I got up from Hubert's lap and sat back down in my chair with a loud groan. "I don't want no divorce and I don't want to leave this lovely house." I sighed again, this time much louder and deeper. "I'll keep praying that we'll have a normal marriage someday. God's been good to us so far. Sooner or later, He has to take pity on you and restore your manhood."

"Well, I don't know about you, but whatever God decides, I'll accept it." Hubert took a deep breath and said something that didn't make no sense to me. "Besides, what is sex anyway? Nothing but 'a beast with two backs.'"

I narrowed my eyes and stared at him. He had said some boneheaded things to me before, but what he'd just said was the worst one of all. "What in the world is that supposed to mean?"

He chuckled. "Mr. DeBow said that. He told me he'd read it somewhere. Mrs. DeBow was going through menopause at the time and suddenly got a little too frisky for him."

"Why would *you* be discussing a *white* man's sex life with him?"

"I didn't bring it up, he did. He likes to discuss his personal life with me. That's how I found out how useless his two sons are. He told me—or griped to me, I should say—that during that time period when his wife was so hot to trot, she would mount him like a jackrabbit as soon as they got in the bed and wear him out almost every night. Even when he was suffering with lumbago! He said that after being married to her for over forty years, 'a beast with two backs' was all sex had become to him. That's how he explained it to me."

I blew my breath out so hard, it sounded like I was whistling. "I declare, I wish *my* back was one of the ones on a beast . . ."

Hubert laughed at my comment, but I was dead serious.

CHAPTER 38
Hubert

When Jessie told me she had bumped into Mr. DeBow at the market last week, I almost peed in my pants. It was such a close call, I knew I couldn't keep using his mama as a excuse too often to stay out of town overnight. I was lucky it hadn't come up in their conversation. I probably wouldn't be so lucky if she ran into him again.

To make myself feel better about all the lies I told Jessie, I took her out to supper Sunday evening. Afterward, we went to the movies and seen *The Wizard of Oz*. It had been out awhile, but our little poo-butt theater was just now running it. I enjoyed it, but Jessie enjoyed it even more. I couldn't remember the last time a movie had made her laugh so much. I was pleased she had enjoyed our evening out. Before we turned in for the night, we got down on our knees by the side of our bed and honored Maggie and Claude with a special prayer. We thanked God for blessing us with two wonderful people for so many years. Jessie added something that brought tears to my eyes. "God, I thank you for bringing me and Hubert together so we can look after each other until we join Maggie and Claude in Heaven."

By Monday, Jessie seemed like her old self. I wanted to do even more to show her how much she was loved and appreciated. On Tuesday evening, I bought her some flowers and smell-goods on my way home from the mill. She liked that. "Hubert, you don't have to keep spoiling me," she gushed.

I raised my eyebrows. "You complaining? I'm sure my mama, your mama, or Yolinda would love to have them flowers and smell-goods if you don't want them," I teased.

She slapped my hand when I reached for the gifts I'd just gave her. "You stop that. I ain't complaining about nothing. I was just making a comment. No other man ever treated me so nice."

"I ain't 'no other man,' and you should know that by now."

"I do. And you can keep on spoiling me."

Thanksgiving was coming up this week. There had been so much turmoil this year, we wanted to celebrate the day alone. Mama and Daddy was going to Toxey to spend the holiday with some used-to-be church members that had recently moved over there. And that busybody Yolinda was going to celebrate with one of her daughters in Branson, so we didn't have to worry about her barging in on us. Jessie's mama had invited us to eat with their family and some of their rowdiest friends and neighbors, but I didn't waste no time turning down her invitation. I explained how we really wanted to be alone that day.

"I ain't surprised or disappointed because there will be a lot of drinking over here and y'all don't touch that stuff no more," her mama said. "I wish the rest of my kids was as virtuous as you and Jessie."

Leroy was spending part of the holiday week in New York visiting some relatives who had moved up there two years ago. Me and him planned to have a belated celebration when he got back the day after Thanksgiving.

Jessie had to work on that upcoming Friday, but Mr. DeBow had gave all the workers at the mill the day off with pay. I told

Jessie I'd use that day off to go to Hartville to pick up some new embalming tools.

I had Karl meet me at the funeral home Wednesday evening. We had to start preparing the body of a elderly woman who had been battling cancer for two years. "This lady used to chase me with a switch for stealing pecans off her tree," Karl said in a sad tone as he stood over the embalming table, where we had laid the woman. "It's a shame she had to go out this way."

I shook my head. "It's a shame that nobody can choose the way they die."

Karl gave me a pensive look. "Did you forget about that man who drunk some poison last month and killed hisself because his wife left him?"

"Oh. I forgot about lost souls like him." I snorted and clapped Karl on the back. "I appreciate how hard you work, but I ain't going to overwork you. I had Tyrone and Floyd work all day, six days a week, for years. I had them hang around just in case somebody couldn't reach me at home and called the funeral home. Well, you ain't got to work on Saturday and Sunday, unless we already got a body here. If somebody can't reach me or you at home, they will just have to keep calling until they reach one of us. When the last two folks died, somebody from the families came to my house to let me know. Besides, us picking up a body a few hours later won't make no difference. We'd still get them prepared in time for their funeral. That's all we need to be concerned about. You can take the day after the holiday off—with pay."

Karl's face lit up like a lightbulb. He reminded me so much of Jessie. He was a foot taller, fifty pounds heavier, and two years older than she was, but they almost looked enough alike to be twins. She was the baby of the family, but she was smarter than her three siblings and had a lot more class. Otherwise, I probably wouldn't have married her.

"All right, boss," Karl said, grinning. "I got a new lady friend I can spend Friday with. Ain't nothing like spending the day after a big holiday with the one you love, right?"

"Right," I agreed.

Me and Jessie had so much to be thankful for, we enjoyed a wonderful Thanksgiving. After we had gobbled up almost everything she had cooked, she went to visit one of her friends who had been in bed after having a miscarriage. I encouraged her to spend as much time with her as possible. She'd had a miscarriage herself, so she understood what her friend was going through and could offer her a lot of sympathy.

While she was gone, I was going over to Toxey and pick up Earl before it got too late in the day. My stepson could never replace Claude in my heart, but I loved him like he was my own. I thought it would be a good idea for him to spend Friday and the rest of the weekend keeping his mama company. I knew Jessie would be pleased.

She tried on a regular basis to get Earl to spend more time with us, but he didn't want to. His only excuse was that he didn't like to come to Lexington no more. We had visited him one evening last week, but he was not in the mood to do much talking. It had been such a nice day, and we took him to one of them outdoor markets to pick up a few things for Minnie to cook for supper.

While me and Jessie was looking at the greens, Earl wandered over to the table where the candy and other things that kids liked was laid out. So far, he hadn't said nary a word since we picked him up a hour earlier. All of a sudden, he came running up to us, panting like a big dog. "Mama, Hubert! There is a all-white *colored* man, with a table next to the cleaning goods, selling peanut brittle!"

"He's what folks call a *albino*, son," Jessie explained. From the baffled expression on Earl's face, I could tell that she had only confused him more. "He's one of God's special children," she added.

"Oh! Just like me!" Earl hollered. He grabbed her hand and pulled her over to the man's table. I shuffled along behind them. When we reached the albino man's table, Earl went right up to him and asked, "Mr. Man, what planet did you come from?"

The man gasped and his eyes got real wide. "I'm from the same planet you come from," he said slowly, looking from Jessie to me.

"I'm sorry, sir. Our son is a little on the slow side and didn't mean no harm," I apologized. "He was born this way."

"That's all right. I was born this way too. Folks ask me crazy questions all the time," the man replied. He looked hurt, so we steered Earl away as fast as we could. We didn't do no more shopping that day, and Earl didn't do no more talking.

Just recalling Earl's innocence made me misty-eyed. My son, Claude, had been so intelligent, I wondered what he could have accomplished if he hadn't died. He had talked about going to college to be a doctor and getting a job at the colored clinic.

I didn't call up Minnie to let her know I wanted to pick Earl up today. I wished I had. When I got to her house, there was nobody home. A lady sitting on the porch next door told me that Minnie and her family had gone to Mobile to spend the holiday with some friends and wouldn't be back home until Sunday.

Jessie was home when I got back to our house. She looked so happy when I told her I had attempted to bring Earl to Lexington so he could spend some time with her while I was in Hartville on Friday and Saturday.

"Hubert, you are so considerate, and I really do appreciate it. I forgot to mention to you that Minnie had told me they was going to Mobile for the holiday. You go on to Hartville tomorrow and get them new tools you need. Don't worry about me. Mama wants me to come over and help her can some chicken necks and backs, so I got plenty to do."

Jessie got up Friday morning and walked to her mama's house, which was just a few streets over. I immediately dialed Leroy's number. It was a few minutes after 9 a.m. He had told me he would get back from New York early Friday morning, around four or five o'clock. I hadn't called him right away because I thought he'd be tired after the drive back to Alabama.

When he didn't answer his telephone after ten rings, I figured he hadn't made it home yet. Just as I was about to hang up, he picked up. His voice was low and weak, I almost didn't recognize it. I figured he had just woke up. "Baby, I am so glad you made it back home," I chirped. "I'll be on my way in a few minutes."

"Hubert, you can't come today—"

I didn't even wait for him to explain. My heart started beating so fast and hard, I thought it was going to explode. "Why not?" I wanted to know. "You don't want to see me? What about the plans we made?"

"I picked up a bug in New York. I'm so sick, I can't keep no food down and can barely stand up."

"Oh, I'm sorry to hear that. Is there anything I can bring you? Some pills or something? I can come over and fix you something to eat and keep you company. I done already told Jessie a good fib about having to drive to Hartville this morning for some new embalming tools."

"Hubert, I hate for you to waste up a good fib. But don't come over here, period. I don't feel like seeing nobody in the condition I'm in, and I don't know if this bug I caught is catchy. Don't worry about me. I can get up and make a sandwich when I get hungry. I just need to rest and take it easy for a few days." Leroy started coughing and didn't stop for almost half a minute. "I . . . I'll call you when I feel better," he rasped. "Now . . . I have to get back in the bed. Bye, baby."

"Bye," I muttered. I hung up and shuffled to the living room and stretched out on the couch. I was so disappointed, all I wanted to do was lay down.

When Jessie walked through the door two hours later, I sat up and told her that the man I was supposed to meet with in Hartville had called me up and canceled our meeting because he had overbooked. "Did y'all reschedule?" she wanted to know.

"Um, he's going to call me and let me know when to come. I'm sure it'll be one day next week."

"I hope he don't overbook again. How can somebody in the business he's in be so careless?" Jessie paused and gave me a pensive look. "I wish everybody was as professional as you. Can you imagine what would happen if you overbooked funerals?"

"I ain't even going to think about that, because it ain't never going to happen."

I insisted on us playing checkers for a few hours so I wouldn't sit around and think about Leroy. But I did. I was so distracted that I couldn't concentrate, so she won all but two games.

I didn't hear from him on Saturday or Sunday, and I was getting real concerned. I didn't care what he said, I had to see him in person, whether he wanted me to or not.

Sunday afternoon while Jessie was visiting Yolinda, I jumped in my car and drove to Hartville. Since Leroy no longer left his door unlocked because of Sadie, when I got to his apartment, I knocked for the first time. He didn't answer, so I knocked some more. When he still didn't answer, I called out his name and tried to open the door, but it didn't budge. I didn't know what to do. I couldn't take a chance and let one of his neighbors see me banging on his door. I had no choice but to leave.

When I got back home, Jessie was taking a bath, so I called Leroy several more times. He still didn't answer. The worst thing I could think of that could have happened to him was that Sadie had returned anyway. If that was the case, then there was nothing I could do but wait until I heard from him.

By the time I got off work at the mill on Monday, I was frantic. If Leroy had got so sick he had to go to the clinic, I wanted to know. If he was too sick to answer his phone or his door, I wanted to know that too. Jessie hadn't come home from work yet, but I expected her any minute. I didn't want to waste no time, so I called the Hartville police station. I told the man who answered that I had a sick friend who wasn't answering his phone and asked him to send a officer to do a wellness check. When I gave him the address, he let out a tired sigh and asked, "Ain't that the street where nothing but colored folks live?"

"Yes, it is, sir. But he's a real nice colored man, so I would appreciate it if you could help me find out what's going on with him."

The man didn't even try to hide his impatience. "I'll let the sheriff know."

I gave him my name and telephone number, but I didn't expect to hear back from the sheriff, or anybody else, anytime soon.

Another hour went by. I hadn't heard back from the police, and Jessie hadn't come home. I went out on the sidewalk and looked down the street to make sure I didn't see her. I rushed back to the kitchen and dialed Leroy's number again. He still didn't answer. I reluctantly called up the police station again, to see if they could give me any information about the wellness check I'd asked them to do.

The same man, who answered the first time, answered again. What he said made me freeze. "You need to get in touch with his family, or one of the local colored undertakers."

"Undertaker?" I could barely get the word out. My tongue couldn't have felt worse if somebody had sliced it in two.

"Yup, I'm afraid so. I don't know which one is handling the arrangements, so you'll have to check with them both."

My voice trembled and tears filled my eyes. "C-can you tell me anything else, sir?"

"Nope, that's all I know. Now you need to get off this telephone, boy. You know it ain't fitting for us to get involved in colored folks' affairs if we don't have to." The man abruptly hung up before I could say anything else.

CHAPTER 39
Hubert

Leroy done died. Just thinking them words made my body feel like it had turned to stone. How much more misery could I stand? I was still holding the telephone; but my hand was so numb, I couldn't feel it.

"Leroy is dead," I whispered to myself. Saying the words was worse than just thinking them. Why was life beating me down so much by taking Leroy away from me? Especially only one week after the second anniversary of Maggie's and Claude's deaths! Had I disrespected somebody in some way, and they'd put a hoodoo curse on me? That would explain all the misery that just kept coming at me. If that was the case, I didn't want to know, because I didn't want to have nothing to do with folks who was into that mess. I would just have to rely on God to take care of me.

For several more seconds, I looked at the phone like it was a skunk, before I finally hung it up. Then my head started swimming. If I hadn't stumbled over to the table and grabbed the back of a chair, I would have fell to the floor. Even after I sat down, I felt like I was going to faint. I told myself that I had to be strong. I needed to get all the information I could about Leroy. Otherwise, I would never be able to accept his death and move on. The thought of him being dead was so overwhelming, I couldn't process it. But why else would the man at the police station tell me to get in touch with his family or a undertaker?

All kinds of thoughts was floating around inside my head. One was that maybe the man at the police station had mixed up Leroy with somebody else. If he really was dead, I wanted to know for sure. I wouldn't believe he was gone until I actually seen his body, or until somebody who would know told me to my face.

I don't know how I was able to get through the rest of the day without fainting. I almost did a couple of times. When Jessie came home a hour later with a live chicken in a crocus sack that she had bought from the man down the street, she immediately went outside to wring its neck so she could fry it for our supper. She was so busy the next couple of hours, she didn't pay too much attention to me.

"Hubert, don't think I'm ignoring you. I just want to get supper done so I can finish washing them clothes I started on yesterday. If I don't, I'll have to put on a pair of your step-ins." She laughed.

"Why don't I finish the laundry and you can focus on supper," I suggested. I would rather get a whupping than wash clothes. But I was willing to do just about anything that would keep me busy.

"Thank you, baby. But that's all right. If you don't mind me saying so, you look mighty distressed right now. If you're constipated, I can get some castor oil from Yolinda and give you a dose. Or, if it's something more serious, I can call up your daddy and have him come over and lay hands on you."

"I ain't constipated and I don't need no laying on of hands. It's just that I was real busy at the mill today. We got a slew of new orders, and twice as many complaints from folks who hadn't received their orders was coming at us, left and right. On top of all that, I had to train a new man in my section. He was so slow catching on, it frustrated me."

When we finished eating supper, I pretended like I had a headache. "I'm fixing to go stretch out on the couch for a while."

"You do that, Hubert. Holler if you want anything. And don't forget to take a pill before you lay down."

When I went to bed for the night, I got less than three hours' sleep. By the time I got up to get ready for work this morning, Jessie had already ate and left the house. She had told me last night that she promised Yolinda she'd stop by her house on her way to the bus stop this morning to drop off some quilt pieces. She had left breakfast for me in the oven. But I didn't have no appetite. I left a note on the kitchen counter to let her know I had to go to Hartville again, but I didn't tell her the reason. I advised her to eat supper without me.

It was another very busy day at the mill on Tuesday. Somehow I managed to make it to the end of the day without going to pieces. As soon as quitting time rolled around, I sprinted to my car. I shot off like a bullet toward the highway.

I knew the two colored undertakers in Hartville, but I drove to Leroy's place first. The barbershop was closed. I didn't bother to go to his apartment this time. I went straight to the undertaker that was the closest. A elderly, dark-skinned woman walking with two canes met me at the door. "Can I help you?" she asked in a raspy tone. Her eyes was red and swollen, so I knew she had been crying.

"Good evening, ma'am. Is the undertaker in? I'm here to get some information about a man named Leroy Everette."

The woman looked me up and down. Her bushy white hair looked like a big ball of cotton. "I taught Leroy in Sunday school when he was a young'un. You kin to him?"

"No, ma'am. Me and him was in the army together. I bumped into one of our friends last night and he told me he'd heard Leroy was sick and might not live long. I couldn't get in touch with none of his family to get more information, so I called the police. They told me I needed to see one of the colored under-takers. I thought I'd come to this one first."

The woman shook her head. "Well, Leroy didn't make it. Bless his soul. He left this world Sunday night. It was bad enough his wife took off with another man and left him to die alone."

"I talked to him Saturday morning. I had no idea he was that sick." It wasn't easy, but I managed to hold back my tears. I knew I was going to cry a river as soon as I was alone.

"One of his aunts told me that he went to New York to cel-ebrate Thanksgiving with some of his other kinfolks. He got sick the day after he got there. He couldn't eat, sleep, or barely walk. My, my, my. I don't know if he went to a doctor up there or not, but he thought he had got better. He drove back home, but was still sick when he got back to Alabama. Come to find out, he had caught the pneumonia. That's the same thing that killed my baby sister. She moved to Detroit last winter and that was the end of her." The woman looked me up and down again. "Who did you say you was?"

"Um . . . I'm Lester Wilson." I didn't think it was a good idea for me to give my real name. I couldn't take a chance on her sharing the information with somebody who knew folks in Lexington. Especially since I lied and told her I'd been in the army with Leroy. Everybody who knew me knew that I'd never been in the military.

"I'm Bertha Mae Crawford. Nice to meet you, Lester. I wish we could have met on a more pleasant occasion."

"I wish we could have too, ma'am. Do you know when they're going to have his funeral?"

"I ain't sure, but I think it's going to be this coming Friday.

Leroy got relatives all over the place and they need enough time to get here. I just hope that whoever he caught that pneumonia from don't come down here and infect some of us at the funeral. God help us if that was to happen!" The old woman had to pause to catch her breath before she went on. "His used-to-be wife, Sadie, is at his place now with his sons. She just called here a few minutes ago. That wench had the nerve to bring her tail back to Hartville yesterday with that fool she left Leroy for! Some women ain't got no shame at all. Anyway, she claims she and them young'uns of his came to help Leroy's folks clean out his place and load up his belongings. I'm sure Leroy's mama would be pleased if you stopped by there when you leave here to pay your respects."

"I wish I could do that. But I have to get back to Mobile. My wife is sick, and I promised her I wouldn't be gone long. What about the calling hours? Maybe I could come back for that."

"I don't have all the information about that. I'm sure Sadie would know. Leroy's telephone ain't been cut off yet, so if you want to talk to her, I wouldn't put it off. She told me she wanted to get everything packed up and hauled away by today or tomorrow. That heifer! I'm sure she'll root through everything and take what she wants. Leroy had some real nice stuff in his place."

"Maybe I will call or go over there. Thank you, ma'am. You have a blessed day." I was about to leave when the old woman grabbed my arm.

"Hold on, young man. If you got a few minutes, I could let you go say your last good-bye to Leroy right now."

My eyes got big. "You don't mind if I do that?"

"Naw, I don't care. You have to be quick about it, though. I was fixing to leave when you showed up." The woman screwed up her face and shuddered. "I can't wait to get up out of here. If this wasn't my nephew's business, I wouldn't have come over here and wait for him to get back in the first place. I believe that there is just as many haints in a funeral home as there is in a graveyard."

"I won't take long."

I followed the woman to a room that had a dim lightbulb hanging from a string in the ceiling directly above Leroy's body laid out on a slab. The closer I got to my beloved, the more my heart raced. When I got up to him, I could only stand to look at his remains for about five or six seconds. I was pleased to see that he looked so peaceful. Without saying a word, I spun around and scurried out the door and jumped back into my car.

CHAPTER 40
Jessie

I was standing in the doorway when Hubert parked in our driveway. He shuffled up the porch steps and then dragged his feet across the living-room floor. He dropped down so hard onto the couch that it squeaked. From his long face, I knew something was wrong.

I eased down onto the couch. "What did you have to go to Hartville for this time? To meet with that vendor that canceled on you last week?"

"Uh, no." Hubert had to pause and swallow the lump blocking the inside of his throat. "One of the men I supervise at the mill told me late yesterday that a man over there that I been knowing for years was on his deathbed. I wanted to reach him in time so I could hug him and tell him good-bye. I headed over there right after I got off work today."

My breath caught in my throat. "My Lord. I'm sorry to hear that. Was it one of the men you been buying embalming fluid and other products from?"

"Um . . . no, it wasn't him. This man's name was Leroy. He was a barber I occasionally went to when I was over there."

"Oh. What did he die from?" I braced myself in case he told me the man had died from being beat up or shot.

"Pneumonia. He caught it while he was visiting some of his kinfolks in New York for Thanksgiving. Poor thing. He didn't really want to go, but they kept riding his back until he gave in."

I breathed a sigh of relief. "Thank God he wasn't murdered! But pneumonia is a awful way to go too. Well, I guess I'd better dig out my bereaving dress. When is his funeral?"

Hubert moaned and rubbed the side of his face. I couldn't understand why he was so broken up over a barber that he occasionally went to. When one of the barbers he'd been going to in Lexington died six months ago, he didn't get upset at all. He didn't even go to his funeral. But Hubert rarely went to funerals that the Fuller Brothers handled. "His family is from Meridian, Mississippi. That's where they'll be having his home-going, so we won't be able to make it."

I shrugged. "I don't see why not. Meridian is about the same distance from us as Hartville and Mobile, and you go to them towns all the time. We need to go and pay our respects. I'm glad I just got your black suit cleaned last week."

"Jessie, if you don't mind, I'd rather not go. It would be too hard for me to look at him laying in a casket."

I narrowed my eyes and gazed at Hubert. "I can't believe what I'm hearing. You look at dead folks laying in caskets all the time. If he was a friend of yours, you owe it to him and his family to be there. I'm sure that if it was the other way around, he'd attend your funeral."

"I know he would. But the thing is, his used-to-be wife will be there. She's married to another man now, but she was still coming to Leroy when she needed money. That woman is even meaner than Blondeen was."

Just hearing that name caused bile to rise in my throat. I had been trying not to mention it anytime soon, and I couldn't bring myself to say it out loud now. "I didn't think anybody could be meaner than *that woman*."

"Well, Leroy's used-to-be is a straight-up bride of Satan. Anyway, she never liked me. The last time I seen her, she accused me of being a bad influence on Leroy."

"Is she trying to put some of the blame on you for them breaking up?"

"Uh-huh."

My jaw dropped. "That woman must be crazy! You must be the most pious, straitlaced man I know. You don't drink, smoke, gamble, and you sure don't chase women. What is it she blames you for?"

Hubert gave me a sad look that was so profound, I almost felt his pain. "She thought I was taking up too much of Leroy's time."

"You and him would go off somewhere after he cut your hair?"

"No, but I'd hang around after a haircut and me and him would stay in his barbershop and play checkers for hours on end. Or we'd go up to his apartment. It was just upstairs above the barbershop."

I gave Hubert a confused look. "Hmmm. I been knowing you all my life and I ain't never knew you to play checkers 'for hours on end' with nobody except me."

"Well, Leroy loved the game as much as you do. After his divorce, he decided to take his time to look for another wife. He'd been married since he got out of the military and wanted to have some time in between to get his bearings back. He even treated me to supper at some of the restaurants he liked to go to. His used-to-be wife didn't like that."

"He didn't have no other men friends to spend time with?"

"Huh? Oh! Leroy had a heap of men friends, like some of his customers, members of his church family, and whatnot!" Hubert was talking so fast, spit was flying out the side of his mouth. "He went fishing, hunting, and he worked on cars with them. But they didn't enjoy playing checkers like me. That woman didn't like them neither."

"Oh. I can see why you don't want to face her at his funeral, and if his other buddies got half as much sense as you, they won't attend the funeral neither. Women like her could cause a scene. Remember when one of my she-devil cousins slapped her dead husband's girlfriend at his funeral when your daddy was in the middle of the eulogy?"

"I'll never forget that. My daddy almost had a fit. I doubt if Leroy's used-to-be would go that far. But I don't want to take that chance."

I stood up and gave Hubert a pitiful look. "You stay put. Supper will be ready in a few minutes."

Right after we ate the pinto beans, smothered chicken, rice, and corn bread I had cooked, Hubert took a bath and went to bed.

While I was washing the dishes, the telephone rang, but I didn't answer it. Five minutes later, Yolinda stormed through our front door. "Jessie, Hubert, where y'all at? Uuuuuh, Jessie! Uuuuuh, Hubert!" she hollered as she made her way from the living room to the kitchen. I was drying the dishes. "How come y'all didn't answer the telephone when I called just now?"

"Was that you? I was sitting on the commode then. The phone had stopped ringing by the time I finished doing my business and made it back to the kitchen."

"Where is Hubert at?" She sniffed and looked toward the living room.

"Keep your voice low. He's in the bed."

"In the bed? Why is he in the bed this early? What's the matter with him?"

"Ain't nothing wrong with him. The man who used to cut his hair sometime when he was in Hartville died. He's taking it real hard."

Yolinda gave me a sympathetic look. "Aw, that's too bad. Can I go to the funeral with y'all? I'm anxious to show off that new frock I bought last weekend. And I might even buy a wig-hat so I can hide my gray hair."

"We ain't going. The woman that the man was divorced from didn't like Hubert, so he don't think it would be a good idea for us to go."

"Say what? How could anybody not like a saintly man like Hubert? She must be a low-down, mean-ass heifer!" Yolinda's face looked so tight; I was surprised it didn't crack. It was hard to believe that she was the same woman who had told me a few months ago how she had helped support a child her dead husband had had behind her back with one of his girlfriends.

"I'm sorry for losing my cool. I just came over to borrow some rouge, not to hear a bunch of sad news. If I don't leave now, I'll get depressed. I got a date tonight, so I better haul ass." She rotated her finger in the air and swooned. "Girl, my man is giving me so much affection now. The last three times I went to his house, we spent more time in the bed than out."

"That's . . . nice. I'm so glad to hear he's staying on track." I must have sounded as sad as I looked because Yolinda's demeanor suddenly changed.

"Let me hush talking about nasty stuff at a time like this." She cleared her throat and gave me a sympathetic look. "I'm sorry to hear about Hubert's friend passing. He had to be a good man if Hubert liked him."

"He had to be," I agreed.

Yolinda left right after I gave her the rouge. I spent the next hour writing letters to some of my out-of-state kinfolks.

When I went to bed, I nudged Hubert, but he didn't move or make a sound. I woke up in the middle of the night and was surprised to see his side of the bed empty. I tiptoed to the bathroom and put my ear up to the door. He was crying up a storm. Him and that Leroy must have had a special friendship because I hadn't heard him cry that hard since Maggie and Claude died.

Hubert's behavior was making me curious. The only person I knew who had grieved so hard for somebody who wasn't kin to him was Glenn Hawthorne. He'd cried off and on for days before, during, and after the funeral of a man who hadn't paid him back the one hundred dollars he'd borrowed so he could set up a still and make his own moonshine.

I raised my hand to knock on the bathroom door so I could ask Hubert if he wanted a pill or some tea, but something told me to leave him alone. If he wanted to tell me more about the Leroy man, he would. He must have owed Hubert some big money. It *had* to be that because I couldn't think of nothing bad enough to upset Hubert so much about the passing of a man he wasn't even related to.

CHAPTER 41
Hubert

I didn't want Jessie to know I was taking Leroy's passing so hard. That was the reason I went in the bathroom last night while she was asleep so I could grieve in private.

When I got up in the morning, I was feeling somewhat better. But there was still a throbbing pain in my head that wouldn't go away no matter how many pills I swallowed. What was I going to do without Leroy?

Almost two weeks had passed, and I was still feeling overwhelmed with grief. I woke up early Sunday morning, but I had to lay in bed a couple of hours longer. I needed for something to distract me, so I decided to go to church today. Me and Jessie hadn't attended regular service in a while. With all that was going on with me now, I thought some spiritual nourishment would do me a heap of good.

I had just put on my blue suit and was in the bathroom shaving when Jessie came in. "Where you going?" she wanted to know.

"Church. You coming with me?"

"No, I promised Yolinda I'd help her clean a bucket of chitlins. I'll stay over there until she cooks them, so I can bring some home. That way, I won't have to cook much for supper this evening."

Within minutes after Daddy started his long-winded sermon, folks started stomping their feet, clapping their hands, and whooping and hollering. It didn't take long for a few women to get overcome and they fainted. But my daddy's words was going in one of my ears and out the other. When the morning service ended, some folks left, but everybody else stayed for the afternoon service, which started up about midafternoon.

The choir was in the middle of the sixth hymn (they never sung less than eight), when one of the ushers rushed up to Daddy and whispered in his ear. His face immediately froze. He closed his Bible and made a motion to the choir to stop singing. And then he let out a painful-sounding moan. It took a few seconds before he started talking again. "Y'all, I have some more distressing news to report. I was just told that the Japanese done dropped a bomb on Pearl Harbor this morning! I declare, this has been a bad year for us. Satan done stopped working overtime and is working in three shifts now." Daddy was so riled up, he strutted to the edge of the stage and stomped his foot so hard, his hymnbook fell off the lectern. "I swear, this world was already in a uproar. That's all the more reason why Jesus needs to hurry up and come back down here and straighten out this mess."

People started looking around and talking in low tones. I heard a lady behind me ask, "Where is Pearl Harbor?" Another person told her it was in Hawaii. "Where is Hawaii at?" a man with a raspy voice asked.

Daddy dismissed the choir first and then he turned back to the congregation. "I don't know what is going to happen next, but we all need to get to our homes and pray." He pointed toward the door. "Now y'all git along!"

I was sitting on the front pew, but I was one of the first ones out the door. My thoughts was all over the place. I was so worried about what was going to happen next, I couldn't wait to get home. I had to drive real slow so I wouldn't hit nobody or run a stop sign. Another reason I was taking my time was because I didn't want Sheriff Zachary to catch me speeding again.

When I got to my house, Jessie was pacing around the living room with a wild-eyed look on her face. She stopped pacing and put her hands on her hips. "Guess what I heard on the radio? The Japanese folks done bombed a harbor in Hawaii!"

I plopped down on the couch so hard that my tailbone ached. "I know. That's why Daddy sent everybody home."

"Do you think America is fixing to go to war?"

"What's wrong with you, Jessie? Do you think a man like President Roosevelt is going to sit on his butt and not do nothing about foreigners destroying American property? If he is as tough as he tries to make the country think he is, he'll have bombs dropping down on Japan like raindrops."

"I declare, if it ain't one thing, it's another." Jessie sniffed and gave me a weary look. "Shame on the president for letting things get to this point. That man needs a good whupping! I guess the folks that voted him into office is mad as hell now. My stomach balls up when I think about all of them young colored men they drafted and put in harm's way in the Great War—and still treated them like fourth-class citizens when and if they made it back home alive! Praise God you are too old for them to drag you into the military."

"If I was still young enough to get drafted, they'd have to drag me kicking and screaming. I couldn't pick up no gun and kill nobody." The blood drained from Jessie's face, and I knew

what she was thinking. "Um . . . shooting somebody by accident in self-defense don't count, right?"

I was surprised at how long it took her to respond. "Right,"
she mumbled. "Death is such a unpleasant subject, no matter
how it happens. By the way, how are you feeling these days
about your barber friend up and dying? You all right now?"

"I'm feeling much better about it," I lied. The truth was, I
felt just as woebegone as I'd felt the day I seen Leroy's body at
that funeral home.

"Sugar, take all the time you need and cry all you want."
Jessie eased down on the couch and crossed her legs. "Uh, I
wasn't going to ask, but I won't rest until I do. It's about
Leroy."

A spasm hit me like a bolt of lightning. If I hadn't been sitting down, I probably would have slid to the floor. "W-what
do you want to ask me about him?"

"Remember how folks say Glenn carried on when that man
died owing him some big money? I've kept quiet for weeks,
but did you lend Leroy some money that he still owed you?
Tell me the truth now. I promise I won't get mad."

"Why you asking me that? You know I don't like to lend
money."

"Well, I can't understand why his passing upset you so
much. That was the only thing I could think of. A lady that
used to work at the nursing home borrowed money from me
and abruptly quit her job and left town before she paid me
back. I had to borrow money from three different people to
pay my rent that month. That was fifteen years ago and I still
get mad when I think about it."

I gave Jessie a sheepish look. "Well, sugar, you got me.
Leroy did owe me some money. A hundred dollars. But don't
worry, we ain't going to end up in the poorhouse."

"A hundred dollars?! That's more than most colored folks I
know make in a month!"

I held up my hand and shook my head. "Don't get too upset. I loaned him that money before me and you got married."

"Oh. Now that I'm your wife, the next time somebody wants to borrow that kind of money from you, we need to discuss it first."

"All right, sugar. But after this, I don't plan on lending nobody no more than a couple of dollars."

CHAPTER 42
Jessie

By the time the Christmas week arrived, things was pretty much back to normal with the folks we knew. I was glad the talk had died down about the attack on Pearl Harbor, and all the rest of the violence going on around the world. Especially since it didn't have no real impact on colored folks in America.

Nobody let the bombing stop them from celebrating Christmas, and Hubert finally seemed to be over losing his barber friend. But one thing that really puzzled me was the fact that since the barber's passing, he had cut his trips to Hartville in half. Last week, he sent Karl over there to pick up a few items, and he told him he wanted him to go again after the holidays. He had never sent Tyrone or Floyd to pick up no products. This was way out of character for him. I didn't want to ask him why, but when my brother came over to eat Christmas supper with us, I decided that the first chance I got, I'd ask him if he knew why.

We had invited my immediate family to eat Christmas supper with us. They couldn't make it, though. They had already decided to spend it in Tuscaloosa with some of our extended family. Karl didn't want to go with them, and he was glad to join us. We had also invited Ma and Pa Wiggins. Not only did they show up three hours before we asked them to, but my mother-in-law also took it upon herself to "help" me and Hubert cook the huge feast we had planned. She slowed us down so much with her suggestions, additional dishes, and complaints, we ended up serving supper a hour later than we was supposed to.

After we'd ate, Pa Wiggins suggested we all go into the living room to sing a few hymns and then get on our knees and pray. Halfway into the first hymn, Karl groaned, shook his head, rolled his eyes, and headed to the kitchen. I waited until the hymn ended before I followed him.

"Don't them folks do enough singing and praying at church?" he asked, snickering as he grabbed a biscuit off a platter on the stove and started chomping on it.

"You know how holy the Wiggins family is, so you stop talking like that," I scolded. I moved closer to him and asked, "Um . . . do you know why Hubert stopped going to Hartville as often as he used to?"

Karl gave me a side-eyed look. "Jessie, he's your husband. Why don't you ask him?"

"I thought about doing that. But when Hubert don't want me to know something, he won't tell me."

"Then what makes you think he'd tell me?"

"Because some men tell other men stuff they won't tell their wives. Maybe I'm overreacting. After all, things have been tough on him lately—finding out about Tyrone and Floyd, and then losing a close friend a few weeks later."

"What close friend?"

"A barber that used to cut his hair from time to time when he went to Hartville."

Karl gave me a confused look. "I never knew Hubert to have no 'close friend.' Not even when we was kids. Maggie was the only one I ever seen him hanging around with."

"Well, he's always liked to be by hisself a lot. Even when he was young."

Karl gave me a look I couldn't figure out. His eyes blinked a few times, and he shook his head, which made me think he knew something I didn't know. "Baby sister, Hubert was never young, not even when he was young."

I rolled my eyes and let out a impatient breath. "What you just said don't make no sense. He wasn't born a grown man."

Karl snorted and gave me a sympathetic look. "I ain't trying to hurt your feelings about your husband, so let me put it another way. You know when somebody calls a kid a 'old soul'? Well, when we was kids, I used to hear folks say that about Hubert."

"Shoot! Mama called me a 'old soul' one time. All she meant was that I was more sensitive about certain things than other kids my age, and that made me seem older than I was."

"Okay. You just described Hubert when he was a little boy and the way he is now. He likes to keep certain things to hisself."

"I know what you mean. But lately he's been wrapped up in hisself more than he usually is."

"Oh yeah? Hmmm. Well, if I was you, I'd keep a eye on him. You know what they say about folks when they get *too* wrapped up in themselves."

I hunched my shoulders. "No, I don't know."

"A person wrapped up in his- or herself, they make a real small package."

I didn't like where this conversation was going and was sorry I had started it. "There ain't nothing wrong with my husband."

"Something is wrong if you think he's too wrapped up in hisself. If you don't help him get over whatever is causing the problem, you are going to have more problems with him." Karl clucked his tongue. "Hubert could even get lax on his job in the bedroom . . ."

"That would never happen!" I said real quick. "He's too much of a man for something like that to happen."

"Well, there is a first time for everything. You just need to show him more affection. And be patient and don't badger him. I'm sure he'll eventually come around."

When everybody left, Hubert helped me put away the leftovers. I was glad there was enough so I wouldn't have to cook no supper tomorrow. "Jessie, I can wash the dishes. You did enough today." He sounded and looked tired, but I decided not to comment on that. It seemed like every time I said certain things, conversations took off in directions I didn't like.

"Hubert, I can do the dishes. I want you to go sit on the couch and relax."

He blinked and gave me a curious look. "Why? Do you think I look tired?"

"No, you don't look tired. I'm just talking out the side of my mouth. You look fine, but I know you still feel bad about all the things that happened last month. So maybe you should go pray some more. That's the best elixir in the world."

Hubert raised his eyebrows and stared at me like I had stepped on his foot on purpose. "Pray some more? After all the singing and praying Daddy made us do a little while ago? Jessie, I'm fine," he insisted, holding his hand up in the air. "Now please leave me be." And then he took a deep breath and gave me a hopeless look. "All right. I'll go stretch out on the couch and get some rest, but I ain't praying no more today. Happy?"

Glenn's elderly mama died two days after Christmas, and him and Carrie wanted to send her out in style. They picked out the most expensive casket Hubert had in stock and a burial frock from the most high-priced women's store in town. Ma Wiggins was going to press and curl the few wisps of white hair that the old woman still had on her head. Carrie had arranged for the man who sang the blues at their house some nights to sing a couple of her favorite spirituals at the funeral on Tuesday. Out of respect for the old woman, who was a used-to-be slave and had never drunk no alcohol in her life, Glenn and Carrie canceled the big party they had planned for New Year's Eve.

Hubert and me was lucky that we had got time off from work for the Christmas and New Year's holidays. We could attend the ceremony without worrying about being fired. It was a long funeral. Glenn's mama had a lot of friends, so there was standing room only. That was why I didn't see Amos and his wife until the service was almost over. They had been sitting only two pews behind me the whole time. While everybody else had their heads bowed for the last prayer, I got up and slunk out the door.

I heard footsteps behind me, but I didn't turn around to see who was following me. If it was Amos, I didn't want to know. I was glad it was Hubert. "Jessie, ain't you going to stay and eat? There's a feast fit for a king and a queen laid out in the dining room. And ain't you going to help console Glenn and Carrie and the rest of their kinfolks? Remember her half brother, Amos? He used to chase you with lizards when we was growing up. He's here with his wife. I'm sure they'd be pleased to get a hug from you."

"Um . . . I just got a bad cramp in my stomach." I hated to tell lies in church, but I didn't have no choice. "I need to get home and take a pill. I don't want to get sick in front of all these folks," I replied with my face scrunched up and one hand on my stomach. I added a cough and a moan to make myself sound sick.

"Oh. I'll let Glenn and Carrie know."

"I wish I could stay—"

"No, not if you ailing. Come on, I'll drop you off at home and I'll come back over here. It's only fitting for me to stay awhile, especially since Glenn is putting out so much money for his mama." Hubert took my arm and started steering me away from the church.

"You coming home right after you eat, or are you going to go with everybody to Glenn and Carrie's house after the burial?"

Hubert's eyes got big, and he looked at me like I was spewing gibberish. "Jessie, it's one thing for me to spend time with the bereaved family at the church. But you know I ain't setting foot in Glenn's house, or any of them other moonshiners'! I don't drink no more, dance, and get rowdy like the folks do in them places. Me and you have our reputations to think about. We have to be careful about where we go." He paused and looked around. And then he whispered, "Folks like us have to be real careful about who we associate with in public and in private."

I didn't waste no time responding. "I seen Carrie at the market one day back in May and she told me to come to her house to pick up some quilt pieces so I could make her a quilt. She didn't have them all cut out at the same time, so I had to make more than one trip over there."

"Oh? I didn't know you'd been over there since Orville died. I remember how you used to go over there and make him come home. How come you are just now mentioning it?"

"I didn't think it was no big deal. I can't tell you every little move I make, especially with you being out of town overnight so much. Besides, I was only there long enough for her to give me them quilt pieces. I thought I'd mention it to you in case somebody tells you they seen me over there, so you'd know why."

Hubert waved his hand. "Pffftt! You picking up quilt pieces ain't a sin. Did you get them all, or do you have to go over there again?"

"She finally had the rest ready in October. I ain't had to go back over there since."

"Did you finish making her quilt?"

"Oh yes. She came to pick it up a couple of weeks before Thanksgiving."

Hubert scratched the side of his head. "If she came to pick

up the quilt, how come you had to go to her house to get the quilt pieces?"

"Oh. Well, Glenn was having problems with his truck at the time, and he got bunions on both feet worse than yours. That's why I didn't ask him to bring them pieces to me. I didn't ask Carrie neither because she don't do much walking since she broke her ankle last year. Since they live so close to Mama, and I walk over there all the time, I'd swing by to see Carrie after one of my visits to Mama." I decided to cover all the bases on this subject so it wouldn't come up no more. "All of Carrie's kids done moved out, otherwise I would have asked her to have one of them bring me them pieces."

Hubert looked so relieved. "Well, in the future, if you need to pick up any more quilt pieces or drop off another quilt over there, let me know and I'll do it. I don't think it's safe for a juicy-butt woman like you to be in a house where so many drunk, frisky men hang out. And, unless Glenn and Carrie ask us for some spiritual advice, we need to feed them with long-handled spoons. Now let's go get in the car so you can get home to take that pill."

CHAPTER 43
Hubert

After we buried Glenn's mama, I swung back over to the church and had my mama fix plates for me and Jessie so she wouldn't have to cook supper this evening. When I got home, she was in the bedroom sitting at her sewing machine, working on something else for the church.

"That was one of the saddest funerals I ever been to. How was the burial?" she asked without turning around to face me.

"No different from all of them others. Glenn got a little overwhelmed and almost fell on top of the casket after it had been lowered into the grave."

"Poor Glenn. He was so close to his mama. I know he'll miss her something terrible."

I sat on the bed and crossed my legs. "Well, a man's best friend is his mama."

Jessie turned around with her mouth hanging open. "Oh?"

"Next to his wife," I clarified. "I wonder how his mama felt about how he turned out."

"What do you mean by that? Glenn is one of the most successful colored men in Lexington. He probably makes more money than you, and you got two jobs."

"I know that. But his mama was a real dignified woman. She couldn't have approved of him becoming a moonshiner."

Jessie sighed and went back to her sewing. "Well, at least he ain't hurting folks and robbing banks. Speaking of banks, I think they've hurt more folks than the moonshiners. Minnie told me that when she went to Branson last week to visit one of her daughters, one of the last two banks they still had over there done failed."

"Well, the newspaper keeps claiming that the Depression is over, but if banks are still going under, I guess it ain't really over for everybody."

"Why don't you get out of your good suit and hang it back up in the closet so it'll stay fresh. That way, I won't have to get it cleaned for the next time you need to wear it. You already got some strands of hair on it from hugging so many folks today."

I brushed off my lapels. "I hope the next time I need to wear this suit, it will be to a wedding."

I rubbed the back of my neck, which felt so tense and tight, I knew I'd have to take some pills for it soon.

I shuffled into the living room and flopped down onto the couch. I was glad Jessie was still in the bedroom so I could be alone for a while and go over some of the thoughts floating around in my head. The main thing on my mind was Leroy. With him gone, I didn't know what I was going to do with myself now. One thing was for sure, my desire to have sex was as strong as ever, but I couldn't do nothing about it right now. The incidents with that mannish woman and the prostitute was still fresh on my mind. I was still too scared to attempt to find another man. I was worried that I might never be able to enjoy pleasure again.

I was going to turn forty-five in a couple of months. I cringed when I thought about how close I was to fifty. I was surprised that I still had such a strong interest in sex at my age.

And I never thought that such a enjoyable activity would end so abruptly for me. But when me and Jessie turned in for the night, something happened that I never expected. She was laying on her side with her back to me. I crawled under the covers and, without giving it much thought, I got closer to her than I meant to and was pressed up against her rump. I wanted to move away, but I didn't, because her booty felt so good.

Before I realized what was happening to me, my pecker got so hard, you could have bounced a dime off it! I thought I had lost my mind. Being turned on by a woman was something I had *never* experienced. I was surprised that Jessie didn't react. She just laid there as quiet as a church mouse and as stiff as a plank. I stayed pressed up against her for at least a hour. She didn't say nothing the whole time and I didn't neither.

I woke up at the crack of dawn and was shocked to feel a damp spot in my underwear between my legs. I hadn't had a wet dream since I was a teenager. If Jessie had seen or felt it first, I would have claimed I'd accidentally peed on myself in my sleep. But when I thought about it, I couldn't decide if it was worse to let her think I'd lost control of my bladder, or that I'd been dreaming I was having sex. That was the reason I eased out of bed before she opened her eyes.

I had another reason for getting out of the bed so fast. Since Jessie hadn't reacted to me getting hard while I was pressed up against her, I wasn't sure if she had felt it or not. I wasn't going to mention my strange behavior unless she brought it up.

I got dressed as fast as I could and went to cook breakfast. A minute after I had set plates and a pot of coffee on the table, Jessie walked in, yawning with her hands high above her head. "Thanks for getting breakfast ready this morning." When we made eye contact, she smiled, but I could tell it was forced.

"I don't mind cooking from time to time. Besides, you was sleeping so hard last night, I decided to let you snooze a little longer."

"I declare, attending a funeral two days before the New Year really wore me out. I'm glad we ain't going to Yolinda's party or anybody else's. I'm going to turn in right after the stroke of midnight."

"Me too," I mumbled. "We must really be getting old if we don't want to do nothing to celebrate the New Year coming in."

"Pffftt." Jessie gave me a dismissive wave. "We ain't that old. Besides, I don't think our age has nothing to do with us wanting to have a quiet evening. Your mama and daddy are twice our age, and they are going to a celebration at the church tonight."

"Well, I'd much rather spend the night alone with you."

The way Jessie suddenly gazed at me from the corner of her eye, you would have thought I was something good to eat. I was glad I couldn't read her mind. I didn't want to know what she was thinking right now, but I had a feeling it wasn't about New Year's Eve. My pecker up against her last night had been too hard for her not to feel it. Or maybe I was flattering myself. She could have been in such a deep sleep, she didn't feel nothing. Either that, or she thought it was my knee. If we was ever going to discuss this subject, I wasn't going to be the one to bring it up.

We ate in silence until we'd both almost cleaned our plates. Suddenly Jessie cleared her throat and chuckled. "What's so funny?" I asked.

"I was thinking about something Minnie said to me when we was kids."

"That Minnie. That sister of yours ain't changed a lick. Every time I see her, she makes me laugh."

"Well, this ain't just funny, it's kind of sad too. One of our aunts, who lives in Houston, was a very pretty woman when she was young. She had been wild all her life and had had more boyfriends than we could count. She got married when she was thirteen, and by the time she was twenty-five, she'd been married four times. Each one of her husbands had been handsome, but lazy, jealous, and unfaithful. My aunt could have married another one like that, but the last one she chose was plumb ugly. I asked Minnie why a pretty woman would marry such a frog."

I took a sip of my coffee before I asked, "What did she tell you?"

Jessie finished chewing a piece of toast and swallowed it before she responded. "She said that good looks fade over time, and if Auntie had married another handsome man, he would have lost his looks too. She was right. Many years later, when I seen her used-to-be-handsome husbands, they was all uglier than the husband who'd been ugly all his life. That man was so sweet. He worked his fingers to the bone at jobs he hated just to give Auntie a good home and everything else she wanted. She was glad she'd married him instead of another fancy man because she knew he would stay with her for life. And she'd told everybody, she wasn't about to grow old alone. As you know, my used-to-be husband was good-looking and treated me worse than you'd treat a snake you didn't like. Folks used to ask me all the time why I stayed with him."

"I used to wonder that same thing myself. Why didn't you leave Orville? He was the meanest man I knew."

A sad look was on Jessie's face now. "I put up with him beating me and running around with other women for over twenty years. I didn't leave him because I didn't want to grow old alone neither. I don't think nothing is worse than growing old alone."

"Jessie, you have always been a good-looking woman. If you had left Orville, I'm sure you could have found somebody else to grow old with."

"Not if I was dead. Orville threatened to kill me if I left him."

"Do you really think he was serious?"

"I did every time he put his shotgun up against my head when I made him mad."

I sucked in my breath and gave Jessie a woebegone look.

"Thank God he didn't live long enough to carry out his threat." We got quiet for a few awkward moments. "I declare, this is a odd conversation. I got a feeling you steered me in this direction to keep from talking about what's really on your mind."

Jessie dropped her head and stared at her plate for a few moments. When she looked up at me, there was tears in her eyes. "I got a lot of things on my mind, Hubert. I want you to know that no matter what happens, or don't happen"—she paused and cocked her head to the side—"I ain't never going to leave you, and I hope you never leave me."

"I thought I had already made it clear to you that I ain't never going to leave you. Our marriage is as solid as a brick. So long as things don't change between us, it'll stay solid."

"Even if we never have sex together?"

That question burned my ears like a hot iron. "I didn't say that. But if we never do it, I still want to be your husband. I'm sure we ain't the only married couple that don't have sex."

"I don't know how many you know, but I don't know none now, and I never have."

"You done forgot about your sister Minnie and her husband? You told me he'd once had the same problem I'm having now."

"Oh yeah. I had forgot about them. But I told you he'd got over his problem in a few months. Do you think yours will be over in another few months?"

I sat up straight in my chair and drew in a long, loud breath. "Well, it might, and it might not."

CHAPTER 44
Hubert

I had never felt so uncomfortable with Jessie before. A couple of minutes dragged by and neither one of us said nothing. It was so awkward to sit at the table and just stare at my plate. But she was doing the same thing. When she cleared her throat, I thought she was fixing to say something, but she didn't.

I wanted to speak, but I didn't know what to say after the conversation we'd just had. I prayed the telephone would ring or that somebody would come to the front door, because this was one conversation I didn't want to continue. While them thoughts was still in my head, Yolinda barged into the house. As much as she usually annoyed me, I could have jumped up and kissed her. "I wanted to come over and wish y'all Happy New Year," she chirped as she pranced into the kitchen and flopped down in the seat next to me. "I been so busy since Christmas, I ain't had a chance to come over here until now. I wanted to drop in before I got busy cooking some of the snacks I plan on serving at my party. I need to get a early start this morning. Don't eat a big supper before y'all come to the house, because I'm going to have everything from baked ham to black-eyed peas."

"We won't be able to make it, but please save us a couple of plates," I said.

Yolinda looked disappointed. "How come y'all ain't coming?"

"With the hectic Christmas we had, and Glenn's mama's big funeral, we been running ourselves ragged for the past few days. We just want to spend the next couple of days and nights relaxing alone," Jessie answered.

Yolinda folded her arms. From the sulky expression on her face, it looked like she was getting more disappointed by the second. "I hope I don't sound nosy, but I'd like to know why y'all looking so glum the week after the Lord's birthday? Did I interrupt a sensitive conversation?"

Jessie waved her hand. "Pffftt. We was just trying to decide what to do the rest of this week."

"And another thing, I ain't been feeling too good. Jessie wants me to take a pill with some ginger tea and relax today," I threw in.

Yolinda gave me a concerned look. "Now that you mentioned it, you do look a might peaked. Look at them dark circles under your eyes. We'll miss y'all at my party, but I understand." A huge grin suddenly showed up on Yolinda's face. "Jessie, would it be too much for me to ask you to go with me to pay a visit to the man down the street that sells the chickens?"

"I thought you was in a hurry to start cooking," Jessie said.

"I am. But I wanted to buy some fresh chickens to go with the other stuff I'm going to cook. I would have made one of my grandkids go with me, but them lazy young'uns ain't even out the bed yet."

"Why do you want me to go with you? You go down there by yourself all the time to buy fresh chickens," Jessie said.

"Because I need three this time, and that's too many for me to try and tote by myself. You can carry the crocus sack with just one chicken, and I'll carry the other one. Please don't dis-

appoint me some more, Jessie." A pout was forming on Yolinda's face.

Jessie was so softhearted, I knew she was going to give in.
But I decided to give her a little prodding anyway. "Sugar, it
would be a shame for you not to go with Yolinda. You could
get a chicken for us to eat this evening," I said with a pleading
look on my face.

Jessie stared at me for a few seconds before she hunched her
shoulders and said, "All right, then. Let me go put on my shoes.
I guess I could use some fresh air. If I'm getting a chicken for us
too, that means I'll have to tote a sack with two chickens."

"Then make sure you pick out a small chicken for us," I suggested.

The reason I wanted Jessie out of the house was so I could
be by myself for a while. I needed to organize my thoughts in
case she brought up my actions in the bedroom last night.

She came back a hour later with a small hen clucking up a
storm and clawing like a demon to get out of the sack. "It's
your turn to wring the neck."

"Okay." She handed me the sack and I went out to the backyard and did what I had to do. I still didn't know what I would
say to her about last night, if she brought it up.

Jessie was soaking her corns in a foot tub full of soapy water
when I came back into the kitchen with the chicken in a
bucket all plucked and ready for her to cut up. "That was one
mean hen! It's been a long time since I had to deal with one
that fought as hard as this one did." I set the bucket in the sink.
"I got scratches from my wrist up to the end of my elbows." I
held my arms out for her to inspect.

She shuddered and reared back in her chair. "My Lord! If I
didn't know no better, I'd think you been fighting with a bear.
Go put some calamine lotion on them scratches so you won't
get infected."

"I will. And then I'm going to go stretch out in the bed for a while."

"Oh? You don't feel good?"

"I feel fine. I just . . . I just want to relax for a little while."

"Hubert, it ain't even noon yet. If you trying to avoid me, you don't have to."

"I ain't trying to avoid you." I couldn't believe I'd said that with a straight face. I didn't want to be around her. I knew that sooner or later one of us would have to bring up what happened last night. I wanted to put it off as long as I could.

"Hubert, don't you want to talk about last night? We can't keep avoiding the subject."

My whole body tensed up. "I . . . I don't know what to say about what happened to me last night," I admitted.

"I don't neither." Jessie let out a loud sigh and swished her feet around in the water.

"If neither one of us knows what to say, then I guess we won't talk about it, right?"

There was a seriously sad expression on her face. "I guess not. Okay, we won't."

I didn't care what Jessie said, I knew it was just a matter of time before the subject came up again.

"Uh, I'm going to get up and walk over to Mama's house. She told me to bring some smell-goods for her to splash on tonight, and she wants me to write some letters for her to a bunch of folks."

Jessie's mama had dropped out of school in the second grade and could barely read and write. Jessie's siblings didn't have the patience to sit for hours scribbling one mundane thing after another. So my mother-in-law depended on Jessie to do it.

"You know how long-winded Mama is, so I'll be gone for quite a while. But don't worry, I'll be back in plenty of time to get supper ready. Besides, I don't want to be out and about when folks start celebrating tonight."

She dried her feet off with a towel, put her shoes on, and left. It was starting to get dark by the time she came home.

The only thing we conversated about over supper was the letters she'd wrote for her mama, and a few other things that didn't mean no more to me than they did her. When we finished eating, Jessie decided to take a long bath. I flopped down on the couch to listen to one of the holiday gospel programs. But the music wasn't holding my attention. I wondered what was going to happen when we went to bed tonight.

I had already started dozing off a couple of hours before New Year arrived. I had to force myself to stay woke until midnight. After me and Jessie toasted with some lemonade, we decided to turn in for the night.

I was laying in bed, trying to get comfortable, while she was in the bathroom. The next thing I knew, she came into the room as naked as a jaybird. Without looking in my direction, she glided over to the chifforobe facing our bed. Her back was to me, so I couldn't take my eyes off her juicy butt while she fiddled around in the top drawer looking for one of her nightgowns. "I sure hope 1942 will be a better year for everybody," she muttered as she continued to root around in the drawer. "I can't believe how fast the years been going by."

"Well, if you want to live a lot more years, you better hurry up and put on something before you catch your death of cold."

"I'm fixing to do just that. I can already feel goose bumps climbing up my legs," Jessie said with a snicker. I couldn't take my eyes off her as she put on a see-through white gown and pranced over to the bed.

"Is that new?"

Jessie rolled her eyes and plopped down on the bed. "My goodness, Hubert. I've had this thing for months. You was with me when I bought it." Immediately after she slid under the covers, she scooted toward me until her hip touched mine.

"I am so glad you don't go out of town so often no more. I declare, I've enjoyed having you to myself at night more often."

I cleared my throat, but my voice came out sounding scratchy anyway. "I've enjoyed it too. Um, I sure ain't ready to go back to work on Friday."

Jessie didn't say nothing. She was so close to me, I could feel her heart beating against my back, and her body felt even better than the last time. We stayed as still as statues and was as quiet as mutes for the next hour. I didn't know if I'd ever get aroused again, at least not with Jessie. But I did. It happened when I least expected it: two minutes later. This time, I did something about it.

CHAPTER 45
Jessie

If Santa Claus was the man on top of me instead of Hubert, I couldn't have been more stunned. All I could do at first was just lay there. I held my breath when he started kissing me on the mouth, while his hands worked fast to get me naked. I was glad it was dark in the room because I didn't want him to see the way my face was scrunched up, because it might have scared him enough to stop. That was the last thing I wanted to happen after I'd suffered as long as I had.

Once he started moving, I did too. The whole time we was going at it, he didn't say nothing, and I didn't neither. But the way he was grunting and moaning, I knew he was enjoying hisself as much as I was.

What surprised me even more was that he was much better at making love than the two men I'd cheated on him with—and my late husband! I was glad he was taking his time, because I wanted this miracle to last as long as possible, in case it never happened again.

When Hubert shuddered and yelped, I knew he was finished. I'd finished a few seconds earlier. I didn't get buck wild and whoop and holler like I usually did when a man satisfied me. I knew that some men didn't like for women to be too loud and frisky in bed. Because of Hubert's sensitive and mysterious medical history with his manhood, I thought it would be smart for me to take baby steps into this new phase of our marriage. I didn't want to say or do nothing that would traumatize him and trigger something that might make him lose his manhood again.

"Baby, that was so good! Was it good for you?" Hubert panted when he rolled off me and clicked on the lamp. I was scared to move, so I just laid on my back and stared at the ceiling. From the corner of my eye, I seen him staring at the side of my face. I guess I was taking too long to answer his question because he tapped my shoulder. "You okay, Jessie?"

"Uh . . . huh," I replied in a hoarse tone. "What about *you*? What you just did, *after all this time*, must have really took a lot of steam out of you."

"I ain't lost nary a bit of steam. I enjoyed myself. I declare, this was a unique experience."

I had never heard a sex act described in such a odd way. I didn't know how to respond to that. "You . . . surprised me."

He chuckled and then he got serious. "I surprised myself too. I hope you don't think I planned this."

I giggled. "I don't care if you did or not. Sex is one of the most natural things in the world between two people, and I think it's better when it ain't planned."

"True. Especially when they both want to do it. But since I didn't *ask* you to let me do it, it ain't the same—"

I cut him off. "Hush up, Hubert. You didn't rape me tonight," I said firmly. "What we just did was wonderful." I pinched my arm to make sure I wasn't dreaming. I had so many questions in my head, I didn't know which one to ask first. I decided on the most logical one. "Do you think your problem is cured?"

Hubert didn't say nothing at first. He just laid there breathing loud for a few moments. "I don't know," he whispered. I wished I hadn't asked him that question, because now he sounded panicky. The sudden change in his demeanor made me panic. I didn't know what I'd do if things returned to the way they'd been since we got married. Even if he only made love to me once in a blue moon, I could learn to be happy with that. Some sex was better than no sex at all.

"I hope it is. It sure was better than the first time," I said in a meek tone.

Hubert suddenly inhaled so hard, I was surprised the air didn't choke him. "I thought you couldn't remember nothing about that incident? I sure can't."

"Oh! I can't recall nothing about it neither!" I softened my tone. "What I meant was, since we was both sober this time and enjoyed it, it had to be better than the first time."

"I see. I just wish I could remember the details of that night. It's so hard for me to accept the fact that I forced myself on you."

I gently patted his arm. "Hubert, that's in the past. We don't need to ever talk about it again."

"I know and I'll try not to bring it up no more. I just wish . . . I just wish you hadn't lost the baby we created that night."

"I wish I hadn't neither . . ." We stayed silent for several moments. I hesitated before I spoke again. "It'll be nice for us to have a real marriage. That is, if your problem is cured."

"It's all up to God."

"Well, if He done restored your manhood, we have a lot of time to make up for." I picked up his hand. As stiff as it was, I thought he'd pull it away, but he didn't. Instead, he took both of my hands in his and squeezed them. Then he kissed me again. He hadn't kissed me on the lips more than two or three times since the day we got married. Now here he was doing it more than once in less than a hour!

"Jessie, let's see how things go. My sudden passion could just be a fluke . . ."

"I don't care if it is. It's a step in the right direction. You could be a complete man now and stay that way."

Hubert shuddered so hard, I thought he was having a spasm. The way he was rubbing his chest, it must have been painful. "You don't think I was a 'complete' man before?"

"I didn't mean no harm. But you have to admit that you wasn't fulfilling your duties as a husband. The incident that happened on your birthday when you got drunk don't count."

"I wish you would forget about me raping you! It's bad enough I have to live with that guilt for the rest of my life."

"Well, you shouldn't feel too bad about it. It wasn't all your fault anyway. I shouldn't have encouraged you to drink so much that night. So half the fault is mine."

"You done told me that before, but it don't make me feel less guilty, Jessie."

It bothered me to know that because of my lies, Hubert thought he was a rapist. I knew in my heart that drunk or not, he would never rape me or nobody else. That and him shooting and killing Blondeen had to be such a heavy burden for him to carry around. I was surprised that the load hadn't wore him down enough to confess what he'd done to his daddy and mama and ask them to help him atone for his sins.

"Uh, if you don't mind, I think we should stop conversating and go to sleep now. We done said enough for tonight. I'd hate for one of us to say something that'll hurt the other one's feelings."

"You're right," I agreed.

He went to sleep right away. It was another hour before I did.

I was so happy me and Hubert had finally consummated our marriage. For the next few weeks, he climbed on top of me almost *every* night. But the first week in February, he abruptly stopped. I had become so spoiled with all the sex I had been getting, I was real disappointed. I didn't want to ask him what had happened. The last thing I wanted to hear was him telling me that his manhood had fizzled out again.

On February 16, the day before his forty-fifth birthday, I started feeling strange while I was at work that Monday. Half a hour before lunch, my stomach started churning and there was a nasty taste in my mouth. I blamed it on the five-day-old leftover pig ears I had nibbled on when I had got up for a midnight snack. When lunchtime rolled around, I felt even worse. Now my head was throbbing and the taste in my mouth was twice as nasty. My supervisor was one of the coldest white women I'd ever come across, so I wasn't about to let her know I wasn't feeling well. With all the elderly, sick patients we had to care for, the last thing she wanted on the premises was a ill worker, especially a colored one. I didn't wait for her to find out how I was feeling. I told the head nurse instead and she told me to go home.

There was a bench at the bus stop, but it was full, so I had to stand while I waited for the bus. I was so queasy, I thought I was going to collapse. The Lexington hospital was four blocks away, but it was for white folks only. They had never admitted any of us, even if we was at death's door.

By the time the bus arrived, I was seeing white dots in front of my eyes. When the bus stopped at the spot where I usually got off, I stayed on it until I reached the stop a block away from the colored clinic. I knew that without a appointment, I'd have to wait a long time before one of the doctors or nurses would be able to see me. So I was going to pretend I was sicker than I was and go directly to the emergency room, where somebody would have to tend to me sooner. I didn't have to do that, though. As soon as I walked through the front door, I passed out.

When I came to, I had on a hospital gown and I was in a bed. I had no idea how long I'd been unconscious, but when I glanced at the window and seen how dark it was outside, I knew I'd been out for several hours. Other than feeling a little dizzy, I felt better now. A doctor and a nurse was standing over me. Since they was both smiling, I figured I wasn't too sick. I took a deep breath and sat up. "What happened?" My throat felt as dry as sandpaper, so my voice was a raspy whisper.

"Mrs. Wiggins, you're going to be fine. I gave you a shot, so you might feel light-headed for a little while," the cute young doctor told me. He was the same one who had tended to Maggie and Claude the night they died. "I want you to come back a week from today, anytime before the noon hour, the earlier the better."

"Was it food poisoning, Dr. Underwood?" I asked. "I ate some five-day-old leftover pig ears last night."

"No, it was not food poisoning." There was a bigger smile on his face now.

"Then what's wrong with me?"

He laughed before he answered my question. "Other than the fact that you're pregnant, there is nothing wrong with you."

My heart immediately felt like it was turning somersaults, and so was my brain. I couldn't believe my ears. I had given up on ever having a child with Hubert, or any other man, for that matter. My periods was very irregular now that menopause was nipping at my heels. I hadn't even had one since last summer. "Huh? Pregnant? I don't know how . . ." I narrowed my eyes and stared at the doctor. "I had no idea I was in the family way! You sure?"

"Yes, I'm very sure, and I'm not surprised you didn't know. A lot of women your age get pregnant and don't realize it until they come here. I had one patient who didn't know she was expecting until she actually gave birth."

"Was her baby all right?"

"Her baby was perfect, and yours will be too. You're a strong healthy woman, so you shouldn't have any problems. But, because of your age, you need to come in every two weeks for the first three months, starting a week from today. I won't be the one to see you when you come in next Monday. I work the night shift, but I'm filling in for another doctor, who had a family emergency today. But don't worry, you'll be in good hands. The results of your blood work will be back by then."

"Okay. Is there a telephone here I can use? I need to call my husband and have him pick me up."

"Mr. Wiggins is already here. He was notified right after you were admitted. He came right away."

"He is going to be as shocked as I am to hear that I'm pregnant. I want to tell him in a special way, like over a nice home-cooked supper."

Dr. Underwood and the nurse laughed. "He already knows. And I have to say that I have never seen a man happier than he is."

CHAPTER 46
Hubert

There was only one place I hated being at more than the graveyard: the clinic. The reason was because it was where I'd been told Claude and Maggie was dead. I hated the smell and I hated seeing all the workers scurrying around like mice. I knew they worked hard and really cared about their patients, but to this day, I was still very disappointed that they hadn't been able to revive my son and wife that evening I brought them in.

It had been hard to leave them at the clinic and go back home. But it was even harder to return with my hearse to collect their bodies. I couldn't wait to get out of this place.

After the doctor had talked to me, I had been left alone in a rinky-dink waiting room with no windows and some outdated magazines to read. When I got tired of reading and sitting on a metal chair, twiddling my thumbs, I got up and started pacing. I was in that room for two hours before a nurse came to escort me to where they had took Jessie.

My stomach churned as we approached the room at the end of a long hallway. It was the same one where they had took Maggie. The nurse left after she opened the door and ushered me in. My stomach was still churning.

I would never forget the twinkle in Jessie's eyes when I seen her. And she seemed to be in really good spirits. She had a smile on her face that reached from one side to the other.

"Hubert, we fixing to have a baby!" She was standing by the side of the bed, buttoning up her work uniform. I could tell she wanted to be the one who told me this good news. She wanted to break the blessing to me.

"I know! The doctor told me!" I rushed up to her and wrapped my arms around her waist. I held her as tight as I could. "This is the best birthday present I ever got!"

"Turn me loose before you squash the baby!" Jessie said with a chuckle.

I hauled off and kissed her on the lips before I let her go. I stared into her eyes for a few seconds. I always knew she was a pretty woman, but at this moment, she looked prettier than ever. "I can't wait to share the news with everybody. Mama and Daddy will be over the moon. We'll tell them tomorrow when they come over to celebrate my birthday with us. Don't you blab to big-mouth Yolinda, or nobody else."

She gasped. "What about my mama? She'll pout until the Rapture if I put off telling her."

I laughed. "I guess I wasn't thinking straight just now because your mama done already been blessed with a heap of grandchildren. My mama and daddy ain't had but one."

"You'd better not let Mama hear you say that," Jessie warned, and then she laughed. "We'll tell your folks first, but we'll have to tell my mama as soon as possible."

Jessie had planned to bake a cake for my birthday, but I talked her into letting me do it. Even though she said she felt fine, I didn't want her to do too much of nothing.

When we got home from the clinic, I led her into the house by the hand, all the way to the living room. We gently eased down onto the couch, sitting side by side. "You sit still, sugar. You need to take it real easy. No cleaning or cooking the rest of today. I'll cook supper."

Jessie let out a sharp laugh and rubbed her belly. "Hubert, what's wrong with you? You know doggone well I ain't going to let you do all the cooking and cleaning. I'll go crazy if I just sit on my butt until the baby comes. And I got to go to work."

"I can't stop you from going to work. But I want you to be extra careful handling them old folks and helping keep that place clean. We done lost one child because you didn't know when to slow down. I don't want to take a chance on you losing this one too. I don't know what I'd do if it happened again."

"You ain't got to worry. I ain't going to lose this baby."

I was surprised that Jessie sounded so confident. But that didn't change the way I felt. "You didn't know you was going to lose the first baby, so how do you know you won't lose this one?"

"I just know."

She sounded so sure of herself, I believed her. But I still insisted on cooking supper this evening.

Mama called Tuesday evening a few minutes after I got home from work. Jessie hadn't made it in yet. "Son, I know you and Jessie was expecting me and your daddy to come over this evening. We hate to disappoint y'all, but we won't be able to make it."

"Oh? Did something come up?"

"Something like that. See, I'm behind on a baby blanket I'm knitting for the upcoming church benefit. We got four expectant first-time mothers in our congregation! It took one five years of trying to finally conceive. God is so good! He eventually blesses every childless married couple . . ."

I knew Mama's last comment was her way of reminding me how bad she wanted a grandbaby. It was on the tip of my tongue to tell her to start making baby blankets for me and Jessie. But I wanted to tell her in person because this would probably be the last time I had news like this to share with her and Daddy.

"If I stay home, I can finish the blanket tonight and turn it in tomorrow. The sisters on the committee will be so pleased."

"I understand how important church activity is to you. But this is one time I wish you'd put that aside for one more day. There is something we need to tell y'all. And I ain't going to do it over the telephone."

Mama took her time responding. "Lord, please don't tell me you and Jessie fixing to bust up! Divorce goes against everything we believe in. God brought y'all together and—"

I had to cut Mama off. "Hush up. We ain't getting no divorce. Me and Jessie's marriage is stronger than ever."

"Is one of y'all sick?"

"Not exactly."

"Not exactly what? Is one of y'all sick or not?"

"No, we ain't sick."

"Then what is it?"

"Mama, like I said, I ain't going to tell you over the telephone. Now, if you insist on staying home to finish that blanket tonight, that's fine. I guess we'll just have to tell Jessie's folks our good news first." My last comment got her.

"Uh-uh. I'll finish the blanket tomorrow. I'll just have to get up real early in the morning. We'll be there right after I soak my corns."

CHAPTER 47
Jessie

As happy as I was about being pregnant, I couldn't really rejoice the way I wanted to, because I wasn't sure who my baby's daddy was!

I had dumped Amos the last week in October, last year. Me and Hubert had had sex for the first time, the first day in January. I had started to gain weight way before then, mostly around my middle. I assumed my body was getting rounder because I'd been eating like a pig for so many months.

When my in-laws showed up this evening to celebrate Hubert's birthday, he ushered them into the living room and steered them to the couch. "Happy birthday, son," Ma and Pa Wiggins said at the same time.

"You sure don't look no forty-five," Ma Wiggins said, beaming proudly. "See what living by the Lord's word, living a chaste life, and inheriting good blood will do for you."

"Humph! That good blood came from my side of the family," Pa Wiggins hurried up and tossed in.

"Don't you take all the credit, you old goat," Ma Wiggins shot back. We all laughed.

Pa Wiggins slapped his hefty thigh and rubbed his hands together. "Well, now. I'm champing at the bit to hear what this mystery is that y'all got to share with us!" he hollered with his eyes stretched open as wide as they could go.

"Me too," Ma Wiggins piped in. She fanned her face with her hand and looked at me like she was about to accuse me of something.

I was glad Hubert didn't give her time to do that. Just as she opened her mouth to speak again, he held up his hand. "Don't say nothing else yet, Mama," he said with a big grin on his face. And then he eased down into the wing chair facing the couch, grabbed my hand, and pulled me into his lap. "Mama, Daddy, I got so much joy in me right now, I could wrap it in eggshells." He squeezed my hand and gazed into my eyes. "Sugar, do you want to tell them, or do you want me to do it?"

"You go ahead," I mumbled. The lump that had blew up in my throat felt like it was the size of a big man's fist. Amos's face flashed in my mind, and a split second later, I seen the face of a baby that looked just like him. Amos's coloring and features didn't even come close to resembling Hubert's. Claude was the only child Hubert had fathered. Amos had six, so he had some potent baby-making batter in his body. It was very possible that he was the daddy. I was glad Hubert said something to interrupt my thoughts.

"Don't y'all get too excited and dance a jig. I'd hate for one of y'all to fall and break a hip. I don't want to have to hoist nobody up off the floor," he said.

"Boy, if you don't get to the point, you'll be the one that'll have to be hoisted up off the floor," Pa Wiggins threatened.

"And I'll give you a whupping while you still on the floor," Ma Wiggins added in a stern tone.

Hubert was still grinning. He took a deep breath and blurted out, "We found out just yesterday that we are finally about to become parents."

My mother-in-law gasped so hard she started choking on some air. Pa Wiggins had to slap her on the back. "I'm fixing to be a grandmamma again?" she croaked. A huge smile appeared on her face.

"See there, Mother. I told you that prayer chain we organized a few months ago would work." My father-in-law crossed his legs and continued. "Jessie, I noticed you been looking a tad stout these days. I didn't say nothing about it because I know how sensitive some women can be about their weight."

"Yeah, I have put on a few pounds," I said in a small voice. "I just thought it was all of them pig ears I been eating."

"I'm so pleased, y'all. A new baby is the most wonderful news ever. I can't imagine how many new blankets I'll be stitching!" Ma Wiggins paused and turned to Pa Wiggins. "Old man, when we get back home, I want you to go out in the shed and dig up Claude's old baby crib."

Pa Wiggins waved his hand at her like he was shooing away a fly. "Pffftt! What's wrong with you, woman? That crib is over twenty years old, and it must have three inches of dust. I'm going to go to the lumber mill and buy some fresh wood and make a brand-new one."

Ma Wiggins rolled her eyes at him and added, "While you at it, you better make a new rocking chair for me so I'll have a comfortable place to rock the baby in." She turned to me and asked, "When is the baby due?"

Me and Hubert looked at each other. My face felt like it was on fire. "I . . . I don't know," I stammered.

My in-laws gasped, Hubert scratched the back of his head and looked at me with a confused expression on his face. "Jessie, didn't Dr. Underwood tell you the due date? It should be around the start of October."

"Um . . . it was real hectic, and he was tending to me and some other patients at the same time. I guess he forgot to tell me," I mumbled as I shifted in Hubert's lap. His "resurrected" manhood felt good pressed up against my butt. If I hadn't been so worried about who my baby's daddy was, I would have got excited. But for the time being, I couldn't be turned on with fifty thousand volts.

"He told you that you was pregnant, but didn't tell you how far along?" Pa Wiggins said with his eyes narrowed. "What kind of doctor is that slack? I keep telling folks that Dr. Underwood is too young to be doctoring. He looks like he's barely out of his teens. They ought to have him doing less serious work until he learn the ropes, like sitting at the front desk filling out forms and helping bathe the patients!" Pa Wiggins blasted.

"Y'all behave now. Dr. Underwood started working at that clinic at least five years ago," Hubert said in a stern tone. "And how would he learn the ropes if they had him filling out forms and bathing sick folks?"

"If he don't know the ropes after working at that clinic for five years, he needs to get a job in another line of work!" Ma Wiggins snapped.

I held up my hand. "Please don't blame the doctor. He might have told me, but I was drowsy and I might not have heard him," I defended. "Or I might have forgot. He gave me a shot and that might have affected my memory." I let out a chuckle, but nobody else seemed the least bit amused.

"Well, when will you find out? I want to know when I can start working on the baby's new layette. I'd like to have everything done by the time he or she gets here. And I got a heap of other shopping to do—toys, play-pretties, and whatnot. There's a wonderful store in Mobile I'd like to go to. I bought most of Claude's things there. Colored folks can only shop there on Monday and Tuesday, so I'd like to get everything in one or two visits."

"I have to go back to the clinic next Monday. I'll find out the due date then." I cleared my throat and stood up. "I'm going to slice the cake and bring out the snacks."

I held my breath until I made it to the kitchen. All I could think about was *who* got me pregnant. One minute, I would scold myself for being foolish enough to get involved with another man. The next minute, I was mad as a hornet at Amos for getting me into this mess!

My hand was shaking when I cut into the birthday cake. I was so light-headed, it felt like I was floating. I knew I would be in the same condition, if not worse, until one of the doctors at the clinic told me when my baby was due.

We sang "Happy Birthday" to Hubert and had a brief prayer session before we ate the sandwiches and potato salad me and Hubert had made. We prayed some more before we started on the cake

I was glad my in-laws didn't stay long.

Hubert was so giddy, it was annoying. He was strutting around the living room like a banty rooster. "I can't wait to tell the guys at the mill. They all got big families and I'm sick of looking at baby pictures and listening to them repeat some of the cute things their kids say. Now I'll be doing the same thing." He stopped in the middle of the floor and put his hands on his hips. "It ain't that late. You want to go over to your mama's house so we can let her and the rest of your folks know?"

"I'd rather stop by there on my way from work tomorrow and tell them."

I loved my family, but they was so loud and uncouth. I really had to be in the mood to deal with them. Right after Karl had moved in with Mama, my sister Annie Ruth divorced her husband and moved in. It had been chaos ever since then. She had a slew of boyfriends coming and going. Her three teenagers had many friends, so the house had a crowd from morning to night, seven days a week. Trying to keep Annie Ruth's rowdy kids under control kept my elderly mother from being bored. As much as Mama "complained" about having to do so much cooking and cleaning, I knew she was glad she wasn't alone.

That was one less thing for me to worry about. But I couldn't wait to tell her and the rest of my family about the baby.

Hubert went to bed. I was in the living room listening to the radio until one of my coworkers called me up and babbled on for over two hours about one mundane thing after another. When she finally hung up, my sister Minnie immediately called. She almost never said hello or identified herself before she started talking. "Jessie, I called to tell you I dreamed about fish last night."

"You called this time of night to tell me that?"

"Yup. My memory ain't what it used to be, so I wanted to tell you before I forgot. Anyway, you know that ever since I was a little girl, whenever I dream about fish, somebody I know is pregnant. And it's usually somebody in our family. I bet it's our bloomer-dropping sister, Annie Ruth. That hussy don't need no more kids. Especially by that snaggletoothed joker she is in love with. Mama will end up helping her raise this new baby too."

I held up my hand, even though my sister couldn't see it. "Hold on now. You don't have to worry about Annie Ruth. Somebody in our family is fixing to have a baby, but it ain't her."

Minnie gasped. "She ain't! Did she tell you she wasn't pregnant?"

"Nope."

"Then how do you know she ain't? Hmmm. Well, I know it ain't me, and it couldn't possibly be Mama, and . . . is it *you?*"

"Yup."

"Great balls of fire! W-when did you find out?"

"Yesterday." I told Minnie about me getting sick at work and going to the clinic.

"You told Hubert yet?"

"The folks at the clinic called him at the mill after they had admitted me. I wanted to be the one to tell him, but the doctor had already broke the news to him before I could. He's as pleased as pie."

"I declare, he ain't the only one. It's going to be so nice to have a baby in the family to fuss over again after all these years! You must be walking on air."

"I am."

Minnie rambled on for ten more minutes before I finally ended the call. I went to use the bathroom, and as soon as I finished doing my business, the telephone rung again. This time it was Mama. "Girl, Minnie just told me the good news! How come you ain't told me?"

"Mama, we just found out yesterday. We spent this evening celebrating Hubert's birthday with his mama and daddy. I was going to stop by and tell you tomorrow."

"A new grandchild! I'm so happy. God is so good to bless me with so many grandchildren. I don't mean to sound greedy, but I hope y'all don't wait too long to make the second one."

"Mama, it was hard enough for us to make this one. We ain't so young no more," I reminded.

Mama started to talk so fast, it sounded like everything she said was one long word. "Well, if it's God's will, y'all will have a second and maybe even a third. I had you when I was three years older than you are now! I got a feeling it's going to be a boy. I hope he looks just like his handsome daddy, don't you?"

Her last sentence made me cringe. "Yeah, me too," I murmured.

CHAPTER 48
Jessie

Four days after we found out I was pregnant, we had already told almost everybody we knew. They was as happy and surprised as me and Hubert was. Mr. DeBow made a special trip to our house on Saturday right after the noon hour. "Good afternoon, Jessie," he greeted, and tipped his hat as I waved him into the living room.

"Hello, Mr. DeBow. It's so nice to see you again," I chirped. "Have a seat and make yourself at home."

He sat down on the couch and kicked off his shoes. "I do declare, Jessie, I am tickled to death to hear about you and Hubert's blessing. I already told him that whenever you give birth, he can take a whole week off with pay. I came over to tell you in person how happy I am for y'all."

I eased down in the chair facing the couch. "Thank you. You didn't have to drive out of your way. You could have just called me up on the phone."

"Uh-uh. I told Hubert when he told me earlier this week that I wanted to congratulate you in person. By the way, my wife is happy for y'all too. She rarely leaves the house these days, otherwise she would have come with me."

"Would you like something to drink?"

His face lit up like a flashlight and his lips divided into a smile so extreme I could see the top edge of his false teeth. "I know I am not supposed to be drinking and driving, but I wouldn't mind having a highball if you have a few laying around."

"I'm sorry, but we don't keep alcohol in the house no more—for religious reasons." I didn't feel bad about lying to Hubert's boss, since I lied so much to everybody else.

"Oh, well. I drink too much booze already. But if—what's that I smell cooking in yonder?" He looked toward the kitchen and started sniffing.

"Pig ears with a pinch of vinegar. I started cooking early so they'll be done in about a minute. I wanted to have supper ready by the time Hubert got back home."

Mr. DeBow suddenly looked like a kid who had been turned loose in a candy store. "Pig ears, huh?"

I nodded.

"Well, if it wouldn't be too much trouble, I would be most grateful if I could take a mess home."

"No problem. I'll put enough in a bowl for more than one meal, and even enough for your wife."

"That would be right godly. Oomph, oomph, oomph. I tell Hubert all the time that he's a lucky man to have married a woman who knows her way around the kitchen. By the way, where is that husband of yours?"

"He had to go pick up a body. We lost another church member last night."

"Dagnabbit! I was hoping to catch him at home. Oh, well. I won't keep you from your kitchen duties. As soon as you can bowl up those pig ears, I'll be on my way."

Five minutes after Mr. DeBow put his shoes back on, he took off, out the door, holding that bowl like I'd filled it up with pieces of gold.

I couldn't stop wondering who my baby's daddy was. By the time Hubert got home, almost every part on my body was in distress. I was laying on the couch when he walked in. I didn't want him to know I wasn't feeling well, so I got up and went about my business, like I always did.

While we was eating supper, we discussed everything from Mr. DeBow's visit to the jelly I planned to make on the weekend. Before I could finish the food on my plate, I had to jump up from the table and sprint to the bathroom to puke. Hubert followed me. The whole time I hovered over the commode like I was a pig at a hog trough, Hubert stood next to me, praying under his breath and rubbing my back.

"Jessie, when you go to the clinic on Monday, ask the doctor for something to help settle your stomach."

"I will," I mumbled.

He suddenly stopped rubbing my back and drew in his breath. "I just thought of something. And it sure is strange."

I gulped and turned around to face him. "What?"

"You didn't have no morning sickness the last time you was pregnant. I can't remember one single time you had to go puke."

"Yes, I did! I puked a heap of times. You was so busy during that time, it must have skipped your mind." Every now and then, I completely forgot about the pregnancy I had faked to get him to marry me.

"Hmmm. I think I do remember you complaining about it once or twice. Just before you had the miscarriage." His voice cracked and he gave me a pitying look. "I'm going to tell Daddy to round up his spiritual warriors and get a prayer chain going. That'll help you carry this baby all the way."

After me and Hubert put away the leftovers, he went back to the funeral home. Him and Karl had to work on one of Daddy's hundred-year-old church members, who had died in his sleep last night. Him and his wife had had eighteen children, so his huge family was planning a very lavish funeral. The service was going to be on Wednesday. By then, I would know the date I was supposed to deliver.

While Hubert was gone, I had plenty more time to think about my predicament. I was a mess, so I didn't feel like having no company. But playing possum on the couch didn't discourage Yolinda and Ma Wiggins when they barged in together before Hubert got back. Ma Wiggins went into the bedroom and got one of the quilts I'd made and covered me up. Then she and Yolinda made themselves comfortable and sat and gossiped for the next hour.

I was so glad when Hubert came back home. This was the first time since we got married that he didn't seem happy to see his mama. And I knew how much Yolinda's presence usually annoyed him. "Ladies, I hate to do this to y'all, but I'm going to tote Jessie into the bedroom and put her to bed, where she'll be more comfortable."

"Good!" Yolinda hollered. "She looks like a slug stretched out on that couch. But she still looks good, even with all the weight she done gained. Come on. I can help you get her to the bedroom. You grab her arms and I'll take hold of her legs."

"We'd better hang around in case some complications come up. I don't know what I'd do if she was to lose this baby," Ma Wiggins choked.

"She ain't that heavy. I carry her all the time, so I don't need no help getting her to the bedroom. If a complication comes up, I can take care of everything," Hubert insisted as he lifted me off the couch.

"Um . . . I ain't that sick," I feebly protested. I was glad Hubert had stepped in. Otherwise, if he hadn't come home when he did, I would have politely asked them to leave. "Ma Wiggins, why don't you give me a call later this evening. Yolinda, you can come back tomorrow. I'm sure I'll feel more like having company then."

"Well, I'll call you before I go to bed, and I'll come back tonight if I can. I was hoping to spend more time over here," Ma Wiggins said with a slight pout.

"I got a long, hot date with my man tomorrow—fishing, shopping, the movies. If it ain't too late when I get home, I'll come back over here." Yolinda paused and added in a snippy tone, "I was hoping to spend a few more hours with you this evening, Jessie."

"Y'all make sure the door shuts on the way out," Hubert said. He didn't say nothing else as he hauled me to the bedroom and eased me onto the bed. He sat down and stroked the side of my face. "Jessie, you need to slow down and take it easy. And I mean it. How do you feel, sugar?"

"Fine. I hope you didn't hurt your mama's and Yolinda's feelings. I didn't know how to tell them to leave, but I like the way you handled it."

"I could tell from the tight look on your face that they was getting on your nerves."

"Was I that obvious?"

"You was to me. I know you so well now, I can almost read your mind. So I advise you not to ever try to hide nothing from me, you hear me?"

I gulped. "I hear you."

Hubert laughed. Somehow I managed to laugh too. But inside, I was falling apart.

Hubert offered to go to work late Monday morning and take me back to the clinic. I told him I didn't want him to take no more time off. We got paid by the hour, and when we didn't work, we didn't get paid. He balked about it for a minute, but it didn't do him no good. I literally pushed him out the door.

The bus ride to the clinic seemed so long. When I finally arrived and got prepped, one of the older doctors on the day shift entered the exam room with a scrunched-up look on his fleshy, wrinkled face. My heart started doing double beats right away.

"Good morning, Mrs. Wiggins."

"Good morning, Dr. Isley. What's wrong? Was there something wrong with my blood work?"

He held up his hand and smiled. "It's nothing serious. Your iron is low, but I'll give you something to help build it up. And I'm going to give you something that'll help with the nausea."

I breathed a deep sigh of relief. No matter who was the father of my child, he or she would be completely mine. If things blew up in my face, I'd be able to face it better with a healthy child.

"This will be your second child, right?"

"Uh-huh."

"You haven't had any other pregnancies?"

That question threw me for a loop. "Um . . . not really."

Dr. Isley raised his eyebrows. " 'Not really'? Can you explain what you mean by that?"

I didn't know nothing about blood work, or what doctors could or could not tell about a woman's body if they examined her. That's why I decided to be up front with Dr. Isley. I had to be prepared in case he said something to Hubert and let the cat out of the bag that I hadn't been pregnant last year and hadn't had no miscarriage, like Hubert and everybody else believed. I would never forgive myself if Hubert found out how deceitful I was. And I could never face my in-laws or my own family again if they found out. Juicy news like this would be enough to keep Yolinda running her mouth all over town from now on.

"Well . . . I had all the symptoms last year and thought I was pregnant. My husband was over-the-moon happy. But it was a false alarm. I didn't want him to know I'd been wrong, so I said I'd had a miscarriage. I figured that a, um, 'act of God' would be easier for him to deal with than him finding out I'd never been pregnant in the first place."

Dr. Isley stared at me so long, with a tight look on his face, I started to fidget. "Oh? Why would you lie about something as serious as that? Especially to your husband."

"See, Hubert is real sensitive and insecure, especially about his manhood. He'd had only one child and had started to think that he wasn't manly enough to have any more. When I was pregnant, or thought I was, he became very confident. And then I found out from one of the doctors here that I'd never actually been pregnant in the first place, and that my late monthly and the symptoms was all related to menopause. I didn't have the nerve to tell him that. I . . . I'm a little sensitive and insecure myself, especially about my age. Menopause meant I was getting old. I hope that's not what I'm going through now. Are you sure I really am pregnant?"

"Mrs. Wiggins, you've been thoroughly examined. You are definitely pregnant."

I sucked in my breath and geared up to bring up the issue that had been on my mind since last week. "I hope I have my baby before summer gets here."

Dr. Isley's eyes got big. "I hate to disappoint you, Mrs. Wiggins. But that's not likely. You're only about six weeks along. If everything goes well, you should deliver in early or mid-October. That is, if you carry the baby to full term."

I couldn't believe my ears! I needed to hear him tell me my due date again. "October? It ain't possible you got the dates wrong, and I'll deliver before then?" I held my breath.

Dr. Isley shook his head. "I didn't get the dates wrong," he said in a firm tone. "Now, I will admit that I can't predict the exact day in October that you'll deliver. I don't think too many doctors can do that yet. We can come pretty close, say within a week or ten days. But I was way off with one of my other expectant mothers. She had her baby two weeks after the date I'd predicted. Why did you ask that question?"

"Um . . . I was just curious. I thought maybe I'd got pregnant around late October last year. I'd felt queasy off and on the rest of the year and put on a bunch of pounds, but I didn't want to say nothing about it to nobody."

"Mrs. Wiggins, you did not conceive before January."

Dr. Isley's words was music to my ears. If the baby wasn't due until October, there was no way Amos could be the daddy! I must have got pregnant the first time Hubert made love to me on New Year's Day morning. I'd been doubly blessed. My marriage had finally been consummated and I'd conceived a child at the same time. I couldn't have been happier if a rich person had died and left me a million dollars.

CHAPTER 49
Hubert

I was disappointed that Jessie didn't want me to take her to the clinic. I didn't argue with her, because I didn't want to do nothing that might stress her out. All I could think about at work was that I was finally going to have a child with my blood.

When I got home from work, she was sitting on the couch, with her legs crossed and her arms folded. I hadn't seen her looking so serene since she was pregnant with the child she'd miscarried.

"I'm glad to see you in such a good mood. You must have some good news to tell me." I held my breath and rubbed my hands together.

"Yup. I'll tell you in a minute." She sniffed and blinked a few times before she went on. "After I left the clinic this morning, I came home and decided not to go to work, after all."

I dropped my jacket onto the wing chair and sat down at the other end of the couch. "You missed a whole day? And you had the nerve to be on my case about us taking off work without pay."

Jessie shot me a hot look and waved her hand. "Aw, shuck it!" she snapped. "So what if we come up a few dollars short this month? It won't be the first time."

"Okay. Now go on. You know I don't like being in suspense. Whatever you have to tell me, tell me now." My breath suddenly caught in my throat and I leaned forward in my seat. "I hope the doctor didn't give you no bad news. Is . . . the baby all right? And what about you?"

Jessie rolled her eyes. "Didn't I just tell you I had good news? Me and the baby are fine. Except for me needing to build up my iron, my blood work didn't detect nothing for us to be concerned about." She paused and started to smile like she was imitating Mona Lisa. "Our baby is due in October."

I almost choked on the lump in my throat. I lifted my head and hands up as high as they could go in praise of God. "Thank you, Heavenly Father!" When I turned my attention back to Jessie, she was shaking her head, and her lips was curling up at the ends like she was about to laugh. I was glad she didn't, because this was the most serious thing in my life right now. "Did Dr. Underwood tell you anything else?"

"I didn't see him. He works the night shift. He was just filling in for another doctor when I seen him last Monday. Dr. Isley tended to me today."

"Good! He's much older and more experienced than Dr. Underwood. I'm sure this news will please Mama and Daddy." I rubbed my hands together again. "Well, I guess we should start thinking about baby names."

"If it's a girl, I'd like to name her Bessie."

I reared my head back and looked at Jessie like she was nuts. "Are you crazy? That's what somebody would name a hog or a cow. We'll call her Lula Mae."

Jessie screwed up her lips like she'd just bit into a spoiled lemon. "Uh-uh. My grandpa had a mule named Lula Mae. What if it's a boy?"

"Well, as long as it took us to get this far, it's only fitting to call him a name he can be proud of."

Jessie hunched her shoulders. "Okay. Like what?"

"Hubert Jr. sounds good to the ear."

"Not to my ear. I think that because this child is such a unexpected blessing, we ought to pick a name from the Bible."

I gave Jessie a thoughtful look. "Hmmm. That makes a lot of sense, I guess."

"Hubert, there is something else I want to say." She didn't give me time to ask what before she told me. "This will be a new beginning for us. We should start out with a clean slate."

"What do you mean? I thought we started out with a clean slate the first time." I didn't know where this conversation was going, but it was making me nervous.

Jessie suddenly looked so somber, it scared me. I was afraid to ask what was on her mind now. I figured she'd tell me if she wanted me to know. I just didn't want to hear nothing that was going to bust the balloon it had took us so long to fill up with air. I held my breath as she went on. "We started out that way. But I did a few things later, that wasn't very Christian-like. And I'm so ashamed of myself, I'd whup my own butt if I could. I mean, it was irresponsible of me to put myself in a position for that man to take advantage of me at Yolinda's party that time."

I dropped my head. "Jessie, don't even think about beating yourself up about what happened to you that night. I forgave you, even though it wasn't your fault. The sucker that pestered you is the one to blame. You are as wonderful and virtuous as Maggie was." It wasn't easy for me to say what I said next. "Besides, I ain't been no angel myself."

Jessie gave me a confused look. "Hogwash! You might not think so, but you've always been one to me, and to everybody else. Shoot! You are the only man I know of that so many women tried to hook when Maggie died. The folks in Lexington got you up on the highest pedestal they ever put a colored man on. And a educated, rich white man like Mr. DeBow wouldn't trust you—over his sons—to take money to his mama if he didn't think you was so humble and saintly. Ain't you proud of yourself?"

"I am," I muttered.

"And another thing, I believe that fidelity is one of the most important things in a marriage. I *know* you ain't never cheated on me with another woman, and never will. Honesty is the next most important thing. I'm telling you here and now that I am so happy right now, I don't care what you done in the past, or in the future. There ain't nothing you could do that would be bad enough for me to leave you. Even if you did get involved with another woman, or robbed a bank—we could work through it with God's help. But I promise you, I ain't giving up on our marriage. A wild horse couldn't drag me away from our lovely house."

Jessie's words was so profound, I felt as special as one of the Lord's disciples. But I was worried that she might take everything back when she heard what I had to tell her. "Sugar, I can think of other things that could break up a marriage—"

Jessie rolled her eyes and said, "You *killed* a woman and I'm still with you. What could be worse than that?"

"I'll let you mentioning Blondeen slide this time."

Jessie drew in a sharp breath and her eyes got big. "Did you . . . kill somebody else?"

"If I did, would that make you leave me?"

She shook her head. "I know you wouldn't kill again, unless it was a accident and self-defense, like the first time. Now if you don't mind, let's end this conversation before one of us says something they'll regret. You want me to get out the checkerboard?" She started to stand up.

"Don't move." I motioned her to sit back down. I cleared my throat and gazed into Jessie's eyes. I had to blink hard to hold back my tears. I wondered if she would keep her promise if I told her the truth about myself. I was about to find out. Not only was it the right thing to do, it was time for me to tell my wonderful wife exactly what kind of man she was married to. It was hard to get started. I felt so detached, it was like another person had took over my body and was about to do all the talking. That was the only way I could confess what I never thought I'd be able to do.

"Hubert, you scaring me."

"I'm scaring myself too. Let me get this over with before I change my mind." I took the deepest breath I ever took in my life before I started talking again.

Jessie sat as stiff as a tree while I told her *everything* I'd been hiding—from my fake marriage to Maggie to my relationship with Leroy. She cringed at certain points. But when I told her how I'd "accidentally" picked up a male prostitute, she ran to the bathroom and puked.

When Jessie got back to the living room, she looked like she'd seen a ghost. "Sugar, you all right?" I asked.

She held up her hand and sat back down. "I'm fine." She rubbed her nose and looked at me with her eyes narrowed. "Did you tell me everything? If you didn't, you need to tell me the rest now. If I'm going to be sick again, I'd like to do it before I get in the bed in case I can't make it to the bathroom in time."

CHAPTER 50
Hubert

I looked Jessie in the eyes and said, "I told you everything." The living room got so quiet, you could have heard a flea sneeze. I was surprised I wasn't sweating the way I usually did when I was in a tense situation. And this was the tensest one I'd ever been in. For a split second, I wished I could take back everything I'd told her. But it was too late. I'd done something I never thought I'd do and now I had to live with the consequences. My head suddenly started throbbing and my chest got so tight, I was surprised it didn't squeeze my heart out. "Jessie, please say something."

She stared at me for several moments before she spoke again. "What do you want me to say?"

I hunched my shoulders. "I don't know. I just dropped a big load on you. You must have something to say about it. It was hard for me to get this off my chest. Now I don't know if it was the right thing to do. But since I did, I need to hear everything you want to say about it."

The way she was looking at me, I was surprised she didn't slap me, or run into the bedroom and start packing her clothes. And

then she exhaled and said in a stern tone, "So you been forni-
cating with men, all this time?"

I didn't like the tone of her voice, but I didn't want to sound
stern myself, so I replied in the most gentle tone I could.
"Well, yeah."

Jessie shook her head. Her lips was moving, but no words
was coming out. Finally she said, "I . . . I can't believe my
ears."

"You better believe your ears, because everything I told you
is the honest-to-God truth."

"You sure you didn't leave nothing out?"

" 'Leave nothing out'? Do you want to hear the details about
each one of my boyfriends and what we done?"

Jessie's eyes got big. The next words shot out of her mouth
like bullets. "I don't need to know all that! I get the picture. If
you been doing this as long as you say you have, you been with
a *heap* of men. If you tried to give me the details about each
one and what y'all did, we'd be sitting here the rest of the day."
She blew out a breath and waved her hands above her head.
"Y'all probably done things I ain't never even heard of, and I
don't want to hear none of that."

"I doubt if I been with as many men as you think. My last
two relationships was long-term. All them other men was here
today gone tomorrow, one-nighters, and—"

Jessie cut me off by holding up her hand. "That's all right."
She looked away and stared at the wall before she said, "Maggie used to brag to me about what a passionate man you was in
the bedroom." She whirled back around to face me with her
eyes narrowed. "She was lying?"

I nodded. "She had to lie. We did and said whatever we
thought was necessary to make our marriage look real. I know
what you think about them lies we told everybody, so if you
want to back out of the promise you just made about never

leaving me, I'll understand. But I hope you want to stay married for the sake of our child."

Jessie's eyes got as big as saucers. "Our child!" she yelled. "How do you think this is going to affect him or her when they find out? Their little friends, and everybody else, will torture them to no end."

Some of Jessie's comments was beginning to exasperate me. I felt like jumping up and stomping my foot and wagging my finger in her face. But I kept my cool. "Jessie, what's wrong with you? Do you think this is something I'd tell my child? I don't know how I'll feel once they get grown, and I don't know if it's something they'd need to know even then, since I'm out of that lifestyle."

"I just thought of something else. Blondeen's uncle and one of her boy cousins was born like you. So some folks believe this condition is hereditary . . ."

"I was born this way. If our child is too, I won't love them no less. My main concern will be trying to keep them safe from the law and the folks that think being like me is the worst thing in the world."

"What about your mama and daddy? Have you thought about telling them?"

When I nodded, my head felt as heavy as a block of cement. "I wanted to tell them a while ago. That was the only thing me and Maggie ever disagreed on. I changed my mind just before she and Claude died. And it's a good thing I did. When the man I had planned to leave Maggie for told his wife and kids he was planning to get a place with me, they took it so hard, he dropped me like a bad habit."

The room got real quiet again. Just as I was about to say something else, Jessie looked toward the kitchen and said, "If we hadn't stopped keeping alcohol in the house, I'd drink some now."

I sighed and nodded. "I would too." I stared at the floor for a few moments, and when I looked back up at Jessie, there was the strangest look on her face. "Claude looked so much like you. I never would have guessed that you wasn't his real daddy."

"That was because we made sure to pick a man that looked enough like me," I said with a shrug. "And we had to pick one that lived in another town so we wouldn't bump into him on a Lexington street. Maggie found him in a joint in Mobile."

"Did y'all ever tell the man about Claude?"

I shuddered and drew in my breath. "Goodness gracious, no! It was bad enough that poor Maggie had to go at it with him so many times to get pregnant. When she found out the deed was done, she never went to see him again. But Maggie said he was a really nice man. He already had several kids that he had to support. I didn't think he'd want another mouth to feed."

Jessie shook her head and fanned her face. "My Lord. I can't see a woman who was as prim and proper as Maggie going at it with a stranger just so she could get pregnant."

"She did. And let me tell you, she didn't like it one bit."

"I didn't know nothing about her being molested when she was a little girl until you told me. And I sure didn't know she never wanted to have sex with another man. She seemed so normal."

"Maggie was normal. I'm sure there are other women who don't want to have sex."

"Me and her was so close, I told her everything. And I thought she told me everything. I don't understand why she kept the truth a secret from me."

"Jessie, if she had told you, I know you probably wouldn't have blabbed to nobody, but we couldn't take that chance."

Jessie stared off into space for a few seconds before she went on. "Your dead boyfriend sounds like he was a real nice man."

"Leroy was the salt of the earth." I sniffled and sucked in a deep breath to keep from going to pieces.

"You was going to leave Maggie for that other boyfriend before you got with Leroy? Would you have eventually left me and moved in with him?"

"No, I wouldn't have. Leroy knew all about you and he was happy with our arrangement the way it was. There was no way I could have moved in with him. He had two half-grown sons that visited him on a regular basis and he couldn't let them find out."

There was a bone-weary expression on Jessie's face as she continued. "If you done told me enough lies to fill up a deep well, how do I know you ain't lying to me now?"

"About what?"

"What if you was to fall in love with another man you'd rather be with than me? And . . . what if you and him was to run off together? Where would that leave me? I don't want to raise a child by myself."

"Like I told you, that lifestyle is over for me. You can believe me, or you can choose not to. I just want to have a *honest* relationship with you, and I can't do that if I'm still lying. I forgave you for that mishap you had with that man you met at Yolinda's party two years ago. Even though it wasn't your fault, you shouldn't have been at that party without me in the first place." Jessie flinched when I narrowed my eyes and looked at her for a long, silent moment. I knew she was uncomfortable by the way she kept blinking her eyes and shifting in her seat. "You owe it to me, and yourself, to let me know if there is anything else scandalous you did behind my back. If you did, I want to hear about it now. I won't be happy if it comes out later."

She stared straight ahead. When she looked back at me, tears was streaming down her face. "I ain't done nothing else behind your back but what I already told you."

CHAPTER 51
Jessie

I was surprised God didn't strike me down dead for being so untruthful. Especially after Hubert had confessed to me about doing some of the most unspeakable things a human being could do. The lie I'd just told him left such a bad taste in my mouth, I gagged so hard, he had to rush over and slap me on the back.

"Jessie, I know how much I just upset you, but you need to get a grip. We can't let you get sick. The baby you carrying is the most important thing in our lives right now."

"I-I'm all right," I stammered. I was nowhere near all right. I felt like the scum of the earth. What Hubert had just told me might have sent another woman screaming up and down the street. She probably would have grabbed a frying pan and beat him to a pulp. And there was no telling what her family would do with what was left of him.

When I looked at Hubert and seen the distressed look on his face, I knew what I had to do. I couldn't go on letting him believe I was something I wasn't. But when I tried to come clean, I couldn't do it. What he had been hiding was bad, but was the mess I was hiding worse? I couldn't decide. But it didn't matter. I was not the woman he thought I was. I just didn't know how to tell him and when.

"Jessie, please say something. This silence is making me nervous."

"I first need to digest everything you told me. I don't really know what else to say right now."

"Well, we do need to talk about it some more. Maybe not right now, but in the next few days."

"Why?"

"If you got any more questions, I want you to ask them while this is still fresh on your mind. I want to put this behind us as soon as possible so we can move forward. That is, if you think you can do that now, knowing what you know about me."

My mouth dropped open. "I can't think of no more questions to ask you right now. Let's let this rest for a little while."

"Jessie, if you got some more questions, the longer you put off asking them, the harder it's going to be for you to ask. And the harder it'll be for me to answer them."

"I know. But this is so deep and serious, I can't promise I won't come up with more questions about it tomorrow, next month, or even next year."

"Well, this ain't something I can leave open-ended for no year. I don't want no loose-ended questions you might have dangling over my head for God knows how long. That kind of suspense would send me to the crazy house."

"Can I at least sleep on it tonight? If I can't think of no more questions by tomorrow or the next couple of days, we won't have to discuss it again. All right?"

"All right, I guess."

"I think I'm going to go to bed now," I said, sounding as weak as a kitten.

"Bed? It's way too early to turn in. It ain't even six o'clock!

Besides, we ain't ate supper. You want me to cook something?"

I glared at Hubert. Not only did I feel like I'd been duped by a snake oil salesman, I felt more angry, sad, and disappointed than I'd ever felt before in my life. The same feelings he would have had if I had told him all the ways I had betrayed him. "I ain't got no appetite. And I don't see how you could be thinking about food either."

"I ain't got no appetite myself, but we still need to eat. You sure you don't want to talk about this no more now?"

"I'm sure."

While Hubert was in the bathroom, I rushed into the bedroom and put on my nightgown. I had my back to him and the covers pulled up to my chin when he came into the room.

When he got in the bed two hours later, he gently tapped the side of my rump. I froze. "Jessie, thanks for being such a understanding woman. You was the best choice I could have made for a new wife."

I appreciated his praises, but I didn't turn around to look at him. As mean as it was of me, I wanted him to feel really bad for all the lying and sneaking around he'd done. "I'm glad you feel that way," I mumbled. "I'm still in a state of shock. I need to get some sleep and refresh my brain so I can process everything. Besides, I need to have all my wits about me when I go to work tomorrow."

"You sure you ain't going to tell nobody what I told you? You know that if folks find out what I used to do with men, I could go to prison. Not to mention all the pain and shame it would cause my mama and daddy and the Church. Yolinda and all the rest of them gossipmongers would have a field day if they knew about me. I'd be better off dead."

I turned over, sat bolt upright, and gave Hubert the most dumbfounded look I could come up with. "Why in the world would I tell anybody what kind of man you really are? Every colored person in this town would be scandalized. You're my husband and I married you for better or worse."

"Does the 'worse' include me being what I am?"

"I ain't going to answer that."

"You don't have to. I know what you're thinking." A hurt look crossed his face. "I'm sorry you still think of men like me in such a unholy way."

"Don't put words in my mouth. To be honest with you, I never thought I would be so tolerant about a affliction like yours. And it ain't easy. I know none of our family and friends would be able to at all."

"Jessie, I don't have no 'affliction.' I'm just as healthy as any other man."

My heart started thumping so hard, I could hear it. "I just thought of some more questions. What if you see other men you want to be with for a one-night thing? Will you backslide?"

"Didn't I tell you how dangerous trying to find a man done got for me? I ain't got the nerve to try it again. I want you to know now that if you tell somebody what I told you, and I find out in time—before they can get to me—I'm going to get up out of this town as fast as I can. I ain't going to spend years and years in no prison, get beat up, or killed. I'll go up North and start a new life with a new name."

I gulped. "Go up North? You said you would never leave me. Now here you are threatening to run off already, change your name, and live another life with a new set of lies. And leave me to raise your child all by myself!"

"Jessie, I hope it don't come to that. I meant what I said about never leaving or lying to you again. But if you rile up folks by blabbing on me, I won't have no choice. Can you imagine what folks would do to me if they found out I been deceiving them all my life? You remember how they beat up Blondeen's uncle and cousin when they found out about them—and ran them out of town. If I didn't leave Lexington, some of them same folks would run me out of town, if they didn't beat me to death first."

I heaved out a sigh that was so deep, it was painful. "Hubert, I ain't going to tell nobody what you told me. Now you hush up and let's get some sleep."

CHAPTER 52
Hubert

It was a rough night for both of us in our bed. Jessie fidgeted like a worm on a fishhook. She got up to use the bathroom two times in a hour. The last time she went, I heard her puking. I played possum so I wouldn't have to say nothing to her when she got back in the bed. I tossed and turned for two hours before I finally dozed off.

When I woke up about three hours later, Jessie was sitting up in bed. I turned on the lamp on my nightstand. Her shadow on the wall looked ominous, and it sure did fit the occasion. The way she was acting, I was really sorry I had told her anything. But I didn't think I could spend the rest of my life keeping so many secrets from my wife. Especially after she told me that there was nothing I could do bad enough to make her leave me.

"Jessie, you need to go back to sleep."

She cleared her throat before she said anything. When she did, her voice was weak and raspy. "I can't. I got too much on my mind." I felt even sorrier that I had caused her some new pain. "I'm a straight-up, God-fearing woman. What you told me goes against every Christian belief I was raised with."

I wrung my hands and held my breath. It helped ease the discomfort in my bosom. "I thought we agreed to talk about it some more after a while."

"If you had told me this in bits and pieces over a few days or a week, maybe it would have been easier for me to swallow."

I looked at Jessie like she was crazy. "You know as well as I do that you wouldn't have let me get by telling you something this serious in bits and pieces. Especially not over that long a period of time."

"Then how come you never told me this before now?"

"I didn't have no reason to. I thought we had the perfect marriage."

"W-what? Shame, shame, shame! How could you have thought our marriage was 'perfect' if you was having sex with men behind my back? And how come you decided to tell me now?"

I was getting more frustrated by the second. I wondered if this was something I should have told Jessie on my deathbed so I wouldn't have had to deal with the fallout. But it was too late, and I was going to deal with it as well as I could. "Jessie, you are the one that said we needed to start over with a clean slate, remember?"

She looked away for a few seconds. "Yeah, I did."

"If you meant it, what was I supposed to do?"

"I just never expected you to tell me what you told me."

"Looka here, this ain't easy for me. Please try and look at things from my point of view."

"I don't think I could do that."

"Well, just imagine you was like me. Say, you was attracted to women. It would be a hard life to live and hide, even for a strong woman like you. All my life, I have regretted my behavior. But I couldn't do nothing about it. Now that I got a chance—with your help—to be a normal man, or something close to that, don't ruin it for me. This is important for both of us."

Jessie gave me a thoughtful look. "I guess nobody would choose to be like you." She paused and glanced at me from the corner of her eye. "Can I ask you a question and will you tell me the truth?"

"I already told you to ask me anything you want. What good would it do for me to lie to you now? What do you want to know?"

"Did you enjoy being with all them men?"

"Well, I guess I did. Otherwise, I wouldn't have done it for so long."

"If that's the case, if you hadn't run into that she-man and that man prostitute that gave you such a bad time, would you still go after men?"

"I . . . I don't know."

Jessie gave me a blank stare. "Let me put it another way." She sucked in a deep breath and sniffed. "If a good-looking man came up to you and acted real nice and sweet, and wanted to, um, be with you, would you do it again?"

I wanted to be as honest as I could be with her now, so I said what was really on my mind. "I really don't know. I don't want to and I'm going to do everything I can *not to*. I been this way all my life and I don't know if I can change completely overnight. I swear to God, if a man was to come at me, and I don't care how handsome and sweet he is, I will tell him right off the bat that I got a wife."

Jessie gasped. "You told some of them men you had a wife. If it didn't make no difference then, why would it make a difference with a new one?"

I was getting tired of this conversation. If Jessie didn't end it soon, I would. "I had a choice then, I have a choice now. I am going to do everything I can not to fall back into them ways. And I mean it from the heart. Don't make this no harder than it already is."

I was surprised and glad Jessie put her arm around my neck and laid her head on my shoulder. "Hubert, I feel so sorry for you. I can't imagine how tortured you must have felt."

"All my life."

"I never met no man or a woman like you, but after listening to you, I have a lot of sympathy for all of y'all. I got a feeling that what you turned out to be was a freak accident of nature. And I'm sure the devil had a hand in it."

"You could be right. But I really meant what I said. I ain't going to lie to you no more. If we ain't completely honest with each other, we got empty vows. Don't you agree?"

"Um, yeah."

"I think we done conversated enough about this tonight. Let's sleep on it. Good night, sugar."

"Good night, Hubert."

I clicked off the lamp and tried to go to sleep, but I couldn't. Except for the night I spent hiding under Leroy's bed, I had never felt more uncomfortable in a bedroom.

Now that me and Jessie had a sex life together, and a baby on the way, I felt like a changed man in so many ways. I would pray as long and as often as necessary to stay changed. It didn't take much to make Jessie happy, and I was going to bend over backward to make sure she stayed happy. I didn't know what was going to happen to our relationship in the future. I was convinced that a baby—and us being honest with each other—would make a big difference. We loved each other, and despite my past, I didn't see no reason why we couldn't be as happy as we'd been so far.

Despite all the discomfort my confession seemed to be causing, I had freed myself from a burden that had weighed me down long enough. I knew in my heart that I had done the right thing.

But I still missed Leroy.

On Tuesday, I asked Mr. DeBow if I could take a extra couple of hours for lunch. He didn't hesitate to allow me to do so. I was happy he had never asked me why I needed a longer lunch all them other times. Each time, I had offered to work overtime without pay to make up the time, but he never took me up on it. I was glad that this was probably going to be the last time I needed extra time to go do something personal, not including my funeral duties. I wanted to go to Hartville so I could ride past Leroy's barbershop, one last time. I thought that the nostalgia would make me feel better. And it would give me much-needed comfort.

There was a padlock on the door, and the windows had been covered up with newspaper. I was tempted to get out of my car and go around the building and gaze up at his apartment door for old times' sake. Leroy had had plain white curtains at his bedroom window. There was some plaid ones there now. Somebody suddenly parted them and I seen a dusky-brown, moon-faced man gazing out. Knowing that a new tenant had already moved into the place where I had enjoyed myself so much, I felt like I was at a funeral. This made everything so final. I couldn't hold back the tears that gushed out of my eyes on my drive back to work.

When quitting time rolled around, I literally ran to my car. I didn't know what to expect when I got home.

Just as I was about to turn onto my street, I seen nosy Yolinda darting off my porch steps. She was the last person I wanted to deal with right now. I made a U-turn and drove around long enough to give her a chance to make it back to her house.

She caught me anyway. As I was parking in the driveway, she dashed back across the street. "Hey, Hubert. I was at loose ends, so I thought I'd visit you and Jessie for a spell. She should be home in a few minutes, right?"

"Right. But me and Jessie got something important to discuss and we need some privacy. Can you visit us tomorrow?"

Yolinda's eyebrows shot up. "Oh? What y'all got to discuss?"

I was exasperated. I knew that if I didn't get away from this busybody in time, I'd hurt her feelings. And I didn't want to do that, since she was Jessie's best friend. "It's kind of personal."

"Personal, my foot. Ain't nothing personal in this neck of the woods. I know as much about your business as you know about mine." Yolinda sniffed and gave me a pensive look. "This have anything to do with the baby y'all expecting?"

If I had been attracted to women instead of men all my life, I would have never had nothing to do with a nosy, meddlesome, inconsiderate one like Yolinda. She could be a thorn in the side of a grizzly. "Uh-huh."

Yolinda rolled her eyes and snickered. "What's so personal about that? I even know how much money you make and how loud you snore when you go to sleep. Maggie told me." She lowered her voice and went on. "And she told me how frisky you was in the bedroom!"

I knew that Maggie had also liked to gossip with her friend-girls as much as Jessie did. I didn't care about her discussing my salary and my sleeping habits, but I resented her telling Yolinda about our sex life—especially since we'd never had one. "It ain't just that. I got a few other things to discuss with my wife that I only want her to hear," I said in a firm tone.

Yolinda rolled her neck and snapped, "Well, ex . . . cuse me." I knew I'd hurt her feelings, but I didn't care, so long as she dragged her nosy tail back home.

CHAPTER 53
Jessie

Yolinda had been right about it going against human nature to keep secrets too long. The ones I'd been holding in had started to wear on me like a cancer. And every person I ever knew that had cancer died from it. Not only did Hubert seem relieved that he had shared his secrets with me, he seemed like a whole new man. And in a way, he was. Coming clean had been a healthy decision for him. He looked as bright-eyed and bushy-tailed as he did the day we got married.

I was glad Hubert had already left for work when I got up Tuesday morning. I needed to be by myself for a while before we conversated some more about what he'd told me, if we ever did discuss it again.

One thing, for sure, was that if he had told me before we got married that he was "funny," I wouldn't have married him. I'd been taught all my life that God created Adam and Eve so that *men and women* could populate the world together. But I had also been taught that Satan was so powerful, he could interfere with a lot of God's plans for human beings. As if all the racism, crime, and diseases wasn't enough.

I was relieved to know that the reason Hubert hadn't been

able to have sex with me wasn't because of a medical condition. But I was unhappy about him sexing up a storm with men at the same time! He'd admitted to having so many lovers since his teens, he'd lost count. I couldn't believe a woman like Maggie had put up with all that. I had misjudged them both. But I still loved Maggie, and I definitely still loved Hubert. I knew it would benefit me to stay with him, especially because of the financial security and prestige I got being his wife. Thanks to him, I had everything a woman wanted, except a normal sex life. Well, maybe it was going to be normal now that he had made such a drastic change in his life.

I didn't have no appetite, so I didn't even bother trying to eat something before I went to work. All kinds of thoughts, old and new, was roaming around in my head. I had known Hubert all my life, but now I realized I didn't know him at all. If I had married a complete stranger, I couldn't have felt more confused, uncertain, and disappointed. It was hard for me to accept the fact that he had been duping me from the beginning.

But the thing at the front of my mind was that I'd done as much duping as he had. So I wasn't no better than he was. I wondered if I told him if he'd still want me to be his wife . . .

I was my usual happy-go-lucky self when I got to work, so none of my coworkers could tell that something was bothering me.

Two patients had died during the night, and two new patients was coming in today, so we was going to be real busy. But the best news was that our head nurse, a mean old heifer who supervised the colored workers and treated us so bad, had got mad at the owners of the facility because they refused to give her a raise and quit on the spot. Every colored worker got downright giddy. The maintenance man even danced a jig when he heard the news.

I avoided my coworkers as much as I could all day. I was

afraid somebody would notice I was worried about something. But I couldn't keep walking around grinning like everybody else who was "celebrating" the departure of that mean nurse.

I spent my lunch break walking through the woods behind the facility. I ignored the baloney sandwich in my purse, which I had brought from home, because food was the last thing on my mind. My stomach was in knots, and the inside of my mouth was so dry, I couldn't eat nothing.

I didn't know if what Hubert had told me was worse than what I'd been hiding from him. What I did know was that the load I was carrying was suddenly so heavy, I knew I had to unburden myself before I broke down.

When I got home from work Tuesday evening and seen Hubert's car in the driveway, my chest tightened. I had hoped that I'd have a little more time to myself so I could decide when and how I was going to confess.

I gave him a tight smile when I walked into the living room, where he was sitting on the couch. "Hello, Jessie," he greeted. I had planned to wait until after we'd ate supper to tell him everything. But my guilt was so deep, I knew I couldn't put it off a minute longer. For a split second, I wished that my bothersome in-laws or Yolinda would drop by. If they did, maybe by the time they left, I'd have changed my mind. I didn't like that thought, though. If I was going to be the wife God wanted me to be, I had to go through with it.

"Hubert, I need to talk to you," I said as I plopped down at the opposite end of the couch.

He held up his hand. "Jessie, I decided that I don't want to talk about what I told you no more. I been wondering all day if I shouldn't have said nothing. I been holding in all them secrets and lies so long, maybe it would have been better if I'd kept them to myself. I am so sorry I was such a lying dog. You deserve so much better."

"Hubert, hush up and please let me talk. What I got to say this time ain't about what you told me."

He gave me a confused look. "It ain't?"

I took the deepest breath I ever took before I went on. "Hubert, I lied to you again," I whispered.

"What about?"

"Uh . . . a heap of things. Last night when you asked me if there was anything else I'd done behind your back, I told you no. That was another lie. I can't go to bed tonight without getting the load off my chest that's about to cave me in. If you did it, I need to do it too. Otherwise, we can't start over with a 'clean slate' so long as my side of the slate got so much dirt on it." The more I talked, the bigger the lump in my throat swole up. But as long as it didn't stop me from getting the words out, I wasn't going to let it stop me.

"Jessie, I don't care what it is you need to tell me. It can't be that bad. Or no more shocking than what I told you." His face suddenly froze. He stood up and got smack-dab in front of me with his hands on his hips. "Unless . . . you fixing to tell me the baby ain't mine."

There was so much terror in his eyes, I had to put a stop to that right away. "You're the daddy, Hubert. I ain't been with another man since October." I stopped talking long enough to catch my breath before I added, "He didn't mean a hill of beans to me!"

Hubert's jaw dropped. He stared at me with his eyes narrowed. "Jessie, don't hold nothing back. I want to know *everything* you ever did that went against our marriage. If I could bare my soul to you with such devastating news, the least you could do is be honest with me all the way. It won't make no difference. I done recommitted myself to you, and ain't nothing going to change that."

"I hope not." I had to get up and go in the kitchen to drink a glass of water before I could go on. Instead of sitting back on the couch where he was now, I eased down in the chair facing him. When I tried to talk, at first my lips refused to move, and my knees was knocking together. Finally the words started rolling off my tongue like water off a duck's back. And I left no stone unturned. When I got to the part about my fake pregnancy that had resulted in a "miscarriage," he had to get up and go in the kitchen and drink a glass of water. When he got back to the living room, he dropped down onto the couch and gawked at me like I'd sprouted a beard.

When he spoke, his voice was so weak and raspy, he sounded like a man twice his age. "I'm glad to know I ain't no rapist. You got anything else to tell me?"

I shook my head. "Honest to God. I'll even swear to it on the Bible if you want me to."

"You ain't got to go that far. I believe you."

I sucked in several deep breaths and stared straight ahead. He was gazing at the floor. When I turned to look at him, I couldn't think of a word to describe the expression on his face. It was hard to decide if he was angry or just hurt. "Say something," I said with my voice trembling.

"I'm surprised you'd get involved with the same man Blondeen was living with at the time," he croaked.

"I know that was a foolish thing for me to do, but I only did it because you wasn't able to do nothing for me in bed," I explained.

"Of all the men in Lexington, why did you have to choose Blondeen's?"

"I didn't know he was her man until I'd already started up with him. Um . . . he was the first one that paid me a lot of attention."

"Did she ever find out about y'all?"

"I ain't sure. If she did know, I'm glad she died before she let the cat out of the bag and told you. I never wanted you to know how trifling I used to be."

"Jessie, you wasn't no more trifling than I was." He was breathing through his mouth.

I was having a hard time breathing at all. "Where do we go from here?"

"Well, for our own peace of mind, I think we should drop this subject for now and forever. I don't want to talk about it no more tonight, next week, or ten years from now. And I mean it."

"That's fine with me. And I . . ." I stopped talking and looked at Hubert with a wan expression on my face. "I just thought of one more thing."

Hubert shook his head and groaned. "Lord, have mercy. What is it?"

"Should we come clean about *everything?*"

"I thought we already did. Look, Jessie—"

I held up both hands and shook my head. "I'm talking about Blondeen."

Hubert's face froze. "W-what about her?"

"Do you want us to go to the police and tell them what really happened to her? We can ask Mr. DeBow to go with us again."

Hubert groaned and covered his face with his hands. When he took his hands away, it looked like all the blood had drained out of his face. "If we do, what good would it do? It sure wouldn't help our marriage. And everybody believes Tyrone and Floyd killed her. As far as I'm concerned, that case is closed. Do you want to reopen it and put her family, not to mention ours, through another nightmare?"

It didn't take long for me to answer. "No, I don't."

"Then let that secret stay a secret."

"All right, then."

"I know it's early, but I need to lay down now, so I'm going to get in the bed. These past couple of days done wore me down to a nub. My whole body is so shocked, I might not be able to stand up without falling."

"What about supper?"

"I done lost my appetite. But if I get hungry later, I'll get up and eat a baloney sandwich."

"I ain't hungry neither."

Hubert stood up and didn't fall, but he surprised me by reaching out his hand to me. "You coming?" Him doing this made me feel a little bit better. I leaped up out of my seat and put my hand in his. With his arm around my shoulder, he steered me into the bedroom.

I finally got a good night's sleep.

Several weeks passed, and I didn't like knowing that Hubert was still attracted to men. I believed him when he said he was done with that lifestyle, though. But I was still going to keep praying about it, because I knew it was going to be hard for him to ignore certain natural urges he'd had all his life. He was what he was, no matter what else he did with me to override his condition. I knew a few folks who had been involved in criminal activity most of their lives. Nobody expected them to change. "Bad blood is hard to cleanse," my pious father-in-law said a few years ago. It saddened me to know that a preacher didn't think people born a certain way could change.

Pa Wiggins was as pleased as he could be when a few of the criminals in Lexington turned their lives around and became respectable members of our community. One of the worst ones even became a preacher and had been saving souls for over fifteen years. If a career criminal could become a changed man and stay changed, I knew Hubert could too.

I didn't plan on ever going back to Glenn and Carrie's house, and I hoped I didn't see Amos at church again, or anywhere else. But the day after Easter, on April 6, I seen Carrie at the market. She told me that Amos's wife had took their kids and ran off to California with a man she'd been seeing on the side since last year! Her eyes pooled with tears as she went on. "My poor brother is devastated. He never even looked at another woman and he treated Nita like a queen—and she still betrayed him! That two-timing hussy had everybody thinking she was so pious! Amos got so upset, he packed up last week and moved to Philadelphia to live with one of our cousins. I'm going to write him a letter this week. You want me to tell him you said hi?"

"Yeah. You tell him that. And let him know I'm happier than ever."

I think I had chose worthless men to fool around with, because deep down I didn't want to be with one I'd consider leaving Hubert for. I felt sorry for Amos, but only a little bit.

I prayed that my marriage would stay strong and that me and Hubert had a healthy child. One thing was for sure, we would raise him or her to be God-fearing, respectable, and productive. But the most important thing of all was, I didn't want our child to be as deceitful as me and Hubert had been.

I prayed that nobody from Hubert's wretched past, or mine, showed up one day and started running off at the mouth to anybody willing to listen.

I prayed that neither one of us backslid and did something else that went against our marriage.

I prayed . . .

EPILOGUE
Hubert

September and October 1942

It had been a long, hot summer. I was glad it was over and that things was going well for everybody I knew.

I told Jessie I wanted her to stay at home when the baby arrived. I thought she would put up a fuss, but she didn't. "Thank you!" she said as she breathed a sigh of relief. "I been dreaming about the day I could quit working. I'm going to turn in my notice at the end of this month."

Now that Jessie was going to be home all day, I told her we needed to move Earl back in with us. She was so pleased to hear that, she couldn't stop grinning. He didn't seem to care one way or the other when she told him. But he was real excited about having a baby brother or sister to play with. He rubbed his hands together and hollered, "It'll be like having a puppy!"

A lot of things happened in September. Mr. DeBow's alcoholic son got sober again and moved back in with his wife, after being separated for five years. The other ne'er-do-well son went to prison for robbing a grocery store with a butcher knife. Mr. DeBow's old-maid niece, who had been taking care of his mama, finally found a man at our annual county fair on Labor Day. He had proposed to her a week after they met. "This is her first and last chance to be happy. She can't take care of Mother any longer because she wants to focus on her marriage," Mr. DeBow told me.

"You know, I'm still willing to take money to her whenever you need me to," I replied.

"That won't be necessary, Hubert. I've finally decided to put her in a nursing home."

Yolinda and her long-term boyfriend got married. They moved to Memphis and bought a house. Before they left town, she told me and Jessie, "If my new husband ever cheats on me the way the first one did and I find out, he'll be looking for a new place to live—if I don't kill him first."

Last weekend, Jessie's footloose brother, Karl, married the woman he had been seeing off and on for a year. They moved into a house one block down the street from ours.

I had stopped making love to Jessie several times a week, but not because she didn't appeal to me no more, or because I wanted to be with a man instead. She was in her eighth month and had gained so much weight, she was as clumsy as a ox. She felt so unattractive, she wouldn't even let me see her naked. "You going to have to content yourself until I drop this load," she teased after our last time.

"I can't help myself. I been waiting a long time to show my love to you, so I'm *waaaay* behind," I reminded.

"Well, you had a good reason. It wasn't . . . um . . . really your fault, so I don't hold nothing against you. Besides, we can make up for that lost time after I have the baby."

I was very understanding. I seen how hard it was for her to move around the house just to do simple things like mopping and sweeping. I started doing them chores myself. My mama and Jessie's mama was always available to help too.

Tyrone was executed the last Friday in September. Floyd

had a heart attack and died the night before his date with Yellow Mama, which was supposed to happen the following Monday. Nobody wanted to talk about their deaths, but I knew it was on everybody's mind. Me and Jessie was just glad it was all over. The families didn't want to have no funerals, no graveside rights, or nothing else. The Fuller Brothers collected the bodies from the prison and drove them straight to the graveyard. I had hired another man to help me and Karl, and since they was the only colored gravediggers in Lexington, they had already dug the graves.

I was still attracted to men, but every time I seen one that appealed to me, I recalled what had happened them two times I'd attempted to pick up somebody. Since no other man had shown interest in me since Leroy's death, I knew it wouldn't be too hard for me to stay on the straight and narrow.

Our son was born on October 31. Earl wanted us to name him after a puppy he'd once owned named Poochie. We agreed to let that be his nickname, but his Christian name was Ishmael.

My life with Jessie was finally complete. Praise the Lord!

LOVE, HONOR, BETRAY

Mary Monroe

ABOUT THIS GUIDE

The suggested questions that follow are included to
enhance your group's reading of this book.

DISCUSSION QUESTIONS

1. Did you think Leroy was asking too much of Hubert to hide under his bed so his ex-wife, Sadie, wouldn't find him (naked!) in Leroy's bedroom?

2. Hubert hid under Leroy's bed for a whole night. Would you go to such lengths for someone you loved?

3. When Hubert attempted to hook up with other men while Leroy's ex was in the picture, it didn't go well. He was almost assaulted, so he decided this was a wake-up call. Did you expect him to "give up" the gay lifestyle and concentrate more on Jessie?

4. Hubert told Jessie before she married him that he could not perform in bed. She was convinced that his problem was temporary and married him anyway. Would you marry someone who told you up front that they couldn't perform in bed?

5. When Jessie started her relationship with her married lover, she didn't mind paying for the motel room and lending Amos money on a regular basis. But when he asked her to help finance his honeymoon, she broke up with him. Did you think she was a fool for staying in the relationship as long as she did?

6. Did the hints throughout the book help you figure out who was killing the Black women?

7. Were you surprised that it was Tyrone and Floyd?

8. Were you horrified to learn the reason they were committing murders?

9. Hubert was devastated when he realized two cold-blooded killers had been hiding in plain sight the whole time. Have you ever been severely betrayed by someone you've known and trusted most of your life?

10. What do you think would have happened if Mr. DeBow hadn't gone with Hubert and Jessie to the police to turn Tyrone and Floyd in?

11. Everyone was horrified when they found out Tyrone and Floyd had also *lynched* the two Black men. What would you think of a person who would commit such a heinous crime against their own race?

12. Were you as surprised as Jessie when Hubert finally made love to her?

13. Jessie was stunned when Hubert told her about his gay background and his sham marriage to his first wife. She chose to stay with him anyway because of the baby they were expecting. Was it necessary for her to confess all of her betrayals to him?